Teaching the N

Series Editor
Ben Knights
Teesside University
Middlesbrough, UK

Teaching the New English is an innovative series primarily concerned with the teaching of the English degree in the context of the modern university. The series is simultaneously concerned with addressing exciting new areas that have developed in the curriculum in recent years and those more traditional areas that have reformed in new contexts. It is grounded in an intellectual or theoretical concept of the curriculum, yet is largely concerned with the practicalities of the curriculum's manifestation in the classroom. Volumes will be invaluable for new and more experienced teachers alike.

More information about this series at
http://www.palgrave.com/gp/series/14458

Charlotte Beyer
Editor

Teaching Crime Fiction

Editor
Charlotte Beyer
University of Gloucestershire
Cheltenham, UK

Teaching the New English
ISBN 978-3-319-90607-2 ISBN 978-3-319-90608-9 (eBook)
https://doi.org/10.1007/978-3-319-90608-9

Library of Congress Control Number: 2018950657

Printed on acid-free paper

This Palgrave Macmillan imprint is published by the registered company Springer Nature Switzerland AG
The registered company address is: Gewerbestrasse 11, 6330 Cham, Switzerland

Series Preface

One of the many exciting achievements of the early years of the UK English Subject Centre was the agreement with Palgrave Macmillan to initiate the series 'Teaching the New English'. The intention of Philip Martin, the then Centre Director, was to create a series of short and accessible books which would focus on curriculum fields (or themes) and develop the connections between scholarly knowledge and the demands of teaching.

Since its inception as a university subject, 'English' has been committed to what is now known by the portmanteau phrase 'learning and teaching'. The subject grew up in a dialogue between scholars, critics, and their students inside and outside the university. Yet university teachers of English often struggle to make their own tacit pedagogic knowledge conscious, or to bring it up to a level where it might be shared, developed, or critiqued. In the experience of the English Subject Centre, colleagues found it relatively easy to talk about curriculum, but far harder to talk about the success or failure of seminars, how to vary modes of assessment, or to make imaginative use of virtual learning environments or web tools. Too often, this reticence meant falling back on received assumptions about how students learn, about how to teach or create assessment tasks. At the same time, we found, colleagues were generally suspicious of the insights and methods arising from generic educational research. The challenge for the extended group of English disciplines has been to articulate ways in which our own subject knowledge and forms of enquiry might themselves refresh debates about pedagogy. The need becomes all the more pressing in the era of rising fees, student loans, the National Student Survey, and the characterization of the student as a demanding consumer of an educational product. The implicit invitation of the present series is to take fields of knowledge and survey them through a pedagogic lens.

'Teachers', people used to say, 'are born, not made'. There may be some tenuous truth in this. There may perhaps be generosities of spirit (or, alternatively, drives for didactic control) laid down in early childhood. But the implication that you cannot train or develop teachers is dubious. Why should we assume that even 'born' teachers should not need to learn or review the skills of their trade? Amateurishness about teaching has far more to do with the mystique of university status than with evidence about how people learn. This series of books is dedicated to the development of the craft of teaching within university English Studies.

Teesside University
Middlesbrough, UK
UCL Institute of Education
London, UK

Ben Knights

Acknowledgements

Thank you to the Series Editor, Professor Ben Knights, for his encouragement and invaluable guidance, and to Benjamin Doyle, Camille Davies, and Tomas Rene at Palgrave for their helpful assistance and advice throughout the process of the production of this book.

Enormous thanks go to all the contributors to this volume for sharing your fascinating insights and experiences. Your work and commitment have made this book. Thank you also to all my colleagues in the wider crime fiction criticism community.

I would also like to acknowledge the inspiration and enthusiasm which I have received from all the students I have taught crime fiction over the years, and whose dissertations and theses I have supervised and examined.

Finally, thank you to my husband Stuart and daughter Sif for their unstinting love and support.

Contents

Notes on Contributors

Charlotte Beyer is Senior Lecturer in English Studies at the University of Gloucestershire, where she teaches crime fiction, postcolonial writing, and modern/contemporary literature. She has published widely on crime fiction, and her forthcoming monograph from McFarland examines the crime short story. Her edited volume *Mothers Without Their Children* (with Andrea Lea Robertson) will be published in 2019 by Demeter Press. Charlotte is on the Steering Committee for the Crime Studies Network and on the Editorial Boards for the journals *Feminist Encounters*, *The New Americanist*, and *American, British and Canadian Studies.*

Malcah Effron is a Lecturer in Writing, Rhetoric, and Professional Communication in the Department of Comparative Media Studies at Massachusetts Institute of Technology. She holds a Ph.D. in English Literature from Newcastle University, England and has published articles in *The Journal of Narrative Theory*, *Narrative*, and *Women & Language.* She also edited *Function of Evil across Disciplines* (Lexington Books, 2017) and *The Millennial Detective* (McFarland, 2011) and has contributed chapters to it as well as to *History of American Crime Fiction* (Cambridge, 2017). She is also the co-founder of the international Crime Studies Network (CSN).

Christiana Gregoriou is an Associate Professor in English Language at Leeds University. She is a crime fiction stylistics specialist and ran the 2016–17 AHRC/ESRC-funded project on the representation of transnational human trafficking in news media, true crime, and fiction.

Most notable are her three monographs (*Crime Fiction Migration: Crossing Languages, Cultures, Media*. 2017; *Language, Ideology and Identity in Serial Killer Narratives*. 2011; *Deviance in Contemporary Crime Fiction*. 2007), and her edited collections (*Constructing Crime: Discourse and Cultural Representations of Crime and 'Deviance'*. 2012; *Language and Literature*, 'Investigating Contemporary Crime Writing' special edition 21(3) 2012.

Sian Harris is the Director of Teaching and Digital Learning in English at the University of Bristol. She was previously in post as an Education & Scholarship Lecturer at the University of Exeter, where she designed and delivered a specialist survey course 'From the Rue Morgue to the Millennium', as well as supervising numerous undergraduate and postgraduate dissertations on detective fiction. Siân's research interests are driven by the dynamic between gender and genre in contemporary fiction, and she has previously published work on A.S. Byatt, Marina Warner, J.K. Rowling, and Ian Rankin.

Rosemary Erickson Johnsen is Professor of English at Governors State University, near Chicago, USA, where she teaches courses in literature and popular culture. Her publications include Contemporary Feminist Historical Crime Fiction (Palgrave Macmillan) and articles on crime fiction, Irish literature, and public scholarship. Her current book project focuses on contemporary Irish and Scandinavian crime fiction; other research interests include Patrick Hamilton and the British inter-war period. She received a National Endowment for the Humanities grant in 2017, and serves on the editorial advisory board of the Journal of Popular Culture. More information is available at rosemaryj.com.

Paul Johnston is a Lecturer in Creative Writing at Liverpool Hope University. He has degrees from Oxford, Edinburgh, and St Andrews universities. He is the author of nineteen critically acclaimed crime novels, two of them award-winners, numerous short stories, and a poetry pamphlet. His novels have been published around the world and translated into many languages. His current work-in-progress is *No Man*, a recasting of Homer's *Odyssey* and Joyce's *Ulysses* as crime fiction. An early version, 'Ulysses of Embra', appeared in *American, British and Canadian Studies*, number 1, 2017.

Nicole Kenley is an Assistant Professor of English at Simpson University in Redding, CA. She received her B.A. from the University of California, Berkeley, her M.A. from New York University, and her Ph.D. from the University of California, Davis. She is currently at work on her first book project, *Detecting Globalization*, which examines American detective fiction's shift from a national literature to a global one post-1970. In addition to detective fiction, her fields of interest include contemporary American fiction, gender studies, and the literature of globalization. Her scholarship has been published in *Mississippi Quarterly* and *Clues*.

Rebecca Martin teaches at Pace University in New York in the areas of crime writing, detective fiction, the gothic novel and female gothic, and film studies. She holds a Ph.D. in English from the Graduate Center of the City University of New York. Her published research is in detective fiction, the eighteenth-century gothic novel, and film studies. Recent publications include two edited collections of essays with Salem Press: *Critical Insights: Crime and Detective Fiction* (2013) and *Critical Insights: Film: Bonnie and Clyde* (2016).

Sam Naidu is an Associate Professor in the Department of English, Rhodes University, South Africa. Her main research and teaching interests are transnational literature, crime and detective fiction, and the oral-written interface in the colonial Eastern Cape. Recent publications are *Sherlock Holmes in Context*, Palgrave Macmillan (2017) and *A Survey of South African Crime Fiction: Critical Analysis and Publishing History* (2017). She has also guest edited a special issue of *Current Writing* on South African crime fiction (2013) and of *The Journal of Commonwealth and Postcolonial Studies* (2017) on postcolonial and transnational crime fiction.

Andrew Pepper is Senior Lecturer in English and American Literature at Queen's University Belfast where he has taught crime fiction at undergraduate and M.A. levels for sixteen years. He is the author of *Unwilling Executioner: Crime Fiction and the State* (Oxford 2016) and *The Contemporary American Crime Novel: Race, Ethnicity, Gender, Class* (Edinburgh 2000) and co-editor of *Globalization and the State in Cotemporary Crime Fiction*. He has also written a series of detective novels set in nineteenth-century Britain and Ireland including *The Last Days of Newgate* (2006) and *Bloody Winter* (2011), all published by Weidenfeld & Nicolson.

Maureen T. Reddy is Professor of English at Rhode Island College in Providence, RI (USA), and has been teaching and writing about crime fiction for thirty years. Her publications on crime fiction include two books, *Sisters in Crime: Feminism and the Crime Novel* and *Traces, Codes, and Clues: Reading Race in Crime Fiction*, and many articles, including a fairly recent piece in *Clues* on Tana French and one in *New Hibernia* on the rise of the Irish hardboiled. Reddy won the Popular Culture Association's Dove Award in 2013 for contributions to the serious study of crime fiction.

Samantha Walton is Reader in Modern Literature at Bath Spa University. Her research concerns the intersection of mental health and ecology in modern and contemporary literature, with particular focus on Scottish literature and popular fiction. Her first book, *Guilty But Insane: Mind and Law in Golden Age Detective Fiction*, was published by Oxford University Press in 2015.

A Chronology of Significant Critical Works

1976 John G. Cawelti, *Adventure, Mystery, and Romance: Formula Stories as Art and Popular Culture*. Chicago: University of Chicago Press.

1980 Stephen Knight, *Form and Ideology in Crime Fiction*. London: Macmillan Press.

1987 LeRoy Panek, *An Introduction to the Detective Story*. Bowling Green, Ohio: Bowling Green State University Popular Press.

1988 Brian Docherty, *American Crime Fiction: Studies in the Genre*. Houndmills: Macmillan Press.

1988 Maureen T. Reddy, *Sisters in Crime: Feminism and the Crime Novel*. New York: Continuum.

1990 Martin Priestman, *Figure on the Carpet: Detective Fiction and Literature*. Houndmills: Macmillan Press.

1993 Stephen Knight, *Continent of Mystery: A Thematic History of Australian Crime Fiction*. Melbourne: University of Melbourne Press.

1994 Sally Munt, *Murder by the Book? Feminism and the Crime Novel*. London: Routledge.

1994 William Reynolds and Elizabeth A. Trembley, eds. *It's a Print!: Detective Fiction from Page to Screen*. Bowling Green, OH: Bowling Green State University Press.

1995 Kathleen Klein, *The Woman Detective: Gender and Genre*. University of Illinois Press.

1997 Jerome Delamater and Ruth Prigozy, eds. *Theory and Practice of Classic Detective Fiction*. Westport: Greenwood Press.

1999 Priscilla L. Walton and Manina Jones, *Detective Agency: Women Rewriting the Hard-boiled Tradition*. Berkeley and L.A.: University of California Press.

1999 Catherine Nickerson, *The Web of Iniquity: Early Detective Fiction by American Women*. Durham, NC: Duke University Press.

1999 Woody Haut, *Neon Noir: Contemporary American Crime Fiction*. London: Serpent's Tail.

1999 Heta Pyrhönen, *Mayhem and Murder: Narrative and Moral Issues in the Detective Story*. Toronto: University of Toronto Press.

2000 Susan Rowland, *From Agatha Christie to Ruth Rendell: British Women Writers in Detective and Crime Fiction*. Houndmills: Palgrave.

2000 Sean McCann, *Gumshoe America: Hard-Boiled Crime Fiction and the Rise and Fall of New Deal Liberalism*. Durham, NC: Duke University Press.

2001 Gill Plain, *Twentieth-century Crime Fiction: Gender, Sexuality and the Body*. Edinburgh: Edinburgh University Press.

2001 Adrienne E. Gavin, and Christopher Routledge, eds. *Mystery in Children's Literature: From the Rational to the Supernatural*. Houndmills: Palgrave Macmillan, 2001.

2003 Maureen T. Reddy, *Traces, Codes and Clues: Reading Race in Crime Fiction*. New Brunswick: Rutgers University Press.

2003 Martin Priestman, ed. *The Cambridge Companion to Crime Fiction*. Cambridge: Cambridge University Press.

2004 Stephen Knight, *Crime Fiction Since 1800: Detection, Death, Diversity*. Houndmills: Palgrave.

2004 John Cawelti. *Mystery, Violence, and Cultural Studies: Essays*. Madison, Wisconsin: The University of Wisconsin Press, Popular Press.

2005 John Scaggs, *Crime Fiction*. London: Routledge.

2005 Lee Horsley, *Twentieth-Century Crime Fiction*. Oxford: Oxford University Press.

2005 Charles Rzepka, *Detective Fiction*. Cambridge: Polity.

2005 David Schmid, *Natural Born Celebrities: Serial Killers in American Culture*. Chicago: University of Chicago Press.

2006 Christine Matzke and Susanne Mühleisen, eds. *Postcolonial Postmortems: Crime Fiction from a Transcultural Perspective*. Amsterdam: Rodopi.

2006 Rosemary Erickson Johnsen, *Contemporary Feminist Historical Crime Fiction*. New York: Palgrave.

2006 Merja Makinen, *Agatha Christie: Investigating Femininity*. Houndmills: Palgrave Macmillan.

2007 Maurizio Ascari, *A Counter-History of Crime Fiction: Supernatural, Gothic, Sensational*. Houndmills: Palgrave.

2008 David Geherin. *Scene of the Crime: The Importance of Place in Crime and Mystery Fiction*. Jefferson: McFarland.

2008 Leonard Cassuto, *Hard-Boiled Sentimentality: The Secret History of American Crime Stories*. New York: Columbia University Press.

2008 Jean Murley, *The Rise of True Crime: 20th-Century Murder and American Popular Culture*. Westport, Conn.: Praeger.

2009 Christiana Gregoriou, *Deviance in Contemporary Crime Fiction*. Houndmills: Palgrave.

2009 Mary Evans, *The Imagination of Evil: Detective Fiction and the Modern World*, London: Continuum.

2009 Claire Gorrara, ed. *French Crime Fiction*. Cardiff: University of Wales Press.

2011 Giulana Pieri, ed. *Italian Crime Fiction*. Cardiff: University of Wales Press.

2011 Andrew Nestingen and Paula Arvas, eds. *Scandinavian Crime Fiction*. Cardiff: University of Wales Press.

2011 Malcah Effron, ed. *The Millennial Detective: Essays on Trends in Crime Fiction, Film and Television, 1990–2010*. Jefferson: McFarland.

2011 Heather Worthington, *Key Concepts in Crime Fiction*. Houndmills: Palgrave.

2011 Marc Singer and Nels Pearson, eds. *Detective Fiction in a Postcolonial and Transnational World*. Farnham: Ashgate.

2012 Lynnette Porter, ed. *Sherlock Holmes for the 21st Century: Essays on New Adaptations*. Jefferson: McFarland.

2013 Sabine Vanacker and Catherine Wynne, eds. *Sherlock Holmes and Conan Doyle: Multi-Media Afterlives*. Houndmills: Palgrave.

2014 Jeanne Slonoiwski and Marilyn Rose, eds. *Detecting Canada: Essays on Canadian Crime Fiction, Television, and Film*. Waterloo, Ontario: Wilfrid Laurier University Press.

2015 Len Wanner, *Tartan Noir: The Definitive Guide to Scottish Crime Fiction*. Glasgow: Freight Books.

2015 Jean Anderson, Carolina Miranda, Barbara Pezzotti, eds. *Serial Crime Fiction: Dying for More*. Houndmills: Palgrave.

2015 Robert E. Crafton, *The African American Experience in Crime Fiction: A Critical Study*. Jefferson: McFarland.

2016 Andrew Pepper and David Schmid, eds. *Globalization and the State in Contemporary Crime Fiction: A World of Crime*. Houndmills: Palgrave.

2016 Katharina Hall, ed. *Crime Fiction in German: Der Krimi*. Cardiff: University of Wales Press.

2016 Mitzi M. Brunsdale, *Encyclopedia of Nordic Crime Fiction: Works and Authors of Denmark, Finland, Norway and Sweden Since 1967*. Jefferson: McFarland.

2016 Margaret Kinsman, *Sara Paretsky: A Companion to the Mystery Fiction*. Jefferson: McFarland.

2017 Sam Naidu and Elizabeth le Roux, *A Survey of South African Crime Fiction: Critical Analysis and Publishing History*. Scottsville: University of KwaZulu-Natal Press.

2017 Heather Duerre Humann, *Gender Bending Detective Fiction: A Critical Analysis of Selected Works*. Jefferson: McFarland.

CHAPTER 1

Introduction: Crime Fiction

Charlotte Beyer

Teaching Crime Fiction

The theme of crime has dominated fictional and cultural representations for centuries. However, it has never been more popular than at the present time. From the reimagining of Arthur Conan Doyle's detective figure Sherlock Holmes in the BBC's *Sherlock* series featuring Benedict Cumberbatch, to the debates surrounding violence against women prompted by Nordic Noir author Stieg Larsson's Millennium trilogy, and the explosion of the true crime subgenre, contemporary crime culture is enjoying increasing popularity. The rise of crime fiction as a literary genre has made an enormous impact on university degree programmes in English Literature and English Studies; yet, it has also been the source of ardent and partisan debates in the academic community, over matters such as value, quality and relevance. Views persist within some parts of the academy, of crime fiction as a sort of guilty pleasure, a frivolous pastime compared with what is considered serious, canonical literature. This predicament is hinted at in a 2016 article by Girgulis,[1] entitled "Popularity of detective fiction course no mystery", about a course on detective fiction taught at University of Calgary in Canada.[2] In the article, McGillivray, a

C. Beyer (✉)
University of Gloucestershire, Cheltenham, UK
e-mail: cbeyer@glos.ac.uk

C. Beyer (ed.), *Teaching Crime Fiction*, Teaching the New English,
https://doi.org/10.1007/978-3-319-90608-9_1

Professor in Medieval Literature, discusses his positive experience of teaching crime fiction and the way in which his course harnesses students' crime fiction enthusiasms. The article also alludes to wider debates in the academe familiar to crime fiction critics and academics. These scholarly debates have often focused on what was perceived as popular culture's lack of seriousness and substance, accompanied by the concern that students of crime fiction would not learn analytical skills such as scansion, traditionally considered central to an English Literature degree. Some academics and students maintain that crime fiction lacks literary merit, and that studying a crime fiction course (or other popular fiction material) is an easy way out from more supposedly rigorous or demanding material. Such assumptions are, of course, questionable,[3] but reflect the compelling observation made by Knight in his lecture, "Motive, Means and Opportunity: Teaching Crime Fiction", that: "it would still be true to acknowledge, and perhaps for us to take some largely unearned credit for, the fact that almost everyone who teaches crime fiction is in some way aware of their action as counter-canonical".

Teaching Crime Fiction sets out to demonstrate why crime fiction has perhaps been an under-estimated genre in the academe, by presenting a series of compelling essays on the many fascinating dimensions of crime fiction in teaching and learning. These essays showcase the rich and growing body of crime fiction criticism and explore the strategies and rewards of teaching this material. However, what this book will not do is further rehearse already dated critical discussions and disagreements over the merits (or perceived lack of them) of crime fiction versus literary fiction respectively. Rather, the starting-point of *Teaching Crime Fiction* is the confident assumption that teaching the new English demands questioning traditional perceptions of literary merit, reordering cultural hierarchies, embracing the field's diversity and recognising that the genre of crime fiction is central to this endeavour.[4] Presenting incisive chapters on crime fiction criticism and the employment of specific teaching and learning pedagogies, the contributors to this book offer their research as well as their practical experience of undergraduate and postgraduate teaching in the academe, in order to promote ways in which this most diverse of literary genres may be taught in the contemporary classroom. Their essays highlight the essential critical abilities and reflective skills which crime fiction students develop through their intellectual engagement with this material.

Developments in Crime Fiction Criticism

Crime fiction has had a complex relationship to mainstream culture: on the one hand frequently deemed too popular or mass culture to be taken seriously; yet on the other hand, due to its focus on criminality, able to explore and expose crime on micro- and macro-levels. The scholarly debates that have shaped crime fiction teaching in the academy in recent decades centre on examining crime and its representation— terms which have been "the foundation for an entire genre of fiction for over one hundred and fifty years".[5] Some of these debates have also highlighted the controversies of crime fiction, such as perceived gratuitous use of violence, or sexual crime against females.

However, Rzepka argues that definitions of crime are not straightforward, and that literary treatment of crime themes is not enough to make a text a crime fiction.[6] Marcus furthermore comments on the distinctions often still drawn by some between literary fiction and crime fiction.[7] These debates raise necessary questions for the characterisation of the genre and the fixity of its definition, but are equally central to our consideration of teaching English in the twenty-first-century university, and the changing perceptions and definitions we are working with in teaching and learning contexts. As we teach students how to become crime fiction scholars and critics through active and reflective engagement with the material individually and collectively, the evolution of the genre and its attending critical modes take on heightened significance. Knight makes a crucial observation, in his Foreword to Malcah Effron's volume, *The Millennial Detective: Essays on Trends in Crime Fiction, Film and Television, 1990–2010*. Commenting on the myths constructed by critics in their attempt to define crime fiction as a lesser genre, Knight states that, "wide as those gulfs between myth and reality might be, the largest and most disabling myth in crime fiction has been that it is not the same as literary studies".[8] Knight further observes that because of its marginalisation in the academy, crime fiction criticism has, until recent decades, lacked input from the most recent and challenging developments in literary criticism.[9] *Teaching Crime Fiction* seeks to counter this absence by demonstrating the breadth and scope of present-day crime fiction criticism and its employment in teaching and learning. Featuring essays on postcolonial crime fiction, crime and stylistics, gender, the crime short story, crime fiction and film, and teaching crime fiction at postgraduate level, and more, this book reflects contemporary critical approaches to crime fiction, and is representative of the riches and diversities of these critical and theoretical perspectives.

One of the considerations academics face when devising a crime fiction course is to what extent the syllabus should be driven by a requirement to represent the genre's canonical texts and historical evolution. The narrative of crime fiction's evolution is traditionally conceived of as starting with the Dupin short stories by American author Edgar Allan Poe, who passed the baton to British writer Wilkie Collins.[10] Priestman further emphasises the significance of Arthur Conan Doyle and his invention of the detective character of Sherlock Holmes, followed by American hard-boiled crime writers such as Raymond Chandler and British Golden Age crime fiction by authors such as Agatha Christie and Dorothy Sayers, who led crime fiction's ever-expanding repertoire and style.[11] These authors all feature centrally in the crime fiction canon and can regularly be found as staple ingredients on undergraduate crime fiction modules, as Pepper notes in Chap. 13 in this book. Critics have argued for the importance of teaching this canon and the history of crime fiction and its growth as a genre, in order to offer students an understanding of the evolution of crime fiction, generically, thematically and stylistically. Scaggs has it that: "Like any literary text, individual works of crime fiction are built from the devices, codes, and conventions established by previous works of crime fiction, and they are therefore crucial to our understanding of these texts in the present".[12] Teaching crime fiction in depth at university requires that specific attention is paid to the mechanisms and dynamics of the genre, and that fundamental questions are investigated and scrutinised, both with regard to its capacity to critique and inform, and concerning the aesthetic and stylistic features of the genre. Thereby students are equipped with the skills and knowledge to critically evaluate crime and its representations, through their investigation of the role and function of crime fiction and its many subgenres in our society and reading culture. The importance of studying and critically evaluating contemporary genres and texts reflect the ethos of teaching the new English and crime fiction's place within it.

More than most other literary forms, the reading and study of crime fiction is driven by readers' enthusiasms.[13] For, as Franks states, "A crime fiction text may be printed on cheap paper and feature a gaudy cover but the pages within can document and discuss the entire continuum of human activity and emotion."[14] The reader enthusiasm dimension can be usefully harnessed to learning outcomes when teaching crime fiction.

Investigating how readers' enthusiasms can be connected with, harnessed and utilised as drivers in teaching and learning is part of this book's project. This connection between literary material and the individual reader is important, Franks argues. In her article, "Motive for Murder: Reading Crime Fiction", Franks offers her personal and professional reflections on the significance of readers' enthusiasm in the study and research of crime fiction. She provides a useful explanation of the attraction or fascination which crime fiction holds—an analysis which is also key to the success crime fiction as a subject is enjoying in the academy. Franks enquires,

> What inspires a reader to pick up a piece of crime fiction over a novel or short story in one of the many other genres that are available? Why do ordinary, generally law-abiding citizens feel such a strong sense of attraction to stories that are dominated by death and other violent crimes?[15]

Franks refers to her teen-age viewing of Howard Hawks' iconic 1946 adaptation of Raymond Chandler's *The Big Sleep* as a formative experience that stimulated her interest in and enthusiasm for crime fiction. Enthusiasm for the genre drives students and academics alike, in their pursuit of the genre, its classic canonical works as well as the most recent works from around the globe. At the same time, readers, students and academics also rightly remain sceptical of what they perceive as flawed or problematic crime fiction texts.

Teaching crime fiction on contemporary undergraduate and postgraduate degree courses has evolved enormously. Since Knight first gave his paper, "Motive, Means and Opportunity: Teaching Crime Fiction", in 1998,[16] much has changed. Critiquing the canon-formation within crime fiction which he observed at the time, Knight deplored the absence from crime fiction courses of feminist crime writers such as Val McDermid and Sara Paretsky, and the emphasis on the literary fiction dimension of detective writing.[17] Drawing briefly on personal anecdote here, my own first attempt, around the year 2001, at constructing an undergraduate crime fiction course (as opposed to merely adding a crime text to a module with an overall different focus) was a six-week option that focused exclusively on contemporary women's detective fiction, with a feminist perspective. The option was part of a contemporary fiction and poetry module which offered options as an acknowledgement of what was seen as the impossibility of presenting coverage in the face of the diversity of contemporary writing. My women's crime fiction option then included texts by

P.D. James, Barbara Vine (Ruth Rendell), Val McDermid, Sara Paretsky and Stella Duffy, and was specifically informed by feminist literary criticism and popular culture criticism, leading me to investigate genre writing as a site for feminist experimentation and resistance. This early venture into teaching crime fiction at undergraduate level suggests that, although Knight's astute assessment of the relative conservativism with which crime fiction was then perceived and taught in the academy was spot-on, gender and genre were on the agenda for change. Feminist interventions in the genre have been immensely significant in radically questioning and altering the conventional narrative patterns, themes and positions of crime fiction. Further vital critical interventions have impacted with equal significance on the teaching of crime fiction in the academy, such as postcolonialism, race theory, ecological concerns, queer theory, language and stylistics, theorising creative writing, and more.

Graff argues that teaching traditionally has not received the attention or been valued by universities in the way that it should be and deserves to be.[18] However, this book's focus on pedagogical scholarship both reflects and confirms Prosser's assertion that "Interest in the scholarship of teaching and learning, pedagogic research in higher education and evidence based practice is growing".[19] The intensifying of interest in teaching and learning is mirrored by the enormous growth of crime fiction courses on undergraduate (and, more recently, also postgraduate) degrees. Commenting on recent teaching and learning scholarship pertaining to romance studies, another popular genre, Fletcher pinpoints the significance of sharing teaching and learning tools and experiences. She highlights "the open exchange of ideas, research findings, and tools for enriching the experience of teachers and, most importantly, students in courses".[20] Following and extending Fletcher's argument, this book demonstrates the validity of crime fiction as a literary genre illustrative of "the new English", and foregrounds the rigour and inventiveness brought to bear on this diverse material by university academics teaching crime fiction. The chapters in *Teaching Crime Fiction* explore the possibilities generated by the diverse and ever-growing body of crime fiction in higher education teaching and learning. We examine the critical enquiries afforded to students enabled by research-led teaching in the field, and evaluate different strategies for involving students in the stimulating experience of creating and applying new knowledge. The essays in this book demonstrate the value of research-led teaching, evaluating various methods and strategies by which research can successfully be brought to the classroom, and explaining and demonstrating the positive impact on student engagement and learning which research-led teaching engenders. Research-led teaching and the scholarship of teaching and learning are not separate endeavours; rather, the two modes go together in the emergent and innovative vision of teaching the new English. The authors here all express an appetite for experimentation and inventive thinking in their pedagogies and teaching practices, looking to enhance innovation in content, assessment and teaching philosophies stimulated by the diversity and scope of crime fiction itself.

Dimensions of Teaching Crime Fiction

Teaching Crime Fiction offers a series of essays authored by prominent crime fiction authors and academics at the forefront of their discipline, presenting compelling accounts of questions and issues encountered in teaching crime fiction, the strategies they utilise in the classroom, and the pedagogical principles that underpin these endeavours. The chapters are broadly devised by theme as this structure provides the most expansive range of exploration possible, as opposed to following a strictly historical approach. In contrast, these essays facilitate discussions of a wide range of crime fiction texts, some canonical, some not, from global contexts. Rather than following a strictly chronological and linear method or approach, the book is structured around specific subgenres, critical approaches, topics (such as gender, sexuality, postcolonialism, history and ecology), undergraduate and postgraduate teaching, and so on. This book offers examinations of what Prosser, citing Boyer, terms "the scholarship of teaching"—namely, "evidence based critical reflection on practice to improve practice".[21] The reflections reported in the chapters here on teaching and learning crime fiction as an important aspect of the new English are informed by personal scholarly research as well as pedagogical research. The latter is especially significant in a higher education context which evaluates our teaching efforts in a variety of ways.

In her chapter on the pedagogy of devising crime fiction modules, entitled "Designing Crime Fiction Modules: The Literature Classroom and Interdisciplinary Approaches", Rebecca Martin examines the priorities and choices which face the lecturer devising a crime fiction module for undergraduate university students. Exploring a number of possibilities for setting course texts ranging from across the crime and detective genre, Martin's chapter comments on the degree of specialisation required by students, and the considerations that this poses on the part of the academic delivering the course in setting the syllabus. Martin furthermore discusses the challenges and opportunities offered by teaching material such as black American crime fiction and true crime, topics and authors that are less frequently encountered on conventional undergraduate crime fiction courses. Martin's pedagogical strategies acknowledge the significance of diversity in the classroom, demonstrating how this dimension is incorporated into the crime fiction modules she devises.

"Plots and Devices", Malcah Effron's chapter on the structuring of crime narratives, examines the mechanics and textual tactics of crime and detective fiction, with a particular emphasis on exploring strategies for teaching students about the significance of the plots and narrative techniques used in crime fiction. Narrative theory is important, Effron argues, since it, "provides a productive avenue for attending to crime fiction plots and genre devices in ways that enrich the reading experience, especially as it is one of the first literary theories to embrace detective fiction as an object of productive study". The theorisation and analysis of narrative elements in crime fiction provides students with important insight into the workings of crime fiction, giving them the vocabulary and the tools to interrogate the writing. Thus, Effron's analysis demonstrates how theoretical concepts and debates in relation to narrative are used as an integral aspect of crime fiction teaching and learning.

Maureen T. Reddy's essay, "Teaching Crime Fiction and Gender", offers an examination of a subject central to crime fiction and teaching crime fiction: namely gender. Taking her starting-point in Judith Butler's argument that gender is performative, Reddy links these ideas to hard-boiled crime fiction and its representation of masculinity and femininity. She examines gender as a central dimension of crime fiction, exploring literary texts which are useful and informative in enabling further questions to be explored. Reddy discusses the theoretical and critical material employed to illuminate these questions in class, thereby providing students with a fuller and more complex context for their investigations of gender in crime fiction. Reddy's chapter thus demonstrates highly effective and innovative ways in which this material can be taught in the university classroom through a textual and critical focus on gender.

In her chapter, "Teaching American Detective Fiction in the Contemporary Classroom", Nicole Kenley tackles the question of how to devise a module, set the syllabus and teach a particular national crime fiction oeuvre. American crime fiction has proved immensely influential, particularly stylistically, but also through its compelling depiction of characters such as the maverick private eye detective. But to what extent is a course on American crime fiction able to go beyond teaching students a superficial sense of familiarity with American-specific styles, themes and tropes? Kenley examines the issue of national specificity in crime fiction, interrogating the construction and representation of national identity. Her essay further demonstrates that the evolution of American crime fiction reflects other literary and cultural developments nationally and internationally, such as modernism and multiculturalism, as well as illustrating enduring themes and concerns.

Sam Naidu's chapter, "Teaching Postcolonial Crime Fiction", offers readers a compelling examination of the specific pedagogical and ethical issues involved in teaching crime fiction derived from a complex postcolonial context, and using postcolonial perspectives. Naidu's analysis focuses specifically on South African crime writing, exploring the questions raised by this body of literature when taught in a South African higher education context. She argues that postcolonial political and cultural contexts force a reconsideration of crime and its linguistic representation, in light of the all-encompassing systemic crimes that the country's fiction reflects. Naidu explores the implications and consequences for teaching and learning resulting from this recognition of the complex and often controversial dimensions of criminality in postcolonial crime fiction.

My chapter, "Cut a Long Story Short: Teaching the Crime Short Story", examines strategies for teaching the crime short story on crime fiction courses, exploring differing facets of this somewhat neglected but now vital and growing subgenre. Taking my starting-point in my own teaching practice and use of a variety of crime short stories on my crime fiction module syllabus, I argue that the crime short story is an evolving fictional form which has the capacity to unveil new and diverse dimensions of the crime genre to students, thereby enhancing their learning. Examining the crime short story's portrayal of gender, location and reimagined detective characters from the canon such as Sherlock Holmes, my chapter demonstrates the variety of approach and thematic content engendered by the crime short story.

In her chapter, "Studies in Green: Teaching Ecological Crime Fiction", Samantha Walton provides a compelling case for the importance of teaching eco crime fiction. She argues that the inclusion of this material on crime fiction modules enable, or perhaps forces, a profound change of approach and focus, both in the selection of primary texts for courses, and in terms of the critical and theoretical modes utilised in the interpretation of the texts. Through a series of examples taken from global crime fiction, ranging from Conan Doyle's *The Hound of the Baskervilles* to contemporary literary works, Walton's discussion demonstrates the compelling nature and content of ecological crime fiction and the critical and theoretical considerations employed in her readings of these works.

Teaching crime fiction in conjunction with film is a popular subject in teaching and learning contexts related to this specific genre. In her chapter, "Teaching Crime Fiction and Film", Siân Harris discusses the ways in which she has utilised film and other visual enrichments as a crucial part of the crime fiction syllabus she offers on her module. The thematic and discursive connections between fiction and film offer a rich subject for exploration and lend themselves eminently to undergraduate teaching of crime fiction. Harris furthermore offers interesting and stimulating examples for learning enrichment, demonstrating how crime fiction teaching may draw on local history as presented by, for example, museums, as well as filmic representations in order to stimulate students' critical enquiry.

Christiana Gregoriou's chapter on crime writing, language and stylistics applies analytical tools for close reading of crime texts which concentrate on vocabulary, uses of language and other textual nuances. Through an intensive and detailed focus on stylistics, Gregoriou's "Crime Writing: Language and Stylistics" demonstrates the capacity of linguistics to engage with the layers of textuality in crime fiction, thereby opening for new dimensions of textual analysis of crime discourses. These techniques are shown to be particularly relevant to students investigating the workings and mechanisms of crime texts as texts. Employing Emmott's frame theory to examine the way in which crime fiction constructs red herrings and other attempts to mislead and trick readers, and Ryan's possible world theory in order to look at the narrative structures that characterise crime fiction, Gregoriou demonstrates the central role of stylistic analysis in teaching students about how crime fiction works discursively.

In his chapter, "The Crime Novelist as Educator: Towards a Fuller Understanding of Crime Fiction", Paul Johnston explores the specific perspectives brought to teaching and learning by the crime novelist as teacher. Using his own experience as a successful crime fiction author as starting-point, Johnston argues that writer/practitioners have the capacity to bring unique and vital perspectives on the crime fiction genre to teaching and learning. The crime fiction writer/practitioner's creative insight into the workings of the genre and the publishing industry enables them to provide wider and more inclusive contexts which students appreciate and benefit from. Providing a range of examples from his teaching experience and writing practice, Johnston gives fresh insight into the unique contribution made to teaching the new English by writer/practitioners.

Teaching students how to read crime fiction, and specifically how to become crime fiction critics is the subject of Rosemary Erickson Johnsen's chapter. In "Teaching Crime Fiction Criticism", Johnsen specifically focuses on the teaching of crime fiction criticism, as a diverse body of critical approaches applicable specifically to detective and crime fiction. Existing critical and theoretical approaches have been profoundly impacted upon and transformed by the particular themes, styles and structures of crime fiction. Johnsen explores strategies for teaching crime in ways which are critically informed and theoretically underpinned. Her chapter also discusses ways in which to encourage an integral research element in taught crime fiction courses, empowering students to see themselves as researchers engaging with critical theory and using secondary sources for modelling this critical reading and research process. She concludes her chapter with an informative and useful exploration of teaching crime fiction at M.A. level, thereby contributing to this book's debates around teaching and learning strategies at postgraduate level.

The discussion in Johnsen's chapter, of teaching crime fiction criticism at postgraduate level, links well with the book's closing chapter by Andrew Pepper. His "Teaching Contemporary US Crime Fiction Through the 'War on Drugs': A Postgraduate Case Study" offers strategies and reflections pertaining to teaching crime fiction at postgraduate level—an increasingly important dimension of teaching the new English. Using a specific body of work within contemporary American crime fiction as his case study, namely novels depicting the American "war on drugs", Pepper's in-depth investigation of the themes and questions presented by these texts demonstrates how crime fiction in the academy may provide a compelling subject for postgraduate investigation. Pepper demonstrates how a course focusing on the connections between the real-life ongoing "war on drugs", true crime and fiction affords postgraduate students insight into contemporary American crime fiction beyond America, examining transnational crime and the crime writing which portrays it.

Conclusion: Fostering Diversity and Critical Inquiry

The chapters in this volume have been explicitly devised in order to address specific topics and areas of interest central to teaching and learning about crime fiction. These topics are regarded as part of an innovative, diverse, forward-looking English subject area teaching diverse undergraduate and postgraduate student groups.[22] The work done in the UK by HEA (Higher Education Academy) and its Subject Centres has been invaluable in exploring the application of teaching and learning pedagogies in universities, as well as contributing to and encouraging pedagogical scholarship.[23] The "Teaching the New English" series, of which this book is a part, reflects and builds on this collective endeavour. Fletcher argues that "engaging in the scholarship of teaching and learning is an opportunity to reflect in a sustained way on one of the most challenging and most rewarding aspects of an academic career – finding ways to help our students learn".[24] To that effect, the essays in this book propose a variety of teaching and learning strategies, ranging from classroom discussions and small-group activities, to inspirational field trips making use of museums and other public facilities, innovative and enquiring assessment forms, the development of online learning communities in virtual environments for the purposes of sharing resources and information, and one-to-one tutorials.[25] Prosser states that scholarship of teaching and learning is practice-based and is carried out "collegially".[26] The acknowledgement of the collegial spirit that drives teaching and learning scholarship is reflected in the vibrant and compelling discussions in this book, as well as more widely at literature festivals, true crime re-enactments and creative writing groups, all of which are evidence of the ever-increasing popularity and appeal of crime fiction for readers, students, scholars and authors.

Notes

1. See also my discussion of this piece in "In Praise of Crime Fiction", Dr Beyer's Page, 25 January 2016. http://beyerpage.blogspot.co.uk/2016/01/in-praise-of-crime-fiction.html Accessed 27 December 2017.
2. Jill Girgulis. "Popularity of detective fiction course no mystery". *The Gauntlet*. 19 January 2016. http://www.thegauntlet.ca/popularity-of-detective-fiction-course-no-mystery/ Accessed 27 December 2017.

3. Richard Bradford, "The criminal neglect of detective fiction". *Times Higher Education*, 4 June 2015. https://www.timeshighereducation.com/content/the-criminal-neglect-of-detective-fiction Accessed 3 January 2018.
4. Katy Shaw, "Introduction". In *Teaching 21st Century Genres*, edited by Katy Shaw. Houndmills: Palgrave, xiv.
5. John Scaggs, *Crime Fiction*. Abingdon, Routledge, 2005. 1.
6. Charles J. Rzepka, 'What is Crime Fiction?" In *A Companion to Crime Fiction*, edited by Charles J. Rzepka and Lee Horsley. Chichester, Blackwell, 2010.1–10. 1.
7. Laura Marcus, "Detection and Literary Fiction". In *The Cambridge Companion to Crime Fiction*, edited by Martin Priestman. Cambridge: Cambridge University Press, 2003. 245.
8. Stephen Knight, "Foreword". In *The Millennial Detective: Essays on Trends in Crime Fiction, Film and Television, 1990–2010*, edited by Malcah Effron. Jefferson: McFarland, 2011. 1.
9. Knight (2011), 2.
10. Martin Priestman, "Introduction: Crime Fiction and Detective Fiction," In *The Cambridge Companion to Crime Fiction*, edited by Martin Priestman. Cambridge: Cambridge University Press, 2003. 2.
11. Priestman, 2.
12. Scaggs, 3.
13. See also Girguilis.
14. Rachel Franks, "Motive for Murder: Reading Crime Fiction". The Australian Library and Information Association Biennial Conference. Sydney: Jul. 2012. 8.
15. Franks, 1.
16. Stephen Knight. "Motive, Means and Opportunity: Teaching Crime Fiction". Professor Stephen Knight. 29 August 2012 https://web.archive.org/web/20170313064908/http:/www.profstephenknight.com/search/label/teaching Accessed 27 December 2017.
17. Knight.
18. Gerald Graff. *Clueless in Academe: How Schooling Obscures the Life of the Mind*. Yale University Press, 2003. 5.
19. Michael Prosser. "The Scholarship of Teaching and Learning: What is it? A Personal View". *International Journal for the Scholarship of Teaching and Learning*, Vol. 2, No. 2 (2008) 2. See also Patricia Cartney. "Researching Pedagogy in a Contested Space". *British Journal of Social Work*, 45 (2015). 1137–1154.
20. Fletcher, 1.

21. Prosser, 1. Cites Boyer, E. L. (1990) *Scholarship Reconsidered: Priorities of the professoriate.* Princeton, NJ: The Carnegie Foundation for the Advancement of University Teaching.
22. See also Northedge, Andrew. "Rethinking Teaching in the Context of Diversity", *Teaching in Higher Education*, 8: 1, 2003. 17–32.
23. Prosser, 3. See also Beyer.
24. Fletcher, 3.
25. See also Shaw's listing of strategies for teaching and learning, xvi–xvii.
26. Prosser, 4.

Works Cited

Beyer, Charlotte. "In Praise of Crime Fiction." Dr Beyer's Page, 25 January 2016. http://beyerpage.blogspot.co.uk/2016/01/in-praise-of-crime-fiction.html Accessed 27 December 2017.

Bradford, Richard. "The Criminal Neglect of Detective Fiction." *Times Higher Education*, 4 June 2015. https://www.timeshighereducation.com/content/the-criminal-neglect-of-detective-fiction Accessed 3 January 2018.

Cartney, Patricia. "Researching Pedagogy in a Contested Space." *British Journal of Social Work*, 45, 2015, 1137–1154.

Fletcher, Lisa. "The Scholarship of Teaching and Learning Popular Romance Studies: What Was It, and Why Does It Matter?" *Journal of Popular Romance Studies*, 3.2, 2013, 1–5.

Franks, Rachel. "Motive for Murder: Reading Crime Fiction." The Australian Library and Information Association Biennial Conference. Sydney: July 2012. 1–9. http://www.academia.edu/2277952/Motive_for_Murder_reading_crime_fiction Accessed 21 May 2018.

Girgulis, Jill. "Popularity of Detective Fiction Course No Mystery." *The Gauntlet*, 19 January 2016. http://www.thegauntlet.ca/popularity-of-detective-fiction-course-no-mystery/ Accessed 27 December 2017.

Graff, Gerald. *Clueless in Academe: How Schooling Obscures the Life of the Mind.* New Haven: Yale University Press, 2003.

Knight, Stephen. "Foreword." In *The Millennial Detective: Essays on Trends in Crime Fiction, Film and Television, 1990–2010*, edited by Malcah Effron, 1–4. Jefferson: McFarland, 2011.

Knight, Stephen. "Motive, Means and Opportunity: Teaching Crime Fiction." *Professor Stephen Knight*, 29 August 2012. https://web.archive.org/web/20170313064908/http:/www.profstephenknight.com/search/label/teaching Accessed 27 December 2017.

Marcus, Laura. *"Detection and Literary Fiction." c 245–268.* Cambridge: Cambridge University Press, 2003.

Northedge, Andrew. "Rethinking Teaching in the Context of Diversity." *Teaching in Higher Education*, 8.1, 2003, 17–32

Priestman, Martin. "Introduction: Crime Fiction and Detective Fiction." In *The Cambridge Companion to Crime Fiction*, edited by Martin Priestman, 1–6. Cambridge: Cambridge University Press, 2003.

Prosser, Michael. "The Scholarship of Teaching and Learning: What Is It? A Personal View." *International Journal for the Scholarship of Teaching and Learning*, 2.2, July 2008, 1–4.

Rzepka, Charles J. "What Is Crime Fiction?" In *A Companion to Crime Fiction*, edited by Charles J. Rzepka and Lee Horsley, 1–10. Chichester: Blackwell, 2010.

Scaggs, John. *Crime Fiction*. Abingdon: Routledge, 2005.

Shaw, Katy. "Introduction." In *Teaching 21st Century Genres*, edited by Katy Shaw, xiii–xx. Houndmills: Palgrave Macmillan.

CHAPTER 2

Designing Crime Fiction Modules: The Literature Classroom and Interdisciplinary Approaches

Rebecca Martin

Introduction

In the litigious culture of the United States, faculty are frequently reminded that the course syllabus is a contract, a legally binding agreement, between the institution and the student. In that sense, one steps into the classroom already aware of an invisible web of obligations and expectations surrounding the presentation of material and conduct of the class. The word "syllabus" itself has a legal usage linked to a brief abstract of cases relevant in particular fields. The syllabus is shaped by the context for which it is devised; all faculty attend to questions of audience (first-year students, advanced undergraduates, graduate students), discipline (the literature classroom, the law classroom, film studies, Indigenous Peoples studies, etc.), or sub-disciplines/subgenres (hardboiled crime fiction, property law, film noir, the Navajo in fiction of the American West, and so on). While crime fiction would seem to be most suited to the literature classroom, it readily overlaps with countless disciplines outside departments of

R. Martin (✉)
Pace University, Pleasantville, NY, USA
e-mail: rmartin@pace.edu

C. Beyer (ed.), *Teaching Crime Fiction*, Teaching the New English,
https://doi.org/10.1007/978-3-319-90608-9_2

English, situating crime writing in a web of interdisciplinary possibilities that offer a very wide range of substantive, relevant connections. These many points of contact make crime fiction a rich basis for classroom collaborations, use as a teaching tool in non-literature classrooms, as well as for the study of literature at every stage from first-year English majors and non-majors to the graduate level and professional schools. While this chapter will focus primarily on approaches to developing crime fiction modules for the undergraduate literature classroom, it will also touch upon ways in which crime fiction is ideally suited to integration with studies well outside the literature classroom, to collaboration in teaching, and to interdisciplinary approaches.

As other chapters in this collection discuss, crime fiction is a relative newcomer to the literature classroom because of the struggle to prove the value of popular fiction in the classroom. Though the argument about mass-market publications and literary fiction continues in the world of critics, peace on that subject prevails in most classrooms where the struggle now takes place around the issue of how to get students to read any books at all. Though not all student-readers are or will be fans of crime fiction, this writing is "popular" in the best sense. It is engaging because it is usually set in a recognizable reality and it provokes curiosity by design. Students may be lured in thinking that popular fiction is an easy read and then will find themselves confronting fiction that keeps their attention, challenges their assumptions about popular fiction and perhaps about literature itself. As they continue to read they build skills and hone talents that are literary in their application but have significance outside the literature class. The study of characterization, narrative and thematic development, narrative voice, point of view, tone, syntax, and word choice sharpen critical and analytical skills and, when writing in the classroom is emphasized, the written communication skills so widely desired upon graduation. Beyond these fundamentally desirable qualities, students will be challenged to make connections and give considered attention to issues outside the classroom, questions about the laws, their social function and their application, and social justice, for example. Questions regarding the law as an ideal and the law as it is often less than perfectly applied, questions about where authority is drawn from and acquires its force, questions about legitimate and illegitimate authority, indeed, about the idea of authority itself, questions about guilt and innocence and the gray areas in between, about punishment, retribution, restoration and redemption, questions about what justice is, whether and how it can be served, all of these can be studied in crime fiction, often by analyzing the figure of the detective and the values that accumulate around that character.

Crime Fiction in Literary Studies

More than a decade ago at my institution, I designed a course in American Detective Fiction to be offered to undergraduates, most but not all of whom were English majors. I have since taught the course numerous times both in the physical classroom and online. The "detective" in each work of fiction may be a professional, such as a private detective or police detective, or a naïve or skilled amateur who investigates a crime for personal reasons. The approach is chronological and, thus, somewhat developmental, moving from Poe's "Murders in the Rue Morgue" (1841) and "The Purloined Letter" (1844) through the popular country house and domestic mysteries of Mary Roberts Rinehart, the successful but marginalized work of Rudolph Fisher during the Harlem Renaissance, the hard-boiled tradition represented by Hammett and Chandler, the noir fiction of Dorothy B. Hughes, and the fatalistic, fantastic works of Chester Himes from the 1950s and 1960s. Generally, the course ends with *Silence of the Lambs* (1988), which introduces a female detective figure, who has the force of the FBI behind her, but whose status as a woman, not only in a traditional man's job but in a world of men, is exploited in creative and provocative ways by Thomas Harris.

The course focuses on the detective figure in each text, analyzing that individual's relationship to and attitude toward the law and the authority behind it and what values the figure seems to stand for, based on the dynamics at play between the detective and official law enforcement during the investigation, as well as the outcome of the case and the actions and reactions of the detective to his or her findings. Those dynamics and readers' interpretation of the implied social commentary will be different depending upon whether it is Rinehart's middle-aged, well-to-do "spinster" (as she calls herself), Rachel Innes, confronting a local police detective during her summer vacation, Chandler's Marlowe confronting corruption in city hall, or Himes's Coffin Ed Johnson and Grave Digger Jones, negotiating their own positions as African American police detectives charged by their white NYPD bosses with keeping peace in the Harlem community. While the characterization and role of the detective figure is emphasized in studying each text, those texts are chosen so that looking at them from different angles also reveals issues of class, gender, and race. The study of the development of detective fiction thus becomes the study of changing attitudes toward women, changing ideas about men's roles, and assumptions about class, race, and ethnicity. In some cases, for instance in Himes's *A Rage in Harlem* (1957) or *Cotton Comes to Harlem* (1965), issues of race and gender are woven throughout in character and narrative; in other cases, social class inflects the portrayal of gender, as in Rinehart's *Circular Staircase* (1908) and in *Silence of the Lambs* (1988). Finally, students can gain a multilayered awareness of changing ideas about what skills and traits or personality are necessary or desirable for criminal investigation, though this is not so much developmental as a case of rounding out a picture that started with the disinterested rationality of Poe's M. Dupin, added the fearlessness and sense of justice imbuing both Hammett's Continental Op and Chandler's Marlowe, and adopted the emotional intelligence of Harris's Clarice Starling. At any point, the addition of new and different texts can alter this balance and can be used to highlight certain points more than others or to introduce new developments in narrative structure, character, or theme. For example, adding Ishmael Reed's *Mumbo Jumbo* (1972) introduces the role of the metaphysical detective and extends the examination of African American novelists' depiction of law and justice. Reed's metaphysical detective, PaPa LaBas, does not depend on rationality or material forensics, but rather his understanding of human beings and his ability to analyze the world's spiritual equilibrium and bring individuals back into harmony. The metaphysical detective takes the long view and does not let himself be too distracted by the foibles and shenanigans of reckless people around him here and now. A module featuring Thomas Pynchon's *Crying of Lot 49* (1965) adds a note of the metaphysical but more significantly introduces the anti-detective novel. In this text the solution to the mystery (and the question of whether there is, in fact, a mystery) seems to recede as one cryptic layer after another is uncovered. The novel overflows with clues that may or may not have meaning and that drive both the detective figure, Oedipa Maas, and the reader on, while perhaps moving the truth farther away and, indeed, undermining the very idea of truth. The revelation seemingly promised at the novel's conclusion may introduce yet another mystery. Finally, the course includes some short fiction but is constructed primarily of novels, so genre is not addressed in any detail, but that particular line of inquiry is enriched by adding a contemporary graphic novel, such as Jules

Feiffer's *Kill My Mother* (2014), that invites students to consider authorial choices that structure a different kind of narrative and challenges them to apply different reading and interpretive skills, taking into account both words and images.

A course such as the one outlined above has a focus on the development of a type of literature, the function of literary devices, and the kind of specificity that assumes in students some level of familiarity with literary analysis and with the culture and history of the nation. However, courses about popular genres also may be of interest to non-majors and to students who approach the study of crime fiction with less preparation in literary study. For those students, the introduction of a greater variety of narratives, some of them closely linked to familiar and contemporary crime stories, can be intriguing and can help them approach what they thought they already knew, but with different eyes. A course such as my Literature of Crime and Criminality, developed for the general student population, introduces students to several genres and emphasizes attention to narrative voice, point of view, and tone in an effort to teach students to approach such narratives with, if not skepticism, at least awareness of the power of narrative assumptions and writers' choice of vocabulary to influence readers' attitude toward actors and events. To that end, the course emphasizes fiction less than crime writing that has some particular claim on truth, such as documentary theater experienced in filmed performance and on the page, the non-fiction novel, and crime reports from a local newspaper, as well as crime fiction in the form of a one-act play, a short story, and one or two novels. The course begins with short works to introduce students to basic tools and concepts for literary analysis, such as characterization, narrative structure, and tone. Students also examine the portrayal of law and those who enforce it, the portrayal of private and amateur detectives and their association with the law and law enforcement, and the investigation of crimes, as well as how the narratives construct the reading and analysis process. Differences among the genres as to the structuring of narratives, the assumption of factuality, the overt or covert presence of the author, and the use of particular structural techniques and word choices to influence readers' responses to narratives are all examined. A selection of Sherlock Holmes stories, chosen based on their relevance to analysis of later texts in the class, and the one-act play, *Trifles* (1916), by Susan Glaspell are the introductory texts. The first familiarizes students with an icon and influential model of the detective and detection while the play provides an intense, concentrated look at how gendered assumptions about crime can undermine and taint detection and the discovery of truth. The choice of novel varies depending on what kind of emphasis or thematic development seems most desirable. Hammett's *Maltese Falcon* (1929) and private eye Sam Spade provide a counterweight to Sherlock Holmes and spark discussion of the cultural context in which hardboiled detective fiction developed, but *Silence of the Lambs* is useful for asserting the continuing relevance of close analysis of the role gender plays in crime, its investigation and its depiction. It connects back very usefully to *Trifles* and to the influence of gender on what is seen and how it is interpreted in an investigation. Jonathan Lethem's novel *Motherless Brooklyn* (1999) and Mark Haddon's *Curious Incident of the Dog in the Night-Time* (2003) introduce fascinating questions about point of view and the perspective that is revealed by an investigator who sees the world in an unusual way. Lethem's Lionel Essrog displays the symptoms of Tourette Syndrome, a frequently disruptive verbal tic, and some compulsive behaviors. Both create difficulties in his detective work, but the Tourette's in particular enhances the novel's rich attention to language and makes Essrog himself uniquely sensitive to language. Haddon's teenage investigator, Christopher Boone, has symptoms of what has been interpreted by critics and readers as Asperger's Syndrome, a form of autism, though Haddon does not identify it as such. Christopher avoids social interactions, is unable to read behavioral signs in others, and does not understand lies. The special appeal of Christopher as a detective, however, is that he focuses on minutiæ that others overlook and asks questions that others would not think to ask. The detective's job is to bring order to a world into which crime has brought chaos. Essrog and Christopher bring readers close to minds that seek to order the world in ways different from more conventional detectives. These characters offer readers new perspectives on genre conventions and significant insights into different kinds of intelligence and observation applied to detection.

Later texts in the course more directly address the relationship between the true and how it is filtered through the writer's consciousness. Truman Capote's non-fiction novel, *In Cold Blood* (1966) and one of Ann Rule's true crime texts, either *Small Sacrifices* (1987) or the *Stranger Beside Me* (1980), challenge students to detect traces of the author's hand in depiction of representatives of law enforcement, the selection of incident, the ordering of events, and in the choice of words to represent the "true" that the designations "non-fiction" and "true crime" signal. It is instructive to ask students to choose from a local newspaper an article about a crime and to analyze the prose, the structure of the narrative, and how the report that is presumed to be "just the facts" differs from other fact-based. Comparing accounts of the same crime from different news sources can also be very instructive. In addition, students explore one of the most recently-developed of the fact-based crime subgenres, that is, the documentary drama or documentary theater. Jacqueline O'Connor, writing in "Performing the Law in Contemporary Documentary Theater" describes it thus: "Documentary theater reconfigures historical events through texts and performances that are partially or completely composed of court transcripts, interviews, newspaper reports, and other documents, and they frequently dramatize excerpts from trial records verbatim."[1] This grounding in documents lends veracity to the account and a sense of historical accuracy. Court transcripts and interviews may provide an immediacy that rivals direct, first-person address in its impact. O'Connor continues, saying "In doing so, these plays transform legal texts into literary texts and legal proceedings into theatrical performance. They demonstrate the ways that art can be constructed from previously existing nonartistic materials, and they highlight the performance aspects of the law."[2] The notion of law as performance, of a trial as an enactment, goes some way to revealing right and wrong, truths and untruths as very much contingent and performative.

This subgenre is particularly exciting to explore with students. They are attracted to the timely nature of the issues dramatized compellingly in plays such as *Zoot Suit* (1978) by Luis Valdez, *Twilight: Los Angeles, 1992* (1993) or *Fires in the Mirror: Crown Heights, Brooklyn, and Other Identities* (1992) by Anna Deavere Smith, and the *Laramie Project* (2000) by Moisés Kaufman and the Tectonic Theater Project. These texts may be explored in print and in filmed versions. All of them open up historical social issues still relevant today. *Zoot Suit* explores the conflict between law enforcement and ethnic expression as exhibited in a 1942 murder trial involving young Los Angeles Mexican American men, and the so-called "Zoot Suit riots." Deavere Smith in *Twilight: Los Angeles, 1992* uses interviews and performance to engage with race, ethnicity, and the slippage between the law and enactment of justice as revealed in the Los Angeles urban uprising of 1992, after the controversial verdict in the trial of Los Angeles police officers in the beating of African American motorist, Rodney King. *The Laramie Project* delves into rural American social attitudes toward homosexuality that underlie discrimination and violence by using community members' statements about the death of gay college student Matthew

Shepard in Wyoming and the trial of two local men for his beating and death. The documentary dramas draw students to original reports of the events, allow them to absorb the questions and issues they raise, to consider how the conflicts are enacted, and to investigate the relationship between a truth seemingly based on factual documents and the reenacting of those events as creative works restructured and designed to appeal to a theatrical or television audience.[3] Finally, the advent and high popularity of investigative journalism series, such as *Serial* (2014–), presented as a serialized podcast narrative, and *Making a Murderer* (2015–), produced as an original online documentary film series through Netflix, have offered even newer forms of crime narrative that raise questions about truth and fiction and about the public's interaction with media and ideas about law enforcement and crime in society. Taken as a whole, the many genres introduced in Literature of Crime and Criminality encourage the exploration of the differing writing practices and reader expectations of the genres and, in the broadest sense, the ideas of law and of justice as concepts that are socially-constructed and, far from being timeless and unchanging, are interpreted and contested by each new generation. The performance of the law and its social, historical context, whether in short stories featuring Sherlock Holmes's conflicts with Inspector Lestrade or in the filmed reactions of Los Angeles citizens of color to a legal verdict that signaled the opposite of "Black Lives Matter," exposes fault lines in the social fabric and encourages thoughtful reexamination of not only the issues and events that are dramatized but of the constructed nature of the texts that present them to an audience. The narratives are creations directed to particular audiences; they are created by an authoring hand, whether that of a playwright, a novelist, an investigative journalist, or a judge in a courtroom crafting a decision, each of whom puts carefully chosen words on a page in a certain order designed to tell a story to particular effect.

Crime writing-as-literary-construct can be traced, of course, much farther back in history. Depending upon the educational context, modules may gain from this deeper sense of history, or from giving this writing practice greater weight by demonstrating its presence in significant historical documents not specifically associated with crime or law, or they may gain from creating a more global context for studying crime fiction. To these ends, instructors may wish to assign texts such as the *Oedipus Rex* or *Antigone* of Sophocles, the Book of Daniel with the story of Susanna and the Elders found in some versions of the Christian Old Testament, *The Merchant of Venice* or another Shakespeare play, or early (thirteenth- or fourteenth-century) or modern versions of the Judge Bao tales from traditional Chinese literature. Many other centuries and cultures provide likely texts and each of them opens up discussion of new cultural contexts and the many variations of law and its enforcement, crime and its investigation, and what is taken to constitute justice or a desirable close to the criminal act. As these examples demonstrate, the cross-cultural study of crime fiction is a rich area of inquiry. Such study might take a comparative, historical approach or might focus on breadth of coverage and explore contemporary crime fiction from all over the world. This comparative study will often discover that the structure of crime fiction does not change very much between cultures but the themes and issues that are highlighted are often very culturally-specific, and certainly the many cultural variations of assumptions about crime, investigation, evidence, and punishment prove particularly fascinating and surprising.[4]

Interdisciplinary Prospects

The examples outlined so far are just a few of the possibilities for course design appropriate to the literature classroom. Numerous other approaches provide rich opportunities for learning, particularly with students who are at more advanced levels in their study of literature. Crime fiction provides provocative texts for the application and study of literary theory, for instance. Much can be learned by analyzing crime fiction through a wide range of theoretical approaches, including psychoanalysis, reader-response, feminist theory, and others. Genre formation and genre theory can be tested in studies of crime fiction texts and their context; such an examination might be particularly fertile because of the long association of the writing of crime fiction with non-fiction sources such as the Newgate Calendar or the real-life exploits of Jonathan Wild in the eighteenth century that provided material for Daniel Defoe's *A True & Genuine Account of the Life and Actions of the late Jonathan Wild* (1725) and Henry Fielding's novel, the *Life and Death of Jonathan Wild, the Great* (1743). Additionally, the gradual separation of detective fiction from the Gothic novel can be a source of insights in the study of the formation of genres and of genre theory, as might the fracturing of crime fiction into multiple subgenres: detective fiction, with its own sub-subgenres, such as cozies, country house mysteries, young adult fiction, and police procedurals, is one; others include the spy novel, courtroom dramas, psychological thrillers, legal thrillers, and more. Studying the historically-grounded link between journalistic practices of crime reporting and the growth of lending libraries in Britain can lead to significant revelations about education, the growth of literacy, the daily lives of women, and audience formation in the eighteenth and nineteenth centuries. The analysis of the anti-detective novel in the context of modernist and postmodern fiction is founded in hybrid texts through which students can examine not only definitions and re-definitions of genre and genre's blurred boundaries, but larger questions of identity formation, even the existence of the individual self, and the existence of truth. In Robbe-Grillet's *The Erasers* (1953), Borges's short story "Death and the Compass" (1942), Pynchon's *Crying of Lot 49*, Auster's *City of Glass* (1985), Peter Ackroyd's *Hawksmoor* (1985), and many others in which the detective figure dissolves or disappears, cause-and-effect are irrelevant, beginnings, middles, and endings may not be discernable, and solutions may never appear. The reading process itself is a search for clues that allow readers to assemble a narrative and follow it to its conclusion. These novels employ the tropes of crime and detective fiction, but frustrate the search for meaning and closure, treating the reader like a detective whose clues seem to make no sense, if they are clues at all, and whose search for a solution and closure is denied, their significance, and existence discounted. Finally, crime fiction affords an ideal vehicle through which to explore narratology, the theory drawn from structuralism and semiotics that analyzes the structure of narrative and identifies points of commonality and divergence in forms of discourse. The basis of crime fiction is the existence of a crime and its investigation, a process that generally ends in a solution. As so many examples above have already shown, though, one of the fascinations of this literature is in its nearly infinite variations. Texts may have many elements in common (for instance a crime, a detective figure, and an investigation), but the arrangement of those elements, the sequencing of events in the plot, the repurposing of tropes and images, offer a unique field of play, a mix of tradition and a space of innovation, that attracts and challenges writers and readers alike and reveals much about the human need for stories. Through narratological study, narrative structures are opened to view, but readers can be examined as well, in their readerly expectations and their degree of tolerance for variation in familiar story elements and narrative patterns.

The many approaches to crime fiction in the literature classroom are matched by the diverse connections that have grown in dozens of other disciplines. Some, such as criminal justice and law, have obvious ties. The use of crime fiction to ground theoretical and field-based teaching about the criminal justice system, law enforcement, and criminology using fictional narratives featuring complex social interactions is longstanding.[5] In criminal justice classrooms, fiction may be introduced with a number of different goals in mind, from studying the gap between popular understanding of law and the realities of law enforcement, for instance, to analyzing popular media versions of famous cases and trials. Skills in problem-solving and critical thinking modeled in crime fiction readily transfer to other studies at the undergraduate level. In law schools, the value of creative storytelling to the study of the principles and application of law gradually has been recognized, resulting in a range of approaches, such as creating stories to reinforce students' understanding of principles of evidence, to different ways to engage students in learning and helping them grasp concepts at a level beyond memorization, to increasing students' awareness of the cultural sensitivities that must inform law enforcement as well as the interpretation and application of legal principles. Peter Brooks, long an influential voice in law and literary analysis, says,

> Our primary interest is to set the study of law in a broad cultural and critical context .... We want to step outside of the law where we can look at it and make students more aware of some of its problematic issues in interpretation and storytelling. You can look at court cases not just for their doctrine, but also for what they're doing to you, for their rhetoric and narrative structure (Couch).[6]

The existence of other interdisciplinary matches, such as linking the practices of multiple media—literature with television, cinema or, now, internet-based entertainment including games and video series produced for the online audience—are well-known sources of insights into adaptation, media studies, audience reception studies, and comparative narratology. It is now possible to read and watch contemporary news accounts of the pursuit, arrest and criminal investigation of O.J. Simpson, study the transcript of the trial, read several books such as legal journalist Jeffrey Toobin's *The Run of His Life* (1997), prosecuting attorney Marcia Clark's *Without a Doubt* (1997) or Simpson's own, *I Want to Tell You* (1995) or *If I Did It: Confessions of the Killer* (2007). Beyond these written accounts, more recently the FX Network's 2016 "true crime anthology" mini-series, *The People v. O.J. Simpson: American Crime Story*, and the nearly simultaneously-released ESPN documentary, *O.J.: Made in America* have been aired. These many texts give very diverse perspectives on the trial and issues of guilt and innocence, and students may profitably analyze the media-mediated spectacle and its textual aftermaths in the classroom. Questions about law, truth, and justice and the narratives that shape public attitudes toward them can be exhaustively studied in this accumulation of texts in various media and genres. This many disputed versions of the truth can result in provocative and enlightening discussions of the boundaries between fiction and non-fiction and the relationship between the goals of the system of laws and competing public ideas about justice. The vast textual coverage of the O.J. Simpson case is but one example of the uses of detective fiction, and crime fiction more generally, to explore topics both broad and deep. This and other cases, whether fiction or non-fiction, open up questions of what constitutes justice: the purpose of laws; the elusiveness of "truth" in crime investigation, in law enforcement, and in the courtroom; the status of documentary evidence; and the question of objectivity. Finally, students may grapple with the fraught issues around whose interest is served by the enactment and enforcement of laws in a system that is, ideally, gender-, race-, ethnicity-, and class-blind.

Looking beyond fields based in traditional narratives, one finds a great deal of interest in and evidence of the successful integration of crime fiction into the study of subjects as diverse as anthropology, architecture, forensic science, gender studies, geography, online game design, and social work.[7] Space does not permit the detailed development of most of these subjects, but two will be singled out for elaboration. To begin, one need look no further than this description of the bachelor of science degree in Game Design offered by Full Sail University of Winter Park, Florida:

> Some people view the world through a narrative lens. They see not just people but players, not just interactions but building blocks of broader stories. If you've ever dreamed of becoming a game designer, and are as passionate about the craft as you are about the end creation—you're not alone. [In] the Game Design bachelor of science program ... you'll cover key industry concepts ranging from aesthetics and immersion to usability and game economics—in addition to foundational topics like storytelling and character development.[8]

When the game goes to market, the result may be something like the action-filled criminal virtual world created in *Grand Theft Auto*, in which the gamer takes the role of a criminal, or in *L.A. Noire*, in which the gamer takes the role of a Los Angeles Police Department detective in the 1940s.

A collection of short stories written by well-known crime story authors may be purchased as an accessory with the latter game and this, with the addition of a few noir and neo-noir films, opens up intriguing possibilities for multimedia study. Finally, there is the relationship between crime fiction and forensic science, which might be explored with a cross-disciplinary contemporary focus. The exploration might consider the prominence of forensic crime shows on television, online, and in cinema, and a similar growth in popularity of forensic-based crime fiction series, such as those written by Patricia Cornwell and Kathy Reichs, which feature a medical examiner and forensic anthropologist, respectively. Neither the television dramas nor the crime fiction offer consumers the realities of forensic science; the process by which the so-called "*CSI* Effect" has infiltrated modern life is, as Lindsay Steenberg has demonstrated in fascinating detail, a "mediated version of forensic science" that has spread across the culture but equates to only a very shallow understanding by the public.[9] The surge in applications to university forensic science programs in the United States in the last decade, referenced by Steenberg,[10] demonstrates one very real effect of this phenomenon and may indicate that modules introducing crime fiction to prospective forensic scientists at the college level or even at earlier levels of education have a strong appeal. Indeed, "Using Detective Fiction to Reinforce Problem Solving Strategies and the Scientific Method"[11] has been designed for middle-school science students in North Carolina, while an integrated curriculum combining law, forensic investigation, biology, and mathematics has been offered to high school students in California.[12] A team-taught course combining chemistry and literature, that is, Introductory Forensic Chemistry joined with American and British Detective Fiction, was recently offered at John Carroll University in Ohio.[13] In a less formal educational context, the *Explore Forensics* website allows participants to reinvestigate famous criminal cases, as in "The Murder of Leeann Tiernan,"[14] learn forensic principles and techniques from a "skilled team of expert authors," and to cooperate or compete with other participants in an interactive, shared-learning environment.[15] While these are very specific examples, they provide a great deal of insight into the many ways crime fiction and crime narratives have become an unquestioned and unavoidable cultural touchstone and the many ways in which they provide an engaging means of learning for students, opportunities for collaborative learning, and stimulating opportunities for interdisciplinary work among faculty.

Conclusion

Lindsay Steenberg begins her study of forensic science and popular culture by saying, "Contemporary popular culture is experiencing a forensic turn,"[16] while Michael Hviid Jacobsen in his *Poetics of Crime* identifies in the current era the "rise of the 'criminological society.'"[17] The contemporary interest in crime fiction and narratives of crime spans all educational boundaries, both in the individuals drawn to it and in its growing integration across disciplines. Steenberg and Jacobsen are both correct in their assessment that modern life provides an immersive experience in texts about crime, from minute-by-minute reports in traditional and electronic journalistic venues, to breaking news of crimes and Amber Alerts received as texts on private cellphones, to the continued success of police and detective shows on television, computers and other electronic devices, and cinema screens. The widespread yet superficial knowledge of forensic techniques and law enforcement they enable in their consumers, the obsession with serial killers, and the pervasive anxiety fueled by fears of generalized violence, sexual assault, war, and global terrorism point to a world that is perceived to be filled with danger and disorder and may be ultimately beyond the knowing, not to mention the control, of the individual. Even those students who do not choose to read or watch texts about crime cannot escape this atmosphere. They may be drawn to courses on crime writing because the subject is popular and is one in which many may feel they are already experts or because they have the feeling that knowing more about narratives of crime will give them more understanding of the world in which they live. Maybe the class simply fits their schedule. Maybe it sounds like a relatively undemanding subject because of its popularity and familiarity. If they come to the study of crime fiction with preconceptions about its familiarity, its narrowness of subject and interest, its dull, restrictive traditions, or the quality of the writing in the genre, such a course will test those preconceptions. In any or all of these cases, though, there is a prospective course module for those students that will engage their intellects and emotions, stimulate their curiosity, tap into issues as relevant as the day's breaking news, help them build their abilities to think theoretically and entertain abstract ideas, and encourage them to practice problem-solving and textual analysis. For students with some literary background, the broad array of texts can introduce them to genre theory and will educate them in the conventions of detective fiction and crime writing, as well as surprise them with the creative space that exists within a single genre. A further benefit is that while participating in a media-rich curriculum that is open to interdisciplinarity, students may engage in learning and enjoyment simultaneously on multiple levels and may achieve a certain amount of new knowledge and useful insights about the world they live in.

Notes

1. Jacqueline O'Connor, "Performing the Law in Contemporary Documentary Theater," in *Teaching Law and Literature*, ed. Austin Sarat, Cathrine O. Frank, and Matthew Anderson (New York: Modern Language Association, 2011), 407.
2. Ibid., 407–408.
3. The juxtaposition of filmed versions of Anna Deavere Smith's *Twilight: Los Angeles, 1992* (2001) and *The Laramie Project* (2002) creates particularly exciting discussion. Both are based on interviews, but Deavere Smith performs all of the characters as part of a filmed one-woman play and *The Laramie Project* is performed by professional actors, some famous, as an HBO television movie. Discussion of performance style and the shaping of the documentary material can be very rich.
4. Readers interested in exploring these options in more depth should consult Rebecca Martin, ed., *Critical Insights: Crime and Detective Fiction* (Ipswich, MA: Salem Press, 2013) or Edward J. Rielly, ed., *Murder 101: Essays on the Teaching of Detective Fiction* (Jefferson, NC: McFarland, 2009).
5. For further discussion of these possibilities, it is suggested that readers consult Michael Hviid Jacobsen, ed., *Poetics of Crime: Understanding and Researching Crime and Deviance through Creative Sources* (Burlington, VT: Ashgate, 2014) and Angela M. Nickoli et al., "Pop Culture Crime and Pedagogy," *Journal of Criminal Justice Education* 14, no. 1 (Spring 2003). While the latter deals with the use of mainstream films in the criminal justice classroom, many of the suggestions are applicable to the introduction of others kinds of crime texts.
6. Readers are referred to the discussions in Beryl Blaustone, "Teaching Evidence: Storytelling in the Classroom," *University Law Review* 41, no. 2 (1992); Kate Nace Day, "Stories and the Language of Law," *in The Future of Scholarly Writing: Critical Writings*, edited by Angelika Bammer and Ruth-Ellen Boetcher (New York: Palgrave Macmillan, 2015); Julie Stone Peters, "Law, Literature, and the Vanishing Real: On the Future of an Interdisciplinary Illusion," *PMLA* 120, no. 2 (March 2005); Robert C. Power, "'Just the Facts': Detective Fiction in the Law School

Curriculum," in *Murder 101: Essays on the Teaching of Detective Fiction*, edited by Edward J. Rielly (Jefferson, NC: McFarland, 2009); and Julie M. Spanbauer, "Using a Cultural Lens in the Law School Classroom to Stimulate Self-Assessment," *Gonzaga Law Review* 48, no. 2 (2013), *John Marshall Law School Institutional Repository, Faculty Scholarship*, accessed June 29, 2017, http://repository.jmls.edu/facpubs/335/, for additional information.

7. For more ideas, consult Rielly, ed., *Murder 101*, and Lindsay Steenberg, *Forensic Science in Contemporary Popular American Culture: Gender, Crime and Science* (New York: Routledge, 2013).
8. "Game Design: Bachelor of Science," *Full Sail University*, accessed June 29, 2017, https://www.fullsail.edu/degrees/game-design-bachelor.
9. Steenberg, *Forensic Science in Contemporary Popular American Culture*, 1.
10. Ibid., 1–2.
11. See Ella Boyd, "Using Detective Fiction to Reinforce Problem Solving Strategies and the Scientific Method," *Yale National Initiative*, accessed June 29, 2017, http://teachers.yale.edu/curriculum/viewer/initiative_07.02.03_u.
12. See ConnectEd: The California Center for College and Career, *Crime Scene Investigation: Integrated Curriculum Unit on Forensics* (Berkeley, CA: ConnectEd, 2010), accessed June 29, 2017, http://www.connected-california.org/files/LJCrimeSceneInvestigation_FullUnit.pdf.
13. See Chrystal Bruce and John McBratney, *Detective Fiction and Forensic Science: A Proposal*, accessed June 29, 2017, http://webmedia.jcu.edu/cas/files/2015/04/ENW.Detective-Fiction-and-Forensic-Science1.pdf.
14. See Suzanne Elvidge, "Forensic Cases: The Murder of Leeann Tiernan," *Explore Forensics*, last modified December 20, 2016, http://www.explore-forensics.co.uk/forensic-cases-murder-leanne-tiernan.html.
15. See "Forensic Science for Beginners," *Explore Forensics*, accessed June 29, 2017, http://www.exploreforensics.co.uk/.
16. Steenberg, *Forensic Science in Contemporary Popular American Culture*, 1.
17. Jacobsen, "Introduction: Towards the Poetics of Crime: Contours of a Cultural, Critical and Creative Criminology," in *Poetics of Crime*, 4.

Works Cited

Blaustone, Beryl. "Teaching Evidence: Storytelling in the Classroom." *American University Law Review* 41, no. 2 (1992): 453–484.

Boyd, Ella. "Using Detective Fiction to Reinforce Problem Solving Strategies and the Scientific Method." *Yale National Initiative*. Accessed June 29, 2017. http://teachers.yale.edu/curriculum/viewer/initiative_07.02.03_u.

Bruce, Chrystal and John McBratney. *Detective Fiction and Forensic Science: A Proposal.* Accessed June 29, 2017. http://webmedia.jcu.edu/cas/files/2015/04/ ENW.Detective-Fiction-and-Forensic-Science1.pdf.

ConnectEd: The California Center for College and Career. *Crime Scene Investigation: Integrated Curriculum Unit on Forensics.* Berkeley, CA: ConnectEd, 2010. Accessed June 29, 2017. http://www.connectedcalifornia.org/files/LJCrimeSceneInvestigation_FullUnit.pdf.

Couch, Cullen. "Teaching the Narrative Power of Law: Program in Law and Humanities Sets Legal Study in Broad Context." *UVA Lawyer* (Fall 2005). Accessed June 29, 2017. http://www.law.virginia.edu/HTML/alumni/uva-lawyer/f05/humanities.htm.

Day, Kate Nace. "Stories and the Language of Law." In *The Future of Scholarly Writing: Critical Interventions*, edited by Angelika Bammer and Ruth-Ellen Boetcher Joeres, 137–145. New York: Palgrave Macmillan, 2015.

Elvidge, Suzanne. "Forensic Cases: The Murder of Leeann Tiernan." *Explore Forensics.* Last modified December 20, 2016. http://www.exploreforensics.co.uk/forensic-cases-murder-leanne-tiernan.html.

"Forensic Science for Beginners." *Explore Forensics.* Accessed June 29, 2017. http://www.exploreforensics.co.uk/.

"Game Design: Bachelor of Science." *Full Sail University.* Accessed June 29, 2017. https://www.fullsail.edu/degrees/game-design-bachelor.

Grand Theft Auto. Accessed June 29, 2017. http://www.rockstargames.com/grandtheftauto/.

Jacobsen, Michael Hviid. "Introduction: Towards the Poetics of Crime: Contours of a Cultural, Critical and Creative Criminology." In *Poetics of Crime: Understanding and Researching Crime and Deviance Through Creative Sources*, edited by Michael Hviid Jacobsen, 1–25. Burlington, VT: Ashgate, 2014.

Kaufman, Moisés. *The Laramie Project.* New York, NY: HBO Home Video, 2002, DVD.

L.A. Noire. Accessed June 29, 2017. http://www.rockstargames.com/lanoire/.

Martin, Rebecca, ed. *Critical Insights: Crime and Detective Fiction.* Ipswich, MA: Salem Press, 2013.

Nickoli, Angela M., Cindy Hendricks, James E. Hendricks, and Emily Osgood. "Pop Culture, Crime and Pedagogy." *Journal of Criminal Justice Education* 14, no. 1 (Spring 2003): 149–162.

O'Connor, Jacqueline. "Performing the Law in Contemporary Documentary Theater." In *Teaching Law and Literature*, edited by Austin Sarat, Cathrine O. Frank, and Matthew Anderson, 407–414. New York: Modern Language Association, 2011.

Peters, Julie Stone. "Law, Literature, and the Vanishing Real: On the Future of an Interdisciplinary Illusion." *PMLA* 120, no. 2 (March 2005): 442–453.

Power, Robert C. "'Just the Facts': Detective Fiction in the Law School Curriculum." In *Murder 101: Essays on the Teaching of Detective Fiction*, edited by Edward J. Rielly, 178–186. Jefferson, NC: McFarland, 2009.

Rielly, Edward J., ed. *Murder 101: Essays on the Teaching of Detective Fiction*. Jefferson, NC: McFarland, 2009.

Smith, Anna Deavere. *Twilight: Los Angeles, 1992, PBS* video, 1:26, June 29, 2012. http://www.pbs.org/wnet/gperf/twilight-los-angeles-full-episode/3972/.

Spanbauer, Julie M. "Using a Cultural Lens in the Law School Classroom to Stimulate Self-Assessment." *Gonzaga Law Review* 48, no. 2 (2013): 365. *John Marshall Law School Institutional Repository, Faculty Scholarship*. Accessed June 29, 2017. http://repository.jmls.edu/facpubs/335/.

Steenberg, Lindsay. *Forensic Science in Contemporary American Popular Culture: Gender, Crime, and Science*. New York: Routledge, 2013.

CHAPTER 3

Plots and Devices

Malcah Effron

Agatha Christie's detective novelist character Ariadne Oliver describes her approach to plotting as follows:

> What really matters is plenty of *bodies!* If the thing's getting a little dull, some more blood cheers it up. Somebody is going to tell something—and then they're killed first! That always goes down well. It comes in all my books—camouflaged in different ways of course.[1]

Christie's fictional surrogate here offers one means that crime writers in a variety of subgenres have actively pursued, or ignored, as works for their plots. However, what Oliver's strategy highlights is that the intrigue of crime fiction is particularly placed in the exposure of a crime, its mechanism of execution, and its perpetrator. The genre is less frequently associated with character, theme, or message than with plot. As such, crime fiction is known as the plot-driven genre *par excellence*, so plot must be included in any crime fiction pedagogy.

This designation, however, has often excluded crime fiction from a place on the academic curriculum. As Peter Brooks notices, plot-level

M. Effron (✉)
Department of Comparative Media Studies, Massachusetts Institute of Technology, Cambridge, MA, USA
e-mail: meffron@mit.edu

C. Beyer (ed.), *Teaching Crime Fiction*, Teaching the New English,
https://doi.org/10.1007/978-3-319-90608-9_3

considerations are often considered superficial because the focus seems to be exclusively on answering the question "what happened?"[2] Detective writers and readers have long perceived this question as central to crime fiction forms, leading High Modernists such as W. H. Auden to condemn it as disposable fiction.[3] Nevertheless, Brooks reclaims attention to plot, arguing that it is not as simple as discovering "what happened." So, attention to plot in a class on crime fiction needs to attend to more than figuring out the solution to the mystery.

Narrative theory provides a productive avenue for attending to crime fiction plots and genre devices in ways that enrich the reading experience, especially as it is one of the first literary theories to embrace detective fiction as an object of productive study. Embracing plot-driven texts—here defined exclusively in terms of those that prioritize solving a mystery—narrative theory reveled in the opportunity, explicitly identified by Tzvetan Todorov, to provide clear illustrations of its claims obscured by more convoluted narrative structures.[4] Consequently, not only does narrative theory enrich the study of crime fiction plots and devices, but the study of crime fiction plots and devices can be used to enrich the study of narrative in general. Applying core concepts from narrative theory to crime fiction, this chapter suggests literary terms to enrich class discussions of crime fiction plots and offers some activities to demonstrate their value to literary studies.

Plot, while seemingly a straightforward term, is actually as complex as its potential structures. Brooks notes that plot can mean "[a] ground plan, as for a building; chart; diagram."[5] This form best maps onto the notion of crime fiction as plot-driven, highlighting how the story assembles discrete points (clues) into an analysis of their relationships (the narrative of the crime). This notion of plot, however, does not dominate textual analysis. In literary studies, at its base level, plot accounts for the events of the narrative, as is indicated by the use of *plot summary* to mean an overview of the story. Yet, plot is not used simply to identify that which is summarized in a plot summary. Tautological definitions aside, determining how to define what aspects contribute to the plot becomes a necessary first step in considering how to study it.

In *Narrative Form* (2003), Suzanne Keen introduces her chapter on plot with multiple definitions, noting that each approach to its definition nuances certain elements. These elements include, and tend to focus on, "narrative's complicated relations with time (chronology), order (and disorder), and generic conventions."[6] In his attempts to reclaim plot's relevance to the academy, Brooks adds to this notion that plot is "an embracing concept for the design and intention, a structure for those meanings that are developed [...] through succession and time."[7] As both Keen and Brooks highlight, discussions of plot center on how storytellers (on any textual level) order events in relation to each other to construct a causal narrative. This definition reasonably explains crime fiction as a plot-driven narrative: the text ends by narrating the crime in an Aristotelian structure with a clear beginning, middle, and end.

For this reason, Tzvetan Todorov identifies a two-tiered plot construction in most crime fiction narratives: *the story of the crime* and *the story of the investigation*.[8] For Todorov, the story of the crime maps onto the events as they happened (*fable* in Formalist terms; *story* in narratological terms) whereas the story of the investigation maps onto how those events are presented to the reader (*subject* and *discourse*, respectively). Todorov uses this correlation to make his claims about narrative theory and the poetics of prose; however, it stops a step too short for a full study of plot in crime fiction. Both the story of the crime and the story of the investigation narrate the causal links, but they operate on two different timelines, distinguishing the two-tiered plot structure of crime fiction from a simple *story-discourse* divide.

While crime fiction scholarship typically follows Todorov's correlation of "the story of the crime" with *story/fable* and "the story of the investigation" with *discourse/subject*, the story of the investigation can be analyzed in terms of its *story* and *discourse*, as well. Typically, the story of the investigation is discussed in terms of form—not content—highlighting the need to disclose all clues that lead the detective to the solution without revealing the conclusion too early in the narrative. Eyal Segal summarizes Golden Age detective writers' (1920s–1940s) attitudes toward this task, noting that these writers have created "elaborate system[s] of disguises and misdirections,"[9] constituting the discourse-level analysis of the story of the investigation plotline.

In outlining the variety of ways that crime fiction writers delay the readers' discovery of the solution, Segal predominantly discusses focalization shifts to leave readers outside the detective's mental processes. This can be done through description, the use of an investigative companion, or the observations of any of the other characters in the texts. Since the rise of an investigative police force and the development of the police procedural, crime fiction incorporates descriptions of professionalized criminal investigations. This involves piecemeal revelations as clues are discovered, rather than through instantaneous conclusions followed by the disappearance of the detective for the duration of the narrative (cf. Doyle's *The Hound of the Baskervilles* [1901–02]). Though Segal does not mention this mode, another facet that the professionalization of the investigator allows for is team collaboration, splitting up the knowledge between sections of the group. For instance, since the 1990s, P. D. James has focalized different chapters through different members of Dalgliesh's, the detective protagonist's, investigative team. Mimetically, these different focalizations demonstrate how investigators can maximize their efficiency by dividing and conquering; structurally it allows the reader the opportunity to piece the puzzle together before the investigators themselves. Such practice ultimately leads to shifting focalization, leading the readers to see through multiple perspectives and asking them to bring together the pieces of the plot rather than leading the readers along a simple explanation of "what happened."

Though these approaches all highlight differing commitments to the detective as primary focalizer, a detective-focalized story of the investigation describes only one primary approach to discourse-level studies of the story of the investigation. Some authors choose to focalize the story of the investigation through the suspects rather than the detectives, allowing the reader to perceive the information as the detective does. Perhaps Wilkie Collins deserves credit for originating this method of focalization in crime fiction in his (self-proclaimed) novel approach to novels in *The Woman in White* (1859). The introduction informs the reader that the story will be told through multiple narrators, calling attention to the narrator-focalizer as witness:

> No circumstance of importance [...] shall be related on hearsay evidence [...] When [the narrator's] experience fails, he will retire from the position of narrator, and his task will be continued [...] by other persons who can speak to the circumstances [...] from their own knowledge.[10]

Collins here shifts narrators to shift focalization. While not all have used Collins's approach, other novelists prioritize witness testimony as a narrative device. For instance, Ngaio Marsh similarly moves between the testimonies of witnesses and suspects as a means of introducing clues without necessarily indicating a clear path to the solution. These narratives come sometimes narrated by the witnesses themselves,[11] and sometimes narrated through Chief Inspector Alleyn's notes.[12] Such moments complicate the story by offering differing accounts of one event, the murder of the primary victim. Focusing on characters as narrators, discussions of character in crime fiction can thus support discussions of plot, and vice versa.

Because crime fiction plots foreground clue-gathering, whether through witness testimony, as in Collins and Marsh, or through forensic analysis, as in Patricia Cornwell or Kathy Reichs, scholars like Todorov claim the story of the crime must take place in the narrative past.[13] Yet, crime fiction narratives do not always limit the narrative present to the story of the investigation. For example, Thomas Harris's *Red Dragon* narrates the simultaneous progress of FBI agent Will Graham and serial killer Francis Dolarhyde.[14] The Dolarhyde narratives create a version of dramatic irony, as the reader has information about the murderer's actions and motives before the detective and can understand the importance of certain clues before or even better than the detective. Yet, this insight only allows the reader to know how, but not who, still requiring the detective's resources to discover the specific individual who committed the crimes. As the who and the why is presented to the readers throughout the experience, the plot in such texts develop intrigue around *how* the criminal will be caught.

Though a traditional history of the crime fiction genre might introduce plot structures like Harris's as postmodern innovations or responses, the criminal's perspective is not a recent addition to the crime fiction plot. Perhaps the most continually popular version of this is *Columbo*, the television series starring Peter Falk, but some of the earliest versions appear during the Golden Age of detective fiction. For instance, R. Austin Freeman's Dr. Thorndyke uses an "inverted" detective story plot,[15] which switches the story from a whodunit to a howdunit. By eliminating the question of "who," these plot structures need the audience to care about how the detective will unravel the threads that will lead directly back to the killer. Howdunits must fully engage the reader in the investigative process, keeping the reader turning pages because of interest in the process rather than curiosity about the culprit.

Both whodunit and howdunit plot structures privilege (devote more space to) the story of the investigation of the crime after its commission, rather than the story of the commission of the crime in the text's narrative present. Todorov has suggested that thrillers collapse the story of the crime and the story of the investigation into the same plot: "[w]e are no longer told about a crime anterior to the moment of the narrative; the narrative coincides with the action."[16] This description works for novels such as Graham Greene's *The Ministry of Fear* (1943), in which most of the criminal intrigue happens during the timeline of the narrative.[17] It works less well for John Buchan's *The Thirty-Nine Steps* (1915), a text often cited as one of the first thrillers,[18] in which the protagonist's escapades are driven by a need to figure out what has happened.[19] Todorov's description of thrillers lends itself nicely to crime fiction narratives about the criminal rather than the detective, as in the case of Patricia Highsmith's Mr. Ripley novels. Yet, the moments of the definition's failure create opportunities to think about the robustness of the crime genre's plot structures, as the form can accommodate so many variations without needing a completely new genre.

As can be seen from this breadth of two-tiered plot structures, a course syllabus could easily be designed around variations of the story of the crime and the story of the investigation. Such a course structure would allow the instructor to break away from the traditional crime fiction pseudo-historical approach that moves from the Golden Age to Hard-Boiled to Police Procedural to Beyond, moving back and forth across the Atlantic. As can be seen even in the brief examples offered above, these forms are not limited to one historical era, national model, or cultural perspective. Additionally, the two-tiered approach would allow an instructor to delve deeply into the narrative difference between the chronological path of events and the order in which the author chooses to disclose them. In particular, it could be productive to include a text more often considered "literature" than "crime fiction," such as William Faulkner's *A Rose for Emily* (1930), which, after all, ends up a crime story. As an a-chronological narrative, Faulkner's text privileges discourse over story and easily demonstrates ways the narrative structure can withhold plot points, both in the story of the crime and the story of the investigation.

Aside from this two-tiered approach, crime fiction can productively be considered in terms of its approach to narrative closure, or how the plot ends. Segal offers a neat definition for closure based on dynamism rather than stasis: "the ending of a narrative text [...] would produce an effect of closure when it brings to a halt the operation of all kinds of narrative interest by filling in all of the significant informational gaps about the represented world that have arisen during the textual sequence."[20] Certainly, as Segal argues, this definition describes the classic detective fiction plot, whose denouement offers an unraveling of all the knots in the investigation by providing a complete narrative of the crime and explaining away all tangents. Typically, "all of the significant informational gaps about the represented world" are filled in through the detective's monologue.

Additionally, in the classic Golden Age form, the crime's solution enables the marriage of two key characters, bringing the text's subplots to a comedic resolution.

Classic detective fiction's strong closure leads scholars to speak of crime fiction as a conservative genre. Scholars argue that for a crime and punishment narrative to have strong closure, it must support the current social order, "restor[ing] to the Garden of Eden."[21] Even crime narratives that begin in a post-lapsarian environment, such as that Raymond Chandler claims for the hard-boiled genre,[22] the criminal is discovered and generally is removed from society. Protagonists operating within hegemonic systems such as the police, the court, or the military understandably are trapped in the ideological systems these infrastructures support. Yet, even activist private investigators, such as Sara Paretsky's feminist detective V. I. Warshawski, rarely conclude by completely overhauling the social system in which the crime occurs. More to the point, even when the protagonist is a criminal, such as E. W. Hornung's Raffles and Elmore Leonard's Chili Palmer, the rule-breaker is redeemed and is reincorporated into the existing social systems.

Despite these kinds of failures, there are some crime fiction forms that push against strong closure conventions. Some police-based novels allow the criminals to escape punishment at the end. For instance, some of Ian Rankin's novels end with the mob boss, "Big Ger" Cafferty still at large (cf. *The Black Book*). Yet, even Cafferty seeks to maintain a current social order, as he helps Rebus with cases as a means of coping with the evolution of gang behavior in Scotland (cf. *Mortal Causes*). Perhaps the most productive work can be seen in texts that actually confront their social systems, especially those that are not known internationally as having ethical institutional practices. As an example, Sam Naidu and Karlien van der Wielen show how Deon Meyer's South African police detectives grapple with defining justice in South African crime fiction, as nationally there is no inherent assumption that what is legal or what is enforced is also what is good.[23] Nevertheless, as Naidu and van der Wielen's work reiterates, even these texts return, at least locally, to some definition of right and wrong through which order might be (re)constructed.

Potentially offering a simultaneous account for why the genre is ideologically conservative, Todorov identifies the inherent structural conservativism of crime fiction: "[d]etective fiction has its norms, to 'develop' them is also to disappoint them: to 'improve upon' detective fiction is to write 'literature.'"[24] Though Todorov's value judgments are outdated, his narratological claims explain the strong resilience of the detective plot form. Those that truly shatter its conventions—such as Gertrude Stein's *Blood on the Dining-Room Floor* (1948) or Paul Auster's *City of Glass* (1985)—are not filed in the crime fiction sections of libraries and bookstores; nor are they generally considered part of the genre, except under Todorov's archaic value system. Nevertheless, the form is flexible enough to admit crime novels that flirt with the boundaries like those Stefano Tani and Patricia Merivale and Susan Sweeney use to categorize anti-detective or metaphysical crime fiction. For instance, while Thomas Pynchon's *The Crying of Lot 49* (1965) is held up as an exemplar of the anti-detective form because it does not offer a conclusion of the case, John Sallis's *The Long-Legged Fly* similarly withholds strong closure, yet the rest of the plot structure follows closely enough that it is still considered part of the crime fiction genre. Similarly, as many scholars have noted, Anthony Berkeley's *The Poisoned Chocolates Case* (1929) offers multiple conclusions, and not only is it considered crime fiction, but it is taken as an exemplar of the Golden Age novel.

Despite these innovations, crime fiction, as a genre is best known for arriving at a denouement in which all is revealed and explained. For this reason, whether speaking of the investigator within the text or the reader outside the text, as Keen describes in relation to Wilkie Collins's *The Moonstone* (1868), "the plot of the novel can be assembled in full only after each deposition has been read and combined in the mind of the reader."[25] This aspect of closure leads Auden to decry the form as both an addictive drug and entirely disposable: "once I begin, I [Auden] cannot work or sleep till I have finished it [but] I forget the story as soon as I have finished it, and have no wish to read it again" (15). In this approach, Auden holds by the common notion of the plot's primary function as a puzzle which once solved—once the trick has been discovered—no longer holds any narrative excitement or interest. Such perspectives, especially by crime fiction authors such as S. S. Van Dine, has long kept the general public from thinking of crime fiction as literature, initially keeping it out of the academy. This attitude persisted because early crime fiction studies refused to reveal endings (cf. Ray B. Browne, John G. Cawelti, and George Grella), making it difficult for scholars to argue compellingly about a whole text. Such prioritization of the conclusion means that, when teaching crime fiction, it is important to decide whether or not students may reveal plot elements that students at different stages of the reading process might not yet have encountered.

One easy solution to this problem is to assign students to read novels as a whole rather than in sections. This approach allows the students to determine for themselves the significant moments in the text rather than the instructor's sectioning overriding the individual reading experiences. This will also allow the students to have more individual reactions to the denouements, as their expectations will be preconditioned by neither instructor guidance nor class discussion. If one is teaching a course in a literature curriculum, this might be an acceptable solution, as many curricula anticipate that students will read an entire work before class discussion. It might even be easier to make this demand if one's students are comprised of Audenesque readers. Yet, there have been many clever assignments that have engaged productively with reading serial narratives on the original publication timeline (not to mention a number of institutions that balk at large weekly reading requirements), so this solution is not a catch-all.

At this point, best practice is largely contingent on the instructor's own reading and analytic goals for the class. For instance, the students could decide at the start of the term that they may only discuss as much content as had been assigned prior to a given class session. This is a practical guideline, as much as it is in the context of any literature classroom. Consider teaching a three-volume novel: should students be limited to only discussing one volume at a time? If yes, then it seems reasonable to extend this practice to a discussion of crime fiction plots. In fact, such limitations can create productive conversations about how the plot develops, forcing students to revisit their understanding of the events in the story at each class session. However, if one prefers to spend more time discussing the full intricacies of the plot, it is helpful to allow students to address the complete structure from the initial conversation. Crime fiction scholarship no longer believes it has any obligation to withhold the ending any more than any other area of literary studies. (Some, like Pierre Bayard, don't even feel obligated to accept the novel's published conclusion.[26]) Despite this, when privileging the incremental unfolding of the plot, students can employ a "spoiler alert" system. Of course, accepting this tactic privileges the perspective that once the solution is found and the trick is revealed, the narrative is "spoiled."

Regardless of the method chosen, the class can pay attention to flexibility of crime fiction plots by thinking about the nature of genre requirements. In this kind of a conversation, ask students to think not only of, but also against the generic codes that have been devised for the genre. When taking an historical approach to genre development, these rules offer a nice place to think about how cultural context affects the function of plot devices. For instance, after reading Ronald Knox's and S. S. Van Dine's rules for writing detective stories, ask students why these limitations were put on the detective genre. Historically, these conventions arose in response to publishing practices, highlighting a social demand for increasing originality in plots. Knox bans "Chinamen" because of their overuse as the criminals in the genre.[27] This can begin a conversation about the cultural biases that led early-twentieth-century writers, such as Sax Rohmer, to gravitate toward a Chinese figure as its villain character. To bring this conversation back to the plot structures that inform crime fiction, call the students' attention to the difference between banning "Chinamen,"—a prohibition ignored in texts like the Hardy Boys *Footprints under the Window* (1937)—and banning stereotyped characters that are overwritten with negative connotations in a contemporary environment. While a ban on "Chinamen" might no longer be appropriate, is it narratively acceptable for crime fiction plots to rely on stereotypes to establish criminality? For instance, compare the use of race in Ngaio Marsh's *Black as He's Painted* (1974) or Henning Mankell's *Faceless Killers* (1990/1997). Such questions bring students back to thinking about the intersections of plot and how these devices can transcend the historical contexts of their specific implementations.

In addition to these rules, used more predominantly now in scholarship than in trade publication, give students some samples of contemporary guides to writing crime fiction. For instance, Carolyn Wheat identifies several plot structures to use when producing crime fiction. Whereas the Golden Age generic guidelines focus predominantly on what *not* to do, these structures are written in a positive, directive fashion. For instance, regarding the denouement, Wheat outlines several kinds of endings writers could use, including "the non-action ending," the "two-layered ending," and "the action ending."[28] Coming under the section title "Endings Are Hard," these examples offer positive approaches to how to resolve a crime fiction narrative. Using Wheat as a sample model for identifying good crime plot structures and the Golden Age authors as another, ask the students to outline a skeleton plot structure for what must happen in order for a text to be part of the crime fiction genre. This activity can work well as a capstone to the semester, allowing them to call on the experience of reading different novels throughout the semester.

Genre-based approaches to plot such as these ask students to focus on what is essential and what is accidental. Use this as an opportunity to promote knowledge transfer from the use of genre when reading to when writing. Comparing the way genres function can help students realize that narrative and argument rest on the same basic process, namely taking readers through an assessment of the causal relations between the parts of the whole. In this process, writers of all genres make individual data points—clues in crime fiction plot—feel meaningfully connected as opposed to coincidentally adjacent. The excitement of discovering "who-dunit" derives from the journey as much as, if not more than, the destination (cf. John Dickson Carr's rant in *The Three Coffins* [1935]), and attention to this journey teaches observation, analysis, and reasoning skills that are necessary for all forms of problem-solving. These are also skills that instructors can have students develop when dealing with a single crime fiction novel in a larger, non-crime fiction curriculum. The points about plot construction transfer not only to the other texts they will read in the class (detective plotting is a good example of hermeneutic analysis), and the papers they will write (the denouement uses evidence to support its argument), but also the basic notion that care and attention can predict and affect outcomes. In a course dedicated to crime fiction, the students can attend to the correlation of plot construction and conventions, using these details to develop a core structure from which to notice variance across the texts in the course. In this capacity, the way detective fiction obscures the presentation of "what happened" can remind the students that, even when one reads for the plot, a story is never as straightforward as it seems.

Notes

1. Agatha Christie, *Cards on the Table.* (New York.: Berkley Books, 1937.; repr., 1984). 57.
2. Peter Brooks, *Reading for the Plot: Design and Intention in Narrative* (New York: Alfred A. Knopf, 1984).
3. W. H. Auden, "The Guilty Vicarage," in *Detective Fiction: A Collection of Critical Essays*, ed. Robin W. Winks (Englewood Cliffs: Prentice-Hall, Inc., 1980).
4. Tzvetan Todorov, *The Poetics of Prose* (Ithaca, N.Y.: Cornell University Press, 1977). 43.
5. Brooks, *Reading for the Plot: Design and Intention in Narrative.*
6. Suzanne Keen, *Narrative Form* (Basingstoke: Palgrave Macmillan, 2003).
7. Brooks, *Reading for the Plot: Design and Intention in Narrative.*
8. Todorov, *The Poetics of Prose.*

9. Eyal Segal, "Closure in Detective Fiction," *Poetics Today* 31, no. 2 (2010). 180.
10. Wilkie Collins, *The Woman in White* (Oxford: Oxford University Press, 1998).
11. Ngaio Marsh, *Death and the Dancing Footman* (London: Published for the Crime Club by Collins, 1942).
12. *Death in Ecstacy* (London: HarperCollins, 2001).
13. Todorov, *The Poetics of Prose.*
14. Thomas Harris, *Red Dragon* (New York: Putnam, 1981).
15. Segal, "Closure in Detective Fiction." 185.
16. Todorov, *The Poetics of Prose.*
17. Graham Greene, *The Ministry of Fear: An Entertainment* (London: Penguin Books, 1973).
18. Christian. House, "How *the Thirty-Nine Steps* Invented the Modern Thriller," *The Telegraph*, October 11, 2015.
19. John Buchan and Christopher Harvie, *The Thirty-Nine Steps*, World's Classics (Oxford England; New York: Oxford University Press, 1993).
20. Segal, "Closure in Detective Fiction." 162.
21. Auden, "The Guilty Vicarage." 24.
22. Raymond Chandler, *The Simple Art of Murder* (New York: Vintage, 1988).
23. Sam Naidu and Karlien van der Wielen, "Poison and Antidote: Evil and the Hero-Villain Binary in Deon Meyer's Post-Apartheid Crime Thriller, *Devil's Peak*," in *The Functions of Evil across Disciplinary Contexts*, ed. Malcah Effron and Brian Johson (Lanham: Lexington Books, 2017).
24. Todorov, *The Poetics of Prose.*
25. Keen, *Narrative Form.*
26. Pierre Bayard and Carol Cosman, *Who Killed Roger Ackroyd?: The Mystery Behind the Agatha Christie Mystery* (New York: New Press, 2000).
27. Ronald A. Knox, "Detective Story Decalogue," in *The Art of the Mystery Story*, ed. Howard Haycraft (New York,: Simon and Schuster, 1946).
28. Carolyn Wheat, *How to Write Killer Fiction: The Funhouse of Mystery & the Rollercoaster of Suspense* (Palo Alto: Perseverance Press, 2003).

Works Cited

Auden, W. H. "The Guilty Vicarage." In *Detective Fiction: A Collection of Critical Essays*, edited by Robin W. Winks, 15–24. Englewood Cliffs: Prentice-Hall, Inc., 1980.

Auster, Paul. *City of Glass*. New York: Penguin Books, 1985.

Bayard, Pierre, and Carol Cosman. *Who Killed Roger Ackroyd?: The Mystery Behind the Agatha Christie Mystery*. New York: New Press, 2000.

Berkeley, Anthony. *The Poisoned Chocolates Case*. New York: Felony & Mayhem Press, 2010. 1929.

Brooks, Peter. *Reading for the Plot: Design and Intention in Narrative*. New York: Alfred A. Knopf, 1984.
Browne, Ray B. *Heroes and Humanities : Detective Fiction and Culture*. Bowling Green, OH: Bowling Green State University Popular Press, 1986.
Buchan, John, and Christopher Harvie. *The Thirty-Nine Steps*. World's Classics. Oxford, England; New York: Oxford University Press, 1993.
Cawelti, John G. *Adventure, Mystery, and Romance: Formula Stories as Art and Popular Culture*. Chicago: The University of Chicago Press, 1976.
Chandler, Raymond. *The Simple Art of Murder*. New York: Vintage, 1988.
Christie, Agatha. *Cards on the Table*. New York: Berkley Books, 1937. 1984.
Collins, Wilkie. *The Moonstone*. Mattituck, New York: Amereon House.
———. *The Woman in White*. Oxford: Oxford University Press, 1998. 1859.
Doyle, Arthur Conan. *The Hound of the Baskervilles*. Mineola: Dover Thrift Editions, 1994. 1901–02.
Faulkner, William. *A Rose for Emily*. New York: HarperCollins, 2013. 1930.
Greene, Graham. *The Ministry of Fear: An Entertainment*. London: Penguin Books, 1973. 1943.
Grella, George. "The Formal Detective Novel." In *Detective Fiction: A Collection of Critical Essays*, edited by Robin W. Winks, 84–102. Englewood Cliffs, NJ: Prentice-Hall, 1980.
———. "The Hard-Boiled Detective Novel." In *Detective Fiction : A Collection of Critical Essays*, edited by Robin W. Winks, 103–20. Englewood Cliffs, NJ: Prentice-Hall, 1980.
Harris, Thomas. *Red Dragon*. New York: Putnam, 1981.
House, Christian. "How *the Thirty-Nine Steps* Invented the Modern Thriller." *The Telegraph*, 11 October 2015.
Keen, Suzanne. *Narrative Form*. Basingstoke: Palgrave Macmillan, 2003.
Knox, Ronald A. "Detective Story Decalogue." In *The Art of the Mystery Story*, edited by Howard Haycraft, 194–96. New York: Simon and Schuster, 1946.
Marsh, Ngaio. *Death and the Dancing Footman*. London: Published for the Crime Club by Collins, 1942.
———. *Death in Ecstacy*. London: HarperCollins, 2001.
Merivale, Patricia, and Susan Elizabeth Sweeney. *Detecting Texts: The Metaphysical Detective Story from Poe to Postmodernism*. Philadelphia, PA: University of Pennsylvania Press, 1999.
Milhorn, H. Thomas. *Writing Genre Fiction: A Guide to the Craft*. Boca Raton: Universal Publishers, 2006.
Naidu, Sam, and Karlien van der Wielen. "Poison and Antidote: Evil and the Hero-Villain Binary in Deon Meyer's Post-Apartheid Crime Thriller, *Devil's Peak*." In *The Functions of Evil Across Disciplinary Contexts*, edited by Malcah Effron and Brian Johson, forthcoming. Lanham: Lexington Books, 2017.
Pynchon, Thomas. *The Crying of Lot 49*. Perennial Classics. 1st Perennial Classics ed. New York: HarperPerennial, 1999.

Rankin, Ian. *Mortal Causes.* New York: St. Martin's Paperbacks, 1994.

———. *The Black Book.* New York: St. Martin's Paperbacks, 1993.

Sallis, John. *The Long-Legged Fly.* New York: Walker Publishing Company, Inc., 1992.

Segal, Eyal. "Closure in Detective Fiction." *Poetics Today* 31, no. 2 (2010): 153–215.

Stein, Gertrude, and John Herbert Gill. *Blood on the Dining-Room Floor.* Berkeley, CA: Creative Arts Book Co., 1982.

Tani, Stefano. *The Doomed Detective: The Contribution of the Detective Novel to Postmodern American and Italian Fiction.* Literary Structures. Carbondale: Southern Illinois University Press, 1984.

Todorov, Tzvetan. *The Poetics of Prose.* Ithaca, NY: Cornell University Press, 1977.

Wheat, Carolyn. *How to Write Killer Fiction: The Funhouse of Mystery & the Rollercoaster of Suspense.* Palo Alto: Perseverance Press, 2003.

CHAPTER 4

Teaching Crime Fiction and Gender

Maureen T. Reddy

Much early hardboiled detective fiction vividly illustrates Judith Butler's theory that gender is entirely performative, with no existence apart from that performance.[1] The original American hardboiled detectives—those detached, cool, solitary men created by Dashiell Hammett and Raymond Chandler in the 1920s and 1930s—repeatedly perform their masculinity (and whiteness and heterosexuality) in opposition to various others in the narratives in which they feature. Indeed, those gender/race performances are arguably the whole point of the hardboiled, whose plots are often far less compelling than are descriptions of the detectives' performative proof of their (white) masculinity. When Sam Spade compliments Effie in *The Maltese Falcon* by saying, "you're a good man, sister," he implies both that masculinity can be performed by those who are not biologically male and that successfully performing masculinity is a worthy goal in itself.[2] The villains of the traditional hardboiled are either men who fail at performing (white, heterosexual) masculinity or women who perform one type of femininity all too well. Think, for instance, of Raymond Chandler's *The Big Sleep*, in which the murdered pornographer is described as "the fag"; in which the gangster who kills Harry and is determined to kill Marlowe,

M. T. Reddy (✉)
Rhode Island College, Providence, RI, USA
e-mail: mreddy@ric.edu

C. Beyer (ed.), *Teaching Crime Fiction*, Teaching the New English,
https://doi.org/10.1007/978-3-319-90608-9_4

Lash Canino, is not-quite-white; and in which the hyper-feminine Carmen presents a murderous threat to men who resist her attempts at seduction.[3] There is no being greater, or rarer, than "a good man"—that man who is "not himself mean"[4]—in the world of Hammett's and Chandler's fiction, with only the detectives fully measuring up to the demands of that particular gender performance.[5] Thinking about the hardboiled in terms of performing gender helps to illuminate why the rise of feminist crime fiction in the U.S. in the last quarter of the twentieth century tended not to follow hardboiled patterns, with even those series that focused on tough private eyes significantly modifying rather than merely adopting the conventions of the hardboiled. That is, performing femininity is at odds with the requirements of the detective role, while a woman detective performing masculinity raises still other problems. Instead, feminist authors of crime fiction featuring female detectives critique the requirements of both roles—femininity and detection—in constructing their characters and plots.[6]

The foregoing may seem entirely obvious to those familiar with Judith Butler's work as well as either the American hardboiled or its feminist revisions, but these ideas are far from obvious to my undergraduate students, many of whom have never encountered either Butler or crime fiction before entering my classroom. For almost a decade, I have been teaching a course called "women, crime, and representation" at Rhode Island College (RIC). The course, which I try to offer once annually, is aimed at undergraduates at the sophomore level or above and is part of my college's general education program in a category we call "connections." Connections courses "emphasize comparative perspectives, such as across disciplines, across time, and across cultures," to quote RIC's website, and are meant to help students further develop their abilities in several core student learning outcomes first introduced at the freshman level. These courses cannot be included in the requirements for any student's major program of study and have few prerequisites; mine, for example, requires only that students have completed at least forty-five credits, including introductory writing and literature courses. I cannot assume, then, that my students have any gender studies background at all or that they have read any crime fiction, although in fact some students are drawn to my course specifically because they are interested in gender studies and/or crime fiction. In the rest of this essay, I discuss how one might use gender theory to analyze crime fiction and crime fiction to illustrate gender theory in the classroom, using this course as one possible example.

My most recent syllabus describes the course this way:

> This connections course examines representations—in fiction, non-fiction, film, and television—of women as criminals, as crime victims, and as detectives. We will consider texts of various national origins and time periods, paying close attention to the similarities as well as differences in their portrayals of women. We will draw on research and analyses done by scholars from a variety of fields, including film and media studies, gender and women's studies, sociology, history, and literature, to help us make sense of these representations and what they might tell us about our society and ourselves. Most of our work in this course could be considered under the broad rubric of cultural studies, the interdisciplinary field begun in the middle part of the twentieth century and focused on the myriad, complex forces through and within which people lead and understand our own lives. We focus for the most part on materials from popular culture, beginning with the 1930s–1940s, but spending the bulk of our time on works created between 1980 and the present.

The course, which is not strictly about crime fiction but includes more crime fiction than any other genre, is divided into four units, beginning with "Dead(ly) Women" and ending with "Female Detectives." The two middle units—"Women Strike Back" and "Political 'Crime'"—focus on a number of non-crime fictional and nonfictional texts, including *Thelma and Louise* and Nawal El Saadawi's *Woman at Point Zero*, that are outside the scope of this book and that I will therefore not discuss here.

During our first class meeting, I briefly explain the underlying premise of the course: that popular culture profoundly influences how we see each other and ourselves. Popular culture is never simple, but instead is often both complex and contradictory, especially when it comes to gender roles, which we often see both reinforced *and* undermined within the same text, whether film or fiction. Further, "reality" is shaped by popular culture; that is, what we believe to be true quite often comes not from our analysis of the world around us but instead from popular culture. When I first began teaching this course, I had to assume that most students would resist these fundamental claims about the importance of fictional representations, but my current students tend to be quite savvy about the influence of popular culture on our perceptions of self and others, in part because of public attention to eating disorders among young people and the connection between girls' self-images and dominant social images of beauty. The students arrive with the assumption that popular culture matters; however, they frequently have a simplistic idea of exactly *how* it matters, one that this course complicates.

At that first class meeting, we spend some time laying out the course's central terms and concepts after I assert that none of the three main words in the course title—"women," "crime," "representation"—is simple or transparent but instead needs some unpacking and discussion. I ask students to participate in trying to construct a shared definition of each of those words with which we can begin the work of the course, while also stressing that we will probably need to revisit and revise those definitions at several points during the term. Invariably, there are several students who quickly insist that defining "women" is easy and who agree on something like "a female over the age of 18," although the numbers of such students have shrunk as awareness of transgender people has increased. I can now count on at least one student challenging the "easy" definition by asking if we are limiting the discussion to ciswomen or if transwomen are included in it. Regardless of other students' responses, this question allows me to steer the discussion toward the vexed role of biological sex in our attempts to define "women" and to ask the class to think about Simone de Beauvoir's famous claim that "one is not born, but rather becomes, woman."[7] My strategy is to leave the definition of "women" open, having shown that we don't in fact share an "easy" definition, and to shift the discussion to the other two terms. This part of the discussion used to be much more difficult, as until recently I was usually the only person in the room to raise the issue of gender identity as a spectrum, not a binary; the rise of public attention to trans issues in the U.S. in the past several years has made teaching gender issues much easier, as fewer students arrive in my class convinced that there are just two sexes. "Crime" turns out to be almost as fraught as "women": students always begin with some version of "an act that is against the law" but other students complicate that—sometimes with my prodding—by asking about unjust laws and, sometimes, unjust regimes. The examples that come up most often in questioning the "against the law" definition of crime are Civil Rights demonstrators against Jim Crow laws in the U.S. and—probably because most students have read *The Diary of Anne Frank* in middle school—people who hid Jews from the Nazis during the Holocaust. If "the law" is not always the final arbiter of crime, what is? I ask students to think about that problem and we move on to our final term, representation. By this point, naturally, students hesitate to go with their first responses, having witnessed first responses to the first two terms being challenged. In an electronic classroom, I pull up the Oxford English Dictionary online and show the definition of "representation," noting that our course is using the second of the three main definitions, which goes like this:

> 2. The description or portrayal of someone or something in a particular way
> *'the representation of women in newspapers'*
> 2.1 The depiction of someone or something in a work of art.
> *'Picasso is striving for some absolute representation of reality'*
> 2.2 [count noun] A picture, model, or other depiction of someone or something.
> *'a striking representation of a vase of flowers'*[8]

If not in an electronic classroom, I simply read this definition aloud. Students sometimes express relief at this point—finally, a word that isn't tricky to define and on which we can all agree!—but I try to trouble that relief a bit by noting that because we can't agree yet on the first two course terms, we are likely to run into trouble discussing "the description or portrayal" of them (women, crime) in course texts.

For logistical reasons, the first text we examine is John Huston's film adaptation of Dashiell Hammett's *The Maltese Falcon* (1941). My course meets twice weekly for two hours each meeting; I cannot ask students to complete an entire novel between the first and second classes, nor do I want to spend more than half of one class period on introductory material. This film works well to get students immediately applying the concepts and terms of the course. I end our discussion of those terms by saying that we will frequently circle back to these issues and then ask students to take careful notes on the film we will begin watching together. In particular, I ask them to think about the course's terms as we watch the first 30 minutes or so of *The Maltese Falcon* together. Exactly how much of the film I show during that first class meeting depends on how much time we have left in the class period after covering the introductory material, as I want to make sure that we have at least ten minutes left after our viewing to begin talking about what we have seen. Even the first 15–20 minutes of *Maltese* offers plenty of material with which to begin that discussion. We finish watching the film during the second class meeting and discuss it in relation both to our course terms and to the title of our first unit, "dead(ly) women." I ask students to comment on the three women in the film—Effie, Brigid, and Iva—in terms of representations of women. How does this film position viewers in relation to these women? Why is it that both Iva and Brigid are dangerous to Sam (Iva calls the police on him, for instance), but that only Brigid's threat must be contained and punished (suggested both by Sam's comments on capital punishment and on the final image of Brigid behind the bars of the elevator)? How do we *know* Effie is a good girl? What are the qualities that make her "good" (this is where "you're a good man, sister" comes in)? How do we square her "goodness" with her seeming lack of sexual attraction? Brigid and the male criminals have exactly the same motive—greed—but the film strongly suggests that Brigid is worse than the men—why? How do we know Sam is superior to all the other men in the film? In what specific ways does each other man fail to measure up to him?

Responding to these questions, which attempt to get at constructions of gender in the film, students frequently mention the distance between our own historical moment and the moment of the film. Many of their comments, particularly about representations of women, begin with some version of "in those days." In those days, women were supposed to do what men said (Effie), women were not supposed to use sex to get what they wanted (Brigid), women were supposed to be loyal to their husbands (Iva), and so on. How do you know that, I ask them, and do you have to know that before seeing the film to understand what is going on in terms of how we are led to make judgments about the characters? If they can get beyond repeating that "everybody knows" how things were in 1941, some students find that they are caught in a logical circle: we know how things were in 1941 *from the film itself* and we judge characters in the film by measuring them against what *the film* tells us about gender requirements through representing gender in specific ways. This is the moment at which I introduce Judith Butler's ideas about gender as performative. If gender were in any way essential, I point out, then there would be no need to acknowledge the decades that intervene between Huston's film and our viewing of it. Judith Butler's idea that the performance of gender constructs gender, versus its "expressing" some essence, can help us to understand what is going on in the film and why we understand it *without* having to read up on women's and men's relative positions in 1941. I usually just summarize those parts of Butler's theory most relevant to our course, but also make available to students her entire essay, "Performative Acts and Gender Constitution: An Essay in Phenomenology and Feminist Theory"

The reading assignment to follow up on *The Maltese Falcon* is Janey Place's important article, "Women in Film Noir."[9] Along with the article itself, I give students some reading questions to help us have a focused discussion during the next class period. The questions are quite broad, and encourage students to keep thinking about *The Maltese Falcon*:

> (1) The options for women in *film noir* are limited, according to Janey Place, and basically come down to the good girl or the spiderwoman. Please identify some of the main characteristics of each category and also that category's typical iconography. How do these categories play out in *The Maltese Falcon*? Does this article help you to understand that film better than you did when we watched it in class?
>
> (2) Place asserts that popular culture functions as myth. She sketches out how myth works and then makes a case about *film noir*. How does *film noir* work as myth, according to Place? What audience fantasy does it indulge? Apply this idea of myth to *The Maltese Falcon*, describing how this film operates as myth. What are its most important mythic elements?

Our third class meeting is devoted to discussing Place's article, focusing closely on these two questions but also considering her other arguments, including points she makes about a resurgence in *film noir* in the 1970s, which I ask students to update to the present moment, when many films and television programs have *noir* elements. What are the social conditions in our time that might correspond to those of the 1930s–1940s that Place limns as what the *film noir* movement responded to?

Those three class meetings—the introductory one on terms, one spent viewing and discussing *The Maltese Falcon*, and one analyzing the film in relation to Janey Place's argument about *film noir*—move us to discussion of our first novel, which is also the final text in the "dead(ly) women" unit: Raymond Chandler's *The Big Sleep*, which I suggest on the first day that students begin reading right away so that they have it completed by the second week of class. The reading questions that I give students on the novel again focus on gender; my instructions ask them only to think about the questions and to note relevant page numbers, not to write out responses:

> (1) *The Big Sleep* (1939) predates the film we viewed together but is a fairly late hardboiled detective novel (Hammett's *The Maltese Falcon* came out about a decade earlier). Consider the novel's female characters in relation to Janey Place's "Women in Film Noir." Are Place's observations about film noir useful in analyzing this novel? Explain why/why not.

(2) In an introduction to a collection of his short stories first published in 1950, Chandler remarks that hardboiled fiction, unlike other murder mysteries, "does not believe that murder will out and justice will be done—unless some very determined individual makes it his business to see that justice is done. The stories [that he, Hammett, and others wrote] were about the men who made that happen. They were apt to be hard men, and what they did, whether they were called police officers, private detectives, or newspaper men, was hard, dangerous work. It was work they could always get. There was plenty of it lying around." In the same essay, Chandler says of these detectives' urban locales, "Down these mean streets a man must go who is not himself mean" Does Marlowe fit his creator's description? In what specific ways does he fit it/fail to fit it?

(3) Janey Place notes that film noir serves a conservative (she calls it "regressive") "ideological function on a strictly narrative level" but stresses that the visual style "often overwhelms (or at least acts upon) the narrative so compellingly" that the bad girl/spiderwoman's dangerous activity is fascinating and exciting. Obviously, novels do not have a visual element that might work against the narrative level. Is there anything in *The Big Sleep* that seems to undermine the "regressive ideological function" of its plot?

On the first of the two days we spend on this novel, I organize what Jennifer Gonzalez calls a "snowball" discussion. As Gonzalez explains,

> Students begin in pairs, responding to a discussion question only with a single partner. After each person has had a chance to share their ideas, the pair joins another pair, creating a group of four. Pairs share their ideas with the pair they just joined. Next, groups of four join together to form groups of eight, and so on.[10]

I split the class in half, assigning one half to the first reading question and the other to the second, and then follow Gonzalez's model, starting with a 15-minute discussion for the first pair and then 10–15 minutes for each addition. The larger groups sometimes need less time than the first pair does because after that first discussion, they are sharing ideas that often overlap. Once each half of the class has gathered into one group, I ask each group to explain to the other group its collective response to the assigned question. After the first group summarizes its response, the other group comments, asks questions, and so on, and then we switch to the second group. I do more planning for this discussion than Gonzalez suggests because I want to make sure that the initial pairs bring together students who have seemed not to be in agreement in our first three classes in the hope that the students who have found the idea of gender as performance useful will persuade their classmates to think about gender in these terms when talking about *The Big Sleep*. The second day of discussion of the novel builds on students' responses to the third question. We also spend some time looking closely at a few striking passages, including the scene in which Marlowe finds Carmen in his bed and rejects her sexual advances, which leads to her hissing and behaving as an animal instead of a human, and which ends with Marlowe destroying the bed in which Carmen has lain once he gets her out of his apartment. Students find these scenes to be excruciatingly belabored in their positioning of women and men as extreme opposites. To conclude this first unit of the course, I ask students to think back to our first class meeting and to summarize where we have been thus far. Can we refine our definitions of the three key terms in our course's title? At this point, most students are willing at least to consider seriously the idea that gender exists only in and through performance, generally feel more confident about what is meant by representation, but often have not altered their definitions of crime

At the end of the first two weeks of the course, we shift away from crime fiction for two units—a total of seven weeks—centered on texts that do not fit the crime fiction genre but that include women in the roles of criminal and criminalized activist, but we continue to focus on and develop the ideas introduced in the first two weeks. I have thought about redesigning the course so that it is all crime fiction, film, and television, and can imagine versions of the course that use only crime fiction to examine the same issues regarding women, crime, and representation, but have not yet tried that out. For the last five weeks of the course—ten class meetings—we turn to texts in which women feature as detectives, but also as crime victims and/or as criminals in several texts. In addition, students work together in groups of four to prepare class presentations on texts that we do not consider as a full class. Although I have changed the specific texts used in this section of the course, each iteration has included at least one text by a woman of color featuring a woman of color as detective, at least one text in which the female detective is a private eye, at least one in which the woman detective is a police officer, and at least one in which the criminal turns out to be a woman. So, for instance, one recent version of the syllabus included Sara Paretsky's *Blacklist* (2003), Paula Woods's *Inner City Blues* (1999), Tana French's *The Secret Place* (2014), and episodes of

Cagney & Lacey (1983), *Prime Suspect* (1991), and *Happy Valley* (2016). I choose the texts for this unit with an eye toward including diverse representations of women and girls and emphases on ideas of both race and gender.

Having experimented with different ways of organizing this unit, I find that beginning with a Paretsky novel—or one of the other feminist-authored series begun in the early 1980s—tends to work best. That choice allows me to set up the historical situation of feminist crime fiction and the shift in the crime text's central consciousness that began during the last quarter of the twentieth century as the framework for the last part of our course. Students are always struck by the awareness of gender expressed by these detectives, and the central role that gender plays in the plots. In *Blacklist*, for example, Paretsky's narrator/protagonist, V.I., comments directly at numerous points on her own and other characters' performances of gender, whether remarking on her own deliberate failure to conform to gender norms, noting the specifics of an upper-class woman's self-presentation as a refined lady, or describing one female sheriff's deputy's sense of female solidarity with V.I. when her boss, the sheriff, tries to demean V.I. in a gender-specific way. I ask students to think about representations of both women and men in Paretsky's novel. Are we seeing a straightforward reversal of the tropes of the hardboiled, with femininity valued over masculinity, or is *Blacklist* doing something else with gender, even perhaps undoing the male/female binary in the gender performances of its characters?

Most students do not think that *Blacklist* goes quite that far, but they do note differences between the texts with which we began and Paretsky's novel that are not attributable mainly to changes between the 1930s and the 2000s. Students tend to be especially interested in this novel's use of larger social issues in its plot, including racism, Islamophobia, the Communist witch hunts of the House of Un-American Activities Committee (HUAC) era and the post-9/11 Patriot Act, and to see that interest as a major shift from the hardboiled texts with which we began the course. Indeed, many of the feminist-authored series featuring female detectives from the 1980s to the present connect the specific crime investigated in a novel with a broad social issue, a shared feature that makes these series part of a counter-tradition, as I argue in *Sisters in Crime: Feminism and the Crime Novel.* Students also observe that the obstacles Spade and Marlowe face in their investigations are not related to their gender, whereas V.I. faces deliberate obstruction from men who object to a female detective. Similarly, although a sole operator, V.I. is not a loner in the extreme way that Spade and Marlowe are: she has close friends and a number of people who assist in the investigation and not merely in the general dogsbody way we see with Effie Perrine. One of these helpers is a Black woman, the sister of the murder victim whose body V.I. finds at the start of the novel. The centrality of race and racism in this novel lead us to consider the ways in which V.I. performs *white* womanhood while remaining aware that her whiteness affords her privileges denied to Black men and women, which is a long way from the unspoken assumption in the Hammett and Chandler texts that whiteness is simply superior to every other racial possibility, just as men are superior to women.

The attention to race in *Blacklist* makes it a good choice to pair with a novel by a woman of color featuring a female detective of color. The novel with which I have had the most success is Paula L. Woods's *Inner City Blues*, which takes place a decade before Paretsky's *Blacklist*, in the midst of the 1992 Los Angeles uprising after an all-white jury acquitted the police officers who were seen on videotape beating Rodney King. More than two decades after the events amid which Woods's novel is set, many of my students don't know who Rodney King is or even that the uprising happened, but two years after the murder of Michael Brown by a white police officer in Ferguson, MO, and the protests that followed, galvanizing the Black Lives Matter movement, my students are well aware of police bias and brutality against Black people. Charlotte Justice, Woods's narrator/protagonist, is a police detective whose family objects to her job and whose co-workers and supervisors object to her being in the job, albeit for different reasons: her family believes she is wasting her education, while many cops believe that cops are by definition white and male, and Charlotte is neither. This novel works well in my course for many reasons, chief among them the narrative's explicit interest in the problematics of racial and gender performance. Charlotte frequently thinks about her own performance of Black femaleness and the hostility anything but a carefully controlled, entirely professional, unemotional, and self-deprecating performance will garner—and even that perfectly controlled performance is often not enough to deflect that hostility. *Inner City Blues* gets at the forces within and through which each of our gender performances is constructed and the complex intersections of gender and race that, along with the weight of history, make policing and Black womanhood a vexed combination. In fact, the villains in this novel are two male police officers; unlike what we observed in the hardboiled, these villains are not marked by their failure to perform a specific version of white masculinity—indeed, students often point out that the villains (one of whom is Black) perform a mainstream version of white masculinity all too well. Some students find the novel's ending disappointing because Charlotte does not solve the central crime and is rescued by her anti-cop brother. However, other students can be relied upon to challenge this view and to argue instead that the novel is much more interesting than a traditional mystery precisely because Charlotte "fails," which they see as forcing readers to think about why and how Black femaleness and detecting/policing are ultimately incompatible in *Inner City Blues.*

In this final unit of the course, I ask students to write an essay that requires them to reflect on some of our last few texts in relation to the ones with which we began. The writing prompt tends to be something like this:

> During the last part of the course, we read three texts and watch three others in which women are in the position of detective, following an historical shift that happened beginning around 1982, when a 'boom' began in female-authored crime fiction featuring female detectives. That shift raised the interesting question of whether gender matters in detective fiction. That is, are these texts substantially different from earlier detective fiction (think of *The Maltese Falcon* and *The Big Sleep* as models) or do female detectives merely fill the shoes of the earlier male ones? Focusing particularly on representations of women—not only the detectives, but also other women characters—consider how gender matters in at least two of the texts from the last unit of our course.

Most students see significant differences in the two sets of texts, and most discuss those differences in terms of constructions of gender and race. Some, however, take an even more interesting approach and examine what they consider to be failures of imagination in one or more of the texts we consider in this unit—these students often write about the police-detective television programs we view together; failures that they sometimes attribute to a writer or director's inadequate understanding of how gender and/or race operate. Whatever their arguments, though, by the end of the course students find thinking of gender and race as performative rather than essential useful. The language of performativity gives them the tools to think about differences between the early hardboiled and its feminist revisions in nuanced and complex ways, as well as to rethink their own conceptions of both "crime" and "representation" in popular culture and why popular culture matters. The fourteen weeks of this course cover a lot of ground, illustrating Judith Butler's theory of performativity in multiple ways. By the end of the course, most students have a new vocabulary for talking about both gender and crime fiction, one that will certainly continue to be useful to them in their academic careers and in their lives beyond academe.

My experience teaching this course multiple times across the past decade have varied considerably, with my current students far more sophisticated in their understanding of the impacts of popular culture on its consumers as well as more aware of the complexities of gender than were the students in the first years of the course. However, one constant has been the efficacy of using a performative understanding of gender to analyze crime fiction, as well as crime fiction to illustrate that theory of gender as performative. In recent years, fewer students enter the class with much experience of reading detective novels, although most have seen numerous detective films and television programs. On the other hand, more begin the course with at least a rudimentary understanding of gender as not "natural." Bringing gender theory and crime fiction together in the way that this course does deepens students' understanding of both.

Notes

1. Judith Butler, "Performative Acts and Gender Constitution: An Essay in Phenomenology and Feminist Theory," *Theatre Journal*, 40, no. 4 (1988), 519–531.
2. Dashiell Hammett, *The Maltese Falcon* (New York: Random House, 1992), 160.
3. Raymond Chandler, *The Big Sleep* (New York: Vintage Crime/Black Lizard, 1988), 100.
4. Raymond Chandler, "The Simple Art of Murder," *Trouble is My Business* (New York: Random House, 1992), vii.
5. See chapter one of Maureen T. Reddy, *Traces, Codes, and Clues: Reading Race in Crime Fiction* (New Brunswick, NJ: Rutgers University Press, 2003), 6–40, for a more nuanced and detailed argument on this point.
6. See the "Loners and Hardboiled Women" chapter of Maureen T. Reddy, *Sisters in Crime: Feminism and the Crime Novel* (New York: Continuum, 1988).
7. Simone de Beauvoir, *The Second Sex* (1949), trans. Constance Borde (New York: Vintage, 2011), 439.
8. *Oxford English Dictionary, s.v* "Representation." Accessed May 6, 2017.

9. Janey Place, "Women in Film Noir," in *Women in Film Noir*, ed. E. Ann Kaplan (London: British Film Institute, 1978), 47–68.
10. Jennifer Gonzalez, "The Big List of Class Discussion Strategies," *Cult of Pedagogy*, October 15, 2015, http://www.cultofpedagogy.com/speaking-listening-techniques/.

Works Cited

Butler, Judith. "Performative Acts and Gender Constitution: An Essay in Phenomenology and Feminist Theory." *Theatre Journal*, 40, no. 4 (1988): 519–531.

Chandler, Raymond. *The Big Sleep*. New York: Vintage Crime/Black Lizard, 1988.

———. "The Simple Art of Murder." In *Trouble Is My Business*. New York: Random House, 1992.

de Beauvoir, Simone. *The Second Sex*. Trans. Constance Borde. New York: Vintage, 2011.

Gonzalez, Jennifer. "The Big List of Class Discussion Strategies." *Cult of Pedagogy*. October 15, 2015. http://www.cultofpedagogy.com/speaking-listening-techniques/.

Hammett, Dashiell. *The Maltese Falcon*. New York: Random House, 1992.

Place, Janey. "Women in Film Noir." In *Women in Film Noir*, edited by E. Ann Kaplan, 47–68. London: British Film Institute, 1978.

Reddy, Maureen T. *Sisters in Crime: Feminism and the Crime Novel*. New York: Continuum, 1988.

———. *Traces, Codes, and Clues: Reading Race in Crime Fiction*. New Brunswick, NJ: Rutgers University Press, 2003.

CHAPTER 5

Teaching American Detective Fiction in the Contemporary Classroom

Nicole Kenley

Introduction

Detective fiction's drive to identify and contain threats makes it a fertile ground for examining the changing concerns of American literature and culture more broadly. Because of this drive, detective fiction directly engages the challenges of twentieth- and twenty-first-century literary and social movements. The course outlined here utilizes two teaching foci, one based on content and the other on genre. The content focus considers what Andrew Pepper frames as the four overarching preoccupations of contemporary American crime fiction: race, ethnicity, gender, and class.[1] Tracking these concepts across the entirety of the course suggests that the genre's obsession is what makes American detective fiction so very American. The second focus, based on genre, examines the generic drive to adapt, subvert, and reinvent previous exemplars of the form. Put together, these approaches allow students to apply the lens of American detective fiction to social and literary movements ranging from feminism to Postmodernism to globalization. Included in this chapter are discussions

N. Kenley (✉)
Simpson University, Redding, CA, USA
e-mail: nkenley@simpsonu.edu

C. Beyer (ed.), *Teaching Crime Fiction*, Teaching the New English,
https://doi.org/10.1007/978-3-319-90608-9_5

of teaching methods for the primary subgenres of American detective fiction, including the hardboiled, the forensic, and the Postmodern, along with the challenges and larger questions these subgenres pose to students. The chapter also presents student feedback informally solicited one year after the conclusion of their course, in order to determine which concepts students found the most useful in working through the course texts. Overall, this chapter presents one template for a thoroughgoing engagement with the genre of American detective fiction across a semester in the hopes that other educators might successfully adapt these method to their own courses.

Framework

While the bulk of the syllabus deals with texts from the hardboiled era of the 1920s–1940s and after, in order to track the growth of the general form into a specifically American one, the course nevertheless begins with a discussion of Edgar Allan Poe's "The Purloined Letter."[2] Although this text is useful for discussing the foundational conventions which subsequent texts will adapt, subvert, and reinvent, introducing these generic parameters is not the primary objective in starting with Poe. (Nor is it to establish Poe as the originator of the genre, which Steven Knight calls one of the many "myths [that] abound in crime fiction studies."[3]) Rather, beginning this way establishes several core components for understanding the genre as an object of study. While scholars of detective fiction are doubtless all too ready to move beyond this debate, it bears outlining at the course's beginning to manage students' expectations of the genre. First, starting with Poe frames detective fiction's literary bona fides. Poe, as a recognized and recognizable member of the canon, imparts to the genre his imprimatur and situates the course texts squarely in the realm of standard American literary curriculum. Next, using "The Purloined Letter" opens the door to bring in analytical examples that establish the rigor with which students can think about detective fiction and the kinds of theoretical concepts that such study can introduce—Jacques Lacan's "Seminar on the Purloined Letter" is an obvious case in point.[4] While presenting the entirety of Lacan's argument (or Jacques Derrida's and Barbara Johnson's responses to it) would doubtless overwhelm students, it is useful to introduce Lacan's idea of the letter as a pure signifier with the ability to orient subjects around it as it shifts. Taking this approach accomplishes three main goals. To begin, this strategy gives the students a handle on a concept that they can use productively throughout the semester. The idea of the Lacanian signifier helps to structure students' thoughts about the genre as a whole, particularly with Dashiell Hammett's *The Maltese Falcon* coming up quickly on the reading list.[5] Further, thanks to encountering Lacan so early on, students understand that not only are they going to be engaging the material with a great deal of rigor, which is not what students may expect from a course dealing with popular texts, but also that preeminent theorists have engaged detective fiction in just this way, underscoring the point about the genre serving as a worthy object of study. Finally, this approach provides a benefit both for students who have yet to take critical theory and for those who have. For students who have encountered theory, Lacan works as a touchstone, a point of familiarity while they encounter a new genre. For students new to theory, learning about the signifier here softens up the ground a bit. Starting with Poe and Lacan sets the stage for the students in terms of the genre's credentials as well as the kind of thinking it can be used to do.

One final framing component for the course from Poe is the relationship between detective fiction, gender, and chivalry. Of the course's four driving thematic elements, gender is the most clearly articulated in the story, and chivalry provides the means for that expression. Poe's Dupin is a *chevalier*, endowed with an honorific which literally means knight. Further, his devotion to his queen and her secrets drives the entire story's plot, and the strategic placement of the letter around the apartment evokes tactical moves by the knight to protect the queen. This chivalric act also serves to highlight the foundational concept of containment for the genre. In this story, authority is threatened, and that threat is then contained by the detective's actions. "The Purloined Letter," then, establishes containment and chivalry as foundational components in the generic framework. Each of these elements will be adapted by later texts and, in the case of gender, reinvention, and subversion will appear first in the hardboiled and next in the reinventions of the hardboiled.

Further, Lacan's reading of "The Purloined Letter" potentially carries a gendered component as well, as John Muller and William Richardson usefully point out in their analysis of his seminar. In Lacan's reading, the purloined letter itself is the signifier, and it structures three different glances around it. These glances represent positions of knowing, from complete ignorance to partial ignorance to knowledge and opportunity. As more becomes known throughout the course of the story, different characters occupy different subject positions. Muller and Richardson read these shifting subject positions as inherently gendered because the first initially belongs to the impotent King, the second to the feminized and promiscuous Queen, and the third to the powerful Minister.[6] Since these positions shift from character to character as they orient around the signifier, degrees of knowledge also become gendered in the text, such that when the Minister shifts to the second subject position, he "is obliged to don the role of the Queen, and even the attributes of femininity."[7] Rehearsing these critical moves with the students at the outset of the course establishes the ways in which, for detective fiction, a discussion of gender dynamics is intrinsic. Overall, positing these fundamentals as the framework for American detective fiction, creates a touchstone against which students can compare subsequent texts to determine the extent to which they adhere to, subvert, and reinvent the genre.

The Hardboiled

From Poe, the syllabus moves quickly to the hardboiled, a subgenre that for many students is synonymous with American detective fiction. While jumping from the mid-1840s to the late 1920s does skip a segment of American detective fiction, it does so to highlight the innovation of what Leonard Cassuto calls "the most important contribution to crime and detective fiction since Poe devised the formula: the invention of the hardboiled."[8] When presented with the works of Dashiell Hammett and Raymond Chandler, students can see Cassuto's point that "ratiocination in the tradition of Poe … remains the trunkline for the main development of American crime and detective fiction: everything else hangs off it, and the main branches don't appear until one travels a certain distance from the roots."[9] In the case of the hardboiled, the "distance from the roots" comes in particularly through the new version of American masculinity that Hammett and Chandler help popularize.

Several critical studies offer differing explanations for the genesis of the quintessentially American characteristics of the hardboiled, citing possibilities from a reaction against the more sentimental mode of nineteenth-century American masculinity,[10] to a rejection of American materialism,[11] to a passionate response to the New Deal's potential to provide justice for diverse groups of outsiders.[12] While these accounts differ, students will be able to recognize the differences that the hardboiled presents from Poe's genteel Dupin in numerous regards, including setting, style, and characterization. The mean streets of San Francisco and Los Angeles, the tough talk and one-liners, the gritty detective and femme fatale—these images will likely ring familiar to students based on their place in the American cultural landscape via film noir. What students may not realize is the extent to which these ideas originate not from film but from pulp magazines. To this end, it can be useful to start with cover images from dime magazines like *Black Mask*, *Dime Detective*, *Weird Stories*, and *Spicy Detective* to offer a visual representation of hardboiled origins, particularly with regard to gender; students typically do not realize the extent to which the hardboiled invests itself in a narrative of hypermasculinity. Cassuto sees this as a twentieth-century American phenomenon, with "gender roles be[coming] severely proscribed after new masculine paragons like Theodore Roosevelt excoriated 'feminized' men as threats to American civilization. These warnings reflected a new context – and new anxieties – attached to being a man."[13] Framing the hardboiled navigation of gender in terms of anxieties helps students to better understand the stakes of the subgenre that so much of subsequent American detective fiction will adhere to, subvert, and reinvent.

Hammett's *The Maltese Falcon* makes a useful first reading because it takes up multiple threads from "The Purloined Letter": it adheres to the generic framework in terms of the Lacanian signifier, diverges from that framework in its chivalry, and introduces new elements of style and characterization. Again, one of the aims in teaching a survey course focused on genre is to introduce students to the generic pleasures of adherence, subversion, and reinvention; they enjoy thinking about the ways in which *The Maltese Falcon* slots into these categories.

The strong emphasis on masculinity and femininity in *The Maltese Falcon* also provides a useful standard for the rest of the semester. Posing Hammett's use of gender as archetypal for the genre allows students to consider the traits those archetypes possess based on the characters of Sam Spade, Brigid O'Shaughnessy, Effie Perine, and Joel Cairo (as well as the ways these characters themselves draw from those lurid pulp images from *Black Mask*). Establishing these uses of gender as generic tropes allows the students to see those same movements of adherence, subversion, and invention with regard to gender as the course moves forward.

Focusing on the hardboiled continues the investigation of gender roles from Poe, and it also allows for a continuation of the debate surrounding high literature and popular culture. Chandler in particular is useful for helping students consider questions both of art and masculinity in hardboiled fiction thanks to his famous investigation of both in his 1944 essay "The Simple Art of Murder,"[14] which serves as a thematic bridge between Hammett's and Chandler's novels. Chandler writes, in his critique of the claim that Hammett (and by association, he himself) are practitioners of a lowbrow form, "There are no vital and significant forms of art; there is only art, and precious little of that."[15] This statement about the nature of art is used as a vehicle to consider how, if at all, detective fiction relates to American literary Modernism, a relatively contemporaneous and far more highbrow movement. Introducing students to Brian McHale's idea of the epistemological dominant of Modernism allows them to see the parallels between American detective fiction and literary Modernism. For McHale, who is working from Roman Jakobson, while Modernism interrogates many issues, its dominant is epistemological, as he demonstrates with what he poses as the Modernist question set:

> How can I interpret this world of which I am a part? And what am I in it? ... What is there to be known?; Who knows it?; How do they know it, and with what degree of certainty?; How is knowledge transmitted from one knower to another, and with what degree of reliability?; How does the object of knowledge change as it passes from knower to knower?; What are the limits of the knowable? And so on.[16]

Presenting this question set encourages students not necessarily to think of the hardboiled as Modernist, but rather to consider detective fiction's function in relationship to Modernism. While in many ways detective fiction, with its formulaic structures and pulp background, runs counter to the Modernist project, the Modernist question set can also double as the driving question set for this period of detective fiction while exposing its lack of diversity. Initiating this discussion with students helps them more usefully conceptualize the parameters of both genre fiction and high Modernism. Further, introducing Modernism at this early juncture helps to prepare students for the Postmodernist turn in detective fiction. In preparation for this moment, it can be useful to stress to students how little these Modernist questions involve the American themes that emerge as central to the texts that appear in the latter half of the twentieth century: race, ethnicity, gender, and class. This point underscores the scope of the generic revision process that takes place and the extent to which the Postmodernist turn enables those revisions.

Continuing with Chandler, "The Simple Art" extends the conversation about masculinity started by "The Purloined Letter" and *The Maltese Falcon*. Chandler writes,

> down these mean streets a man must go .... The detective in this kind of story must be such a man. He is the hero, he is everything. He must be a complete man and a common man and yet an unusual man. ... a man of honor, by instinct, by inevitability, without thought of it, and certainly without saying it. He must be the best man in his world and a good enough man for any world.[17]

This oft-cited passage displays Chandler's version of hardboiled chivalry, a "hero" who earns his knighthood despite being "common," whose masculinity is either so inviolable or so anxiety-inducing that the word "man" is used to describe him seven times in just over a hundred words. *The Big Sleep* and *Farewell, My Lovely* both work well as a novel for this section of the course, as each presents a slightly different focal point.[18] *The Big Sleep* foregrounds the chivalric aspect, while *Farewell, My Lovely* more directly invites questions about different modes of masculinity, including the homoerotic.

Catherine Ross Nickerson writes that "what Chandler opened up was a new way of looking at crime narratives, or rather looking *through* them, as lenses on the culture and history of the United States."[19] For the first essay, students investigate the substance of Nickerson's claim through writing on the topic of Chandler's chivalric formula for masculinity, interrogating what it really stipulates, whether or not even Chandler's own Philip Marlowe meets its specifications, its creation of a specifically American mythos, and most importantly the relationship between masculinity and American detective fiction. To this point, of the four thematic hallmarks of American detective fiction, only gender has been truly inescapable in the course texts, and it bears examining at length in writing before the students encounter the next iteration of the hardboiled, one which considers race, ethnicity, and class alongside gender. To fully prepare students for the subsequent unit, it is useful to invite their critiques of Chandler's model. Eliciting the limits and problematics of "The Simple Art" and its constitutive characteristics is not intended to chastise Chandler, but rather to help students see the necessity of the next round of generic adherence, subversion, and reinvention.

Hardboiled Reworkings

The next section of the course presents challenges to and reworkings of the hardboiled style. Pepper writes that, particularly in America, "detection is a means of social control as well as social revolution. The detective is opposed to dominant values and yet part of the machinery through which those values are affirmed. He or she undercuts but also reinscribes relations of domination and subordination."[20] This unit deals with novels that use race, ethnicity, gender, and class to perform those revisions while maintaining the hardboiled framework. These novels perform crucial work of their own and also prefigure the next two modules of the course, the forensic and the Postmodernist. American authors like Sue Grafton, with her rough-and-tumble protagonist Kinsey Millhone, pave the way for other American female forensic detectives such as Patricia Cornwell and Kathy Reichs, and teaching *E is for Evidence* also foregrounds the interplay of physical and digital evidence that will figure so prominently in the forensics unit of the course.[21] Further, Grafton and Walter Mosely, creator of the Easy Rawlins series, each help to establish the ontological questions that will be crucial for the Postmodern iterations of the genre. Grafton and Mosely work well together in discussing the extent to which the hardboiled formula can be stretched. Pairing these authors presents the hardboiled as an enduring subgenre, with its own tropes to be utilized, adapted, or subverted. The students appreciate the formulaic and serial nature of these texts, with one student joking that despite Grafton's title, in fact, "E is for Exposition." Grafton and Mosely, thanks to the ways in which they adhere to, subvert, and reinvent the conventions of the subgenre, work when positioned for students as a stepping stone between the hardboiled and the forensic.

Though chronologically his work appears later, Mosely appears first on the syllabus in order to compare his *Devil in a Blue Dress* to *The Maltese Falcon* and *Farewell, My Lovely* to engage questions of race, masculinity, and class.[22] The extent to which Mosely adheres to, subverts, or reinvents Chandler in particular is a debatable question; students can engage it by considering Lee Horsley's assertion that *Devil in a Blue Dress* produces a "highly politicized rewriting of" *Farewell, My Lovely*, "asking readers to return with an altered sensibility to their conception of the original."[23] As an African-American in the 1940s, Easy Rawlins is not just a different race but also a different social class than Philip Marlowe, and the intersection of his race and class works as asset and liability in Rawlins' detecting, allowing him entrance into some spaces while precluding that entry in others, while also reflecting backward on Chandler as Horsley suggests. Andrew Pepper, writing about crime fiction, believes that "the question of whether America is better conceived of and understood in terms of its enabling diversity or its crippling divisions has, in turn, fed into and energised debates about the nature and depth of racial, ethnic, class and gender differences."[24] The "altered sensibility" that Horsley notes comes from Mosely's engagement with Pepper's claim. Through reading *Devil in a Blue Dress*, students come to realize that Mosely's novel inserts race and class into an American literary subgenre that relegated these questions to the margins; Mosley's revisions put a novel that recognizes diversity into conversation with a novel that encourages divisions. These questions of race and detection recur when reading Henry Chang's *Chinatown Beat*.[25] Mosely also plays with modes of hardboiled masculinity, helping students think through whether Easy Rawlins fits more in Sam Spade or Philip Marlowe's mode of masculinity. Tension between Easy's masculinity and those of the white hardboiled detectives allows students to engage the concept of intersectionality at an early juncture in the course. These questions prepare students for the transition to Sue Grafton's treatment of hardboiled femininity.

The booming American market for female-authored, female-starring detective fiction in the late 1970s through mid-1990s serves as a useful introduction for Sue Grafton's work. As Priscilla Walton and Manina Jones point out in their seminal study *Detective Agency*, from 1975 to 1980, there were 166 female-authored American crime novels, only 13 of which had female detectives. By contrast, from 1981 to 1985, when Sue Grafton, Sara Paretsky, and Marcia Muller began to gain popularity, 299 American crime novels were written by women, with 45 female detectives. After this boom period, the number of novels written by women and the ratio of female detectives kept increasing, reaching 1252 American crime novels written by women with 366 of them featuring female detectives, from 1991 to 1995. The market changes so dramatically that within 20 years, roughly one third of all American detective novels published feature female protagonists.[26] Framing this popularity at the outset engages the question of whether or not hardboiled American detective fiction as a genre can actually accommodate female detectives. Clearly, the market swell indicates a desire in the readership for these new detective figures. Students are surprised to learn, then, about the critical debate surrounding what Kathleen Gregory Klein terms the "struggle between gender and genre."[27]

Students read Klein's assertion that "the conventional private eye formula inevitably achieves primacy over feminist ideology: the predictable formula of detective fiction is based on a world whose sex-gender valuations reinforce male hegemony"[28] and then consider, based on what they have read, they believe it is true that "either feminism or the formula is at risk."[29] This question, not surprisingly, can produce lively classroom conversation, which has the potential to demonstrate the relevance of detective fiction to contemporary social debates. To conclude this unit, students reflect on the extent to which either *E is for Evidence* or *Devil in a Blue Dress* adheres to, subverts, or reinvents the hardboiled formula present in either *The Maltese Falcon* or *Farewell, My Lovely*. Further, they speculate on the future of the genre based on these texts as a way to position the upcoming changes forensic detective fiction will present.

The Forensic

The final two sections of the class are framed to work together as a unit based on forensic detective fiction's relationship to globalization and Postmodernism. Both globalization and Postmodernism begin to impact American detective fiction around the same time as the contemporary forensic trend, yet they are often thought of as working at cross purposes. Yet while globalization and Postmodernism each suggest that crimes simply may not be resolvable, the rise of forensic detective fiction points yet again to detective fiction's foundational drive toward containment. In an America increasingly beset by threats of terror as well as the changes wrought by a rapidly expanding tech industry, forensic detective fiction enters to transform these unfamiliar elements into strategies of containment and control. Or does this narrative belie an insuperable current of uncertainty? The novels for this section of the course suggest that forensic authors vary widely in terms of their relationship to threats and their desire to contain them. These texts exist on a continuum of containment, with Patricia Cornwell at one end representing the idea that forensics offer a genuine strategy for effecting control of threats, and Kathy Reichs at the other end, expressing extreme doubt about the possibility of forensic science to genuinely contain or control crime. Jeffrey Deaver offers a midpoint along this continuum. Presenting students with the idea of the continuum of containment for forensic detective fiction provides not only a framework for thinking through a potent and popular subgenre but also a bridge to Postmodernist and global detective fiction, which will engage the concept of crimes as unsolvable and uncontainable.

Of particular use in explaining and exploring these concepts is the relationship between forensic detective fiction and technology. Beginning with Cornwell's *The Body Farm*,[30] students investigate the methods of detection used and the ways in which they differ from both the ratiocinative strategy of Dupin and the pavement-pounding of the hardboiled gumshoes. In shifting the detective's profession from private investigator to forensic pathologist, Cornwell creates a new emphasis on the function of evidence and the detective's relationship to it. Scarpetta's savvy use of forensic techniques and technologies seems to provide a ready answer to the challenge of physical crime, with traces of criminal activity, no matter how minute, always inscribed on the world in which those crimes were committed. In teaching, *The Body Farm* illustrates this nicely, with the solution to its grisly crime hinging on a physical imprint left on a corpse, but many Cornwell novels prove this point effectively. Beginning with Cornwell and this comfortable model of forensics allows for a reversal of students' expectations with the transition to Deaver and Reichs. These next two authors show students that, as with the other subgenres they have read, forensic detective fiction is more complicated than they may have assumed based on understanding of it gleaned from the American cultural consciousness.

Jeffrey Deaver, particularly in his newer novels, focuses less on physical and more on digital evidence. His texts call attention to the dangers of computer technology and the misleading qualities of seemingly reliable data, while still maintaining faith in the ability of the detective (rather than merely the technology he or she wields). *The Broken Window* illustrates this simultaneous trust in and undermining of new digital technologies through its focus on data mining and the difficulties of containing digital crime, though again other Deaver novels could also achieve this purpose.[31] In *The Broken Window*, Deaver's quadriplegic detective Lincoln Rhyme demonstrates the powers and the limits of digital technology, arguing that the success of these technologies remain contingent on the skillful detective. One student wrote, one year after the class ended, that her favorite novel was "Jeffery Deaver's *The Broken Window* because it dealt with the limitations of technology's data and metadata; it pushed back against ... the current idea that modern technology is all encompassing of every aspect of humanity." In this way Deaver serves as a midpoint between Cornwell's firm belief in the power of technology and Reichs' doubt that crime can be effectively contained.

For Kathy Reichs, the same forensic technologies used in Cornwell and Deaver point instead to the incredible difficulty of turning information into answers—the more the technologies reveal, the more questions they create. *Spider Bones* emphasizes this particular point because of its sharp contrast with what students expect from the forensic in general and what they read in Cornwell in particular.[32] Initially, Reichs' work seems like a close copy of Cornwell's, down to the remarkable set of similarities between their protagonists Temperance Brennan and Kay Scarpetta (similarities which can be productively scrutinized in class). However, with careful reading, students can realize that the ways in which the two writers use forensic technologies are in fact dissimilar. Scarpetta places deep trust in forensics, while Brennan does not immediately accept forensic results as gospel. In *Spider Bones*, the gold standard of DNA evidence itself is questioned and ultimately shown to be imperfect. In portraying this fallibility, Reichs situates her texts on the far end of the continuum of containment, suggesting that, despite the aid of a savvy detective, forensic technologies can guarantee neither answers nor, by implication, security. For their second essay, students consider, broadly, some of the differences in the ways that these forensic novels think about their technologies and the ways in which those differences matter, ultimately coming up with their own models for conceptualizing these technologies. Asking students to create their own models for how forensic detective fiction works pushes them to go beyond that common American cultural notion that forensics resolves all problems. Breaking through this misconception empowers students: at this point in the course, they know enough about American detective fiction and its history to challenge modes of understanding it.

Postmodernism and Globalization

Introducing students to concepts such as epistemological question sets and the potential impossibility of solution before arriving at the final unit of the course prepares them for thinking about America's relationship to Postmodernism and global crime, both of which run counter to the kinds of moves they are by now expecting detective fiction to make. Paul Auster's deeply allusive meditation on the urban detective, *The New York Trilogy*,[33] affords the students an opportunity to think about what would happen if suddenly, instead of caring about solutions and containment, the genre instead decided that the very notion of solution proves to be an absurdity and the quest for that solution guarantees nothing except the detective's gradual descent into madness. Here students encounter the corollary to McHale's Modernist epistemological question set: his Postmodernist ontological question set. McHale thinks that the dominant of Postmodernism is ontological, and that it prompts questions such as:

> Which world is this? What is to be done in it? Which of my selves is to do it? ... What is a world?; What kinds of worlds are there, how are they constituted, and how do they differ?; What happens when different kinds of worlds are placed in confrontation, or when boundaries between worlds are violated?[34]

Auster's text places all of these questions in play, and the students seem to enjoy using a challenging concept to deal with such an abstruse, metafictional, wholly unexpected version of detective fiction. Further, these questions allow for a greater interrogation of the questions of race, ethnicity, gender, and class that shape contemporary American detective fiction; "which of my selves is to do it?" points to the intersectionality of these four components and their creation of different lived realities. The students seemed to find this way of thinking through Modernism and Postmodernism useful. One student wrote that, for her, "the concepts of epistemological and ontological dominants of Modernism and Postmodernism" remained with her after the course concluded. Again, using American detective fiction to explore important movements in contemporary literature more broadly both better prepares students for additional coursework and helps them to realize the genre's flexibility.

To conclude the course, students read two texts that demonstrate both the complex relationship between Postmodernism and globalization and additional ways in which the genre begins to think about global crime. These seemingly disparate texts are Henry Chang's *Chinatown Beat* and Michael Chabon's *The Yiddish Policemen's Union*.[35] Despite the fact that one text is set in a post-9/11 New York City (in, of course, Chinatown) and the other is set in a fictional Jewish state established in Alaska post-World War II, the texts raise a surprising number of similar concerns relevant to globalization and global crime. Each text thinks in great detail about race, ethnicity, and class. Each text thinks about national borders, their permeability, their constructedness, and their limits. Each text thinks about ethnicity, intersectionality, cultural practice, religious practice, and the impact these factors have on a detective's ability to pursue solutions in distinct communities. Each text thinks about global crimes such as trafficking and border crossing, as well as strategies to contain these crimes. Each text seems to suggest that, in order to succeed at all in a global landscape, the detective must be a hybrid entity, able to gain access to a variety of different communities, and a Postmodern subject capable of entertaining the notion of a multiplicity of contingent, perhaps mutually contradictory, solutions to any given crime.

Chinatown Beat follows nicely on the heels of *The New York Trilogy* because it reveals a completely different version of contemporary New York detection. An oft-quoted passage from the beginning of *The New York Trilogy* begins "New York was an inexhaustible space, a labyrinth of endless steps, and no matter how far he walked, no matter how well he came to know its neighborhoods and streets, it always left him with the feeling of being lost."[36] Henry Chang's police detective Jack Yu, in contrast, successfully solves crime largely thanks to his depth of knowledge about and connection to its Chinatown. Because he was raised in Chinatown (and is himself ethnically Chinese and bilingual), Yu has access to sources of information that are virtually inaccessible to his colleagues in the New York Police Department. He talks to everyone from street vendors to street hustlers, and these information sources allow him to tap into the Triads, the gangs/international smuggling networks that control crime. At the same time as he takes advantage of his diversity, Yu also encounters division, isolated from his white colleagues because of his race and ethnicity and from his Chinese community because of his class and his employer. For students, Yu compares usefully to Mosely's Easy Rawlins because of his access to multiple communities, but he also eclipses Rawlins as a node in an international network. Students find it productive to discuss the issue of whether or not Chang's detective can be categorized in a new way, as a global detective rather than an American one, despite his physical grounding in New York City.

Concluding the course with Michael Chabon's *The Yiddish Policemen's Union* brings things to a neat end. The text ties strongly back to the hard-boiled model, brings forward examples of the kinds of Postmodernist questions McHale asks, dwells on issues of race, class, gender, and ethnicity, and stretches the boundaries of the genre—the question of which world this is, in particular, resonates with the text's additional genre of speculative fiction. Chabon creates a fictional Jewish state in Sitka, Alaska, and populates it with Jewish and Native Alaskan detectives. At this point in the course, students can take the lead in identifying the ways in which Chabon's novel adheres to, subverts, and reinvents the genre, and they tend to succeed in this task. One student recollects, "My favorite book from detective fiction was *The Yiddish Policemen's Union*. The way the novel wrestled with intersectionality, gender, borders and the consequences of crossing them, war, and finding a sense of belonging/identity put it at the top of my list. ... It also paid homage to the classic hard-boiled detective in a way that was both classic and more complex than solving crimes with fists." Responses of this nature demonstrate engagement with concepts from both Postmodernism and globalization.

As a final writing task, in their third essay students consider two questions: the ways in which Chabon's, Chang's, and Auster's texts fit into McHale's model of Postmodernism, and the extent to which these novels can be considered American. Encouraging students to think about adherence, subversion, and reinvention throughout the semester yielded positive results here. One student writes, "For me, the concept that has stuck with me the most is the idea that books don't always fit so perfectly into the box of a single genre. For example, we discussed *The Yiddish Policemen's Union* as a Postmodern detective novel. However, I was able to argue in an essay that perhaps it was less Postmodern than it tried to claim. I have used this same concept for various other classes." That a class on genre and categorization can produce an enduring concept of slippage and counter-readings attests to the flexibility and utility of genre in general and detective fiction in particular.

Conclusion

Ultimately, a survey course in American detective fiction provides students with more than a semester-long look into a niche genre. Instead, the students encounter many of the concerns of twentieth- and twenty-first-century American fiction more broadly, thinking through gender, race, class, ethnicity, technology, intersectionality, high culture v. popular culture, Modernism, Postmodernism, and globalization, as well as the generic drive to adapt, subvert, and reinvent.

When asked about the benefits of the course after one year, the students' responses represented both the benefits of thinking about a topic in depth, and a breadth of thinking that one might not expect from so focused a course. Reflecting on the benefits of an in-depth study for her understanding of genre, one student writes, "While having an American Literature survey course helps with the general understanding of American Literature, Detective Fiction allowed me to take a deeper look at specific aspects of different genres and all the subgenres within the detective fiction realm. It was really great to have the opportunity to compare and contrast individual aspects of different novels and to understand what allowed them to remain detective fiction while still moving between subgenres." Another student expanded upon the utility of the course for thinking broadly about American literature. He writes, "Taking American Detective Fiction broadened my understanding of Modernism versus Postmodernism in a general way, contributing to my ability to read and understand texts from both literary movements and especially from 20th and 21st century American literature. As a 21st century American, this awareness has also given me a greater understanding of the impact of my own time and culture on the way I read and understand texts." Given these results, it is reasonable to believe that future iterations of the course, perhaps incorporating even more current examples of how detective fiction makes sense of the ever-changing world, will help students to process the complexities of the American literary and cultural landscape.

Notes

1. Andrew Pepper, *The Contemporary American Crime Novel: Race, Ethnicity, Gender, Class* (Edinburgh: Edinburgh University Press, 2000).
2. Edgar Allan Poe, "The Purloined Letter" (First Page Classics, 2017), Kindle edition.
3. Steven Knight, "Introduction" in *The Millennial Detective: Essays on Trends in Crime Fiction, Film, and Television, 1990–2010,* ed. Malcah Effron (Jefferson, NC: McFarland & Company, 2011), 1.
4. Jacques Lacan, "Seminar on 'The Purloined Letter,'" in *The Purloined Poe: Lacan, Derrida, and Psychoanalytic Reading*, ed. John P. Muller and William Richardson (Baltimore: Johns Hopkins University Press, 1987), 28–54.
5. Dashiell Hammett, *The Maltese Falcon*, in *The Complete Works* (New York: Library of America, 1999), 387–586.
6. John P. Muller and William Richardson, "Lacan's Seminar on 'The Purloined Letter': Overview," in *The Purloined Poe: Lacan, Derrida, and Psychoanalytic Reading*, ed. John P. Muller and William Richardson (Baltimore: Johns Hopkins University Press, 1987), 63.
7. Muller and Richardson 65.
8. Leonard Cassuto, "The American Novel of Mystery, Crime, and Detection," in *A Companion to the American Novel*, ed. Alfred Bendixen (Malden, MA: Blackwell Publishing, 2012).

9. Ibid., 292.
10. Leonard Cassuto, *Hard-Boiled Sentimentality: The Secret History of American Crime Stories* (New York: Columbia University Press, 2009).
11. Larry Landrum, *American Mystery and Detective Fiction: A Reference Guide* (Westport, CT: Greenwood Publishing Group, 1999).
12. Sean McCann, *Gumshoe America: Hard-Boiled Crime Fiction and the Rise and Fall of New Deal Liberalism* (Durham, NC: Duke University Press, 2000).
13. Cassuto 2012 297.
14. Raymond Chandler, "The Simple Art of Murder," in *Later Novels and Other Writings* (New York: Library of America, 1995), 977–992.
15. Ibid., 978.
16. Brian McHale, *Postmodernist Fiction* (New York: Routledge, 1987), 9.
17. Raymond Chandler, "The Simple Art of Murder," in *Later Novels and Other Writings,* (New York: Library of America, 1995), 991.
18. Raymond Chandler, *The Big Sleep*, in *Stories and Early Novels*, (New York: Library of America, 1995), 587–764; Raymond Chandler, *Farewell, My Lovely*, in *Stories and Early Novels*, (New York: Library of America, 1995), 765–984.
19. Catherine Ross Nickerson, "Introduction," in *The Cambridge Companion to American Crime Fiction*, ed. Catherine Ross Nickerson (Cambridge: Cambridge University Press, 2010), 2.
20. Pepper 7.
21. Sue Grafton, *E is for Evidence* (London: Pan Macmillan, 2008).
22. Walter Mosley, *Devil in a Blue Dress* (New York: Washington Square Press, 2002).
23. Lee Horsley, Twentieth-century Crime Fiction (Oxford: Oxford University Press, 2005).
24. Pepper 2.
25. Henry Chang, *Chinatown Beat* (New York: Soho Press, 2007).
26. Priscilla Walton and Manina Jones, *Detective Agency* (Berkeley: University of California Press, 1999), 28–29.
27. Kathleen Gregory Klein, *Women Times Three: Writers, Detectives, Readers* (Bowling Green: Bowling Green State University Popular Press, 1995), 88.
28. Ibid., 89.
29. Ibid., 98.
30. Patricia Cornwell, *The Body Farm* (New York: Berkley Publishing Group, 1994).
31. Jeffrey Deaver, *The Broken Window* (New York: Simon and Schuster, 2008).

32. Kathy Reichs, *Spider Bones* (New York: Pocket Books, 2010).
33. Paul Auster, *The New York Trilogy* (New York: Penguin, 1990).
34. McHale 10.
35. Michael Chabon, *The Yiddish Policemen's Union* (New York: HarperCollins, 2007).
36. Auster 4.

WORKS CITED

Auster, Paul. *The New York Trilogy*. New York: Penguin, 1990.

Cassuto, Leonard. "The American Novel of Mystery, Crime, and Detection." In *A Companion to the American Novel*, edited by Alfred Bendixen, 291–308. Malden, MA: Blackwell Publishing, 2012.

Chabon, Michael. *The Yiddish Policemen's Union*. New York: HarperCollins, 2007.

Chandler, Raymond. "Farewell, My Lovely." In *Stories and Early Novels*, 765–984. New York: Library of America, 1995.

———. "The Big Sleep." In *Stories and Early Novels*, 587–764. New York: Library of America, 1995.

———. "The Simple Art of Murder." In *Later Novels and Other Writings*, 977–992. New York: Library of America, 1995.

Chang, Henry. *Chinatown Beat*. New York: Soho Press, 2007.

Cornwell, Patricia. *The Body Farm*. New York: Berkley Publishing Group, 1994.

Deaver, Jeffrey. *The Broken Window*. New York: Simon and Schuster, 2008.

Grafton, Sue. *"E" Is for Evidence*. London: Pan Macmillan, 2008.

Horsley, Lee. *Twentieth-Century Crime Fiction*. Oxford: Oxford University Press, 2005.

Klein, Kathleen Gregory. *Women Times Three: Writers, Detectives, Readers*. Bowling Green: Bowling Green State University Popular Press.

Knight, Steven. "Introduction." In *The Millennial Detective: Essays on Trends in Crime Fiction, Film, and Television, 1990–2010*, edited by Malcah Effron, 1–4. Jefferson, NC: McFarland & Company, 2011.

Lacan, Jacques. "Seminar on 'The Purloined Letter'." In *The Purloined Poe: Lacan, Derrida, and Psychoanalytic Reading*, edited by John P. Muller and William Richardson, 28–54. Baltimore: Johns Hopkins University Press, 1987.

Landrum, Larry. *American Mystery and Detective Fiction: A Reference Guide*. Westport, CT: Greenwood Publishing Group, 1999.

McCann, Sean. *Gumshoe America: Hard-Boiled Crime Fiction and the Rise and Fall of New Deal Liberalism*. Durham, NC: Duke University Press, 2000.

McHale, Brian. *Postmodernist Fiction*. New York: Routledge, 1987.

Mosley, Walter. *Devil in a Blue Dress*. New York: Washington Square Press, 2002.

Muller, John P., and William Richardson. "Lacan's Seminar on 'The Purloined Letter': Overview." In *The Purloined Poe: Lacan, Derrida, and Psychoanalytic Reading*, edited by John P. Muller and William Richardson, 55–76. Baltimore: Johns Hopkins University Press, 1987.

Nickerson, Catherine Ross. "Introduction." In *The Cambridge Companion to American Crime Fiction*, edited by Catherine Ross Nickerson, 1–4. Cambridge: Cambridge University Press, 2010.

Pepper, Andrew. *The Contemporary American Crime Novel: Race, Ethnicity, Gender, Class*. Edinburgh: Edinburgh University Press, 2000.

Poe, Edgar Allan. *The Purloined Letter*. First Page Classics, 2017. Kindle Edition.

Reichs, Kathy. *Spider Bones*. New York: Pocket Books, 2010.

Walton, Priscilla, and Manina Jones. *Detective Agency*. Berkeley: University of California Press, 1999.

CHAPTER 6

Teaching Postcolonial Crime Fiction

Sam Naidu

Postcolonial Crime Fiction, Context and Pedagogy

Definition of Postcolonial Crime Fiction

Postcolonial crime fiction can roughly be defined as crime fiction which explores the crimes of colonialism and neo-colonialism, and which includes the perspectives and values of previously colonised subjects, whilst utilising a literary aesthetic and epistemology which are modified by the specific postcolonial context. Whilst postcolonial crime fiction is clearly evolving from a long-established tradition of crime and detective fiction, it has established itself as a robust sub-genre which reacts to but is not limited by the rise of detective fiction in the 'west'. This rise in the nineteenth century, with its emphasis on reason and epistemology, evinces an Enlightenment notion of the inviolability of rationality and its links to 'western' concepts of civilisation. A character such as Sherlock Holmes thus comes to function as the arch-symbol or emissary of an imperial project which aims to maintain 'the idea' and suppress 'the horror' by

S. Naidu (✉)
Department of Literary Studies in English, Rhodes University,
Grahamstown, South Africa
e-mail: S.Naidu@ru.ac.za

C. Beyer (ed.), *Teaching Crime Fiction*, Teaching the New English,
https://doi.org/10.1007/978-3-319-90608-9_6

uncovering 'the truth'.[1] The creation of nineteenth-century crime fiction in the metropole was in part a reaction to colonialist concerns about the threats of barbarism and dissolution embodied by the colonised subject. Combining the emerging discourses of science in the nineteenth century with a hermeneutic strategy based on the laws of reason and logic, classic detectives such has Holmes arrived at the 'truth'. In these fictional worlds of the colonial era, rationality triumphs in the face of threats and anxiety symbolised by crime, and through the canny use of narrative, civilisation and order are restored. But what happens when authors start to question this celebration of reason, and its attendant images of racial, class, gender and sexual normativity? The answer is the birth of postcolonial crime fiction, which more often than not questions and subverts notions of colonial order, civilisation and 'truth' by portraying a world in which crime is only ever provisionally solved.

The genetic/generic links between classic crime fiction and postcolonial crime fiction are obvious. As Pearson and Singer acknowledge, postcolonial crime fiction "interrogate[s] the imperial histories and racial ideologies that helped spur their own generic development".[2] Despite of or because of its genealogy, postcolonial crime fiction performs a clear social and political function, as Yumna Siddiqi's description contends:

> a recent spate of postcolonial novels that use the format of the mystery or detective story but tweak it or turn it inside out in what becomes a narrative of "social detection", to borrow a phrase from Frederic Jameson, a "vehicle for judgments on society and revelations of its hidden nature".[3]

Siddiqi identifies, with the help of Jameson, the shift here as being from the detection of a single crime to social analysis and another ontological focus: "the hidden nature" of society. In addition, postcolonial crime fiction not only engages overtly and critically with socio-political issues, it also aims to revision the forms of classic crime fiction to better address the concerns of a postcolonial context. Wendy Knepper describes the mechanics of the postcolonial detective genre as a "manipulation or subversion of generic conventions as a purposeful, political activity".[4] Just as the content shifts focus to ontological questions, postcolonial crime fiction manipulates the formal conventions of 'classic' detective fiction to reflect the exigencies of the postcolony. As a result, settings rife with disorder and political instability, denouements which are open-ended, detectives who fail to detect, and perpetual quests for social justice are characteristic of postcolonial crime fiction.

In their seminal text, *Postcolonial Postmortems: Crime Fiction from a Transcultural Perspective*, Matzke and Mühleisen ask "[W]hat, then, does the 'postcolonial' bring to the genre of crime fiction apart from well-known discourses of 'resistance', 'subversion' and 'ethnicity', all of which are undoubtedly valid and form an important part of the debate?"[5] Their book goes a long way towards answering this question, as the essays contained in it examine how postcolonial crime fiction

> [suggests] that power and authority can be investigated through the magnifying glass of other knowledges, against the local or global mainstream, past and present, or against potential projections of a dominant group and a (neo)imperial West. Many authors have thus broadened the theme of investigation to address issues of community, beliefs and identity constructions across geographic and national boundaries, including gender and race relations. Others have broadened the genre by inventing recognizable subcategories which relate to the social, political and historical formations of their specific postcolonies.[6]

In other words, by focusing on present crimes whilst uncovering their historical dimensions, and by zooming out from individual crimes to investigate socio-political ones, postcolonial crime fiction in general has the potential to resist dominant ideologies and epistemologies, to question narrow cultural or geographic affiliations, to continue the struggle against 'western', white hegemonic discourses, and to inscribe new, empowered subject positions for the previously marginalised and oppressed. In postcolonial Africa it is evident that, as Andersson argues, crime fiction authors use "their sleuths to make statements about the political past of their particular country, and to criticize the way in which the colonizers' interests were absorbed by, and are often reproduced by, the colonized".[7] Corrupt postcolonial governments, failed attempts to mimic or jettison the colonial ethos, unstable economies and dysfunctional infra-structures are ubiquitous themes in African postcolonial crime fiction, as are hybrid subjectivities and syncretic detecting methods.

Matzke and Mühleisen include South African crime fiction in their designated category— crime fiction from a transcultural perspective—because of its power for postcolonial intervention, specifically its interrogation of neo-colonial racial and cultural relations. Contemporary South African crime fiction indisputably evinces this interventionist function. Not only has South African crime fiction almost always engaged with the country's race relationships, inequities and politics, more recently it has developed further to include ethnic, class, gender and transnational inflections. In particular, its content and form demonstrate that here, ratiocination, central to classic crime fiction, can play only a minor role in the interpretation of real-life crime or even the solving of fictional crime. This is mainly because the social order, which in classic crime fiction depicting social settings of long-standing stable democracies is reinstated after the process of logical reasoning is complete and the individual crime is solved, does not exist here and never has. Of great concern, as reflected in the literature, is that, more than two decades after the inception of a formal democracy, the country continues to be destabilised by crime, unemployment, economic vulnerability, poor infrastructure and varying forms of social injustice. Currently, postcolonial crime fiction in general, and South African postcolonial crime fiction in particular, demonstrates a rising diversity and experimentation as it proliferates in wide-ranging geo-cultural locations and mutates into a transnational literary phenomenon, exhibiting a postmodernist questioning, of reason, together with a postcolonial questioning of reason's relationship to authority, social order and notions of justice.

South Africa: A Postcolonial Context?

The region of Southern Africa, occupied by a number of indigenous peoples such as the Khoi and San, and also by the Bantu people who supposedly migrated to the area from the north was, since the sixteenth century, colonised by the Portuguese, the Dutch and then the British. During the formal colonial era, which lasted more than three hundred years, numerous wars were fought between the European colonisers and the indigenous peoples, slavery was established and widescale appropriation of land occurred. Accompanying the brutal physical colonisation was the 'civilising mission' of the Christian missionaries and various other discursive, epistemic colonising efforts which resulted in the subjugation of a huge, diverse population of black African people by a small white minority. In the twentieth century, the white minority government made up mainly of descendants of Dutch colonisers (the Afrikaans people or Boers), and the descendants of British colonisers, institutionalised a complex legal, economic and social system of segregation known as apartheid. For most of the twentieth century, apartheid was harshly and inhumanely enforced, but after years of violent anti-apartheid struggle and tense negotiations, a new, much-celebrated constitution was formulated and South Africa became a democracy in 1994, with Nelson Mandela as its first black, democratically elected president. Formally, South Africa is a postcolonial nation, and moreover it is also referred to as a post-apartheid state, with the two systems of oppression, colonialism and apartheid, being deeply imbricated. Teaching crime fiction in such a context necessitates engaging with these historical, systemic crimes, which feature as key themes in the literature.

The legacies of colonialism and apartheid are, however, painfully manifest in the current racial, economic and cultural differences which beleaguer South Africa. The bulk of the country's wealth still resides with the minority white population and the current government, with its ill-equipped and often unscrupulous members, has proven deeply incompetent and corrupt resulting in disaffection and cynicism. One of the most keenly felt neo-colonial ills is that of endemic poverty and unemployment, resulting in a pandemic of crime and corruption. Currently, the country's universities are wracked by protests calling for free education and the 'decolonisation' of the higher education system. General consensus, from scholars,[8] the media, political commentators and the populace, is that South Africa is still haunted by its past of gross injustices and heinous race-based crimes and abuses. So, with this current climate of deep-seated dissatisfaction, turbulence and violent eruption of protests, the term postcolonial appears both inaccurate and unseemly. Used, however, to denote that very condition of the postcolony—its haunted state of neo-colonial oppressions and power imbalances, the continued abjection of a group of peoples who were previously colonised, the historical relationships between colonial crimes and current crimes—the term postcolonial is not entirely inapposite. If the term postcolonial, when applied to South Africa, means a region which was once colonised and which continues to suffer the social injustices which are born of systemic oppression and marginalisation, despite ostensible or official liberation, then it is applicable.

Crime fiction, as defined in the previous section, written and taught in this context, therefore becomes a valuable hermeneutic and pedagogic tool with which to make sense of this often bewildering context, and perhaps transform it. Teaching South African postcolonial crime fiction in the South African postcolonial context is about interrogating, with students who have inherited this legacy and who live this reality, crimes of the colonial and apartheid eras, and how those past crimes impinge on the present. What becomes apparent is that South African crime fiction, in terms of socio-historical context and narrative imperative, is uniquely positioned.

There is no retrospective social order to be metonymically restored through deductive reasoning, but there are the aspirations of justice, safety, security and stability to imaginatively project, and a new ethical and moral topography to be mooted.

Towards a Postcolonial Pedagogy

To teach postcolonial crime fiction in a postcolonial context such as South Africa a distinctively tailored postcolonial pedagogy is required. For a teacher of English literature, this entails, first and foremost, recognising that, as Slemon puts it, "colonialist literary learning is at the primal scene of colonialist cultural control, and that a pedagogy of the book plays a necessary and material role in the strategic production of willing subjects of Empire".[9] Slemon argues that acknowledging the complicity of English literature and of the English language in colonialism is a starting point, opening up within

> English Studies itself – the *place* of colonial management – a cognitive space in which the subject-to-be-educated reads the effects of ideology in *both* personal and political dimensions, and finds within that space [...] something that functions as a "room for manoeuvre".[10]

This "room for manoeuvre" is required equally for teacher and learner. Thereafter, this quandary, resulting often in a healthy ambivalence which perpetually re-defines the discipline and attendant teaching philosophies and practices, gives rise to an approach which is highly critical and cognizant of colonial and apartheid history, whilst also aiming to foster generative skills and knowledge based on the principle of hope.

In conceiving of a postcolonial pedagogy which does justice to both the literature which is the object of enquiry and the context of teaching, bell hooks' concept of "engaged pedagogy" has been highly influential and informative.[11] "Engaged pedagogy" is made up of the following components: re-conceptualisation of knowledge; linking of theory and practice; student empowerment; multiculturalism; and incorporation of passion. According to hooks, this approach is aimed at addressing issues of race, gender and class biases, and it is offered as a counter-strategy to the "transfer-of-knowledge" pedagogy which "socializes students into existing power relations while undermining creativity and a reflective stance".[12] Underpinning this pedagogy is the general charge to challenge old hegemonies, deconstruct old epistemologies, recognise cultural diversity, respect the social reality of students, and to foster non-hierarchical, non-authoritarian ways of interacting in the classroom. An engaged pedagogy "addresses student alienation resulting from a monocentric – Eurocentric – curriculum and pedagogical orientations".[13] In addition, students' lived realities, emotional responses and idiosyncratic knowledge-making capacities are incorporated into the teaching-learning process. A postcolonial pedagogy arising out of this thinking has, therefore, to acknowledge racial, class, gender, sexual, ethnic, linguistic and various other differences, and whereas difference was previously deployed in colonial discourse to 'other' and thereby subjugate, now in the postcolonial context, difference needs to be positively re-articulated, understood and validated.

Teaching in a postcolonial context as riven by social hierarchies as South Africa is, one has to actively engage in questioning the ideological basis of knowledge and knowledge production, the relationship between abstract theories and lived realities, the agency of the students, the diversity of the student body, and the need for an empathetic and holistic classroom strategy. In short, one is involved in a project which is focused on "the decentering of the west globally, embracing multiculturalism, [which] compels educators to focus attention on the issue of voice. Who speaks? Who listens? And why?"[14] Awareness of one's own relative position of authority, of the power dynamics and of often disconcerting differences in the classroom inform a postcolonial pedagogy. Moreover, appreciating that the epistemologies which prevail originate in the 'west', but which, in an era of globalisation can no longer be described reductively or simplistically as 'western', and resisting the reification of one type of (academic or abstract) knowledge is described by Gerry Turcotte as militating against a neo-colonial "totalizing educational system" through the "interrogative function of a postcolonial pedagogy".[15] Turcotte advocates understanding the "belonging and alienation that marks the colonial condition", and the use of literary texts to engage with this simultaneous belonging and alienation and hybridity of one's students.[16] Like hooks, Turcotte, writing about the Australian postcolonial context, also aims to "unsettle/dismantle the entrenched institutionalized hierarchies of power that are marked by the academy [and] tug at the boundaries that separate the academy from the community".[17] Thus the aim of a postcolonial pedagogy is an inclusive, democratic classroom in which belonging is promoted without sacrificing the unsettling knowledge which results from encountering difference and the unfamiliar, be it in the social space or in the literature.

Using a postcolonial pedagogy to teach postcolonial crime fiction in a postcolonial context means adopting a cognizant stance from which to critique the past, question the present, trouble generic, disciplinary boundaries, disrupt conventional roles of teacher and learner, breach the divide between academia and community, desacralise the concept of knowledge, and empathetically develop independent critical thinkers of the future. Through reading, analysing, researching, writing about, discussing and orally presenting on postcolonial crime fiction, students are guided through a reparative process which helps them understand the past and its relationship to the present, and which instils in them a desire to 'detect' their worlds and pursue social justice.

Case Study: Sleuthing the State: South African Crime and Detective Fiction

Course Description

What follows is a description of a course taught at third-year level in the Department of Literary Studies in English Literature, Rhodes University, South Africa. The principles of a postcolonial pedagogy described in the previous section are highlighted where necessary. In 2011 the course, described as focusing on the significance of South African crime fiction in cultural and literary terms, was conceived, planned and incepted. Students were told that this literature seeks to address weighty themes such as the trauma of a society in transition, which has been fractured by violent crime, whilst engaging fans of crime fiction with compelling and inventive renditions of the genre. In addition, it was explained that the purpose of the course is to examine how historically and globally, crime fiction has been lauded for its interpretive function, but taken together with its origins in the metropole and its commercial success, this praise raises questions about credibility, necessitating an examination of crime fiction's ambiguous ideological position. Students were encouraged to take the course so that they can engage with debates about English literary studies as a place of colonial management, and about the artistic merit of popular literature. The selection of primary texts was based on two sub-genres identified as widely written and read in South Africa: literary detective fiction and crime thriller fiction. It was explained that both sub-genres would be historicised (going back to nineteenth-century British and American antecedents), and then formally analysed. Also, texts were chosen (*Devil's Peak* Deon Meyer 2007,

Daddy's Girl Margie Orford 2009, *Cold Sleep Lullaby* Andrew Brown 2005 and *Lost Ground* Michiel Heyns 2011) due to their level of engagement with the South African postcolonial context, popularity and critical acclaim. Students were alerted that, of particular interest, are the perspectives these texts offer on evolving and ambivalent attitudes to 'truth' and justice, the relationship amongst power, authority and self, and the correlations between literary form and the potential for socio-political comment.

With this description and statement of purpose, students were made aware that they would be engaged in a formal, literary analysis of the novels, as well as in a socio-political study of postcolonial South Africa. They were also encouraged to question, from the outset, the efficacy and appropriateness of crime fiction as a hermeneutic tool. In terms of credit weighting, this course is a substantial proportion of their total English 3 mark (25%) and involves considerable commitment (two notional hours per week for one thirteen-week semester). To enrol for this course, students need to have 'learning in place' or display the 'requirements of prior learning'. In this case this means they need to have completed English 2 in order to have the requisite knowledge about the historical periods of literature, aesthetic movements, genres and elements of prose narratives. In English 1, they would have done Colonial and Postcolonial Literatures and would therefore have a basic understanding of postcolonial literary studies, which this course aims to develop further.

Assessment for the Course

The assessment for the course is mainly of a formative nature comprised of a three-step process which I call: Foundation; Developing a Voice; and Becoming a Research Scholar. By 'Foundation', what I mean is that they are given practical information which operates as a basis for their learning experience. Students are given a comprehensive handout with all relevant information including dates of seminars, topics for each seminar, guidelines for presentations, and descriptions of assessment tasks. They are also provided with a primary and secondary reading list and a detailed 'time-line' depicting the development of crime and detective fiction. On this time-line postcolonial crime fiction is clearly marked. The Initial Writing Assignment is designed to give them an opportunity to create the foundational knowledge they need to complete the rest of the course. The 'Foundation' dimension of the learning process is aimed at empowering students with basic skills and knowledge.

'Developing a Voice' is probably the most significant aspect of this specific example of engaged pedagogy. Students do two oral presentations for this course. The purpose is to develop each student's confidence to articulate an argument, and to promote conversations and debate in the classroom. For their presentations, students write a proposal on a topic of their choice related to the texts being studied, present to their peers (they are encouraged to use visual aids and props creatively), then they receive feedback from their peers and me. Both presentations are meant to build towards a research essay, so students are also guided on how to synthesise information and develop their presentations into a complex, research essay. With this pedagogical approach, the conventional hierarchy of the classroom is disrupted. I sit back whilst students present and then discuss afterwards. I complete a presentation assessment form which the student receives, but during the presentations and ensuing discussions the students take centre stage. The opportunity to be an active participant in the cognitive space, the focus on voice, the call for passionate engagement, the recognition of different types of self-produced knowledge, which constitute the 'Developing a Voice' dimension, are crucial to creating an inclusive, democratic classroom.

At the end of the course, students submit a research essay based on the foundational knowledge acquired through the Initial Writing Assignment, the autonomous ideas and independent research they conducted for their presentations, and the critical feedback they received from peers and me. The thinking here is that, having developed a voice, students are equipped, in the short-term to become research scholars, and in the long-term to become critical, articulate members of a thriving democracy. They prepare detailed research proposals which I discuss with them at length, which teaches them to collate their research material in order to produce a sustained and comprehensive essay. The essays produced in this manner are noticeably more competent and complex than the assignments they produce without this scaffolded and empowering process.

For this engaged pedagogy to work, a system of appropriate assessment tasks needs to be satisfactorily completed. Students are asked to complete an Initial Writing Assignment [20%], to do two oral presentations [15% each], and the final research essay [50%]. For each of these assessment tasks they are given detailed guidelines and a set of assessment criteria. Feedback sheets with constructive comments from me, as well as collated comments from the members of the group, are presented to students after a presentation so that they can receive affirmation, reflect and address weak areas.

Student Evaluations

For the purposes of critical self-reflection, student evaluation is carried out at the end of every course. Students are given a questionnaire to anonymously fill out in their own time. The questionnaire contains the following questions: What did you most enjoy/benefit from in the Sleuthing the State course?; What were the challenges/problems you encountered in this course?; Do you consider contemporary South Africa to be a postcolonial context? Elaborate; How did this course help you understand this context?; Does this course adequately engage with our context?; What is your view on HOW this course engages with its context? Comment on how SN has conceived of the course, how it is structured and how it is taught?; What can be done to improve the course?; What specific skills and knowledge have you gained from this course?;What do you think SN's constraints are when TEACHING such a course?; Any other comments?

In terms of the content of the course, the student evaluations are overwhelmingly positive. Students are grateful for their exposure to this kind of literature, which forces them to confront painful and controversial aspects of their socio-political context. They are critical of the background and lineage of the genre, yet are able to appreciate the particular value of postcolonial crime fiction. Some students expressed their delight in discovering that 'local' literature has so much to offer. They view the course as pertinent, not just to postcolonial South Africa, but to a wider social context. Significant is their appreciation of postcolonial crime fiction's tendency to interrogate the historical crimes which are often the root cause of present-day crimes, and many students comment on how the literature highlights that the inequities of the colonial and apartheid eras persist. Many students mention how the course allows them to engage creatively and critically with such social ills as poverty and sexual violence.

As for the method of teaching, most students respond favourably to being given a clear foundation, and to the challenge of developing their own voices. As one student put it:

> Sam creates an environment which strongly encourages her students to critically engage with her topic matter, reverting to asking specific individuals to speak if a pause has continued for too long a stretch. This method allows people to form their own voices within the discussions, and, I feel, increases the confidence of her students. [...] The use of presentations made for an interesting shift from the typical essay submission structure of the English undergrad course, and allowed for students to develop skills not only in

> presenting, but also in debate and critical conversation. Engaging with the content within her class always proved an enjoyable and enlightening experience due to the rapport created between her and her students.[18]

Here there is evidence that engaged pedagogy is appreciated by students who feel nurtured and supported in a learning environment which does not alienate them or discredit their individual input. Alternative forms of knowledge production, a focus on voice, empathy, pleasure and passion seem to have been achieved through the adoption of an engaged pedagogy.

However, the most difficult and challenging aspect of the course, based on some student responses, is the oral presentations. A number of students find this assessment task too "direct" or "immediate" and they are "intimidated" by performing in front of their peers. Some also express an emotional affect when dealing with traumatic subject matter, which makes formal oral presentations even more daunting. As one of the key outcomes of the course is to develop students' voices, this response raises a crucial challenge. In future, methods of support and encouragement need to be devised so that the classroom is a safe space of belonging, where the power dynamics encourage individual participation however diverse student abilities may be, and where different knowledges and forms of expression thereof are constantly validated.

On the whole, teaching postcolonial crime fiction has been a tough but rewarding experience. In the words of one student

> the method of instruction included challenging lines of questioning regarding the state of South Africa in current day, as well as facilitated self-reflexivity of the students. Because of this, there was not only an abstract academic discussion surrounding our context, but also an exploration of the individual's responsibility to the community, including that of the individuals within the course.

This realisation on the part of the student that the course is aimed at developing both the personal and political dimensions of students as autonomous, critical thinkers, is particularly encouraging. The shift away from abstract learning to an appreciation of personal agency and accountability expressed here is ratifying and heartening. There is a clear sense that what is learned in this course is, in some form or another, put into practice. Student evaluations have been germane to the evolution of this course and often, the learners articulate most cogently what the teacher plans, implements and hopes will be the outcomes of the course. Sometimes, the learners perceive the unsettling nature of learning and the dangers inherent in the process:

> As a lecturer, mentor and teacher she provides scholars with a space for errors, for growth and above all, respect. Without respect for one another Sam Naidu would not be able to teach this course. This course has many traps in which to offend an individual, for example, socio-political commentary can become rigid, and those speaking could feel anxious about offending people in a post-1994 demographic which means that respect between one another is very important.

This student captures, in her own voice, the main aim of an engaged pedagogy—a classroom which has room for manoeuvrability, and which is characterised by respect for all its members.

Response to Student Evaluation and Conclusion

Although students are candid about finding the course challenging at times, they emphasise that the texts and the pedagogy allowed them to meaningfully and critically engage with South African postcolonial crime fiction and with South Africa as a postcolonial context. They also highlight the values of specific disciplinary skills such as being able to identify genres and aspects of form. Most affirming is their appreciation of the space created for them to speak, develop their own voices and share knowledge. I am particularly pleased that some have independently made the connection between "abstract academic discussion [and] an exploration of the individual's responsibility to the community". Ultimately, the aim was to develop a dynamic teaching/learning experience informed by bell hooks's "engaged pedagogy", an experience which calls on "everyone to become more engaged, to become active participants in learning",[19] and, based on student evaluations over the years and the continued popularity of the course, this has been achieved.

One of the challenges to consider is negotiating between facilitating the creation of knowledge whilst providing enough of the basic tools to enable students to do this. As some students point out, the foundational knowledge aspect of the course can be improved to provide clearer explanations of aspects of literary form. Another consideration, not arising out of the student evaluation, but from my own reflection on the course is the choice of texts. Christian warns in the introduction to *The Post-Colonial Detective* that "these novels, though set in post-colonial countries, are written by white males, have male detectives, and have detectives who are members of a police force".[20] Although the current texts are varied in their representations of race and gender, the authors are all white, middle-class and educated. In the future, the list of primary texts will be modified to reflect greater cultural and generic diversity as crime fiction continues to flourish in South Africa.

Finally, in the current climate of disruption, disaffection and uncertainty in higher education in South Africa, it is particularly important to retain some of the ideals of a postcolonial pedagogy, to remind myself that education is about mutuality and partnership, about passion and community, that it is about "the practice of freedom, [which] enables us to confront feelings of loss and restore our sense of connection".[21] Bearing in mind that there is still profound loss and instability plaguing South Africa, education—if the higher educational infrastructure survives this current epoch of violent protests—is one way to connect and heal. Although the future is uncertain and not particularly bright, through teaching postcolonial crime fiction in a postcolonial context using a postcolonial pedagogy, we, the students and I, have managed to create a space that is "life-sustaining and mind-expanding"[22] that denounces oppression and abuse, and, to echo Paulo Freire, cultivates hope.[23]

Acknowledgements I wish to thank Dr Sue Southwood of the Rhodes University Centre for Higher Education Research Teaching and Learning for her kind assistance with the writing of this chapter. And I am always grateful to my students, who make teaching a constantly exciting learning experience.

Notes

1. See Joseph Conrad's *Heart of Darkness* for a detailed thesis on the relationship amongst 'The Idea', (Imperialism), 'The Horror' (embodied in the character of Kurtz), and 'The Lie' (the lie told to preserve 'the Idea').
2. Nels Pearson and Marc Singer, eds., *Detective Fiction in a Postcolonial and Transnational World* (Aldershot: Ashgate, 2009), 8.
3. Yumna Siddiqi, "Police and Postcolonial Rationality in Amitav Ghosh's *The Circle of Reason*", *Cultural Critique* 50 (2002): 176.
4. Wendy Knepper, "Confession, Autopsy and the Postcolonial Postmortems of Michael Ondaatje's *Anil's Ghost*", in *Postcolonial Postmortems: Crime Fiction from a Transcultural Perspective*, ed. Christine Matzke and Susanne Mühleisen (Amsterdam: Rodopi, 2006), 36.

5. Christine Matzke and Susanne Mühleisen, eds. *Postcolonial Postmortems: Crime Fiction from a Transcultural Perspective* (Amsterdam: Rodopi, 2006), 8.
6. Matzke and Mühleisen, *Postmortems*, 5.
7. Muff Andersson, "Watching the Detectives", *Social Dynamics* 30.2 (2004): 149.
8. For an example, see S.J. Ndlovu-Gatsheni and W. Chambati, "The Idea of South Africa and Pan-South African Nationalism", in *Coloniality of Power in Postcolonial Africa: Myths of Decolonization* (Oxford: African Books Collective, 2013).
9. Stephen Slemon, "Teaching at the End of Empire", *College Literature* 20.1 (1993): 153.
10. Slemon, "Teaching", 159.
11. bell hooks, *Teaching to Transgress: Education as the Practice of Freedom* (New York: Routledge, 1994).
12. N. Florence, *bell hooks' Engaged Pedagogy: A Transgressive Education for Critical Consciousness* (Westport: Bergin and Garvey, 1998), 9.
13. Florence, *Transgressive Education*, 130.
14. hooks, *Teaching to Transgress*, 40.
15. Gerry Turcotte, "Compr(om)ising Postcolonialisms: Postcolonial Pedagogy and the Uncanny Space of Possibility", in *Home-Work: Postcolonialism, Pedagogy and Canadian Literature*, ed. C. Sugars (Ottawa: University of Ottawa Press, 2004), 2.
16. Turcotte, "Compr(om)ising Postcolonialisms", 155.
17. Turcotte, "Compr(om)ising Postcolonialisms", 158.
18. Students quoted in this chapter have given written permission for their comments to be used anonymously for the purpose of an academic study.
19. hooks, *Teaching to Transgress*, 11.
20. Ed Christian, ed. *The Post-Colonial Detective* (Basingstoke and New York: Palgrave, 2001), 4.
21. bell hooks, *Teaching Community: A Pedagogy of Hope* (New York: Routledge, 2003), xv.
22. hooks, *Teaching Community*, xv.
23. See Paulo Freire, *Pedagogy of the Oppresssed*. Translated by Myra Bergman Ramos (New York: Herder and Herder, 1970).

Works Cited

Andersson, Muff. "Watching the Detectives." *Social Dynamics* 30.2, 2004. 141–153.

Christian, Ed, ed. *The Post-Colonial Detective*. Basingstoke and New York: Palgrave Macmillan, 2001.

Florence, Namulundah. *Bell Hooks' Engaged Pedagogy: A Transgressive Education for Critical Consciousness.* Westport: Bergin and Garvey, 1998.

hooks, bell. *Teaching to Transgress: Education as the Practice of Freedom.* New York: Routledge, 1994.

———. *Teaching Community: A Pedagogy of Hope.* New York: Routledge, 2003.

Knepper, Wendy. "Confession, Autopsy and the Postcolonial Postmortems of Michael Ondaatje's *Anil's Ghost.*" In *Postcolonial Postmortems: Crime Fiction from a Transcultural Perspective*, edited by Matzke, Christine and Susanne Mühleisen, 35–58. Amsterdam: Rodopi, 2006.

Matzke, Christine and Mühleisen, Susanne eds. *Postcolonial Postmortems: Crime Fiction from a Transcultural Perspective.* Amsterdam: Rodopi, 2006.

Pearson, Nels and Singer, Marc, eds. *Detective Fiction in a Postcolonial and Transnational World.* Aldershot: Ashgate, 2009.

Slemon, Stephen. "Teaching at the End of Empire." *College Literature* 20.1, 1993. 152–161.

Siddiqi, Yumna. "Police and Postcolonial Rationality in Amitav Ghosh's *The Circle of Reason.*" *Cultural Critique* 50, 2002. 175–211.

Turcotte, Gerry. "Compr(om)ising Postcolonialisms: Postcolonial Pedagogy and the Uncanny Space of Possibility." In *Home-Work: Postcolonialism, Pedagogy and Canadian Literature*, edited by Cynthia Sugars, 151–166. Ottawa: University of Ottawa Press, 2004.

CHAPTER 7

Cut a Long Story Short: Teaching the Crime Short Story

Charlotte Beyer

Introduction: The Crime Short Story

The crime short story is a diverse literary form which provides a unique textual space for thematic and formal innovations.[1] With postmodernist challenges to generic boundaries,[2] and the subsequent re-evaluation of the division between high and popular culture,[3] the genre-busting qualities associated with short fiction have found new momentum in the specific genre of the crime short story. The upswing in interest in the crime short story genre has also been noted by critics and the media.[4] This chapter explores the rich learning opportunities provided for students by thorough study of the crime short story, arguing in favour of the canon-expanding propensities of this particular literary form being given fuller treatment in the designing and teaching of crime fiction courses.

In my own experience of teaching a second-year crime fiction course containing a mixture of novels and short stories, and assessed by coursework, I have found that teaching crime short stories provides a welcome opportunity to explore the cultural and thematic diversity, linguistic

C. Beyer (✉)
University of Gloucestershire, Cheltenham, UK
e-mail: cbeyer@glos.ac.uk

C. Beyer (ed.), *Teaching Crime Fiction*, Teaching the New English,
https://doi.org/10.1007/978-3-319-90608-9_7

experimentation and stylistic multiplicity of crime writing. Instead of merely presenting the established crime fiction canon of more or less predictable crime novels and their attending critical perspectives, a crime fiction course making more extensive use of crime short stories can help introduce students to a plurality of themes and crime fiction authors from various national and cultural contexts, as well as provide an opportunity for research-led teaching. The crime short story poses interesting challenges for the ways in which the crime fiction genre is conventionally conceived of and taught on university literature courses. Commenting on the pedagogical dimensions afforded by the short story in teaching and learning contexts, Ailsa Cox states, "As a self-contained form, the short story lends itself particularly well to close reading and seminar discussion. Questions of style, imagery, structure and narrative strategy can be addressed through a single text"—pedagogical aspects which I shall also discuss in this chapter.[5] Nevertheless, in crime fiction teaching and learning contexts, the crime short story as a specific subgenre has often been overlooked, apart perhaps from token exceptions such as Poe's Dupin stories, and this marginalisation is mirrored in what Myszor terms a "critical neglect" of short stories more generally.[6] This chapter seeks to redress this imbalance, by focusing explicitly on the crime short story and its function in teaching and learning, examining the thematic and formal questions it poses and the pedagogic and practical reflections it gives rise to. Through this approach, my discussion demonstrates the richness and complexity of the crime short story, exploring how it can be successfully harnessed to extend and enrich the study of crime fiction at undergraduate level.

Theorising and Teaching the Crime Short Story

Scholarly research into the crime short story as a genre has focused on identifying specific literary traits, calling for further examination of this diverse and intriguing genre.[7] My teaching of the crime short story is informed by short story scholars such as Cox, Liggins et al., and Priestman, as well as feminist genre criticism and crime fiction criticism more generally. This part of the chapter offers some reflections on what this specific subgenre contributes to my crime fiction course, and how teaching the crime short story expands students' knowledge of crime writing. I employ a range of teaching strategies in mediating this material, such as informative lectures, small group work, individual tutorials, online learning communities, showing supplementary film, documentary material and interviews with authors, and devising coursework assessments which allow for student reflection and encourage individual and independent research. Through these various strategies, students are encouraged to develop their own critical and reflective positions as crime fiction critics, to articulate sophisticated critiques of the material, and to identify their specific personal and scholarly interests within the field of crime fiction.

The crime short story has undergone constant evolution since its inception. Priestman traces the rise of crime fiction back to the rise of the short story genre in the period from the 1840s to 1920.[8] Myszor's parameters of definition similarly encompass the period from circa 1840 to the present day.[9] Cox points out that many critics have attempted to define the short story in formal as well as historical terms,[10] an approach reflected by Liggins et al., who also open their monograph on the British short story with a discussion of the genre's definition. Hunter states that, up until the modernist period, short fiction had been conceived of "as a condensed novel, and the art of writing it lay in the skill with which the author could squeeze the machinery of plot and character into the reduced frame of a few thousand words".[11] He concludes that "The short story was a doll's house, a fully realized world in miniature".[12] However, modernist writers began to reimagine the short story, transforming its function and form into something quite distinct from the novel-length narrative, removed from the "doll's house" model. According to Myszor, fin-de-siècle social and cultural developments were closely linked to these shifts in the short story genre. He states that: "There was less need for stories 'to be worthy of telling' [...] or to be attached to a moral, as they often had been in the past. The short story was now ready to stand alone as a 'slice of life'".[13] The examples examined here reflect these important changes. Modernist authors began to view the brevity of the short story as key to its "great richness and complexity" and experimental potential,[14] thus contributing in important ways to the evolution of the crime short story.

The rising popularity of the crime short story in recent decades, seen for example in the Akashic Noir series and a number of other themed crime short story collections to be treated in this chapter, has no doubt been enabled by the plurality of writers and perspectives it encompasses.[15] This openness to diversity is highlighted by Randolph Cox, who states, in his evaluation of the crime short story and its functions, that "the key to the detective short fiction market lies in the scores of recent minority and women writers who in the last two decades, especially, have reshaped the classic hard-boiled detective into a different breed".[16] The contemporary crime short story affords a means by which issues of difference and identity can be explored and problematised in the classroom. Weber argues that the teaching of social theory is facilitated more effectively when theoretical concepts and ideas are illustrated through literature,[17] making the classroom into what Fletcher calls a "'site of inquiry' for students and teachers".[18] The crime short story is well-suited to these pedagogical purposes, since, as well as illustrating various stylistic and aesthetic approaches, it can also be used in teaching to inform and debate, using representations of race/ethnicity, class, gender, location, textual experimentation and more. The classroom analysis and discussion of a crime short story opens up for a more general debate about the specifics of the short story genre, its textual workings and dynamics, and how these might compare with novel-length works studied on the course. Students are able to compare and contrast the workings of the textual dynamics in those two textual forms, as crime short stories lend themselves uniquely to student engagement with location and form, in ways that are often different from crime fictions of novel length in terms of plot, character, generation of suspense, and resolution. The crime short fiction format helps to maintain a concentrated focus, by helping students to pay attention to specific ideas, concepts, aesthetic strategies, stylistic traits, moments, tropes and so on. Rather than getting bogged down in narrative details and complexities, the crime short story facilitates a closer focus centred on brevity and specificity.

In the following, I present a series of case studies taken from my crime fiction course; firstly, teaching the canon through Poe and "Golden Age" crime short stories; and secondly, crime short stories exploring place and reimaginings of iconic detective figure Sherlock Holmes through contemporary crime short stories. Many of the works used in these course sessions I have also published on. These scholarly publications are added to the course syllabus and inform my teaching of the material as well as my discussions here. In other words, my teaching is research-led; however, it would be equally true to say that my research is teaching-led. What this means, among other things, is that I identify gaps in scholarship in relation to the texts I teach, and, where feasible, I strive to produce publications on those texts. This helps students in identifying secondary sources for their assessment as well as for further study, but also demonstrates to them what research-led teaching might mean in practice.[19] Thereby, I hope to demonstrate to students on the course that we are all researchers, and that the processes of learning, exchanging information and debating are ongoing and in process—for me, as well as for them. These practices and reflections form part of my pedagogy in "teaching for diversity" and "sharing meaning" with students.[20]

Teaching the Canon

The undergraduate crime fiction course I currently teach follows a roughly chronologically organised outline, illustrating to students how the crime short story has evolved alongside, and responded to, novel-length crime fiction. Edgar Allan Poe's Dupin stories from the 1840s are frequently taught on crime fiction course syllabi, because of the stories' focus on central crime topics such as ratiocination and criminal psychology. Commenting on the importance and influence of Poe on crime fiction, Leitch states that "Poe is universally regarded as the father of the detective story, and his place as a pioneer of the short story is scarcely less secure".[21] Through its crime plot, Poe's 1841 crime short story "The Murders in the Rue Morgue" calls attention to problematic themes at the heart of crime fiction, namely violence and victimisation of marginalised and disenfranchised characters. Teaching this crime short story helps in highlighting the gender-political dimensions of the genre. As Harrowitz states, "The story presents the conflict between our view of different civilizations and our desire to identify scapegoats",[22] leading in this case to the story's preference for the grotesque plot twist of a murderous orangutan rather than confronting the problem of patriarchal violence against women. The graphic depiction of violence in "The Murders in the Rue Morgue" has become one of the staple elements of much crime fiction, as Franks also argues.[23] These aspects of Poe's crime short stories serve an important didactic purpose, highlighting the idea of patriarchal society as a crime scene, and drawing attention to the use of the female body as a site for exploitation. Poe's Dupin stories illustrate to students the evolution of detective figures in crime fiction, including in the crime short story, while at the same time calling attention to some of the genre's enduring problematics and thorny questions, such as the representation of violence against women. Classroom debates of important gender-political questions such as violence against women and cultural difference help to develop students' critical vocabulary, and serve to demonstrate how crime fiction, far from being merely escapism, engages with social and cultural concerns.

Agatha Christie's *The Mysterious Mr. Quin* (1930) short stories from the Golden Age period have been identified by Priestman as significant in the evolution of the crime short story.[24] Specific Mr. Quin stories which I have taught include "The Coming of Mr. Quin", "The Bird with the Broken Wing", "The World's End", and "The Face of Helen".[25] As I discuss elsewhere, the Mr. Quin stories offer compelling insight into British social and cultural values in the 1920s–1930s, presenting male and female characters which problematise, challenge and disrupt gender norms.[26] These investigations are used to prompt students, to help them recognise that Golden Age crime writing, far from being merely "cosy" or predictable, features moments of disruption and transgression. The Mr. Quin stories introduce students to another, less familiar but no less compelling, part of Christie's oeuvre. In a teaching context, including these stories helps to address the problem of replicating works and repeating syllabi used on other crime fiction courses currently taught in universities. Contextually, Christie's short stories help students to situate crime writing within the wider modernist period, illustrating how themes and stylistic traits from that period's "high art" may recur or echo in the crime fiction of the period.[27] Through teaching Christie's Mr. Quin stories, I encourage students to further explore themes such as the representation of gender and its subversion, the country house mystery, the problematisation of female artistic creativity, class structures and their implications for crime, and cultural difference, within a short story setting.[28] The engagement with these Christie stories, which are different in tone from standard clue puzzle mysteries and the conventional plot-centred whodunits of the period, challenges students to reconsider their assumptions regarding Agatha Christie and the Golden Age. Following their previous study of Poe's crime short stories on the course, students are eager to investigate the Mr. Quin short fictions, and are quick to point out perceived limitations of the stories in terms of length, plot, and character development as well as their strengths. Students are often particularly interested in the amateur detective character of Mr. Satterthwaite and his complicated relationship to the elusive harlequin figure Mr. Quin, whose character challenges the boundaries of realistic representation in crime fiction, as Priestman notes,

> Christie's engagement with the short story's particular qualities emerges most clearly with a detective duo specifically designed for the form: the observant Mr Satterthwaite and his elusive, half-unreal alter ego Harley Quin, in the stories collected as *The Mysterious Mr Quin*.[29]

Our examination of Christie's Mr. Quin stories helps us to interrogate the construction and depiction of gender in crime fiction, promoting debate and reflection regarding its centrality to the genre. In the seminars, students explore representations of gender in the Mr. Quin short stories, analysing the differing positions characters adopt in response to patriarchal, social and class pressures, and how these are linked to the theme of crime.[30] Furthermore, the Mr. Quin stories are introduced in order to demonstrate contrasts between different generic modes. Students are fascinated by the contrasts between Golden Age crime fiction, its stylistic dimensions, settings, and thematic preoccupations, and the American hard-boiled crime fiction novels which they also study on my course. In classroom discussions, we reflect on these apparent contrasts and contradictions in representations of masculinity, the detective role, and the development of distinctive stylistic traits in the two crime fiction modes. Through their reflective engagement with Christie's Mr. Quin stories, students examine the blurring of boundaries between literary fiction and popular writing and the representation of gender, power and agency in early twentieth-century class-ridden, gender-restricted Britain. Students are thus further equipped to assess the capacity of various crime fictions to act as a site of critique, acknowledging that this capacity, far from being exclusive to contemporary crime fiction, is a vital element of the crime fiction genre that has historical precedent and significance.

Recent Reimaginings

Experimentations with the crime short story form, and the focus on themes such as gender roles and investigation of artistic practice signalled in Christie's Mr. Quin stories, evolve in the contemporary crime short stories examined towards the end of the course. As we progress towards contemporary material, students consider a range of recent crime short stories. This section discusses two different examples of teaching the twenty-first-century crime short story, one focusing on place, setting and literary locus, the other on the detective figure of Sherlock Holmes. This contemporary material invites students to consider crime short stories by various authors which reflect present-day urban settings or connect with popular culture.

Concerning the representation of place in crime fiction, Geherin argues that crime texts provide "ideal opportunity" for analysing the meanings of setting, particularly because, he states, "in realistic crime fiction, there is often an intimate connection between crime and its milieu, which thus comes to play a prominent thematic role".[31] These considerations form the starting-point for the course's exploration of the Edinburgh setting depicted in stories from the 2009 anthology *Crimespotting: An Edinburgh Crime Collection*, which provide students with an insight into Scottish crime fiction, also known as "Tartan Noir". Published in support of the charity OneCity Trust, the anthology signposts its social engagement, demonstrating, as I state elsewhere, how crime fiction affords a textual space for articulating social and cultural critique, through use of a specific setting and geographical location.[32] In seminar work focused on close readings, students investigate the geography of crime and the stylistics employed by different Tartan Noir crime fiction authors in their representations of crime settings. I now want to turn to two of the stories I have taught from the *Crimespotting* anthology, in order to more closely examine important dimensions of the crime short story illustrated by these texts; namely gender-political uses of subgenre and controversial thematic content of contemporary relevance. One of the *Crimespotting* short stories we have studied on the course is Kate Atkinson's "Affairs of the Heart". This story perfectly illustrates the emerging awareness of the genre of Domestic Noir, with its emphasis on gender politics, the family and the private sphere.[33] Domestic Noir is a relatively recently-coined critical term, joining the ever-growing number of subgenres emerging within crime fiction, and has been defined by the crime writer Julia Crouch:

> Domestic Noir takes place primarily in homes and workplaces, concerns itself largely (but not exclusively) with the female experience, is based around relationships and takes as its base a broadly feminist view that the domestic sphere is a challenging and sometimes dangerous prospect for its inhabitants.[34]

Atkinson's crime short story employs the Domestic Noir subgenre to explore and expose patriarchal dynamics within the traditional family, using humorous subversion to portray the drastic violent action taken by the mother and her daughters in the story to avenge themselves on a tyrannical and domineering husband and father.[35] In class, we examine how Atkinson's story alludes to fairy-tale motifs such as Bluebeard,[36] and uses stereotypical motifs from crime fiction, such as the murder in the library and the femme fatale, but playfully transforming these motifs into feminist mimicry and pastiche through the use of humorous subversion. Atkinson's text thus illustrates how the crime short story through its experimentation can alter the dynamics of the conventional Domestic Noir. Denise Mina's short story "Chris Takes the Bus" is another *Crimespotting* story which is effective in a crime fiction teaching and learning context, due to its thematic focus on the controversial issue of male rape.[37] Sexual crime against women is a frequent theme in crime fiction, as Heather Worthington explains[38]; however, Mina importantly tackles the culturally silenced subject of sexual crimes against males. The brief, fragmented text describes a young man's attempt to escape by bus to London from Edinburgh, after having recently been raped. In class, we examine how Mina's "Chris Takes the Bus" employs textual experimentation though its innovative use of the short story form, combined with challenging thematic crime content. As I discuss elsewhere, the story's unresolved ending leaves many of the questions usually posed in crime novels unanswered, by refusing closure and withholding description of the crime itself from the narrative.[39] The textual technique of withholding information is an important aspect for crime fiction students to explore as part of their actively engaged study of the text. Key to the plot, yet absent from the crime narrative itself, withheld information serves to engage student readers in asking questions and reading actively. Students reflect on the wider implications of an alienating and divisive urban environment, sexual crimes going unpunished and the open-endedness of Mina's story.

The second example of teaching the contemporary crime short story is a recent addition on my crime fiction course. This case study centres on teaching twenty-first-century crime short stories which explore or recast the character of Sherlock Holmes, an iconic detective figure within the genre. Teaching these contemporary recastings of Sherlock Holmes serves to foreground literary and cultural links between the established crime fiction canon and our early-semester reading on the course of Conan Doyle's *Hound of the Baskervilles* and contemporary reconfiguring of the detective figure, and to assess the textual, cultural and political realignments that drive these innovations.[40] The stories furthermore demonstrate to students the multiplicity of literary style and thematic content employed by various writers in their depictions of Holmes' character, including uses of intertextuality and textual echoes, gender-political and international dimensions. For this purpose, selected crime short stories from Laurie R. King and Leslie S. Klinger's edited work, *A Study in Sherlock: Stories Inspired by the Holmes Canon* (2011), are employed. Two of the texts I have taught from the King and Klinger anthology are Lee Child's hard-boiled crime short story "The Bone-Headed League"[41] and Margaret Maron's crime short story "The Adventure of the Concert Pianist".[42] In class, we discuss Child's story as an illustration of textual echoes and intertextuality, and the title's allusion to Conan Doyle's "The Red-Headed League".[43] Students investigate how Child's crime short story exposes the creation of cultural clichés through crime fiction, in its depiction of iconic London settings associated with Holmes and its humorous references to Cockney rhyming slang. Linking to our previous study of Chandler on the course, we study how, through its use of postmodernist intertextual allusions, Child's story illustrates the evolution of a maverick detective character who "rank[s] high on insubordination".[44] Students respond to Child's story and its parodic constructions of Britishness and the character of Holmes, by evaluating the ironic twist of the story's ending, while considering the questions it raises regarding the reader's expectation of crime fiction and closure.[45] In contrast, Maron's story "The Adventure of the Concert Pianist" specifically puts gender on the agenda. Set in the late nineteenth century, the text reflects contemporary neo-Victorian literary trends.[46] Maron's crime short story explores the implications of removing the main focus of the narrative, the iconic male detective Sherlock Holmes, leaving instead the landlady Mrs. Hudson, a perceived minor character, an older woman, in the role of detective.[47] The study of Maron's story paves the way for an examination of the gender-political dimensions of Sherlock Holmes, such as the fresh insight the story provides into the otherwise overlooked character of Mrs. Hudson who turns out to be capable of solving crime using her emotional intelligence, employing methods which are different from Holmes', but equal in substance.[48] Classroom discussions focus on ways in which Maron's story challenges conventional literary constructions of the detective figure, specifically in relation to Sherlock Holmes. These texts facilitate a discussion with students of the manifold reasons behind the continued popularity of Sherlock Holmes, and the aspects of his character that intrigue readers and audiences across the world, as well as our own individual responses to this canonical figure. Such reflections and more form the basis of students' ongoing engagement with detective figures and the politics of their representation and evolution in the contemporary crime short story.

Conclusion: Challenging Conventions

The crime short story deserves a central place in the literary crime landscape which we teach, and there is much scope for extending student learning and furthering critical enquiry through extended use of this subgenre. May argues that "In the early twenty-first century, as multicultural studies and postcolonial theories privilege the socially conscious novel, teaching the short story – a poetic form that has never been amenable to sociological or political criticism – becomes a difficult and thankless task".[49] However, this has not been my experience; I have found the form useful for exploring social and political dimensions in crime fiction. Peach notes that "The comparative lack of attention that the literary short story receives on degree courses in the UK reflects its low status in the larger publishing world".[50] However, particularly since the publication of Peach's essay in Cox' 2011 volume in this series on teaching the short story, there is a sense that this situation has changed, and that the textual landscape charted on degree courses is more varied than his assessment suggests. Rather, the examples employed in this chapter, of crime short stories and their application in teaching and learning contexts, reflect the point made by Liggins et al. that,

> the short-story form has offered liberation from the formal restrictions of the novel, inviting experimentation and subversion of the norms of the mainstream. The fluidity of the form has rendered it an effective outlet for the exploration and negotiation of gender, race, class, and sexual identity.[51]

As we have seen, classroom study of the crime short story opens up new dimensions of the crime fiction genre. The examination of subgenres and forms thus plays a crucial role in teaching crime fiction, contributing to greater understanding of the genre and the means by which its conventions and patterns may be challenged and reassessed. Teaching the crime short story is much more than merely "cutting a long story short".

Notes

1. Rebeca Hernández, "Short Narrations in a Letter Frame: Cases of Genre Hybridity in Postcolonial Literature in Portuguese", In *Short Story Theories: A Twenty-First-Century Perspective*, edited by Viorica Patea. Amsterdam, Rodopi, 2012. 154.
2. Iftekharruddin states: "Postmodernism is a complex entity that encompasses a wide range of philosophical, social, linguistic, and literary interests and attracts a variety of practitioners including social theorists, poststructuralists and psychoanalysts." Farhat Iftekharuddin. "Fictional Nonfiction and Nonfictional Fiction". In *The Postmodern Short Story: Forms and Issues*, edited by Farhat Iftekharuddin; Joseph Boyden, Mary Rohrberger, Jaie Claudet. No. 124. Greenwood Publishing Group, 2003. 4.

3. Raymond Williams, "On High and Popular Culture". *New Republic*, 22 November 1974. https://newrepublic.com/article/79269/high-and-popular-culture Accessed 16 July 2017.
4. See Tom Nolan, "Short Stories, Hard Covers: New Partners in Crime Fiction". *The Wall Street Journal*, 9 May 2007. https://www.wsj.com/articles/SB117867237969196688 Accessed 26 December 2017.
5. Ailsa Cox, "Introduction", In Teaching the Short Story, edited by Ailsa Cox. Houndmills, Palgrave, 2011. 1.
6. Frank Myszor, *The Modern Short Story*, Cambridge, Cambridge University Press, 2001. 7.
7. Martin Priestman, Part III, Chapter 11. In *The Cambridge Companion to the English Short Story*, edited by Ann-Marie Einhaus, 159–171. Cambridge: Cambridge University Press, 2016. Kindle. See also Charlotte Beyer, 'Bags Stuffed with the Offal of Their Own History': Crime Fiction and the Short Story in *Crimespotting: An Edinburgh Crime Collection'. Short Fiction in Theory and Practice*, Vol. 3 No. 1. 37–52.
8. Priestman, 159.
9. Myszor, 8.
10. Ailsa Cox, "Introduction", *Writing Short Stories: A Routledge Writer's Guide*, Abingdon, Routledge, 2005; 2016. Kindle.
11. Adrian Hunter, *The Cambridge Introduction to the Short Story in English.* Cambridge: Cambridge University Press, 2007, p. 1.
12. Hunter, p. 1.
13. Myszor 26.
14. Hunter, p. 1.
15. Iftekharuddin, 5.
16. Randolph J. Cox. "Detective Short Fiction", in *The Facts on File: Companion to the American Short Story*, edited by Abby Werlock and James Werlock. New York: Infobase Publishing, Cox, 2010. 185.
17. Weber, Christina D., Literary Fiction as a Tool for Teaching Social Theory and Critical Consciousness". *Teaching Sociology*, Vol. 38 No. 4, 2010, 351.
18. Lisa Fletcher, "The Scholarship of Teaching and Learning Popular Romance Studies: What is It, and Why Does It Matter? *Journal of Popular Romance Studies*, 2013, 3.2.1–5. 4.
19. I have cited those of my publications here that apply to this discussion, specifically in relation to teaching the crime short story.
20. See Northedge, Andrew. "Rethinking Teaching in the Context of Diversity", *Teaching in Higher Education*, 8: 1, 2003. 17–32. Northedge uses these terms as part of his discussion of pedagogy.
21. Thomas Leitch, "On the Margins of Mystery: The Detective in Poe and After". In *Contemporary Debates on the Short Story*, edited by José R. Ibáñez Ibáñez, José Francisco Fernández, Carmen M. Bretones. Bern: Peter Lang, 2007. 25. See also Myszor, 15; Leitch, 34.

22. Nancy A. Harrowitz, "Criminality and Poe's Orangutang". In *Agonistics: Arenas of Creative Contest* edited by Janet Lungstrum, Elizabeth Sauer. Albany: State University of New York Press, 1997. 188.
23. Rachel Franks, "Hardboiled Detectives and the Roman Noir Tradition". In *Violence in American Popular Culture*, Volume 2, edited by David Schmid, Santa Barbara, CA: Praeger, 2015. 97.
24. Priestman, 166.
25. All in Agatha Christie, *The Mysterious Mr. Quin*, London: HarperCollins, 2003.
26. Charlotte Beyer, "'With Practised Eyes': Feminine Identity in *The Mysterious Mr. Quin*". In *The Ageless Agatha Christie: Essays on the Mysteries and the Legacy, edited by* Jamie Bernthal. Jefferson: McFarland, 2016. 61–80.
27. Beyer, "Practised". See also Merja Makinen, *Agatha Christie: Investigating Femininity*. Houndmills: Palgrave, 2006.
28. I also refer to these themes in Beyer "Practised", 62.
29. Priestman, 166.
30. Beyer "Practised", 76.
31. David Geherin, *Scene of the Crime: The Importance of Place in Crime and Mystery Fiction*, Jefferson, NC: McFarland, 2008. 8.
32. See my article on the anthology: Charlotte Beyer, "'Bags Stuffed with the Offal of Their Own History': Crime Fiction and the Short Story in *Crimespotting: An Edinburgh Crime Collection*". *Short Fiction in Theory and Practice*, Vol. 3 No. 1. 39.
33. Kate Atkinson. "Affairs of the Heart". In *Crimespotting: An Edinburgh Crime Collection*, edited by Kate Atkinson et al. Edinburgh: Polygon, 2009. 13–34.
34. Julia Crouch, "Genre Bender". Blog, http://juliacrouch.co.uk/blog/genre-bender. Accessed 6 January 2018.
35. Beyer, "Bags", 40–41.
36. Beyer, "Bags", 40.
37. Denise Mina, "Chris Takes the Bus". in *Crimespotting: An Edinburgh Crime Collection*, edited by Denise Mina et al., Edinburgh: Polygon, 2009. 195–200.
38. Heather Worthington, *Key Concepts in Crime Fiction*. Houndmills: Palgrave, 2011. 50.
39. Beyer, "Bags", 48.
40. These issues are also explored in Vanacker and Wynne.
41. See my article, in which I discuss this story; Charlotte Beyer, "Sherlock Holmes Reimagined: An Exploration of Selected Short Stories from *A Study in Sherlock: Stories Inspired by the Holmes Canon*". *Oscholars* (Special issue on Conan Doyle). https://oscholars-oscholars.com/doyle/.

42. I also discuss this story in my chapter: "'I, Too, Mourn The Loss': Mrs Hudson and the Absence of Sherlock Holmes". In *Sherlock Holmes in Context* edited by Sam Naidu. Houndmills: Palgrave. 61–82.
43. Beyer, "Reimagined", 7.
44. Raymond Chandler, *The Big Sleep*. London: Penguin, 2011. 9. I also make the connection to the hard-boiled detective anti-hero in Beyer "Reimagined", 8.
45. Beyer, "Reimagined", 8.
46. Louisa Hadley, *Neo-Victorian Fiction and Historical Narrative: The Victorians and Us*. Houndmills: Palgrave, 2010. 5.
47. Beyer, "I, Too", 62.
48. Beyer, "I, Too", 74.
49. Charles May, "Teaching the Short Story Today". In *Teaching the Short Story*, edited by Ailsa Cox. Houndmills: Palgrave, 2011. 149.
50. Linden Peach, "Women Writers". In *Teaching the Short Story*, edited by Ailsa Cox. Houndmills, Palgrave, 2011. 61.
51. Andrew Maunder, Emma Liggins, Ruth Robbins, *The British Short Story*. Houndmills: Palgrave. 16.

Works Cited

Atkinson, Kate. "Affairs of the Heart." In *Crimespotting: An Edinburgh Crime Collection*, edited by Kate Atkinson et al., 13–34. Edinburgh: Polygon, 2009.

Beyer, Charlotte. "'Bags Stuffed with the Offal of Their Own History': Crime Fiction and the Short Story in *Crimespotting: An Edinburgh Crime Collection.*" *Short Fiction in Theory and Practice*, 2013, Vol. 3, No. 1, 37–52.

———. "Sherlock Holmes Reimagined: An Exploration of Selected Short Stories from *A Study in Sherlock: Stories Inspired by the Holmes Canon.*" *Oscholars*, 2015. https://oscholars-oscholars.com/doyle/

———. "'With Practised Eyes': Feminine Identity in the Mysterious Mr. Quin." In *The Ageless Agatha Christie: Essays on the Mysteries and the Legacy*, edited by Jamie Bernthal, 61–80. Jefferson: McFarland, 2016.

———. "'I, Too, Mourn The Loss': Mrs Hudson and the Absence of Sherlock Holmes." In *Sherlock Holmes in Context*, edited by Sam Naidu, 61–82. Houndmills: Palgrave Macmillan.

Chandler, Raymond. *The Big Sleep*. London: Penguin, 2011.

Child, Lee. "The Bone Headed League." In *A Study in Sherlock: Stories Inspired by the Holmes Canon*, edited by Leslie S. Klinger and Laurie R. King, 87–94. New York: Bantam Books, London: Titan Books, 2011.

Christie, Agatha. "The Coming of Mr. Quin" (1930). In *The Mysterious Mr. Quin*, 1–23. London: HarperCollins, 2003.

———. "The Face of Helen" (1930). In *The Mysterious Mr. Quin*, 229–257. London: HarperCollins, 2003.

———. "The Bird with the Broken Wing" (1930). In *The Mysterious Mr. Quin*, 297–328. London: HarperCollins, 2003.

———. "The World's End" (1930). In *The Mysterious Mr. Quin*, 329–359. London: HarperCollins, 2003.

Cox, Ailsa. "Introduction." In *Teaching the Short Story*, edited by Ailsa Cox, 1–12. Houndmills: Palgrave Macmillan, 2011.

Cox, Randolph J. "Detective Short Fiction." In *The Facts on File: Companion to the American Short Story*, edited by Abby Werlock and James Werlock, 182–185. New York: Infobase Publishing, 2010.

Fletcher, Lisa. "The Scholarship of Teaching and Learning Popular Romance Studies: What Is It, and Why Does It Matter?" *Journal of Popular Romance Studies*, 2013, Vol. 3, No. 2, 1–5.

Franks, Rachel. "Hardboiled Detectives and the Roman Noir Tradition." In *Violence in American Popular Culture*, Volume 2, edited by David Schmid, 95–117. Santa Barbara, CA: Praeger, 2015.

Geherin, David. *Scene of the Crime: The Importance of Place in Crime and Mystery Fiction*. Jefferson, NC: McFarland, 2008.

Graff, Gerald. *Clueless in Academe: How Schooling Obscures the Life of the Mind*. Yale University Press, 2003.

Hadley, Louisa. *Neo-Victorian Fiction and Historical Narrative: The Victorians and Us*. Houndmills: Palgrave Macmillan, 2010.

Harrowitz, Nancy A. "Criminality and Poe's Orangutang." In *Agonistics: Arenas of Creative Contest*, edited by Janet Lungstrum and Elizabeth Sauer, 177–196. Albany: State University of New York Press, 1997.

Hernández, Rebeca. "Short Narrations in a Letter Frame: Cases of Genre Hybridity in Postcolonial Literature in Portuguese." In *Short Story Theories: A Twenty-First-Century Perspective*, edited by Viorica Patea, 155–172. Amsterdam: Rodopi, 2012.

Hunter, Adrian. *The Cambridge Introduction to the Short Story in English*. Cambridge: Cambridge University Press, 2007.

Iftekharuddin, Farhat. "Fictional Nonfiction and Nonfictional Fiction." In *The Postmodern Short Story: Forms and Issues*, edited by Farhat Iftekharuddin, Joseph Boyden, Mary Rohrberger and Jaie Claudet. No. 124, 1–22. Greenwood Publishing Group, 2003.

Leitch, Thomas. "On the Margins of Mystery: The Detective in Poe and After." In *Contemporary Debates on the Short Story*, edited by José R. Ibáñez, José Francisco Fernández and Carmen M. Bretones, 25–48. Bern: Peter Lang, 2007.

Makinen, Merja. *Agatha Christie: Investigating Femininity*. Houndmills: Palgrave Macmillan, 2006.

Maron, Margaret. "The Adventure of the Concert Pianist." In *A Study in Sherlock: Stories Inspired by the Holmes Canon*, edited by Leslie S. Klinger and Laurie R. King, 230–249. New York: Bantam Books, 2011.

Maunder, Andrew, Liggins, Emma and Robbins, Ruth. *The British Short Story.* Houndmills: Palgrave Macmillan.

May, Charles. "Teaching the Short Story Today." In *Teaching the Short Story*, edited by Ailsa Cox, 147–160. Houndmills: Palgrave Macmillan, 2011.

Mina, Denise. "Chris Takes the Bus." In *Crimespotting: An Edinburgh Crime Collection*, edited by Denise Mina et al., 195–200. Edinburgh: Polygon, 2009.

Myszor, Frank. *The Modern Short Story.* Cambridge: Cambridge University Press, 2001.

Northedge, Andrew. "Rethinking Teaching in the Context of Diversity." *Teaching in Higher Education*, 2003, Vol. 8, No. 1, 17–32.

Nolan, Tom. "Short Stories, Hard Covers: New Partners in Crime Fiction." *The Wall Street Journal*, 9 May 2007. https://www.wsj.com/articles/SB117867237969196688 Accessed 26 December 2017.

Peach, Linden. "Women Writers." In *Teaching the Short Story*, edited by Ailsa Cox, 60–75. Houndmills: Palgrave Macmillan, 2011.

Poe, Edgar Allan. "The Murders in the Rue Morgue" (1841). Poestories.com. nd. https://poestories.com/text.php?file=murders Accessed 4 January 2018.

Priestman, Martin. "The Detective Short Story", Part III, Chapter 11. In *The Cambridge Companion to the English Short Story*, edited by Ann-Marie Einhaus. 159–171. Cambridge: Cambridge University Press, 2016. Kindle edition.

Vanacker, Sabine and Wynne, Catherine eds. *Sherlock Holmes and Conan Doyle: Multi-Media Afterlives.* Houndmills: Palgrave Macmillan.

Weber, Christina D., "Literary Fiction as a Tool for Teaching Social Theory and Critical Consciousness." *Teaching Sociology*, 2010, Vol. 38, No. 4, 350–361.

Williams, Raymond. "On High and Popular Culture." *New Republic*, 22 November 1974. https://newrepublic.com/article/79269/high-and-popular-culture Accessed 16 July 2017.

Winspear, Jacqueline. "A Spot of Detection." In *A Study in Sherlock: Stories Inspired by the Holmes Canon*, edited by Leslie S. Klinger and Laurie R. King, 359–383. New York: Bantam Books, London: Titan Books, 2011.

Worthington, Heather. *Key Concepts in Crime Fiction.* Houndmills: Palgrave Macmillan, 2011.

CHAPTER 8

Studies in Green: Teaching Ecological Crime Fiction

Samantha Walton

Reading ecological crime fiction and reading crime fiction ecologically demand a shifting of focus to features of a text often dismissed as backdrops to human activity: rivers, forests, landscapes, climate or the planetary ecosystem. It provokes an adjustment of temporalities, urging scholars to situate human activity in seasonal, anthropological, evolutionary and deep timescales. Crime and detective fictions are inherently concerned with the ways in which ambiance, location, history and place-memory may be factors in crime and provide clues towards a mystery's solution. Every crime novel is set *somewhere*, and investigation of that *somewhere* is a good place to start introducing students to wider questions posed by ecological reading. What forms of knowledge are best suited to excavating obscured histories of a landscape, and how are past transgressions built into the fabric of a place? Is the environment passive, or active, in the unravelling of the crime, and what kinds of relationships do characters and other agencies form with the world in which crimes are commissioned, investigated and solved? With these questions as starting points, students can be encouraged

S. Walton (✉)
Bath Spa University, Bath, UK
e-mail: s.walton@bathspa.ac.uk

C. Beyer (ed.), *Teaching Crime Fiction*, Teaching the New English,
https://doi.org/10.1007/978-3-319-90608-9_8

to think beyond the immediate and engaging human dramas of crime fiction, and to begin to explore the roles that other-than-human factors and agencies play in criminal transgressions and the process of detection.

Ecocriticism

In order to support students through this process of refocusing attention on environmental and ecological themes, the forms of reading practised in crime fiction studies need to be brought into dialogue with the field of ecocriticism. An ecocritical reading, in the most general sense, approaches texts in two ways. Firstly, it reads any literary text with attention to the representation of the non-human world, including landscape, weather, flora, fauna and any other features commonly referred to as 'nature'. Secondly, any text that explicitly engages with environmental and conservation issues—for example, a work of nature writing focused on species decline—may be open to, or insist on, an ecocritical reading. Current trends in ecocriticism offer many specialised ways of approaching texts: for example, through attention to interspecies relationships, ecological interconnectedness or the vital materiality of the living world. At the root of these reading practices is the question of whether, by deepening understanding of culture–nature interrelations and contributing to behavioural change, literature may contribute to efforts to improve and mediate the real-world conditions of environmental crisis. Ecocriticism has its roots in environmentalism, and continues to engage with the ethics and politics of literary representation, asking challenging questions about culture's efficacy as a political tool or barometer of change. To this extent, it is a world-facing critical practice, and its methods and concerns are comparable to, and often compatible with, approaches adopted in feminism, critical race theory and queer studies.

The study and teaching of crime fiction has, historically, moved through distinct stages which coordinate with major trends in literary criticism. A teacher of crime fiction will find it easy to introduce students to approaches inherited from narrative theory, new historicism and psychoanalysis, and to urge students to attend to representations of gender, sexuality, race and class within a text. In each case, they will be able to draw from a wealth of literary scholarship. Bringing environmental criticism into dialogue with crime studies is a fruitful exercise, and a timely one, given the current conditions of environmental crisis and the specific anxieties young people have about the state of the planet. However, there are at present limited books and articles to refer students to as models of ecocritical analysis of crime fiction.[1]

In its earliest days, ecocriticism was concerned with theories of nature and reactions to industrialisation found in Romantic poetry and American Transcendentalism. As the field grew, its focus diversified. Scholarship has built up around 'popular' genres including science fiction, horror, computer games, and the emerging genre of climate change fiction or 'cli-fi', which engages with climate change effects such as sea-level rise, food shortages and mass extinction.[2] Teaching ecological crime fiction may involve extrapolating from this wealth of adjacent material. For example, cli-fi novels may incorporate tropes and formulas associated with crime fictions, such as the psychological thriller (as in *The Rapture* (2009) by Liz Jenson) and corporate conspiracy (see *Odds Against Tomorrow* (1959) by Nathaniel Rich). The intertextuality and genre-borrowing of cli-fi suggests ways of introducing environmental themes into the teaching of crime fiction, for example, through exploring how established formulas have been adapted to address new cultural understandings of climate change and current political responses to the scientific consensus.

Beyond this, I would like to suggest two possible themes for development in teaching of ecological crime and detective fiction: firstly, the construction of nature as 'other' in classic crime narratives; and the challenge environmentalism poses to the genre's traditional commitment to upholding law and assigning responsibility. There are, of course, many other approaches that could be explored, and in the conclusion I suggest ways of situating ecological concerns within the long tradition of detective narratives.

Nature in 'Classic' Detective Fiction

It is rarely noted that the rise of detective fiction coincided pretty exactly with the development of conservation and environmental movements, including: late eighteenth- and early nineteenth-century Romanticism, the American wilderness preservation debates of the 1890s, the British reforestation movement of the 1920s, and the emergence of ecological consciousness and anxieties about toxicity and pollution from the 1960s onwards. In spite of this, it would seem that 'classic' crime and detective fiction of the nineteenth century and Golden Age has been notably quiet on the subject of environmental degradation and the human exploitation of the living world.

When writers have paid attention to nature, it has often meant using the countryside, natural formations and non-human animals as plot devices which pose an imminent threat or an obstacle to safety. This tendency does not mean that the novels are of no interest to ecocritics: instead, it will be useful for students to address negative or highly stylised representations of nature in crime fiction. In doing so, they can be asked to consider the role that literature might have played in shaping, or challenging, dominant cultural understandings of nature during an era of unprecedented destruction of natural habitats and species extinction.

For example, in numerous Golden Age detective novels, forests, oceans, deserts and rivers provide a blockade which keep law enforcement out and return the entrapped cast to an anxious, Hobbesian state of nature: Agatha Christie's *Murder on the Orient Express* (1934) and *Death on the Nile* (1937) prove cases in point. What influence might such representation have on readers, and what attitudes to wild places might it encourage? Students can draw from their own culturally, socially and geographically distinct experiences of the texts under consideration, and of the kinds of places represented in crime fiction, in order to explore these questions. Though most students are unlikely to have firsthand experience of living in an isolated country mansion, many may have grown up or stayed in rural places or, if their background is firmly urban, have acquired a stock of perceptions about secluded dwellings and small rural communities from a range of literary and non-literary sources. To what extent have they absorbed tropes concerning the danger of wild and peri-urban places, and if they do fear these places, where do those fears come from? The discussion could be expanded to address the many popular regional detective series which make use of idyllic heritage landscapes such as North Wales, Shetland, the Calder Valley and the Dorset coast as backdrops for organised crime, sexual violence and murder.[3] Psychologist Laurel Watson contends that "a sociocultural context that objectifies women and their bodies is related to their sense of safety and security in the world".[4] How might a slew of detection narratives connecting natural landscapes with murder and rape influence women's perceptions of their safety and security in National Parks, conservation areas and rural places? While environmental organisations such as the Woodland Trust and The Wildlife Trusts try to inspire engagement in conservation through appealing to people's love of nature and wild places, crime fictions frequently equate these places with lawlessness, depravity, transgression and danger.

A module focused on the othering of nature in crime fiction would do well to address Arthur Conan Doyle's *The Hound of the Baskervilles* (1902), located between the dark streets of London and the wilds of Dartmoor.

The arrival of the horrific hound in this landscape of standing stones, mists and mire is a gothic revenge narrative *par excellence*, and the role of the detective is to see past the aura of mystery in order to force the irrational into the natural order of cause and effect. But does nature simply provide atmosphere? Is it a force to be tamed, or is something more complex going on? Ecocriticism has long debated the role of hierarchical binaries in the cultural construction of nature: reason, civilisation, masculinity and the urban have been extensively contrasted with the supernatural, wildness, femininity and nature.[5] In an ecocritical reading of *The Hound of the Baskervilles*, students can be encouraged to isolate and examine the use of reinforcing binaries: for example, Holmes is depicted as paragon of reason, masculinity and civilised urbanity, versus nature as 'other': the hound can be read as an avenger of male violence and a threat to the patrilineal transfer of property; and the moor itself is depicted as an abject and inherently threatening environment, which not only provides a backdrop to human activity, but shapes and alters it.

Doyle's novel also debates different ways of perceiving and instrumentalising non-human nature. Starting with the obvious—the abuse of the hound—students can be asked to find examples of the ways in which nature is exploited to further human ends. The question of what it means to 'exploit' nature is sure to come up. What about the extensive representation of the moors as terrifying and desolate? What possible effects could such artistic licence have on the real moors and wetlands of Britain? Dr. Watson, never one to miss an opportunity for vivid scene-setting, describes the moors as a "barren waste" emitting "decay and miasmatic vapour". He even suggests that the moor's depopulation is connected to microclimate, rather than changes in the economics of tin-mining: the long-gone miners were "driven away, no doubt, by the foul reek of the surrounding swamp".[6]

Ecocritic Rob Giblett has argued that the "pejorative Christian view of wetlands is largely responsible for the destruction of wetlands in the west for the past millennium".[7] Wetlands have been framed as a kind of abject and watery hell, inherently threatening to human health and social order. Not unrelatedly, fens and wetlands have been drained and reclaimed as part of city-expansion projects from the early modern period onwards. With this in mind, students can consider the impact that literary tropes have had, and might in future have, on wider cultural perceptions of places, particularly threatened ecosystems such as wetlands. Does Doyle's novel simply reproduce such negative tropes, or does it challenge them?

One of the few characters to understand the ecological value of the mire is Jack Stapleton. As amateur naturalist and proto-cultural geographer, he is the novel's unlikely ecocritical hero; unlikely, because he is also the keeper of the hound and the killer. Through Stapleton, students can debate the value, and the danger, of scientific knowledge. While many ecocritics have asserted the importance of working with the sciences to share knowledge and bring about holistic behavioural change, others have rejected science as a practice bound up with forms of mastery and domination inherent to patriarchy, colonialism and capitalism.[8] Stapleton is the epitome of the fanatical scientist, exploiting women, nature and non-human animals to achieve dominion. But what about Holmes? He is also a scientific genius, and has the role of disillusioning characters, forcing them to see nature clearly and scientifically, not in the gothic light with which Watson has painted it. The novel's key moment of natural disenchantment is the realisation that the hound is a starved pup rather than a hellish avenger, but the moor is a more complex entity, resistent to Holmes' disenchanting lens. Holmes manages to survive there secretly during investigations, and plans an ambush to catch Stapleton in the act of releasing the hound. However, a white wall of fog advances, leaving the hound running free and giving Stapleton the chance to slip away unchecked. Stapleton escapes into the mire and most likely drowns, meaning he is bought to natural, but not human justice. The mire acts as a kind of avenger, though remains a mysterious and sinister agency, abject, other, and beyond human ken: walking across it, it is "as if some malignant hand was tugging us down into those obscene depths".[9]

Long-established tropes are connected to the writing of landscapes. Alongside Doyle's representation of fens, students may be introduced to broader terminology such as the pastoral and anti-pastoral, the wilderness and the sublime, eco-gothic and the littoral.[10] Each of these approaches offers rich avenues for analysis of crime fiction's representations of threatened and threatening landscapes, and consideration of what impact such a popular genre might have on environmental consciousness of its readership.

Environmentalism, Law and Responsibility

In an introduction to ecocritical methodology, Patrick Murphy urges scholars to study "nature-oriented mystery novels—with or without detectives, and perhaps even without murders—in order to understand the degree to which environmental consciousness and nature awareness has permeated popular and commercial fiction".[11] In the face of newer crime fictions which explicitly engage with environmental themes, Murphy's characterisation of crime fiction as a passive benchmark of a discourse's spread seems somewhat superficial. In teaching ecological crime fiction, students may be encouraged to consider the extent to which writers engage critically with the issues their investigations raise, in particular concerning the legality and ethics of protest, the attribution of responsibility, and the capacity of investigation and denouement to prompt social and political change.

A valuable text for introducing these issues is Ruth Rendell's *Road Rage* (1997), which fictionalises a protest against a major road-building project in the heart of Sussex. The setting will be recognisable to anyone who followed the Newbury Bypass and Twyford Rising campaigns in the 1990s, spurred by Margaret Thatcher's massive Roads for Prosperity building programme. In *Road Rage*, activists live in trees and tunnels while Chief Inspector Wexford and his wife Dora join respectable middle-class sympathisers committed to peaceful campaigning and rousing local interest. Not content with such legal measures, radical environmental activists team up with a family of wealthy property owners and stage a kidnapping, stating the bypass's cancellation as their demand. *Road Rage* offers an instructive insight into middle-class outrage at government policy, revealing how environmentalism has come to appeal to politically diverse groups: local conservatives concerned about preserving wildlife habitats as well as England's pastoral splendour; radical environmentalists who espouse a deep ecological philosophy; and the corruptible rich who will go to any lengths to protect house prices.

Although Rendell eulogises pastoral England and expresses commitment to protecting heritage landscapes through peaceful protest and legal wrangling, *Road Rage* reproduces reactionary stereotypes of environmental activists as Luddites, fanatics, hypocrites and terrorists. She models her protesters on the much-decried Animal Liberation Front, who were particularly active between 1996 and 2002.[12] Students will have no trouble determining the book's ideological commitments. The perspective of the police—sympathetic, but averse to disruption and civil disobedience—is framed as neutral and common-sense, while observation and penetration of activist groups is all in a day's work for coppers who see no ethical problems with such comprehensive surveillance. Given that between 1987 and 2010, male police spies infiltrated environmental and animal rights groups, forming inappropriate sexual relationships with women activists, students could be prompted to consider how the novel contributes to a wider social discourse which normalises the heavy-handed and intrusive policing of campaigners.[13] The relationship between local issues and wider systemic change is also raised by the novel: while the activists support an overhaul of economic and political order, the legitimate campaigners might be accused of adopting a 'Nimbyist' ('Not In My Back Yard') attitude to local conservation. The differences between objectors' positions and values will be worth thrashing out with students, ideally underpinned with reading in ecological philosophy such as Timothy Morton's *The Ecological Thought* or Ursula Heise's *Sense of Place and Sense of Planet*. Both of these texts, in distinctive ways, address how we are all enmeshed—materially and ethically—in interconnected world ecology, so that no issue or danger is ever only local or global.

Teaching could also address comparable texts which explore the legal and ethical challenges that direct action poses in ways more sympathetic to environmental activists. Although not a mystery novel, *The Monkey Wrench Gang* by Edward Abbey can be read as crime fiction from the 'criminal' perspective. Published in 1975, it proved hugely influential on the nascent environmental movement, inspiring the formation of radical groups committed to direct action. Abbey's novel follows an eclectic gang of anti-hero eco-activists engaged in sabotage against the logging industry in the American West. Their targets are not just machinery, but the legal frameworks, land-investments and profit incentives of modern capitalism. Crime fiction has often been characterised as a genre committed to upholding the rule of law and bourgeois *status quo*.[14] Reading *The Monkey Wrench Gang* as crime fiction poses a challenge to this formula, as criminal damage to machinery and other misconduct is perpetrated as a protest against a greater offence: that being committed by industries destroying the wilderness for profit.

The Monkey Wrench Gang's commitment to illegal activity for the sake of the greater good could open up challenging discussions with students about the relationship between law and ethics, social order and environmental justice in crime narratives. This is all the more relevant given that environmental activists engaging in direct action have begun to turn the terminology of the legal system to their ends when prosecuted for direct action. In a landmark English case of 2008, Greenpeace successfully used the 'lawful excuse' defence to answer charges of criminal damage. Its protesters had climbed a chimney to protest Kingsnorth Coal Power Station's carbon emissions (amounting to 200,000 tons a day). In defence, they claimed that they had acted to protect property around the world, which will be more significantly impacted by climate change that the power station was by their minor transgression.[15] The jury found them not guilty, demonstrating that English law could be stretched to accommodate cases in which indirect and long-term risks are seen as justification to act in ways that damage property in the small scale. More recently, pleas of necessary action have been entered by defendants involved in direct actions which aim to draw attention to corporate responsibility for climate change.[16] As climate activist Claire Whitney states: "Taking action is not an issue of moral righteousness but an act of self-defence".[17]

Introducing students to Rob Nixon's term 'slow violence' will help make sense of the different scales of impact, responsibility, risk and justice involved in these discussions. Slow violence is "a violence that occurs gradually and out of sight, a violence of delayed destruction ... incremental and accretive, its calamitous repercussions playing out across a range of temporal scales".[18] An 'act' of slow violence might be deforesting a hillside or allowing dangerous chemicals to seep into groundwater. Unlike the individual acts of violence traditionally prioritised in crime narratives, slow violence might be attributable to decision-makers acting on behalf of a company—as, for example, in cases of corporate manslaughter—or come under the self-regulating models of corporate social responsibility practised (often in superficial ways) in business. Looking to fiction, students may be asked: how can the narrative structures of the crime genre—mystery, investigation, denouement—and its ways of theorising knowledge, agency and responsibility be extended to consider questions of slow violence in a global context? How can justice be conceived and enacted when antagonistic actors and agencies may no longer be the 'evil geniuses' of classic detective fiction, but corporations, governments, communities, or even systemic dynamics that have no clear personal or institutional form or locus of legal and moral responsibility?

Many crime and detection novels, TV dramas and films are highly sophisticated in their excavation of the systemic dynamics of oppression: for example, Jane Campion's treatment of misogyny and sexual violence as underpinning intergenerational power dynamics in the television series *Top of the Lake*, series 1 and 2 (2013–present) or Maj Sjöwall's and Per Wahlöö's magisterial critique of capitalism and the failings of the Swedish welfare state in the Martin Beck series (1967–1975). However, novels and series which address environmental issues have had mixed success in tackling the interconnected economic and legal systems, public and political apathy, and ideological and cultural factors contributing to climate change and environmental crisis.

On the one hand, crime novels are inherently able to handle analysis of clues and forensic evidence without seeming to dump information on readers. These features can be seen in a number of recent novels, including the gargantuan *Requiem* by Clare Francis (1991), which takes on a Monsanto-esque agrochemical pollutor from the perspective of environmentalist-cum-detective and investigator Daisy Field; and Antti Tuomainen's *The Mine* (2015), which uncovers corruption and environmental pollution in Northern Finland from a journalist's perspective. Each novel succeeds in conveying considerable information about environmental degradation through the collection and analysis of soil samples, testing of water, analysis of atmospheric data, compilation of evidence from environmental reports and so on, which might seem extraneous and tedious in a realist novel without mystery elements. Indeed, the realist novel has been the subject of considerable criticism because of its lack of engagement with environmental themes.[19] Unlike most realist literary novels, which generally remain focused on localised interpersonal dramas, crime novels are able to plunge into an investigation of international corruption and concealed industrial hazards, and "see the invisible" damage of industrial pollution.[20]

However, the legacy of the Golden Age formula—the corpse and crime scene—hangs heavily over environmental crime fiction. When a murder is at the centre of a text, critiques of societal injustices and toxic discourses still tend to be connected to instances of individual moral failing. As Richard Kerridge states, "Detective stories usually start with simple 'whodunnit' questions which grow into intricate threads of connection" but "at the denouement these stories tend to collapse that intricacy back into a simple confrontation".[21] According to this criticism, Francis's *Requiem* deserves particular praise for enquiring into the multiple, complex, entangled interests which create the context for industrial malpractice and ecological pollution in a comparable way to the television series *The Wire*'s excavation of the USA's drug trade and its law enforcement's war on drugs. At over 800 pages, *Requiem* might prove a challenge for teaching. Nonetheless, Francis's capacity to handle interlocking and international narratives addressing politics, environmentalism, farming, conservation, environmentalism, global poverty, charity, medicine and law produces a more intricate narrative than most. Furthermore, the connections the book makes between ecological and human health could be used to guide students through discussion of the merits and weaknesses of strongly ecocentric or anthropocentric approaches to storytelling. While crime fictions can often be accused of being purely human-centered in their approach to transgression and justice, Francis's novel prompts consideration of the interdependence of social and environmental justice, without forsaking suspense, danger and other kinds of human interest.

Published two years later, John Grisham's *The Pelican Brief* (1993), has been influential in establishing the key tropes of many modern environmental crime thrillers: a clash of interests between powerful oil executives (or other polluting industries) and environmentalists leads to a murder, blackmail and further transgression, with the involvement of government and law enforcement in cover-up and conspiracy. In both *Requiem* and *The Mine*, investigators are threatened while whistle-blowers and activists are attacked or found dead in mysterious circumstances. These novels' exposure of corporate indifference, greed and malpractice may seem melodramatic were it not for the real-world dangers faced by environmental defenders. Global Witness reports that 200 environmental activists were killed in twenty-four countries in 2016, with the most fatalities in Brazil, Columbia and the Philippines.[22] The upsurge of environmental conspiracy novels may be a sign that writers, publishers and readers are becoming alert to the risk of protesting environmental harm and corporate interest; however, this new subgenre's tendency to focus on Western nations also evades the reality that such danger is almost exclusively and disproportionately experienced by indigenous people and communities in the Global South. In teaching environmental crime dramas, it is essential to draw students' attention to the wider geopolitical realities of environmental crisis and activism, and to the places and communities devastated by resource extraction.

Bringing postcolonial ecocritical practices to bear on texts will help students to uncover the interconnected and mutually-reinforcing crimes—both historical and on-going—which underpin and produce environmental injustice.[23] Teaching Helon Habila's *Oil on Water* (2010) could prompt discussion of the ways in which numerous factors contribute to the commission of a crime. Although not strictly a crime novel, it portrays the kidnapping of a British oil executive's wife through the eyes of a journalist, Rufus, who uncovers the interlocking interests which support the devastating oil industry in the Niger Delta. Remote multinational corporations participate in the destruction of indigenous communities, water pollution, civil war and the undermining of Nigerian democracy. The novel's messy ending gestures to the vastness and complexity of these crimes and injustices, which the novel is unable to fully understand, manage or contain. Imre Szeman has written of the defining features of the new genre of 'petrofictions' (novels focused on the global oil industry such as *Oil on*

Water) as follows: "The very best petrofictions being produced today understand oil not as a problem to be (somehow, miraculously) ameliorated, but as a core element of our societies".[24] While classic crime and detective plots can be seen, possibly simplistically, as offering both denouement and closure with the discovery of the killer and the restoration of the *status quo*, crime fictions which engage with the oil industry might only ever be able to offer detection plots without a meaningful form of resolution: that is, until global societies and economies have ceased to be dependent on oil. In teaching novels by Francis, Tuomainen and Habila, students can be encouraged to meditate upon the unresolvability of crimes connected with massive, systemic injustice, and these texts' refusals to offer easy conclusions. Do students find these non-resolutions satisfying, and what kinds of behavioural change at the individual and collective level do these novels advocate?

Conclusion

In *The Ecological Thought*, Morton outlines his theory of ecological enmeshment, in which the human is connected to and co-constituted with non-human nature; living, dead and synthetic matter; environmental processes; and each other. According to Morton, understanding this complete enmeshment involves adopting the perspective of a noir detective: "The noir narrator begins investigating a supposedly external situation, from a supposedly neutral point of view, only to discover that she or he is implicated in it".[25] Reading environmental crime fictions as 'econoir', and bringing the sensibilities of noir fiction to bear on environmental issues, entails collapsing nature/culture binaries and realising that we can never look on at 'nature' or 'the environment' from an outsider perspective. Reading crime fiction ecologically may also involve adopting a radically different perspective on the genre's defining tropes and features, and its possible future developments. How will the detective sift through connected and disconnected material to determine a clear chain of effect and responsibility when ecological entanglement proves that we are all enmeshed? Will we witness a shift from police and journalist investigators to scientists and environmentalists as "the subject supposed to know" finds themselves measuring groundwater pollution or handling climate data?[26] Might non-human agencies, corporations and 'assemblages'—orderings of heterogeneous elements including bodies, energies, acts and intentions—come to take the place of the traditional criminal genius?[27] In the age of Anthropocene, in which human activity is affecting the geological record and altering earth conditions for unimaginable futures, will individual crimes still matter, or will writers and readers of crime fiction come to experience the 'derangement of scale' that Timothy Clark associates inevitably with the opening up of such vast geographical and temporal vistas?[28]

Bringing the study of crime fiction into dialogue with ecocriticism, ecological philosophy and the current conditions of our environment crisis tests the capacities of the genre as a form dedicated to examining transgression, knowledge, justice and the possibility of a different future. It will be challenging, but it will ultimately engage students in some of the most demanding ethical, aesthetic and political questions of our time.

Notes

1. See Sam Naidu. "Crimes against Nature: Ecocritical Discourse in South African Crime Fiction", *Scrutiny2* 19, no. 2 October 2014: 59–70; Martindale, Kym "Murder in Arcadia: Towards a Pastoral of Responsibility in Phil Rickman's Merrily Watkins Murder Mystery Series", *Frame* 26, no. 2 November 2013: 23–36; Walton, Jo Lindsay and Samantha Walton eds. "Crime Fiction and Ecology". Special Edition of *Green Letters: Studies in Ecocriticism* 22, no.1 (February 2018).
2. See Richard Kerridge. "Ecothrillers: Environmental Cliffhangers". In Laurence Coupe ed. *The Green Studies Reader*. Oxford and New York: Routledge, 2000: 242–249; Trexler, Adam. *Anthropocene Fictions: The Novel in a Time of Climate Change*. Charlottesville, VA: University of Virginia Press, 2015.
3. See *Hinterland*. Produced by Ed Thomas. SC4, 2013-present; *Shetland*. Produced by Christopher Aird, Elaine Collins and Kate Bartlett. BBC Scotland. 2013-present; *Happy Valley*. Produced by Nicola Shindler, Sally Wainwright and Matthew Read. BBC One. 2014-present; *Broadchurch*. Produced by Jane Featherstone and Chris Chibnall. ITV. 2013–2017.
4. See Laurel B. Watson et al. "Understanding the Relationships Among White and African American Women's Sexual Objectification Experiences, Physical Safety Anxiety, and Psychological Distress". *Sex Roles* February 72, no. 3–4, February 2015: 91–104.
5. Countless texts take up this theme. Students could be directed to Soper and Haraway for a more detailed discussion.
6. Arthur Conan Doyle. *The Hound of the Baskervilles*. London: Penguin, 2001; 56, 153, 154.
7. Rod Giblett. "Theology of wetlands: Tolkien and Beowulf on Marshes and their Monsters", *Green Letters: Studies in Ecocriticism* 19, no. 2 March 2012: 132–143; p.143.

8. See Ursula Heise "Science and Ecocriticism", *The American Book Review* 18 no. 5 July–August 1997: 4.
9. Doyle, 144, 156, 153.
10. See Terry Gifford. *Pastoral.* Abingdon. Routledge, 1999; and William and Andrew Smith eds. *EcoGothic.* Manchester: Manchester University Press, 2013.
11. Patrick Murphy. *Ecocritical Explorations in Literary and Cultural Studies.* Plymouth: Lexington, 2009, 143.
12. See Stefan H. Leader and Peter Probst. *The Earth Liberation Front and Environmental Terrorism; Terrorism and Political Violence* Vol. 15, Iss. 4, 2003.
13. This story and subsequent trials and investigations have been extensively reported upon in *The Guardian.* For example see: Rob Evans and Paul Lewis, "Undercover police officer unlawfully spied on climate activists, judges rule", *The Guardian* Wednesday 20 July 2011: Web. https://www.theguardian.com/environment/2011/jul/20/police-spy-on-climate-activists-unlawful [Accessed 9 October 2017].
14. See Stephen Knight. *Form and Ideology in Crime Fiction.* London: Palgrave, 1980.
15. John Vidal, "Not guilty: the Greenpeace activists who used climate change as a legal defence", *The Guardian.* Thursday 11 September 2008 https://www.theguardian.com/environment/2008/sep/11/activists.kingsnorthclimatecamp [Accessed 9 October 2017].
16. See Rebecca Nathanson "Climate Change Activists Consider the Necessity Defence", *The New Yorker.* 11 April 2015. https://www.newyorker.com/news/news-desk/climate-change-activists-consider-the-necessity-defense [Accessed 9 October 2017].
17. See Tom Levitt "Climate Activists Face Jail Over Ratcliffe Coal Plot", *The Ecologist.* 14 December 2010 http://www.theecologist.org/News/news_round_up/694507/climate_activists_face_jail_over_ratcliffe_coal_plot.html [Accessed 9 October 2017].
18. Rob Nixon. *Slow Violence and the Environmentalism of the Poor.* Cambridge MA: Harvard University Press, 2011, 2.
19. See Amitav Ghosh, *The Great Derangement.* Chicago: University of Chicago Press, 2016.
20. Barbara Adam. *Timescapes of Modernity: The Environment and Invisible Hazards.* London: Routledge, 1998, 19.
21. Kerridge, 247.
22. See "Defenders of the Earth", *Global Witness.* (13 July 2017) https://www.globalwitness.org/en/campaigns/environmental-activists/defenders-earth/ [Accessed 09.10.17].
23. See Graham Huggan and Helen Tiffin. *Postcolonial Ecocriticism.* Abingdon: Routledge, 2015.

24. Imre Szeman. "Introduction" to Petrofictions Special Issue. *American Book Review* 33, no. 3 March–April 2012: 3.
25. Timothy Morton. *The Ecological Thought*. Cambridge: Harvard, 2010, 16–17.
26. Slavoj Zizek. *Looking Awry: An Introduction to Lacan Through Popular Culture*. Cambridge, MA: MIT Press, 1992, 57.
27. See Jane Bennett. *Vibrant Matter: A Political Ecology of Things*. Durham and London: Duke University Press, 2010.
28. See Timothy Clark. *Ecocriticism on the Edge*. London: Bloomsbury, 2015.

Works Cited

Abbey, Edward. *The Monkey Wrench Gang*. London: Harper Collins, 2006.

Adam, Barbara. *Timescapes of Modernity: The Environment and Invisible Hazards*. London: Routledge, 1998.

Bennett, Jane. *Vibrant Matter: A Political Ecology of Things*. Durham and London: Duke University Press, 2010.

Clark, Timothy. *Ecocriticism on the Edge*. London: Bloomsbury, 2015.

Doyle, Arthur Conan. *The Hound of the Baskervilles*. London: Penguin, 2001.

Francis, Clare. *Requiem*. London: Pan, 2013.

Garrard, Greg. *Ecocriticism* 2nd Edition. Abingdon: Routledge, 2011.

Ghosh, Amitav. *The Great Derangement*. Chicago: University of Chicago Press, 2016.

Giblett, Rod. "Theology of Wetlands: Tolkien and Beowulf on Marshes and Their Monsters." *Green Letters: Studies in Ecocriticism* 19, no. 2 March 2012: 132–143.

Gifford, Terry. *Pastoral*. Abingdon. Routledge, 1999.

Grisham, John. *The Pelican Brief*. London: Arrow, 2010.

Habila, Helon. *Oil on Water*. London: Penguin, 2011.

Haraway, Donna. *Simians, Cyborgs, and Women: The Reinvention of Nature*. New York: Routledge, 1991.

Heise, Ursula. *Sense of Place and Sense of Planet*. Oxford: Oxford University Press, 2008.

——— "Science and Ecocriticism." *The American Book Review* 18 no. 5 July–August 1997: 4.

Hughes, William and Andrew Smith eds. *EcoGothic*. Manchester: Manchester University Press, 2013.

Huggan, Graham and Helen Tiffin. *Postcolonial Ecocriticism*. Abingdon: Routledge, 2015.

Kerridge, Richard. "Ecothrillers: Environmental Cliffhangers." In *The Green Studies Reader*, edited by Laurence Coupe, 242–249. Oxford and New York: Routledge, 2000.

Knight, Stephen. *Form and Ideology in Crime Fiction*. London: Palgrave Macmillan, 1980.

Martindale, Kym. "Murder in Arcadia: Towards a Pastoral of Responsibility in Phil Rickman's Merrily Watkins Murder Mystery Series." *Frame* 26, no. 2 November 2013: 23–36.

Morton, Timothy. *The Ecological Thought*. Cambridge: Harvard, 2010.

Murphy, Patrick. *Ecocritical Explorations in Literary and Cultural Studies*. Plymouth: Lexington, 2009.

Naidu, Sam. "Crimes Against Nature: Ecocritical Discourse in South African Crime Fiction." *Scrutiny2* 19, no. 2 October 2014: 59–70.

Nixon, Rob. *Slow Violence and the Environmentalism of the Poor*. Cambridge, MA: Harvard University Press, 2011.

Rankin, Ian. *Black and Blue*. London: Orion, 1997.

Rendell, Ruth. *Road Rage*. London: Arrow Books, 1997.

Soper, Kate. *What Is Nature: Culture, Politics and the Non-Human*. Oxford: Blackwell, 2000.

Szeman, Imre. "'Introduction' to Petrofictions Special Issue." *American Book Review* 33, no. 3 March–April 2012: 3.

Trexler, Adam. *Anthropocene Fictions: The Novel in a Time of Climate Change*. Charlottesville, VA: University of Virginia Press, 2015.

Tuomainen, Antti. *The Mine*. London: Orenda Books, 2016.

Walton, Jo Lindsay and Samantha Walton eds. "Crime Fiction and Ecology." Special Edition of *Green Letters: Studies in Ecocriticism* 22, no.1 February 2018.

Zizek, Slavoj. *Looking Awry: An Introduction to Lacan Through Popular Culture*. Cambridge, MA: MIT Press, 1992.

CHAPTER 9

Teaching Crime Fiction and Film

Sian Harris

The images flicker as the scene opens on a masked thief, who stands behind a drawing-room table, loading valuable objects into a large sack. A man in a dressing-gown then enters the room and interrupts the robbery, but the thief vanishes into thin air. The man sits down to smoke a cigar, and the thief promptly reappears. The man draws a gun from the pocket of his dressing-gown, shoots at the thief (who instantly disappears again), and retrieves his property. However, his victory is short lived. The thief returns, the sack vanishes from the man's grasp, and thief and sack disappear for a final time. The man in the dressing-gown is left alone, and clearly baffled.

This short, silent sequence—lasting little more than thirty seconds—was produced in 1900 for the Mutoscope, an early viewing device that was a popular feature in piers and arcades. The title of the film was simple: *Sherlock Holmes Baffled*.[1] While not the most auspicious of beginnings for the great detective's on-screen career, it signalled the start of an enduringly productive, complex and mutually beneficial relationship between crime fiction and film. This chapter sets out to explore how studying crime fiction alongside film and television can inform and illuminate the reading, and provide a more complex appreciation of genre convention and narrative code. Based on my experience of course design and delivery,

S. Harris (✉)
University of Bristol, Bristol, UK
e-mail: sian.harris@bristol.ac.uk

C. Beyer (ed.), *Teaching Crime Fiction*, Teaching the New English,
https://doi.org/10.1007/978-3-319-90608-9_9

it considers three core texts as 'case studies' that each promote a distinct set of learning objectives, and offer alternative pathways to discussion and analysis. The texts are drawn directly from the syllabus of "Crime and Punishment: Detective Fiction from the *Rue Morgue* to the *Millennium*", a module offered to final year students in the English department at the University of Exeter (UK) between 2012 and 2017.

Following on from *Sherlock Holmes Baffled*, the first case study considers the benefits of teaching contemporary television alongside classic fiction, through encouraging students to rethink the adaptive relationship between Conan Doyle's *The Hound of the Baskervilles* (1902) and the BBC's *Sherlock* episode 'The Hounds of Baskerville' (2012). The emphasis is on finding ways to disrupt what Ariane Hudelet has labelled "the traditional 'compare and contrast' technique that often leads to a descriptive tendency and a return to traditional hierarchies between the source text and the adaptation copy",[2] and to work towards a more sophisticated understanding of the intertextual dynamic. The second section focuses on the ways in which Howard Hawks's *The Big Sleep* (1946) can offer not only a counterpart to Raymond Chandler's 1939 novel, but also provides an extended insight into the period, and highlights questions of stardom and celebrity through a focus on paratextual culture. This includes an account of how teaching might be informed by archive material. The third case study considers teaching texts in translation, drawing on Stieg Larsson's *The Girl with the Dragon Tattoo* (2005) and Niels Arden Oplev's 2009 adaptation. Finally, the chapter will briefly outline how the module's inclusion of film has been received by students, and explore how their comments and contributions have helped to improve the experience.

While the chapter is primarily concerned with teaching crime fiction in adaptation, this is not intended to negate the merit and interest value of original crime drama, and it is worth pausing for a moment to consider this. Original film and television texts have had a striking impact in shaping popular understandings of crime, criminality, and investigative methods. This might be epitomised by the so-called '*CSI* effect', described by Schweitzer and Saks as the process through which the *Crime Scene Investigation* series has "raised the public's expectations for the kind of forensic-science evidence that could and should be offered at trials to such heights that jurors are disappointed by the real evidence with which they are presented".[3] Original crime drama also provides ample material for aesthetic and intellectual as well as sociological analysis, as in the case of David Fincher's neo-noir *Se7en* (1995), or Jane Campion's haunting

Top of the Lake (2013). However, while the merits of these stand-alone texts afford a tempting digression, in my experience the practical demands of teaching in an English department will often mean that adaptations offer the most immediately productive lines of enquiry, and this is reflected in the choice of texts ahead.

Sherlock and Teaching Multiplicity

In May 2012, Guinness World Records declared that Sherlock Holmes was "the most portrayed literary human character in film and TV", with the character inspiring 254 on-screen versions, including portrayals by John Barrymore, Basil Rathbone, Peter Cushing, Christopher Lee, Charlton Heston, Robert Downey Jr. and Jonny Lee Miller.[4] Furthermore, while this collection of Holmeses is already extensive, it is merely partial, excluding as it does the myriad additional versions of the character that have appeared in cartoons, video games, musical and theatrical productions, advertising campaigns and radio plays. It is perhaps universally inevitable that students will have encountered the image and iconography of Conan Doyle's detective protagonist long before they have had the chance to read the text. Indeed, when first impressions have already been formed by such a range of adaptations—from television series to Halloween costumes—reactions to the actual text can be striking. Some students have reported a sense of anti-climax; while others have been deeply impressed by the capacity for a story they assumed they knew to prove surprising.

The scale of the character's visibility and adaptability can thus seem daunting, especially on a survey course that attempts to cover the development of crime fiction from the mid-nineteenth to the early twenty-first century. The challenge of distilling a complex literary subject into a manageable yet comprehensive syllabus is nothing new—as Albert Schinz wryly complained in a 1926 edition of *The Modern Language Journal*, "you cannot put an elephant in a rabbit hole"[5]—but the diverse range of potential Holmeses can also present the opportunity for a refined understanding of adaptation in practice. After all, scholars working in adaptation studies have long cautioned against the kind of study that:

> "assumed an awareness of the original on the part of the audiences, assumed the superiority of the original, cast the new text solely in its relationship to the original" and espoused an "overarching concern with the notion of 'fidelity' to the original … [that] thus also ignored larger cultural and economic realities".[6]

Assigning 'The Hounds of Baskerville' alongside *The Hound of the Baskervilles* immediately exposes the limitations of that approach. While, as noted, one can assume the audience (the students) will be aware of the character, they are far more likely to know the BBC version, and its idiosyncratic, lateral approach to the source material provides a disruptive take on the concept of "fidelity".

The *Sherlock* series, created by Steven Moffat and Mark Gatiss, first aired in 2010, and relocates Conan Doyle's characters to twenty-first-century London. *The Guardian* designated this as a "re-imagining",[7] while *The Telegraph* described it as "a loose riff",[8] and *The Washington Post* suggested that the characters are "such a part of the cultural currency that we are secure that they can survive a re-minting'".[9] While a more classic version, such as the Granada Television production *The Adventures of Sherlock Holmes* (1984–1994), might risk incurring a reductive focus on the fidelity of the plot and the dialogue, *Sherlock*'s abrupt departure from tradition helps to channel discussion towards the evolution of investigative methods, or the portrayal of the detective's psyche. Indeed, Neil McCaw has suggested that *The Adventures of Sherlock Holmes*'s purported accuracy is itself "inherently and cripplingly subjective" as the series is "haunted by a ghoul of its own making, striving for the impossible dream of definitive, Conan Doylean episodes".[10] *Sherlock*'s rejection of this 'ghoul' is most evident in the 'memory palace' scene, in which Sherlock's (Benedict Cumberbatch's) thought process is made manifest through graphics and imagery. Described by one reviewer as a "*Minority Report* routine",[11] the scene provides a visual account of the detective's mental process that can be seen both as a demonstration and a contradiction of his rational intellect. The precision and speed with which Sherlock rejects 'dead end' answers and arrives at his realisation speaks to a phenomenal capacity for deduction. However, while the destination proves correct, the apparently random and arbitrary nature of the journey—that detours via scraps of music, history, and breeds of canine—can be read as undermining his ultimate authority over the information. The scene also exposes the limits of the insight permitted to the reader, whose access to Holmes's mind is always mediated by Watson's narrative. The distinction has fuelled especially rewarding discussions of narrative perspective, particularly as the course progresses and students can draw comparisons between Conan Doyle's "narrated" detective and, for example, the wry intimacy of Raymond Chandler's first person prose.

Sherlock then rejects a linear relationship to the original, and instead embodies the process as envisaged by Linda Hutcheon when noting that "adaptation has run amok".[12] In the spirit of this, the module has also asked students to engage with less official acts of adaptation or re-imagining, and identify examples of *Sherlock* fan fiction that can be included in the seminar debates. Writing in *The Baker Street Journal*, Betsy Rosenblatt has suggested that "fan fiction seems to flow inevitably from the Canon",[13] but I posit that this 'flow' can also be better understood through rhizomatic rather than linear models. In seminar discussions, it has, for example, often been the case that considering the treatment of sexuality in fan fiction has provided the foundation for a far more nuanced reading of the Holmes/Watson relationship in both the series and the original stories. The series itself appears astute to this dynamic, as highlighted by Tom Steward:

> [*Sherlock*] suggests ambivalence towards the eroticization of the characters that is simultaneously sceptical of and respectful towards the slash conventions of fan fiction. The resultant ambiguity [...] nods to and plays with fan discourses of a homosexual subtext in fiction's central partnership.[14]

This central ambivalence as to the status of the "canon" underlines the sense of co-dependency between narrative forms, as the television series plays up to fan mythology while also relying on it to ensure the "game" is recognised, in a pattern that echoes the parallel relationship between the series and the books.

To summarise then, the key objectives in teaching *Sherlock* on 'Crime and Punishment' have been to disrupt possible common assumptions about the privileging of original texts, chart the complexity and diversity of the text's variations, and encourage readings that take account of fandom and cultural capital as well as literary precedent. However, far from diminishing the role played by the original text, this focus on multiplicity refreshes its significance, and ultimately facilitates a more active critical approach.

The Big Sleep and Teaching Paratexts

This second case study turns the spotlight onto the 1946 Howard Hawks adaptation of Raymond Chandler's 1939 novel *The Big Sleep*, starring Humphrey Bogart and Lauren Bacall. Whereas the approach to teaching

Sherlock set out to disrupt an overly simplistic 'compare and contrast' analysis, here, the emphasis shifts again, and uses the film as a means to consider historical contexts and consumerism. *The Big Sleep* has been referred to as the "fullest, richest, most resonant" private eye film,[15] and its enduring reputation as a Hollywood classic makes it the perfect vehicle for dissecting studio-era Hollywood culture. This section sets out the teaching opportunities afforded by a focus on how the crime film can be read in terms of both stardom and marketing, a methodology best articulated by Deborah Cartmell:

> Rather than simply comparing the film to the book, it can be more revealing for students to read the paratexts as well, to compare the film to its promotional materials, how these exploit or undermine literary pedigree, how they translate the characters into 'stars', how they tease us with the promise of our favourite film genres, such as romance, comedy and adventure, how they speak to the tastes of a contemporary audience, and how they locate themselves within a particular consumer culture.[16]

Here, my own teaching practice has benefitted immeasurably from the resources at Exeter's Bill Douglas Cinema Museum. The museum holds a collection of over 75,000 items relating to film and the moving image, from examples of early 'Magic Lantern' technology to contemporary publicity material and press packs. Students on the "Crime and Punishment" module have been able to spend a seminar in the archives, viewing items such as a photocopy of the shooting script for *The Big Sleep* (including a very different ending), or a 'War Bond' postcard of Bogart, at home with a spaniel. While some items have an obvious relevance or value, others seem more ephemeral, as explained by Lisa Stead:

> Entering this kind of archive involves embarking on an investigation that takes the researcher beyond a fixed notion of a singular 'text' to be researched or discovered in film historiography, and into the material culture that both surrounds and constitutes cinema history.[17]

The museum's collection of movie magazines has provided a valuable gateway into charting the impact of *The Big Sleep*. In a 1946 edition of *Picturegoer*, an article ponders the rise of the "tough" heroine, announcing that "the era when movie heroines had to be sweeter than a chocolate sundae and wind up in the hero's arms appears to have run its course". *The Big Sleep* is one of several examples of films in which "a star was given a part of a pretty, bold and ruthless woman".[18] The contrast between this 'ruthless woman' and her ice-cream sweet predecessor is pronounced, and as Helen Hanson has pointed out, the comparison comes out in favour of the former: "*Picturegoer*, addressed to a predominately female fan community, confidently assumes the tough heroine has an exciting appeal to women".[19] Beyond the articles that feature the film directly, the magazines also include a wealth of features and advertisements that provide further context in regard to 1940s' beauty ideals, aspirations and commercialism. The bookshop scene in *The Big Sleep*, which features beautiful Dorothy Malone removing her dowdy glasses and releasing her tied-back hair before enjoying a dalliance with Marlowe, acquires a curious dimension of pathos when viewed alongside countless advertisements that promise the perfect complexion/figure/smile. However, while these museum resources are limited to local users, other forms of paratext could be more universally incorporated into teaching the crime film.

Most obviously, *The Big Sleep* was marketed on the strength of Bogart and Bacall's on- and off-screen connection. They had starred together for the first time in *To Have and Have Not* (Hawks 1944), and *The Big Sleep* was intended to replicate that chemistry. This can be demonstrated in seminars through a consideration of the publicity material. The original film poster has the tagline "The picture they were born for!" and the names 'Bogart and Bacall' are printed in block capitals, twice the height of the lettering used for the film's title. This is reiterated by the trailer, which follows a clip of the couple kissing with an insistently enthusiastic caption sequence "They're together again! That man Bogart! And that woman Bacall! Are that way again!" Studying these promotional paratexts helps to contextualise the actors' star profile as a couple, as well as explaining the creation of new scenes, written to showcase their talent for flirtatious repartee. The film trailer also strategically evokes intertextual connections. Bogart starred as Sam Spade in the 1941 version of *The Maltese Falcon*, cornering the market in depictions of the hardboiled private eye, so that the characters of Marlowe and Spade have arguably been "customarily regarded as congeneric expressions of the homogenius screen presence we have come to think of simply as 'Bogie'".[20] This close association would culminate in the 1980 parody *The Man With Bogart's Face*, in which Robert Sacchi plays "Sam Marlowe". The trailer for *The Big Sleep* actually pre-empts this hybridisation, beginning in the 'Hollywood Public Library' as Bogart explains to an attractive librarian that he is "looking for a good mystery, something off the beaten track, like *The Maltese Falcon*". She presents a copy of *The Big Sleep* and promises it "has everything *The Falcon* had and more". The scene knowingly plays up the close affinity between the texts, culminating with Bogart opening the book and drifting into a voiceover: "Sometimes I wonder what strange fate brought me out of the storm to that house that stood alone in the shadows". The lines are not taken from Chandler's book, and voiceover is notably absent in the actual film. Notable because, although the film is often labelled as 'noir' it lacks many of the formal devices that define the genre: "the influence of German expressionism is absent, there's no hard-boiled narration, no angst-ridden hero, no distorted camera angles, no nightmares, no ominous shadows, no flashbacks".[21] Given this technical departure, the use of voiceover in the trailer echoes Cartmell's description of advertising that "tease[s] us with the promise of our favourite film genres", and takes on an arch quality that cuts through the banality of the dialogue.

In highlighting the value and teaching applications of paratextual material and archive resources, this case study of *The Big Sleep* has identified ways in which the discussion of crime film and fiction can be productively opened out to include questions of stardom and cinema-going culture. This allows for a better understanding of the audience as well as the film, and calls attention to the strategies and emotions that direct the bond between them.

The Girl with the Dragon Tattoo and Teaching in Translation

Here, the chapter moves on to the burgeoning field of crime fiction and film in translation. According to research commissioned by the International Man Booker Prize in 2016, the total number of books in translation purchased in the UK increased by 96 percent between 2001 and 2015, with the rising popularity of Scandinavian crime fiction widely credited as a key factor in that rise. Waterstones fiction buyer Chris White said that authors like Stieg Larsson and Jo Nesbo had "helped to break down any psychological barriers or pre-conceptions which readers may have had about translated fiction".[22] However, this focus on accessibility risks neglecting the elements that can be lost in translation, as evidenced in this final study of Stieg Larsson's 'breakout' novel *The Girl with the Dragon Tattoo* (published 2005, translated into English 2008) and its Swedish adaptation, directed by Niels Arden Oplev in 2009.

Already, setting out the chronology of translation and adaptation suggests that Barry Forshaw was right to identify the film as playing a key role in the success of the English-language novel: "the Swedish trilogy of films made from the novels of Stieg Larsson were an essential part of a battering ram that pushed the author's astonishing posthumous fame to such giddy heights".[23] English readers who encountered the book in 2008 had only a year to wait to see the characters on-screen, while those who watched the film first were immediately able to access the novel. The timing was undoubtedly mutually beneficial— the novel was listed by Nielsen as the best-selling book of 2010, while the film was nominated for three BAFTAs (winning 'Best Film Not in the English Language') and returned a global gross worth of almost $105,000,000. The film also provides a way to centre the text's Swedish identity. When reading the novel, it is perhaps more possible to 'switch off' from the awareness that this is a text in translation, but watching (and more importantly, listening to) the subtitled film provides a running reminder. Karen Seago has written persuasively of the ways in which crime fiction in translation can be a site of instability, as "cross-border movements, translations, interpretations and cross-fertilisations of detective stories are particularly interesting and offer access to intercultural and intracultural anxieties, cultural and social shifts and the emergent construction of a popular literary form".[24] Including the film is then a way of fostering instability, and troubling the imposition of complete translation. On a more pragmatic note, Swedish itself can sound wonderfully strange to an audience of students who have (in my teaching experience) never studied or spoken the language—this would be far less likely with a film in French or German.

However, one does not need to be fluent to recognise that, almost immediately, the process of translation has been editorial. The opening credits culminate with the film's title(s) displayed on the screen—"Män som hatar kvinnor" / *The Girl with the Dragon Tattoo*. The film's Swedish title is that of the original book: "Men who hate women". The rationale for the name change has been widely critiqued. *The Economist* suggests it was "considered too scary for foreign audiences",[25] while *The New York Times* offers the more cutting explanation that it was too redolent of the books' issues with convincing characterisation, "a label that just about captures the subtlety of the novel's sexual politics [...] nearly every man in the book under age 70 is a violent misogynist".[26] Meanwhile, the visual impact of the two titles together at the start of the film has attracted less attention, although it delivers a jarring series of juxtapositions with

Swedish/English, Adulthood ('Men' and 'Women') / Infantilisation ('Girl'), and Brutality/Fantasy. These tensions and contrasts are more apt to the text than they may appear. Forshaw has identified a central duality to British perceptions of Scandinavian crime fiction, that pits the cliché of "the unspoilt vastness of the fjords, gambolling reindeer and modern, well-designed towns inhabited by blonde-haired, healthy types" against its darker parallel of "long nights that [...] present the perfect stage for simmering familial resentments and violent dispatch'".[27] The gap between the title and subtitle echoes this duality and helps deliver a sense of the uncanny at work in each version of the text.

Despite the noted shortcomings of the English-language title, it does direct the reader/viewer's attention successfully towards Lisbeth Salander, and the combination of Larsson's character via Noomi Rapace's critically acclaimed performance has also provided plenty of teaching material. If the art of Humphrey Bogart lies in convincing the viewer that Philip Marlowe (and indeed Sam Spade) just happens to look *exactly* like Humphrey Bogart, Rapace's talent lies in the opposite direction, as the actress disappears behind the character's exaggerated image. Extending the comparison to Benedict Cumberbatch's socially detached interpretation of Sherlock offers further discussion material, for as the module progresses the actors increasingly emerge as another form of 'text' for analysis. The placement of the three films in the syllabus—in weeks three, seven and ten—also means that comparative discussions are ideally placed to punctuate the module and provide the chance to check in on developing ideas, as well as helping to disrupt the illusion of chronological progress. After all, 'The Hounds of Baskerville' first aired three years later than the film of *The Girl with the Dragon Tattoo*.

The initial objectives in teaching *The Girl with the Dragon Tattoo* as fiction and film were geared towards the value of translation, encouraging students to look beyond British and American crime writing, and highlighting how an individual text can become (sometimes problematically) emblematic of industry trends—be it a vogue for 'Scandi-noir' or for books with the word "Girl" on the cover. In practice though, what has also emerged as an equally valuable line of discussion has been the opportunity this affords for comparative analysis with other film texts. So while the chapter has treated the crime film texts as separate 'case studies' in order to clarify the different questions and objectives that they explore, in the final analysis it is worth balancing this against the myriad ways in which the texts can also complement and illuminate each other.

Student Responses

Over the course of the 'Crime and Punishment' module I worked with around 190 students—some of whom were hardcore crime fiction devotees, others who opted for the course on a more passing whim—and all of whom informed the ongoing development of the option. In recognition of their hard work and valued feedback, this chapter will conclude by briefly flagging up some of the key points that they raised over the years.

The general response has been wonderfully positive, but there has been room for improvement along the way. It was my first cohort of students who really taught me to appreciate that they started the course with very mixed levels of experience in film analysis. Some had already taken first and second year options that introduced them to sequence analysis and technical vocabulary, and a sizeable number had also benefitted from a specialist option in adaptation itself. Meanwhile, others had never analysed a film before, and were understandably concerned that this could put them at a disadvantage. Trying to balance their needs and interests particularly shaped my approach to teaching *Sherlock*. The compact structure and distinctive style of the episode made it an accessible introduction to cinematic close reading—the overt flourishes of the "memory palace" sequence ensure that film novices can see the techniques in action, while expanding the discussion out towards less official narrative strands provided a new challenge for the confident. When the first crime film text on a syllabus could also be the first film text that a student has ever encountered, it needs to afford some flexibility. The question of resources when working on contemporary popular culture was also an issue in the earlier years of the course's development. When the module launched, it was a particular challenge to source scholarship on *Sherlock* and *The Girl with the Dragon Tattoo*. The passage of time and the labour of fellow academics has changed this situation dramatically, but the earlier demands of taking a more lateral approach to research was in many ways a worthwhile learning experience,[28] and proved beneficial to those students who went on to analyse similarly contemporary texts in their final dissertations.

With that in mind, perhaps the best feedback to the presence of film on the module has come in the form of the dozens of students who have opted to build on this interest, and draw film and television texts from outside the syllabus into their final research essays.[29] This has included examples of adaptation and original drama, as well as some particularly strong work on alternative texts, such as graphic novels and video games.

This range of original material has in turn exposed further questions about the borders of form and genre. I have enjoyed thought-provoking essays on the construction of masculinity in *Luther* (2012–), on the politics of appetite and consumption in *Hannibal* (2013–15), and on the ways in which Rooney Mara's wardrobe from the American remake of *The Girl with the Dragon Tattoo* (2011) influenced high street fashion collections. Teaching crime fiction and film has thus not only afforded me the chance to draw research interests more directly into teaching, but to see that become a process of dialogue as students take the teaching as the basis to develop their own research interests. For the students, this has been an opportunity to rethink their own experience as cultural consumers, and (as noted) in many cases it has led on to shape their dissertation research, or drive an interest in postgraduate study. For myself, it has been a chance to not only continue expanding my reading list, but to hone research interests in new media. To end on a note of reflection, I do feel that the genuine reciprocity the course delivered was directly facilitated through the inclusion of film texts—that they made it simultaneously more accessible and more complex—and that the value of this added dimension cannot be underestimated when considering strategies and syllabuses for future teaching in the genre.

Notes

1. *Sherlock Holmes Baffled* was directed by Arthur Marvin, but the names of the two actors are not known, and for many years the film was believed lost, until a copy was rediscovered in 1968.
2. Ariane Hudelet, "Avoiding 'Compare and Contrast': Applied Theory as a Way to Circumvent the 'Fidelity Issue". *Teaching Adaptations,* eds. Deborah Cartmell and Imelda Whelehan, (Basingstoke: Palgrave Macmillan, 2014), p. 42.
3. N.J. Schweitzer and Michael J. Saks, "The *CSI* Effect: Popular fiction about forensic science affects the public's expectations about real forensic science", *Jurimetrics,* 47.3 (2007) 357–364.
4. Anon, "Sherlock Holmes awarded title for most portrayed literary human character in film & TV", *Guinness World Records,* 14 May 2012, http://www.guinnessworldrecords.com/news/2012/5/sherlock-holmes-awarded-title-for-most-portrayed-literary-human-character-in-film-tv-41743. Accessed 5 August 2016.
5. Albert Schinz "The Problem of the One-Year Literature Survey Course Again", *The Modern Language Journal,* 10.1 (1926) 345–348.

6. Kevin J. Wetmore Jr., "Adaptation: Review", *Theatre Journal*, 66.4 (2014) 625–634.
7. Vanessa Thorpe, "Sherlock Holmes is back… sending texts and using nicotine patches", *The Guardian*, 18 July 2010, https://www.theguardian.com/tv-and-radio/2010/jul/18/sherlock-holmes-is-back-bbc. Accessed 5 August 2016.
8. Serena Davies, "*Sherlock*, BBC One, Review", *The Telegraph*, 23 July 2010, http://www.telegraph.co.uk/culture/tvandradio/bbc/7907566/Sherlock-BBC-One-review.html. Accessed 5 August 2016.
9. Anne Midgette, "The Art of the Update", *The Washington Post*, 10 September 2010 http://voices.washingtonpost.com/the-classical-beat/2010/09/the_art_of_the_update.html. Accessed 5 August 2016.
10. Neil McCraw, *Adapting Detective Fiction: Crime, Englishness, and the TV Detectives*, (London: Continuum, 2011) p39.
11. John Teti, "*Sherlock*: 'The Hounds of Baskerville'", *The AV Club*, 13 May 2012, http://www.avclub.com/tvclub/sherlock-the-hounds-of-baskerville-73734. Accessed 5 August 2016.
12. Linda Hutcheon, *A Theory of Adaptation*, (New York: Routledge, 2006) xi.
13. Betsy Rosenblatt, "Sherlock Holmes Fan Fiction", *The Baker Street Journal*, 62.4 (2012) 33–43.
14. Tom Steward, "Holmes in the Small Screen: The Television Contexts of *Sherlock*", *Sherlock and Transmedia Fandom: Essays on the BBC Series*, eds. Louisa Ellen Stein and Kristina Busse (Jefferson: McFarland, 2012) p141.
15. James Monaco, "Notes on *The Big Sleep*, Thirty Years After", *Sight and Sound* 44.1 (1974) 34–38.
16. Deborah Cartmell, "Teaching Adaptation Through Marketing: Adaptations and the Language of Advertising in the 1930s", *Teaching Adaptations*, eds. Deborah Cartmell and Imelda Whelehan, (Basingstoke: Palgrave Macmillan, 2014) p165.
17. Lisa Stead, "Letter Writing, Cinemagoing and Archive Ephemera", *The Boundaries of the Literary Archive: Reclamation and Representation*, eds. Lisa Stead and Carrie Smith, (Farnham: Ashgate, 2013) p. 140.
18. Anon, "Will the Goody-Goody Heroine Survive?" *Picturegoer*, October 1946. The Bill Douglas Cinema Museum.
19. Helen Hanson, "The Big Seduction: Feminist Film Criticism and the *Femme Fatale*", *The Femme Fatale: Images, Histories, Contexts*, eds. Helen Hanson and Catherine O'Rawe, (Basingstoke: Palgrave Macmillan, 2010) p. 241.
20. Virginia Wright Wexman, "Kinesics and Film Acting: Humphrey Bogart in *The Big Sleep* and *The Maltese Falcon*", *Journal of Popular Film and Television*, 7.1 (1978) 42–55.

21. Philip French, "*The Big Sleep* – Review", *The Guardian*, 2 January 2011, https://www.theguardian.com/film/2011/jan/02/the-big-sleep-review. Accessed 5 August 2016.
22. Chris White qtd. in Alison Flood, "Translated fiction sells better in the UK than English fiction, research finds", *The Guardian*, 9 May 2016, https://www.theguardian.com/books/2016/may/09/translated-fiction-sells-better-uk-english-fiction-elena-ferrante-haruki-murakami. Accessed 5 August 2016.
23. Barry Forshaw, *Death in a Cold Climate: A Guide to Scandinavian Crime Fiction*, (Basingstoke: Palgrave Macmillan, 2012), p. 186.
24. Karen Seago, "Crime (fiction) in translation", *The Journal of Specialised Translation*, 22.1 (2014) 2–14.
25. T.W. "Translating film titles: It wasn't the dragon tattoo", *The Economist*, 18 August 2010, http://www.economist.com/blogs/johnson/2010/08/translating_film_titles. Accessed 5 August 2016.
26. Alex Berenson, "Vanished", *The New York Times*, 14 September 2008, http://www.nytimes.com/2008/09/14/books/review/Berenson-t.html. Accessed 5 August 2016.
27. Barry Forshaw, p9.
28. For more on this topic, see Rachel Carroll, "Coming Soon… Teaching the Contemporaneous Adaptation", *Teaching Adaptations*, eds. Deborah Cartmell and Imelda Whelehan, (Basingstoke: Palgrave Macmillan, 2014).
29. The course is assessed by a 2000-word critical analysis of a protagonist *not* studied on the course, a 20-minute group presentation, and a 3000-word final essay. The rubric for the presentation and the final essay asks that students consider at least two texts, at least one of which must be from the syllabus.

Works Cited

Anon. "Sherlock Holmes Awarded Title for Most Portrayed Literary Human Character in Film & TV." *Guinness World Records*, 14 May 2012, http://www.guinnessworldrecords.com/news/2012/5/sherlock-holmes-awarded-title-for-most-portrayed-literary-human-character-in-film-tv-41743. Accessed 5 August 2016.

Anon. "Will the Goody-Goody Heroine Survive?" *Picturegoer*, October 1946. The Bill Douglas Cinema Museum, Exeter.

Berenson, Alex. "Vanished." *The New York Times*, 14 September 2008, http://www.nytimes.com/2008/09/14/books/review/Berenson-t.html. Accessed 5 August 2016.

Cartmell, Deborah. "Teaching Adaptation Through Marketing: Adaptations and the Language of Advertising in the 1930s." In *Teaching Adaptations*, edited by Deborah Cartmell and Imelda Whelehan, 157–170. Basingstoke: Palgrave Macmillan, 2014.

Davies, Serena. "*Sherlock*, BBC One, Review." *The Telegraph*, 23 July 2010, http://www.telegraph.co.uk/culture/tvandradio/bbc/7907566/Sherlock-BBC-One-review.html. Accessed 5 August 2016.

Flood, Alison. "Translated Fiction Sells Better in the UK than English Fiction, Research Finds." *The Guardian*, 9 May 2016, https://www.theguardian.com/books/2016/may/09/translated-fiction-sells-better-uk-english-fiction-elena-ferrante-haruki-murakami. Accessed 5 August 2016.

Forshaw, Barry. *Death in a Cold Climate: A Guide to Scandinavian Crime Fiction*. Basingstoke: Palgrave Macmillan, 2012.

French, Philip. "*The Big Sleep* – Review." *The Guardian*, 2 January 2011, https://www.theguardian.com/film/2011/jan/02/the-big-sleep-review. Accessed 5 August 2016.

Hanson, Helen. "The Big Seduction: Feminist Film Criticism and the *Femme Fatale*." In *The Femme Fatale: Images, Histories, Contexts*, edited by Helen Hanson and Catherine O'Rawe, 214–228. Basingstoke: Palgrave Macmillan, 2010.

Hudelet, Ariane. "Avoiding 'Compare and Contrast': Applied Theory as a Way to Circumvent the 'Fidelity Issue'." In *Teaching Adaptations*, edited by Deborah Cartmell and Imelda Whelehan, 41–55. Basingstoke: Palgrave Macmillan, 2014.

Hutcheon, Linda. *A Theory of Adaptation*. New York: Routledge, 2006.

McCraw, Neil. *Adapting Detective Fiction: Crime, Englishness, and the TV Detectives*. London: Continuum, 2011.

Midgette, Anne. "The Art of the Update." *The Washington Post*, 10 September 2010, http://voices.washingtonpost.com/the-classical-beat/2010/09/the_art_of_the_update.html. Accessed 5 August 2016.

Monaco, James. "Notes on *The Big Sleep*, Thirty Years After." *Sight and Sound*, 44.1 (1974) 34–38.

Rosenblatt, Betsy. "Sherlock Holmes Fan Fiction." *The Baker Street Journal*, 62.4 (2012) 33–43.

Schinz, Albert. "The Problem of the One-Year Literature Survey Course Again." *The Modern Language Journal*, 10.1 (1926) 345–348.

Schweitzer, N.J. and Michael J. Saks. "The *CSI* Effect: Popular Fiction About Forensic Science Affects the Public's Expectations About Real Forensic Science." *Jurimetrics*, 47.3 (2007) 357 364.

Seago, Karen. "Crime (Fiction) in Translation." *The Journal of Specialised Translation*, 22.1 (2014) 2–14.

Stead, Lisa. "Letter Writing, Cinemagoing and Archive Ephemera." In *The Boundaries of the Literary Archive: Reclamation and Representation*, edited by Lisa Stead and Carrie Smith, 139–156. Farnham: Ashgate, 2013.

Steward, Tom. "Holmes in the Small Screen: The Television Contexts of *Sherlock*." In *Sherlock and Transmedia Fandom: Essays on the BBC Series*, edited by Louisa Ellen Stein and Kristina Busse, 133–148. Jefferson: McFarland, 2012.

Teti, John. "*Sherlock*: 'The Hounds of Baskerville'." *The AV Club*, 13 May 2012, http://www.avclub.com/tvclub/sherlock-the-hounds-of-baskerville-73734. Accessed 5 August 2016.

Thorpe, Vanessa. "Sherlock Holmes Is Back... Sending Texts and Using Nicotine Patches." *The Guardian*, 18 July 2010, https://www.theguardian.com/tv-and-radio/2010/jul/18/sherlock-holmes-is-back-bbc. Accessed 5 August 2016.

T.W. "Translating Film Titles: It Wasn't the Dragon Tattoo." *The Economist*, 18 August 2010, http://www.economist.com/blogs/johnson/2010/08/translating_film_titles. Accessed 5 August 2016.

Wetmore, Kevin J. "Adaptation: Review." *Theatre Journal*, 66.4 (2014) 625–634.

Wexman, Virginia Wright. "Kinesics and Film Acting: Humphrey Bogart in *The Big Sleep* and *The Maltese Falcon*." *Journal of Popular Film and Television*, 7.1 (1978) 42–55.

CHAPTER 10

Crime Writing: Language and Stylistics

Christiana Gregoriou

Introduction

Crime fiction is undoubtedly a persistently thriving and popular genre. Mirroring this interest, English language and literature students remain keen to explore this genre and its continuing popularity, whether coming to the genre as reading fans, as aspiring crime fiction writers in their own right, or as eager analysts of its generic form and structure. This chapter proposes a stylistic approach to crime fiction, stylistics being "the practice of using linguistics for the study of literature",[1] and one that requires knowledge of the workings of language alongside an interest in literary genres and their effects and conventions. Stylistic methodology and theory prove particularly suitable when it comes to unpacking this genre's techniques, hence offering students an insight into the mechanisms contributing to crime fiction remaining a genre with popular appeal. This chapter starts with an exploration of the plot and discourse distinction through which students could begin to explore crime fictional story structure, before then delving into Emmott's frame theory,[2] which can shed light on the ways in which crime texts (mis)direct readers. It then turns to considering the importance of narrative style and viewpoint choice in relation to characterisation and reader sympathy. Ryan's possible world theory

C. Gregoriou (✉)
Leeds University, Leeds, UK
e-mail: C.Gregoriou@leeds.ac.uk

C. Beyer (ed.), *Teaching Crime Fiction*, Teaching the New English,
https://doi.org/10.1007/978-3-319-90608-9_10

is subsequently introduced,[3] the ways in which it can also shed light on crime fiction narrative structure discussed. In doing so, I discuss the typical crime fiction effect of suspense, before lastly focusing on linguistic tools with which such suspense can also be generated. It is whilst practising using such crime fiction-related stylistic techniques, that students' understanding of this genre's very workings can be deepened.

Plot and Discourse

The term 'plot' is generally understood to refer to the sequence of chronologically-ordered events which generate a narrative, with 'discourse' encompassing the manner or order through which the plot is narrated, the latter often disrupting the basic chronology of a story.[4] In short, plot is the logical ordering possible of events, with discourse being the order in which the events are actually narrated by the story teller. In simple story-telling, such as children's literature, the two tend to coincide. However, as argued in Gregoriou,[5]

> the 'plot' of crime stories usually does not coincide with the 'discourse', and the effect of this generic convention is important. The pleasure of reading prototypical crime fiction (where the actual discourse starts post-death) depends on being unfamiliar with the actual plot throughout; knowing *all* of what has happened in chronological order would eliminate the element of surprise. This pleasure of delayed recognition at the end is in fact where the largest attraction of the genre lies.

Here are the bare bones of a three-character short story that can be used to illustrate this, and one inspired by the Turkish crime film *Once Upon a Time in Anatolia* (directed by Nuri Bilge Ceylan in 2011). For ease of reference, the story events are numbered as well as given in chronological order. To enable student engagement, copies of the story could be printed, and cut up into ten strip-events. Students could work in groups of two or three, each group being given a single story copy, and hence a single ten-strip set to play with:

<u>Event 1</u>: In 1998, Walter marries Jessica.
<u>Event 2</u>: In June 2001, Jessica starts an affair with Walter's friend, Ben.
<u>Event 3</u>: In late 2001, Jessica gets pregnant.
<u>Event 4</u>: In 2002, Jessica gives birth to a baby boy.

Event 5: On 4 March 2004 (8:50 pm), Ben admits the affair and claims the boy is his.
Event 6: On 4 March 2004 (9 pm), the men fight and Ben fatally injures Walter.
Event 7: On 5 March 2004, Walter dies from injuries.
Event 8: On 6 March 2004, Jessica reports Walter missing.
Event 9: On 7 March 2004, the police discover Walter's body.
Event 10: On 8 March 2004, the police start investigating Walter's murder.

As crime fictional stories go, one could argue that this story is not terribly engaging, particularly if one arranges, and reads, the story-strip in plot (i.e. 'chronological') order. If one puts events in this logical sequence, they get to miss any sort of revelation at the story's end—it is all too predictable. In short, it is no good knowing what happened in the order in which it happened, not less being given the crime fictional story motive at the narrative's start, and there is no whodunit to offer an answer for. Students could here be asked to consider what sort of discourse (i.e. 'narrative design') would instead work best, the paper pieces rearranged accordingly to experiment with. Leaving out the reference to the affair (event 2), or Ben's admitting of the affair (event 5), and his injuring Walter (event 6), until the story's end would be more whodunit crime fiction-appropriate:

Event 1: In 1998, Walter marries Jessica.
Event 3: In late 2001, Jessica gets pregnant.
Event 4: In 2002, Jessica gives birth to a baby boy.
Event 7: On 5 March 2004, Walter dies from injuries.
Event 8: On 6 March 2004, Jessica reports Walter missing.
Event 9: On 7 March 2004, the police discover Walter's body.
Event 10: On 8 March 2004, the police start investigating Walter's murder.

And then, readers discover:

Event 2: In June 2001, Jessica starts an affair with Walter's friend, Ben.
Event 5: On 4 March 2004 (8:50 pm), Ben admits the affair and claims the boy is his.
Event 6: On 4 March 2004 (9 pm), the men fight and Ben fatally injures Walter.

Following this revised event-ordering, the reader comes to interpret the reference to the boy differently. Assuming a stereotypical child-bearing context, where Jess has a baby with someone readers assume, or are aware, she was having sex with, the reader would now assume that the boy was Walter's son rather than either of the two men's, and references to the boy could be read as clues to the solving of the narrative whodunit. Students could be asked to explore the order in which story events could potentially be related to the reader, suggesting possible strip reorderings, and hence asked to ponder the extent to which suspense-generation, surprise and misreading are related to each strip reordering. It is crime fiction whodunits not being written in chronological order that enables plot twists, story-rethinking and retrospective identification of story clues. The next section also explores misreadings, but this time through a theory revolving around what are known as story 'frames'.

Frames

Emmott distinguishes between two sorts of information that story readers absorb about characters and scenes: 'episodic', information she argues is likely to change in the course of the narrative, with 'non-episodic' being the information that remains unchanged.[6] Borrowing and yet adapting these terms for a crime fictional context, I instead define 'episodic' as that information which proves immediately relevant to a crime fictional storyline, with 'non-episodic' being that information which does not to prove so, regardless of whether the information in question is true elsewhere, or indeed throughout the text.

Background information to do with one having children, for instance, might not initially be thought of as hugely relevant to the solving of the crime fictional narrative storyline above, and hence classified in this sense as non-episodic. Misclassifying information into the episodic and non-episodic categories is where much of the effectiveness of crime fiction lies. Red-herrings lead readers to classify non-episodic information episodically, as here defined. In other words, red-herrings lead readers to read something unimportant to the crime problem solving as if it were indeed important. Classifying episodic information non-episodically, on the other hand, is also an effective mechanism. Here, readers are misled into considering important information relating to certain characters as initially non-pertinent to the crime, only to later find out that this indeed functioned as a clue which was meant to be altogether left unnoticed at the start. Return to the reordering 1, 3, 4, 7, 8, 9, 10, 2, 5 and 6. Leaving out the reference to Jessica and Ben's affair (event 2), or Ben's admitting of the affair (event 5), and his injuring Walter (event 6) until the story's end could force the reader to reclassify their original understanding of Walter's child as potentially Ben's instead, which would also show that the reference to Jessica having a son needed classifying as episodic, i.e. crime-pertinent, after all. Emmott uses the term 'frame repair' to refer to instances where "a reader becomes aware that they have misread the text either through lack of attention or because the text itself is potentially ambiguous".[7] What the reader faces in this reordering is what Emmott refers to as 'miscuing' of the signals needed in order to understand the episodic information offered, with repairs forcing readers to not only replace the 'erroneous' frame when they discover the problem, but to also reread or reinterpret the text with the 'correct' frame from the point at which the switch should have taken place.[8] In short, this reordering forces readers to reinterpret the reference to Jessica's child when they are made aware of her affair. Repairs over a whole stretch of text, and those indeed across the whole of the text, can be thought of as frame 'replacements' instead; the frames require such large-scale fixing, that the reader might as well reread/replace them from scratch. Students could engage with crime fictional storyline analysis, considering the misclassification of information that particular readings enable alongside the kinds of repairs/replacements to the relevant frames needed. (On the use of character under-specification for manipulative rhetorical purposes, writer garden path strategising, reader assumption-making in relation to character plot status, and the strategic backgrounding of characters in relation to scenario-dependent roles, see Alexander[9]; Emmott and Alexander[10]; Emmott, Sanford and Alexander[11]; and see also Emmott and Sanford.[12]) Crime fiction frame analysis allows students to track their narrative comprehension, appreciate the crime fiction formula and gain insights into generic effects. The next section considers the generation of suspense, which can also relate to misreadings.

Narration and Viewpoint

There are important narrative choices authors make when telling a crime fictional story, over and beyond the order in which events are reader-related, and the information misclassification or misreadings that such a choice can generate. Going back to the narrative given above, a writer could opt to give it in the first person, with a character-narrator telling their own story, perhaps even unreliably so. Alternatively, the story could be told in the third person, and at a little distance, with the narrator being distinguishable from the character whose story is being shared. With this latter choice, a further distinction that needs to be made is that between the events being narrated either internally or externally: "Internal narrative is mediated through the subjective viewpoint of a particular character's consciousness, whilst in an external narrative events are described *outside* the consciousness of any participating character".[13] Where events are narrated internally, readers have access to one or more characters' viewpoint. Among other things, linguistic indicators of point of view include evaluative lexis, that is, as to something being 'awful', any expressions of certainty/uncertainty, with verbs used such as 'must' and 'might' and adverbs such as 'probably', and indicators of characters' thoughts and perceptions. Such viewpoint can be spatio-temporal, that is, as to something being 'here' or 'there', perceptual, with verbs used such as 'saw' or ideological, such as the earlier reference to something being 'awful'. Short's viewpoint stylistic toolkit offers a list of such linguistic features which can be checked against any single text, enabling students to pinpoint whose viewpoint a text portrays and whether any viewpoint shifts occur.[14] Whereas first person narration is, by definition, internal, and allows access to the consciousness of the character-narrator to which it is limited, third person narration can be either internal or external. Third person external narration denies readers such access to character minds, access that would allow readers to sympathise with the characters in question. Students could be asked to ponder over these choices. If one was to realise the above story in whichever event order via the prose fiction medium, what would the effect be if events were narrated from one character perspective as opposed to another, or indeed several such perspectives? Would Ben's version of events be read differently from Jessica's, for instance? And what kind of effect does access to character consciousness and viewpoint allow? Would giving the story from Ben's point of view perhaps allow him to redeem himself as to Walter's residual death? Through such examination, students can begin to appreciate the ways in which choice of narrative style tends to influence the reader's reaction and judgement over the events described. Viewpoint access also affects characterisation. Access to character consciousness can add to characterisation impression, and related reader assumptions, not less affect where reader sympathy lies. Students could be asked to return to crime fictional narratives and explore their narrative style, and viewpoint-related choices, even engaging in the rewriting of certain extracts from alternative character perspectives before commenting on the revised story's effect. In so doing, students gain insights as to the ways in which the type of narration an author employs (first as opposed to third, internal as opposed to external, from one participating character's perspective as opposed to that of another character or several other characters) affects their sympathy towards the story characters.

Possible Worlds

I next turn to explore 'possible worlds' theory, associated with the work of narratologist Marie-Laure Ryan. Possible worlds, though originally associated with the disciplines of philosophy and logic, have come to find their way to the literary and even linguistic analyses of fictional text. Possible worlds are here defined metaphorically as 'conceivable states of affairs', and the actual or real world, in which the reader is presently reading this text about theory and crime writing, is only one of a multitude of possible ones. Fictional worlds are worlds within the universe projected by the text's storyline. When it comes to fiction, possible worlds include what is called the fiction's actual world (what actually takes place/what happens in the stories we read), but also various 'versions' of this fictional world, many of which are private to characters/character-specific. Ryan describes fictional possible worlds as different versions of the fictional world, otherwise known as the 'Text actual world' or TAW.[15] The TAW may or may not correspond to what characters believe to be true, known as 'Knowledge worlds', what characters speculate, anticipate or hypothesise about, known as 'Prospective Extensions of Knowledge worlds', characters' plans/'Intention worlds', moral commitments/'Obligation worlds', wishes/'Wish worlds', and fantasies/'Fantasy Universes'. The below is the opening from Hawkins' crime novel *The Girl on the Train*[16]:

RACHEL

Friday, 5 July 2013

Morning

There is a pile of clothing on the side of the train tracks. Light-blue cloth – a shirt, perhaps, jumbled up with something dirty white. It's probably rubbish, part of a load fly-tipped into the scrubby little wood up the

> bank. It could have been left behind by the engineers who work this part of the track, they're here often enough. Or it could be something else. My mother used to tell me that I had an overactive imagination; Tom said that too. I can't help it, I catch sight of these discarded scraps, a dirty T-shirt or a lonesome shoe, and all I can think of is the other shoe, and the feet that fitted into them.

The extract takes the form of first person narration, with the events mediated through character Rachel's consciousness, which allows readers access to what she is looking at and presuming about in a rather privileged way. In possible theory terms though, the scene could be described in terms of Rachel formulating speculation/'Prospective Extensions of Knowledge' worlds in relation to the TAW's pile of clothes that take focus; in short, she forms a number of hypotheses as to where the clothes have come from. As Ryan argues,[17] for there to be symmetry, balance or stability, there needs to be perfect correspondence between the TAW and all possible worlds in the fictional universe. In other words, if, for instance, everyone is content, with knowledge shared and wishes fulfilled, the characters are all in a state of bliss. Having said that, Ryan argues that a conflict between these sorts of worlds is necessary to get a plot started. Conflicts could take many forms. We could have the TAW clash with a character's private world, or clashes between different characters' private worlds, or internal conflict across one character's private worlds. Without such conflicts, there would be no need for action. And without any need for action, we would have no plot. It is for this reason that readers often encounter narrative plots where characters want who or what they have not got, a conflict between the TAW and their wish world, or face moral dilemmas in their course of actions, a conflict between their obligation world and their intention world perhaps, or where different characters' expectations/'speculative extensions' clash, or where individual character knowledge and plans differ in some way. Readers can encounter several such conflicts taking place simultaneously, all of which are created and resolved at different times. Even more so, various fantasy novels, science fiction narratives and fairy tales are surrounded by phenomena that oppose our natural laws and therefore the TAW by definition is in conflict with the real world the readers inhabit. To return to the Walter and Jessica crime fictional story above, there is a conflict between the TAW and Jessica's obligation world; in having an affair, she is doing what she is not supposed to. Also, for the vast majority of that story, there is also a conflict between the TAW in which

Jessica is having the affair, and Walter's knowledge world in which he remains unaware of the affair. This conflict does not get resolved until event 5 (the story's 4 March 2004 8:50 pm), when Ben admits the affair and claims that Jessica's boy is, in fact, his. Assuming that Jessica is indeed unaware of Walter's whereabouts until 6 March, which is why she reports him missing then (event 8), there is yet one more conflict between the TAW, in which Walter is dead, and Jessica's knowledge world, where she lacks this knowledge. It is not until the police discover Walter's body (event 9) that this conflict is resolved. The start of the police's investigation into Walter's murder (event 10) marks the start of yet another conflict. The police are unaware as to who killed Walter, there being a conflict between the knowledge world of, say, Ben, who is aware of the fight that took place, and the police's knowledge world, as they are not aware of this altercation. Presumably the story would come to a close once all knowledge is shared, with everyone knowing all there is to know.

Whodunit crime novels very often offer such conflicts between detectives' wish world or obligation/intention world with respect to finding out who the killer is, and the TAW within which the identity of the killer is yet unknown by most characters, apart from most often just the killer him/herself. A lot of hypotheses and speculations are drawn from various members of the investigative team which conflict with the TAW until one of those speculations about someone's possible guilty status comes to match it, and at which point the whodunit problem is resolved. Crime fictional storylines also tend to feature conflicts between the killer's knowledge world and the investigative team's different knowledge world/s, until the two sets of worlds come to match; only then is knowledge shared. Again, students could engage with crime fictional storyline analysis, inspecting what possible world conflicts crime writers are creating and resolving at various points, and considering the extent to which given story endings leave any such conflicts unresolved. In Hawkins' *The Girl on the Train*, for instance, Rachel's questions over the clothes pile remain unanswered by the novel's end, hence the episodic classification of the clothes at first read later needing rethinking along non-episodic, unimportant terms. Rachel's later questions regarding who killed the character of Megan indeed come to be answered, though. As she suffered a blackout the night Megan disappeared, Rachel hypothesises whether she herself killed Megan in an alcoholic rage, a hypothesis that turns out to not coincide with the TAW as she proves innocent of murder. Major unresolved possible world conflicts tend to generate open ended rather than closed narratives; after all, possible world conflicts generate suspense. Students engaging in possible world theory analysis can come to appreciate how various world conflicts generate reader expectations, drive plots and affect their reactions to the unfolding storyline.

Consider the opening of Bill Robertson's crime flash fiction "Tomorrow has been cancelled" below,[18] featuring two men about to come together in a violent confrontation because of their presumably illegal dealings. I numbered its sentences for ease of reference:

> (1) The rain pelted down, plastering the streets in furious torrents. (2) Nicolson could feel the cold water soaking through his socks as he tried to walk faster. (3) He could see Jarrett just ahead. (4) The man was walking stooped over, collar turned up against the downpour oblivious to the fact that he was being followed. (5) Nicolson increased his pace to draw closer and reached inside his jacket to pull out his gun.

These five sentences relate the events in the third person, and all from Nicolson's viewpoint; readers encounter references to him feeling things (i.e. the cold water), and seeing things (i.e. Jarrett). Though Jarrett seems oblivious to the fact that he is being followed, this could well be read as an assumption on Nicolson's part. There is hence a possible world theory conflict in terms of Nicolson's expectation world, that is, his speculation of Jarrett being oblivious to his presence, and Jarrett's knowledge world, where he might not be so. If readers understand Jarrett to be oblivious to the fact that he is being followed, then the sentences also reveal a conflict between Jarrett's knowledge world, in which he is walking in the streets alone, and the TAW, in which he is followed. Also, in readers being made aware of Nicolson pulling out a gun, there appears to be another conflict: between Nicolson's intention world, where he appears to be wanting to threaten, harm or get something from Jarrett, and the TAW where he is yet to do so. Readers read on to discover whether Jarrett is made aware of Nicolson following him, and of the latter's intention world, but also whether Nicolson's intention in relation to Jarrett is realised. Readers as yet do not have access to enough knowledge with which to fully interpret the scene, and it is through engaging in possible world theory analysis that they can begin to explain this scene's ambiguity. Though the narrative gives readers access to Nicolson's perspective, these opening lines are suspenseful; readers are as yet unaware as to whether the two men know each other—though the reference to 'Jarrett' by name suggests that Nicolson knows him—and what exactly it is that Nicolson wants. This chapter's last section lists further effective tools for such suspense, this time with a closer focus on language.

Language and Suspense

Unlike anaphoric references, which are explained by going back to what was said earlier in the text, cataphoric references make the reader wait for an explanation of references still to come, hence these, too, generating suspense. It is for this reason that cataphora's forward-pointing helps shape the viewers' scope of expectation.[19] Let us return to the flash fiction opening, this time reordering the piece's sentences as such:

> (1) The rain pelted down, plastering the streets in furious torrents. (4) The man was walking stooped over, collar turned up against the downpour oblivious to the fact that he was being followed. (5) Nicolson increased his pace to draw closer and reached inside his jacket to pull out his gun. (2) Nicolson could feel the cold water soaking through his socks as he tried to walk faster. (3) He could see Jarrett just ahead.

Compared to the original piece's opening, which reveals Jarrett's identity on sentence 3, the above reordered sequencing generates an air of suspense regarding who Nicolson is following. Besides, Jarrett's name is not given until in the sentence here ordered last. According to this alternative sequencing, the 4th sentence's 'the man' and 'he', here ordered 2nd, are cataphoric: these pose a question (i.e. who is being followed?), the answer to which is delayed.

Grammatical structures can also be revealing in terms of what is known as transitivity. As Mayr notes,[20] "[t]he idea behind analysing Transitivity is to explore what social, cultural, ideological and political factors determine what Process type (verb) is chosen in a particular type of discourse". She adds that "[r]elations of power may be implicitly inscribed by the relationship between *Actor* and *Goal*". To exemplify, active material processes (of the 'X stabbed Y' kind) can be reformulated into passive voice structures (of the 'Y was stabbed [by X]' kind), the suppletion of agentless passives by intransitive clauses (of the 'Y died' kind), and nominalisations—the turning of verb processes into noun phrases which background the process to its product (of the '*The stabbing* proved fatal' kind). To return to the above sentence reordering, further to this sequencing's 'the man' cataphorically making the reader wait for a later disclosure of who 'the man' that is being followed actually is, the agentless passive ('he was being followed'—the clause is in the passive voice with the agent deleted) similarly disguises for the duration of the sentence who, and indeed how many, are doing the following, not to mention whether the follower knows 'the man' or not (which, given the access to Nicolson's viewpoint later on would have been revealed with reference to the other as 'Jarrett'). Lastly, the extract's rain is itself interpretable. Further to being detrimental to both men's vision, and hence adding drama, references to it are ripe with metaphor. The rain 'pelt[s] down' with 'furious torrent' which draws on pathetic fallacy, metaphorically alluding to Nicolson's fury and pending violence, whilst references to the water as 'cold' also suggest the man's own coldness/ruthlessness. A close understanding and analysis of language, and in this case grammar, would allow students to not only investigate the text's suspenseful effect but, importantly, inspect the precise mechanism behind it. Literary linguistic insight allows students to begin to appreciate the workings of such ever fascinating crime fiction texts, illuminating not only students' understanding of these texts, but offering students creative writing ideas whilst deepening their genre appreciation.

Conclusion

Much like crime fiction itself, the discipline of stylistics continues to thrive. In transforming crime fictional texts into accounts of their experience, into events that happen, and which the readers actively participate in, stylistics offers genre students an invaluable toolkit. Whether exploring event-ordering, textual frame- and world-construction, viewpoint or suspense-generating linguistic choices, the techniques on offer would allow students to access, observe and respond to these literary experiences, hence enriching understanding of the mechanisms of a much loved, but also now newly-understood, genre.

Notes

1. Paul Simpson. *Language, Ideology and Point of View* (London: Routledge, 1993), 3.
2. Catherine Emmott. *Narrative Comprehension: A Discourse Perspective.* (Oxford: Oxford University Press, 1997).

3. Marie Laure Ryan. *Possible Worlds, Artificial Intelligence and Narrative Theory*. (Bloomington and Indianapolis: Indiana University Press, 1991a); Marie Laure Ryan. "Possible Worlds and Accessibility relations: a semantics typology of fiction", Poetics Today 12 (3) (1991b): 553–76; and Marie Laure Ryan. "The Text as World Versus the Text as Game: Possible Worlds Semantics and Postmodern Theory", *Journal of Literary Semantics* 27 (3) (1998): 137–63.
4. Paul Simpson and Martin Montgomery. "Language, Literature and Film", In *Twentieth Century Fiction: from Text to Context*, edited by Peter Verdonk and Jean Jacques Weber, 138–64. (London: Routledge, 1995), 141; William Labov, "Uncovering the event structure of narrative", In Georgetown University Round Table on languages and Linguistics 2001, edited by Deborah Tannen and James E. Alatis, 63–83, (Washington DC: Georgetown University Press, 2001).
5. Christiana Gregoriou. *English Literary Stylistics*. (Basingstoke: Palgrave, 2009), 99.
6. Emmott, *Narrative Comprehension*, 122.
7. Emmott, *Narrative Comprehension*, 225.
8. Emmott, *Narrative Comprehension*, 160.
9. Marc Alexander. "The Lobster and the Maid: Scenario-dependence and reader manipulation in Agatha Christie", Online Proceedings of the Annual Conference of the Poetics and Linguistics Association (PALA), 2008, accessed April 24, 2017, http://www.pala.ac.uk/uploads/2/5/1/0/25105678/alexander2008.pdf.
10. Catherine Emmott and Marc Alexander. 2010. "Detective Fiction, Plot Construction, and Reader Manipulation: Rhetorical Control and Cognitive Misdirection in Agatha Christie's *Sparkling Cyanide*", In *Language and Style: In Honour of Mick Short*, edited by Dan McIntyre and Beatrix Busse, 328–46. (Houndsmill: Palgrave Macmillan, 2010).
11. Catherine Emmott, Anthony J. Sanford and Marc Alexander. "Scenarios, Characters' Roles and Plot Status: Readers' Assumptions and Writers' Manipulations of Assumptions in Narrative Texts", In *Characters in Fictional Worlds: Understanding Imaginary Beings in Literature, Film and Other Media*, edited by Jens Eder, Fotis Jannidis, and Ralf Schneider, 377–99. (Berlin: Walter de Gruyter, 2010).
12. Catherine Emmott and Anthony J. Sanford. *Mind, Brain and Narrative*. (Cambridge: Cambridge University Press, 2013).
13. Paul Simpson. *Language, Ideology and Point of View*. (London: Routledge, 1993), 59.
14. Mick Short. *Exploring the language of Poems, Plays and Prose*. (London: Longman, 1996).
15. Ryan (1991a, 87).

16. Paula Hawkins. *The Girl on the Train*. (London: Random House, 2015).
17. Ryan. *Possible Worlds, Artificial Intelligence and Narrative Theory*, 20.
18. Bill Robertson, "Tomorrow has been cancelled", *Black and White World*, 8 September 2012, accessed 24 April 2017, https://billrobertson55.wordpress.com/2012/09/08/tomorrow-has-been-cancelled/.
19. Hans J. Wulff, "Suspense and the influence of Cataphora on Viewers' Expectations", In *Suspense: Conceptualisations, Theoretical Analyses and Empirical Explorations,* edited by Peter Vorderer, Hans J. Wulff and Mike Friedrichsen, 1–18, (New York: Routledge, 2009), 2.
20. Andrea Mayr, *Language and Power: an introduction to institutional discourse*. (London: Continuum, 2008), 18.

Works Cited

Alexander, Marc. "The Lobster and the Maid: Scenario-Dependence and Reader Manipulation in Agatha Christie." In *Online Proceedings of the Annual Conference of the Poetics and Linguistics Association (PALA)*, 2008, Accessed 24 April 2017, http://www.pala.ac.uk/uploads/2/5/1/0/25105678/alexander2008.pdf.

Emmott, Catherine. *Narrative Comprehension: A Discourse Perspective*. Oxford: Oxford University Press, 1997.

Emmott, Catherine and Alexander, Marc. "Detective Fiction, Plot Construction, and Reader Manipulation: Rhetorical Control and Cognitive Misdirection in Agatha Christie's *Sparkling Cyanide*." In *Language and Style: In Honour of Mick Short*, edited by Dan McIntyre and Beatrix Busse, 328–46. Houndmills: Palgrave Macmillan, 2010.

Emmott, Catherine, Sanford, Anthony J. and Alexander, Marc. "Scenarios, Characters' Roles and Plot Status: Readers' Assumptions and Writers' Manipulations of Assumptions in Narrative Texts." In *Characters in Fictional Worlds: Understanding Imaginary Beings in Literature, Film and Other Media*, edited by Jens Eder, Fotis Jannidis, and Ralf Schneider, 377–99. Berlin: Walter de Gruyter, 2010.

Emmott, Catherine and Sanford, Anthony J. *Mind, Brain and Narrative*. Cambridge: Cambridge University Press, 2013.

Gregoriou, Christiana. *English Literary Stylistics*. Basingstoke: Palgrave Macmillan, 2009.

Hawkins, Paula. *The Girl on the Train*. London: Random House, 2015.

Labov, William."Uncovering the Event Structure of Narrative." In *Georgetown University Round Table on Languages and Linguistics 2001*, edited by Deborah Tannen and James E. Alatis, 63–83. Washington, DC: Georgetown University Press, 2001.

Mayr, Andrea. *Language and Power: An Introduction to Institutional Discourse.* London: Continuum, 2008.

Robertson, Bill. "Tomorrow Has Been Cancelled." *Black and White World*, September 8, 2012, Accessed 24 April 2017, https://billrobertson55.wordpress.com/2012/09/08/tomorrow-has-been-cancelled/.

Ryan, Marie Laure. *Possible Worlds, Artificial Intelligence and Narrative Theory.* Bloomington and Indianapolis: Indiana University Press, 1991a.

Ryan, Marie Laure. "Possible Worlds and Accessibility Relations: A Semantics Typology of Fiction." *Poetics Today* 12 (3) (1991b): 553–76.

Ryan, Marie Laure. "The Text as World Versus the Text as Game: Possible Worlds Semantics and Postmodern Theory." *Journal of Literary Semantics* 27 (3) (1998): 137–63.

Short, Mick. *Exploring the Language of Poems, Plays and Prose.* London: Longman, 1996.

Simpson, Paul. *Language, Ideology and Point of View.* London: Routledge, 1993.

Simpson, Paul and Montgomery, Martin. "Language, Literature and Film." In *Twentieth Century Fiction: From Text to Context*, edited by Peter Verdonk and Jean Jacques Weber, 138–64. London: Routledge, 1995.

Wulff, Hans J. "Suspense and the Influence of Cataphora on Viewers' Expectations." In *Suspense: Conceptualisations, Theoretical Analyses and Empirical Explorations*, edited by Peter Vorderer, Hans J. Wulff and Mike Friedrichsen, 1–18. New York: Routledge, 2009.

CHAPTER 11

The Crime Novelist as Educator: Towards a Fuller Understanding of Crime Fiction

Paul Johnston

The popularity of both crime fiction and creative writing as subjects studied in higher education has led to crime writers being appointed to teach the writing of crime fiction.[1] However, crime fiction as the subject of academic study is still mainly taught by academics who specialize in literature.[2] Crime writers—the term is commonly used to refer to crime novelists rather than writers of true crime—often have degrees, undergraduate and postgraduate, but gain their knowledge of crime fiction from private reading rather than academic study. They can bring much to the university-level study of the genre in which they write, including insights into the process of writing, the importance of reading widely across the genre, the influence of the marketplace, and the interplay between crime fiction and film/ TV. This chapter discusses these issues and suggests potential learning outcomes.

Much depends on practitioner-educators' knowledge of the genre; on their capacity to impart that knowledge to students; and on their ability to step back from personal creative practice and cast a critical eye on the

P. Johnston (✉)
Liverpool Hope University, Liverpool, UK
e-mail: johnstp@hope.ac.uk

C. Beyer (ed.), *Teaching Crime Fiction*, Teaching the New English,
https://doi.org/10.1007/978-3-319-90608-9_11

oeuvres of their predecessors and peers. I have recently become a full-time academic, in creative writing rather than crime fiction, having published nineteen crime novels. I studied classics and Modern Greek literature as an undergraduate, and then completed Masters degrees in the theory and practice of criticism and comparative literature, and in applied linguistics (for which I wrote a paper on Arthur Conan Doyle's "The Dancing Men"). Finally, I gained a PhD in creative writing, half of which consisted of an extract from a crime novel that was subsequently published (*Carnal Acts*, published under the pseudonym Sam Alexander); and the other half a critical analysis of that work that included reflection on my own practice. However, my first two degrees were completed several years before I started to write fiction, meaning that although I suspect my reading of Aristotle, Plato, Barthes and Derrida and others informed my novels, I have a limited understanding of exactly how.

My case is that crime writers can gain insights into the genre that differ from those accessible to literary academics. Differ, I stress; such insights are not better or more significant but potentially complementary, leading to the fuller understanding of my title. In an ideal world, every English or Media department would accommodate both literary critics and practitioner-educators because the arts of literary criticism and creation are in effect two sides of the same coin. Creative writers create texts within the genre, using innate ability and knowledge gained from reading, working in marketplaces that vary from country to country, and seeing their work become films or TV series. Critics come to the texts when they are completed and necessarily have different points of view.

There are two theoretical obstacles to writers using their experience as a pedagogical method. The first is the Intentional Fallacy, according to which the author's intention is irretrievable and irrelevant.[3] In response to Wimsatt and Beardsley, who directed attention solely to the text, I would say that the author's intention can be retrieved by the author her/himself, at least to some degree, and that it has relevance as a means of explicating the text, even if only as a mark of failure to achieve objectives. The second is the Death of the Author, which is said to be necessary in order for the reader to be born.[4] Barthes's chief concerns were the complex codes according to which the text was woven and can potentially be unwoven. I would contend that the author can assist with that process from outside the text; this in no way reduces the role of the reader in the creation of meaning.

Stephen Knight has identified three areas of importance: "the Why, What and How of teaching crime fiction".[5] Professor Knight also writes, "Perhaps those touchy-feely Creative Writing courses should be called Uncritical Writing courses", which suggests there is some way to go before practitioner-educators, the purveyors of such courses, are accepted by the literary critical old guard. I will bring my hybrid skills, such as they are, to bear on each field, always with the provisos that creative writers often have little conscious understanding of their practice and that reflecting on it can bear strange fruit.

Why Teach Crime Fiction?

First, students want to learn about crime fiction and other manifestations of popular literature that in the past were deemed unworthy of academic study. It is now widely accepted in the academy that crime fiction is significant in psychological, social, political and other ways. Second, crime fiction has literary value, though defining such value inevitably runs up against perceived genre limitations and the personal taste and judgement of individual readers. I do not intend to rehearse the tedious arguments concerning highbrow and lowbrow writing. A single example will suffice: Man Booker Prize winner John Banville has for several years been writing crime novels under the pseudonym Benjamin Black. As mentioned, I have used a pseudonym myself, but that was a brazen attempt at reinventing myself as a different kind of crime writer, with minimal success. This raises important issues to address with students about why literary authors and others use pseudonyms—they may provide greater artistic freedom, wider critical and public access or different authorial personae.

One of the specific approaches that creative writers provide to crime fiction education is a heightened awareness of and deeper familiarity with the market. The strategies and activities of publishers, agents, reviewers, bookshop chains, bookshop assistants and book-buyers, as well as of other authors, are part of writers' professional lives. Crime writers offer more insights because there are more of us—according to data from Nielsen Book Research, crime, thrillers and adventure (cognate though admittedly quite disparate genres) were top in hardback, e-book and audio sales and close behind general fiction in the composite paperback bestseller list.[6] The market defines much in genre writing and has traditionally been paid insufficient attention in literary studies. A published crime writer can inform students about the various markets for novels, how they operate, how they influence genre conventions, what editors want (and how they persuade sales teams that the book will sell), what book-chains want and what readers want. The last, I suggest, are the most important judges. While literature scholars have begun to pay attention to how markets operated in the time of Austen, Dickens and so on, the only people in direct contact with their readers are authors, who disregard feedback at their peril. Such interaction between creator and consumer is not unique to crime fiction, but because of the plethora of bookshop events and crime writing festivals, it takes on wider and deeper dimensions than both literary—that is, non-generic fiction—and other genres. So, too, crime writing has been commodified for over two centuries, an early example being *The Newgate Calendar*, which, according to Worthington, used "sensational crime and criminal lives to make maximum profits".[7] Although it was purportedly true crime, much of the material was presented in frame-narratives and made use of sensation, as in contemporary Gothic fiction, directing itself towards readers who developed the ability to process an amalgam of the factional and the fictional.

What is the interface between crime writer and reader, and why is it worthy of mention? In terms of the market, readers tell authors—often pulling no punches—what they think of their books, series, protagonists, themes, settings and so on. This input can change how the author writes in future, as well as strengthening the grip of genre conventions—it is rare for crime readers to demand more outré approaches to character, plot or language; rather, they are interested in the well-being of beloved protagonists and sidekicks, and the continuation of favourite series.[8] Of course, authors pay attention to reviewers' comments too, but "ordinary" readers are often more direct in their approval and disapproval. In any case, reviewers are readers too. Authors should consider giving readers what they want. In order to do so, they must find out the object of their desires—and then decide whether to fulfil them or not.

Dove has argued that detective and crime fiction demand specific readerly skills and experience, with the reader entering into a "dyadic relationship" with the author.[9] In particular, the reader acts as detective, following clues, discounting red herrings and weighing up who is potentially guilty, as well as responding to the genre's conventions. This ties in with the commercial nature of crime fiction: "because of the economics of the popular market, it is the reader who determines success or failure and who therefore exerts a decisive influence on the evolution of the genre itself".[10] According to Iser, reading is not "a one-way process, and our concern will be to find means of describing the reading process as a dynamic *interaction* between text and reader".[11] This is particularly the case in crime fiction because questions are posed to the reader by the text more than in much other fiction. A practitioner-educator can bring out the importance of understanding how readers function, enabling students to appreciate individual texts, sub-genres and the overarching genre, as well as *their* interaction.

Consideration of why we teach crime fiction also raises philosophical questions. It is generally accepted that literature enhances the lives of readers by improving their understanding of self and world, stimulating the imagination, and increasing empathy. All these suggest that teaching it is a worthwhile activity, even if "the pleasures of reading indeed are selfish rather than social".[12] But is teaching crime fiction a beneficial activity? A convincing argument can be made on ethical grounds that rape, murder and robbery are not suitable subjects for writing consumed by millions of readers. However, an opposing argument can be made on psychological grounds, that the same millions benefit by understanding how the conscious and subconscious minds of humankind work, even when presented via fictional characters. In any case, the broadening of definitions of culture and the greater attention paid to popular modes of expression has changed attitudes. Chandler's declaration that "The academicians have never got their hands in it [the detective or mystery novel]" no longer stands.[13] Over the past century, crime novels have been seen as relaxation (but then, so are romances, with rather less blood spilled), play or puzzles (the so-called Golden Age), examinations of police work (were there ever "bulls" like those in James Ellroy's work?), purveyors of the return to the Garden of Eden (W. H. Auden), studies of psychology and psychopathy (Patricia Highsmith and, with less subtlety, Thomas Harris), and many other things. As a practitioner-educator, I encourage students to consider why authors have chosen to write specific pieces of crime fiction, as well as why they work in the crime genre more generally. Such speculation can be valuable as a precursor to informed critical judgements. Some novelists may be in it mainly for the money. Others may be trying to find out about themselves. For some the puzzle element is sufficient motivation to write. Others are interested in social, ethical, political or philosophical issues.

Writers consider such questions with varying degrees of profundity before, during and after the creation of crime fiction. In advance of writing my dystopian novels set in an independent city state of Edinburgh in the 2020s, I spent time researching Plato's ideas about the ideal society in

The Republic and George Orwell's about a less-than-ideal one in *Nineteen Eighty-Four*.[14] I informed myself about the technical aspects of such world-building, but also considered the ethical questions raised in the story. It is at least theoretically possible for a totalitarian regime to work for the benefit of citizens. It is possible to eradicate serious crime, at least in a thought experiment. The rights of the individual can be set against the needs of the state in a balanced way—or can they? Literary scholars can produce answers to these questions, but they are unlikely to be always the same as the practitioner-educator's.

The metaphor of state and citizen bodies in my novel *Body Politic* has been noted by critics, but my conception of the multiple roles and presentations of the body, pre- and post-mortem, in my fiction and that of others is more nuanced than literary scholars have so far detected.[15] My use of philosophical ideas is in line with developments in the genre: "The mutual influence of philosophy and crime fiction is manifold".[16] An ideas-driven crime novel that influenced my own is Philip Kerr's *A Philosophical Investigation*, a highly original work that refers to Wittgenstein and other major thinkers.[17] Writers, then, are able to point students directly towards influences while literary critics have to rely on textual and, if they regard it as valid, extra-textual evidence.

Crime fiction undoubtedly has literary qualities: Edgar Allan Poe's genre-defining grotesquery, Arthur Conan Doyle's strange combination of *fin-de-siècle* ennui and extreme rationality, Agatha Christie's complex plotting, Dashiell Hammett's hardboiled language and social commentary, Raymond Chandler's romantic melancholy and so on. There has been much scholarly work on these and other writers.[18] While some critics find the aesthetic standards of crime fiction to be negligible, the prevailing view is that the best writing is worth teaching because of its relevance to readers, its reference to contemporary issues, its technical subtlety and the light it casts on the depths of the human soul. Again, the practitioner-educator is in a good position to supplement the judgements of literary scholars with insights gained from the creative process and from applications of theories of creativity. Everyone has a Muse, a mentor and a major motivation; as well as writers they react against violently: personal experiences can provide students with detailed insights.

Crime fiction's political and ideological dimensions as presented by novelists can also be meaningful to students. Crime writing, I suggest, is primarily about the abuse of power, initially as carried out on the living body as a totality (e.g. physical and mental abuse, grievous bodily harm, slavery) and often leading to the death of that body. The metaphor of the ideologically conditioned 'body politic' in my Edinburgh series is reiterated by titles that refer to physical attributes or constituent substances: bone, water, blood, dust, heads and hearts, and skeleton.[19] Descriptions of quotidian life in a supposedly benevolent dictatorship invite readers to make comparisons with their own life experience and, if so inclined, to consider how power is exerted on them and by whom/what. The writer, having considered these questions in depth during the creative process is well placed to stimulate debate.

Order is often restored by the end of crime novels, leading to the maintenance of the prevailing status quo, especially in Golden Age fiction after the First World War: Agatha Christie's first novel, *The Mysterious Affair at Styles*, written and set during the First World War, succeeds in side-lining the conflict as Poirot solves a family murder.[20] Hardboiled writers tend to create more open-ended fiction. The battered survivors in Dashiell Hammett's *The Glass Key* have few illusions that social and political conditions will improve.[21] Thus, although many crime novels are conservative, even those whose authors might think otherwise, it is wrong to assume that the genre as a whole espouses traditional values and virtues. Porter observes that crime fiction "is a genre committed to an act of recovery, moving forward to move back".[22] This is hard to apply to the novels of Maj Sjöwall and Per Wahlöö, Ted Lewis or Derek Raymond—or to mine, as I point out to readers and students.

Which Crime Fiction Should We Teach?

A simple but not simplistic answer would be "anything you like", considering the importance of readers' directed but personal responses to texts. However, it is impossible to avoid recognizing the existence of a canon, or rather multiple canons, of important works—although defining "important" is potentially divisive. Critical acclaim comes first for some readers, even if such acclaim comes many years after publication. Others use the bestseller lists as sources of future reading. And for many the identity of the author (perhaps a moonlighting fantasy novelist such as J. K. Rowling, a.k.a. Robert Galbraith) is paramount.

It is also the case that each country will have its own canon—even countries such as the UK and the USA that nominally speak, write and read the same language. Since the rise of gender, queer and postcolonial studies, account should be taken of crime fiction writers, countries and characters that were ignored, dismissed or abused in the past. Anyone drawing up a reading list or curriculum must beware of their own assumptions and unconsidered biases. This is another area where the practitioner-educator can supplement the pedagogical process—reflection on the position of their own writing in the various canons can be informative, as well as salutary. As every novelist is only—to a greater or lesser extent—an expert on their own oeuvre, I will give examples from my Quint Dalrymple series.

An observant reader, or one familiar with the works of Plato and Orwell, will consume my texts in a different way to other readers. The reason I chose to write in the crime genre, and in the specific hardboiled tradition using a wisecracking first-person narrator, was to engage readers who were familiar with the conventions and tropes of both genre and sub-genre.[23] Intertextuality—defined as "the range of processes by which a text invokes another, but also the way texts are constituted by their relationships with other texts"[24]—is a particular feature of crime fiction. Conan Doyle refers and responds to Poe, Christie to Doyle, many—perhaps too many writers in the twenty-first century—to Christie and so on. In my case, *Body Politic* and its sequels are full of references to Doyle, Hammett, Chandler, Kerr and others. It surprised me that few readers pick up on this, which goes to show that the author may retain the keys to the kingdom of her/his imagination but should not keep the doors permanently locked. Unless a scholar writes a concordance to my novels, such intertextual links "will be lost in time, like tears in rain".[25] Which would not necessarily be a bad thing. Popular fiction may now be "immortal" because of digital technology, but much of it will soon cease to have relevance to the readers at whom it was directed (the contemporary market). Still, while they are still alive, practitioner-educators can provide detailed information about their creative practice.

A canon—whether broadly agreed in the academy, based on sub-genres, or even on individual writers' preferences—suggests a historical perspective. I have mentioned Poe, Doyle and others, most of whom would be members of a 'great canon' of crime fiction. But do we need to teach crime fiction of the past, given that it remains alive in the intertextuality of modern works? I would argue that it is not essential to teach the history of the genre, though I can see the relevance of doing so in the academy. My experience of creative writing pedagogy is that students read very little and are often reluctant to tackle texts written in non-contemporary language. It may even be better to start by teaching modern crime fiction and subsequently go backwards in time; but how to define 'modern'? The criterion is not only language accessibility, although most students would find Christie easier to cope with than Sayers in terms of style. Also important are themes. In the UK, writers such as P. D. James and Ruth Rendell, who started in the 1960s, paid more attention to social issues than earlier crime writers, as have many since (e.g. Minette Walters and Ian Rankin: the latter's state-of-the-nation novel *Black and Blue* is taught in Scottish schools).[26] Crime fiction in general has become overtly more engaged with contemporary life and issues—I say 'overtly' because many novels still offer the reader limited narrative experimentation and firm closure remains a requirement, particularly for bestsellers. Students can be led by the practitioner-educator to understand these matters with special reference to writers, styles or sub-genres that interest them.

Another learning approach is to concentrate on the presentation of the body and crime fiction. Modern culture in general puts great emphasis on bodies and issues of gender and sexuality. Crime fiction education can direct students' attention to the various ways bodies are made manifest in different sub-genres—for example, in Thomas Harris's *The Silence of the Lambs*, Patricia Cornwell's *Postmortem*, Raymond's *I Was Dora Suarez*, Minette Walters's *The Sculptress*, Val McDermid's *The Mermaids Singing*, my own *Body Politic* and John Connolly's *Every Dead Thing*.[27] Useful comparison can be made between the very different attitudes towards the body—and, of course, the mind as the creation of the body's neurological structure—in the above novels with those prevalent in the works of Christie and her successors. In the ideal seminar room, authors will be present to provide insights into their novels.

How Should We Teach Crime Fiction?

My experience of educating creative writers—I use the word "educate" in the sense of drawing out what is already within early writers, rather than the more top-down "teach"—is that lectures are insufficiently interactive. In literature courses with large numbers of students it may be impossible to use only seminars and/or workshops, in which case lectures should allow for questions and feedback throughout. This strategy increases both attention and the retention of material, as will "breaks, or changes of approach, about every 15 minutes".[28] Ways of checking that students have read set texts can be devised—quizzes, short written tests, or work to be handed in, perhaps in response to a question or questions that cannot easily be found on the Internet. Seminars should be as informal as possible, with chairs arranged in a circle and the 'leader' having no greater role or authority than any other group member. The practitioner-educator may have a certain status in students' eyes that other academics do not: it is important that emphasis is placed on ways of writing fiction rather than the writer's standing. This should be done as informally as possible in order to channel creativity.

The subject matter of seminars held by practitioner-educators may vary from that of other academics. I will concentrate on beginners, as subsequent years can be seen as further storeys built on. Judging that students have a basic understanding of crime fiction tropes gained as much from films, TV series (including extrapolations from fiction such as the BBC's *Sherlock*), computer games, and comics as from novels, I initially encourage them to come up with a list of the genre's salient features. Students then modify the list during subsequent sessions, responding to specific experiences of writing raised by the practitioner-educator. I include at least some sessions that investigate the multimedia nature of the genre. For instance, students read a Conan Doyle story and watch the 'equivalent' TV version, such as "A Scandal in Bohemia" and "A Scandal in Belgravia". The similarities and differences between the different presentations of the story point to the ubiquity of some crime fiction tropes. I encourage students to consider why Conan Doyle wrote the story the way he did—with reference to market conditions of the time—and what roles are available to the reader. Similarly, the ways in which the TV episode was written and presented and its intertextual references to the original story and other crime works are identified. Writers whose books have been televised are able to contextualize these by reference to their own experience and authorial strategies.

Regarding curriculum design, the primary distinctions are: (1) a historical overview; (2) an examination of themes and tropes; and (3) critical analyses of selected texts and/or authors. Clearly there is shared ground between these, and my method of teaching crime fiction unabashedly cherry-picks—thus, both using and subverting the great and other canons. I would discuss (not necessarily in chronological order) Edgar Allan Poe ("The Murders in the Rue Morgue", 1841), Arthur Conan Doyle ("The Dancing Men", 1903), Agatha Christie (*And Then There Were None*, 1939, and the 2015 TV series), Raymond Chandler (*The Big Sleep*, 1939, and the 1946 film), Patricia Highsmith (*Strangers on a Train*,1950, and the 1951 film), *Chinatown*, 1974, (the film as a summing-up of and commentary on the hardboiled tradition), Mario Puzo (*The Godfather*, 1969, and the 1972 film), James Ellroy (*L.A. Confidential*, 1990, and the 1997 film), P. D. James (*Death of an Expert Witness*, 1977, and the 1983 TV series), and Ian Rankin (*Black and Blue*, 1997, and the 2000 TV episode). I refer students throughout to my own novel *Body Politic*, which contains intertextual references to all the above, as well as to other contemporary British and American writers in the genre (e.g. Mark Billingham, Val McDermid, John Connolly and James Sallis, all of whom have different experiences of sub-genres). I also invite agents and editors of contemporary crime fiction to explain in person what makes for them a successful novel.

Although historical, critical and thematic dimensions may be included, the creative process is to the fore. Students are required to consider why and how crime fiction is written, and for which market(s). They are encouraged to write creative responses to the texts, choosing whatever form suits them, whether an academic essay on specific texts or themes, a pastiche in prose or poetry, a reflective piece or a relevant piece of their own creative writing. Flexibility of exercises reflects the blank page without questions or prompts that every fiction writer faces. This may sound 'touchy-feely' and 'uncritical', but I argue the opposite—opening students' minds to the imagination, techniques and responses, both in terms of readers and markets, leads them to perform creative acts that bring them closer to the creative writers they are studying. Living authors such as Ian Rankin, Val McDermid, Mark Billingham, Laura Wilson and John Connolly may be invited to attend sessions to provide insights, and students attend bookshop or library events at which there are always question and answer sessions. Finally, authorial experience of the editing, copyediting and proofreading phases of the publishing process, as well as of publicity, marketing (including author websites) and social media use, are discussed, enabling students to work on their own texts in a more informed way, as well as to consider where they might publish their writing. Blogs, interactive stories, screenplays and plays, and the use of social and other forms of new media make this easier than in the past.

I believe that all literature students should write at least some creative texts of their own. Fiction, especially the broad and multifaceted genre of crime, offers boundless opportunities. Students who have studied with practitioner-educators as well as literary scholars gain a fuller understanding of fictional criminal practices, taking in the views and experiences of the author on the page and in the marketplace. This should enable them to find their own writing 'voices', inside and outside the academy, as well increase their awareness of themselves as readers and creators of meaning. Some may even become competent writers of crime fiction.

Notes

1. Examples are the successful novelists Claire McGowan, senior lecturer on the MA in Creative Writing (Crime Novels) at City, University of London, and Henry Sutton, senior lecturer in creative writing and director of the MA in Creative Writing (Crime Fiction) at the University of East Anglia.
2. An exception is Dr Andrew Pepper, senior lecturer in English at Queen's University Belfast, who is also the author of five crime novels.
3. See William K. Wimsatt and Monroe C. Beardsley, "The Intentional Fallacy", in *The Verbal Icon: Studies in the Meaning of Poetry* (Lexington: University of Kentucky Press, 1947), 3–18.
4. See Roland Barthes, "The Death of the Author", in ed. Séan Burke, *Authorship: from Plato to Postmodernism, A Reader* (Edinburgh: Edinburgh University Press, 1995), 125–130. [Originally published in French in 1967.]
5. "Motive, Means and Opportunity: Teaching Crime Fiction", Stephen Knight, accessed 27 June 2017. http://www.profstephenknight.com/2012/08/motive-means-and-opportunity-teaching.html.
6. Format Share of Top 20 Genres (Volume), UK 2015, 41, https://quantum.londonbookfair.co.uk/RXUK/RXUK_PDMC/documents/9928_Nielsen_Book_Research_In_Review_2015_The_London_Book_Fair_Quantum_Conference_2016_DIGITAL_FINAL.pdf?v=635995987941118341, accessed 27 June 2017.
7. Heather Worthington, "From *The Newgate Calendar* to Sherlock Holmes", in *A Companion to Crime Fiction*, eds. Charles J. Rzepka and Lee Horsley (Chichester: John Wiley, 2010), 15.
8. The series is a major feature of crime fiction. I have written three, one of which I returned to after seven years (Alex Mavros) and another after fourteen years (Quint Dalrymple). Many readers regarded their original ends as premature and demanded their return—which hardened my resolve to write different books until publishers stepped in on the readers' behalf. The other series featured crime novelist turned hard man investigator Matt Wells. He has not yet returned, though there have been requests that he do so.
9. Dove, *The Reader and the Detective Story* (Bowling Green: Bowling Green State University Popular Press, 1997), 156.
10. Dove, *The Reader…*, 37. Dove equates detective and crime fiction because "the differences are negligible" (*The Reader…*, 1), a highly questionable statement, but one that can be discussed elsewhere.

11. Wolfgang Iser, *The Act of Reading: A Theory of Aesthetic Response* (Baltimore: Johns Hopkins University Press, 1978), 107.
12. Harold Bloom, *How To Read and Why* (London: Fourth Estate, 2001), 22.
13. Raymond Chandler, *Raymond Chandler Speaking*, eds. Dorothy Gardiner and Kathrine Sorley Walker (London: Allison and Busby, 1984), 70.
14. I am grateful that my work on Plato was recognised in an academic chapter: Carla Sassi, "'Quis custodiet Athenas Boreales?' Paul Johnston's Platonic Dystopia", in *Why Plato? Platonism and Twentieth Century Literature*, ed. Daniela Carpi (Heidelberg: Winter, 2005), 199–209.
15. Paul Johnston, *Body Politic* (London: Hodder and Stoughton, 1997).
16. Joseph Hoffmann, *Philosophies of Crime Fiction* (Harpenden: No Exit Press, 2013), 11.
17. Philip Kerr, *A Philosophical Investigation* (London: Chatto and Windus, 1992). See my essay on the novel in *Books To Die For*, eds. Declan Burke and John Connolly (London: Hodder and Stoughton, 2012), 392–395.
18. See, for example, Gill Plain, *Twentieth-Century Crime Fiction: Gender, Sexuality and the Body* (Edinburgh: Edinburgh University Press, 2001); Lee Horsley, *Twentieth-Century Crime Fiction* (Oxford: Oxford University Press, 2005) and Peter Messent, *The Crime Fiction Handbook* (Chichester: John Wiley, 2013).
19. Paul Johnston, *The Bone Yard* (London: Hodder and Stoughton, 1998); *Water of Death* (London: Hodder and Stoughton: 1999); *The Blood Tree* (London: Hodder and Stoughton, 2000); *The House of Dust* (London, Hodder and Stoughton, 2001); *Heads or Hearts* (Sutton: Severn House, 2015); and *Skeleton Blues* (Sutton: Severn House, 2016).
20. Agatha Christie, *The Mysterious Affair at Styles* (London: John Lane, 1920).
21. Dashiell Hammett, *The Glass Key* (New York: Knopf, 1931).
22. Derek Porter, *The Pursuit of Crime: Art and Ideology in Detective Fiction* (New Haven: Yale University Press, 1981), 29.
23. I originally wrote *Body Politic* in the third person and found the tone was too dry. Rewriting in the first-person was a more arduous process than I anticipated, a point about editorial work that I often make to students.
24. John Frow, *Genre* (Abingdon: Routledge, 2006), 48.
25. From Rutger Hauer's final speech as the "replicant" Roy Batty in Ridley Scott's *Blade Runner* (1982). *The House of Dust*, the fifth novel in the Dalrymple series, is an extended homage to Scott's film.
26. Ian Rankin, *Black and Blue* (London: Orion, 1997).
27. Thomas Harris, *The Silence of the Lambs* (New York: St Martin's Press, 1988); Patricia Cornwell, *Postmortem* (New York: Scribner's, 1990); Derek Raymond, *I Was Dora Suarez* (London: Melville House, 1990);

Minette Walters, *The Sculptress* (London: Pan, 1993); Val McDermid, *The Mermaids Singing* (London: HarperCollins, 1995); Paul Johnston *Body Politic* (London: Hodder and Stoughton, 1997); John Connolly, *Every Dead Thing* (London, Hodder and Stoughton, 1999).

28. Elaine Showalter, *Teaching Literature* (Oxford: Blackwell, 2003), 49.

Works Cited

Alexander, Sam (Paul Johnston), *Carnal Acts*. London: Arcadia, 2014.

Barthes, Roland, "The Death of the Author." In *Authorship: From Plato to Postmodernism*, edited by Séan Burke, 125–130. Edinburgh: Edinburgh University Press, 1995.

Bloom, Harold, *How to Read and Why*. London: Fourth Estate, 2001.

Chandler, Raymond, *The Big Sleep*. New York: Knopf, 1939.

Chandler, Raymond, *Raymond Chandler Speaking*, edited by Dorothy Gardiner and Kathrine Sorely Walker. London: Allison and Busby, 1984.

Christie, Agatha, *The Mysterious Affair at Styles*. London: John Lane, 1920.

Christie, Agatha, *And Then There Were None*. London: HarperCollins, 2007 [originally published as *Ten Little Niggers*, 1939].

Connolly, John, *Every Dead Thing*. London: Hodder and Stoughton, 1999.

Coppola, Francis Ford (dir.), *The Godfather*. Paramount, 1972.

Cornwell, Patricia, *Postmortem*. New York: Scribner's, 1990.

Dove, George N., *The Reader and the Detective Story*. Bowling Green: Bowling Green State University Popular Press, 1997.

Doyle, Arthur Conan, "A Scandal in Bohemia." In *The Adventures of Sherlock Holmes*. London: George Newnes, 1892.

Doyle, Arthur Conan, "The Dancing Men." In *The Return of Sherlock Holmes*. London: George Newnes, 1905.

Ellroy, James, *L.A. Confidential*. New York: The Mysterious Press, 1990.

Frow, John, *Genre*. Abingdon: Routledge, 2006.

Friend, Martyn (dir.), *Rebus: Black and Blue*. STV, first broadcast 26 April 2000.

Hammett, Dashiell, *The Glass Key*. New York: Knopf, 1931.

Hanson, Curtis (dir.), *L.A. Confidential*. Warner Bros, 1997.

Harris, Thomas, *The Silence of the Lambs*. New York: St Martin's Press, 1988.

Hawks, Howard (dir.), *The Big Sleep*. Warner Bros, 1946.

Highsmith, Patricia, *Strangers on a Train*. New York: Harper and Brothers, 1950.

Hitchcock, Alfred (dir.), *Strangers on a Train*. Warner Bros, 1951.

Hoffmann, Joseph, *Philosophies of Crime Fiction*. Harpenden: No Exit Press, 2013.

Horsley, Lee, *Twentieth-Century Crime Fiction*. Oxford: Oxford University Press, 2005.

James, P.D., *Death of An Expert Witness*. London: Faber and Faber, 1977.

Johnston, Paul, *Body Politic*. London: Hodder and Stoughton, 1997.

Johnston, Paul, *The Bone Yard*. London: Hodder and Stoughton, 1998.
Johnston, Paul, *Water of Death*. London: Hodder and Stoughton, 1999.
Johnston, Paul, *The Blood Tree*. London: Hodder and Stoughton, 2000.
Johnston, Paul, *The House of Dust*. London: Hodder and Stoughton, 2001.
Johnston, Paul, *Heads or Hearts*. Sutton: Severn House, 2015.
Johnston, Paul, *Skeleton Blues*. Sutton: Severn House, 2016.
Johnston, Paul, "Philip Kerr's *A Philosophical Investigation*." In *Books to Die For*, edited by Declan Burke and John Connolly, 392–395. London: Hodder and Stoughton, 2012.
Kerr, Philip, *A Philosophical Investigation*. London: Chatto and Windus, 1992.
Knight, Stephen. "Motive, Means and Opportunity: Teaching Crime Fiction." http://www.profstephenknight.com/2012/08/motive-means-and-opportunity-teaching.html
McDermid, Val, *The Mermaids Singing*. London: HarperCollins, 1995.
McGuigan, Paul (dir.), "A Scandal in Belgravia." *Sherlock*, series 1 (BBC, first broadcast 1 January 2012).
Messent, Peter, *The Crime Fiction Handbook*. Chichester: John Wiley, 2013.
Plain, Gill, *Twentieth-Century Crime Fiction: Gender, Sexuality and the Body*. Edinburgh: Edinburgh University Press, 2001.
Poe, Edgar Allan, "The Murders in the Rue Morgue." In *The Fall of the House of Usher and Other Writings*. London: Penguin, 2003 [1841].
Polanski, Roman (dir.), *Chinatown*. Paramount, 1974.
Porter, Derek, *The Pursuit of Crime: Art and Ideology in Detective Fiction*. New Haven: Yale University Press, 1981.
Puzo, Mario, *The Godfather*. New York: G.P. Putnam's Sons, 1969.
Rankin, Ian, *Black and Blue*. London: Orion, 1997.
Raymond, Derek, *I Was Dora Suarez*. London: Melville House, 1990.
Sassi, Carla, "'Quis Custodiet Athenas Boreales?' Paul Johnston's Platonic Dystopia." In *Why Plato? Platonism and Twentieth-Century Literature*, edited by Daniela Carpi, 199–209. Heidelberg: Winter, 2005.
Scott, Ridley (dir.), *Blade Runner*. Warner Bros., 1982.
Showalter, Elaine, *Teaching Literature*. Oxford: Blackwell, 2003.
Viveiros, Craig (dir.), *And Then There Were None*. BBC, first broadcast 26, 27 and 28 December 2015.
Walters, Minette, *The Sculptress*. London: Pan, 1993.
Wimsatt, William K. and Monroe C. Beardsley, "The Intentional Fallacy." In *The Verbal Icon: Studies in the Meaning of Poetry*, 3–18. Lexington: University of Kentucky Press, 1947.
Wise, Herbert (dir.), *Death of an Expert Witness*. ITV, first broadcast 8 April–20 May 1983.
Worthington, Heather. "From the *Newgate Calendar* to Sherlock Holmes." In *A Companion to Crime Fiction*, edited by Charles J. Rzepka and Lee Horsley, 13–27. Chichester: John Wiley, 2010.

CHAPTER 12

Teaching Crime Fiction Criticism

Rosemary Erickson Johnsen

Introduction

Over twenty years ago, crime-fiction scholar Heta Pyrhönen observed that being able to follow "the critical discussions evolving around the genre demands a working knowledge of the main currents of literary criticism on the part of the reader."[1] While this remains true to some degree, crime fiction criticism has matured sufficiently to achieve a degree of independence in its contribution to overarching critical conversations. Pyrhönen's 1994 study, with the deceptively modest title of *Murder from an Academic Angle: An Introduction to the Study of the Detective Narrative*, is invaluable to anyone teaching crime-fiction criticism. Grouped into sections on narrative form, thematic concerns, and cultural contexts, the book covers crime-fiction criticism from its emergence among fans and practitioners right up to the early 1990s' "metaphysical detective narrative." Its chronologically-ordered bibliography illustrates key moments and unexpected overlaps in the development of crime-fiction criticism.

That crime-fiction criticism has matured in the twenty-first century can be seen in the ways work by canonical figures is being supplemented through processes of recovery and re-argumentation, and how earlier

R. E. Johnsen (✉)
Governors State University, University Park, IL, USA
e-mail: RJohnsen@govst.edu

C. Beyer (ed.), *Teaching Crime Fiction*, Teaching the New English,
https://doi.org/10.1007/978-3-319-90608-9_12

interpretations and emphases are refuted or re-contextualized. Crime fiction has experienced powerful growth in recent decades, particularly as an international phenomenon, and there has been a corresponding complexity in the critical enterprise. Growth encompasses production, popularity, and movement across national and linguistic borders, and success in these areas has been paralleled by an altering relationship with literary fiction. Internationalization encompasses not only subjects of study but also the scholarly conversation. It is impossible to overlook the increasing availability of English-language translations, which now go well beyond the few safe names (e.g., Georges Simenon's Maigret and Maj Sjöwall and Per Wahlöö's Martin Beck series) that used to constitute the market, and the past decade's scramble for another Nordic noir hit has brought into English translation some mid-list titles. Internationalization also applies to the scholars who are participating in the conversation; work in crime-fiction scholarship often transcends traditional boundaries of national literatures, and conferences and publications attest to the international communities at work. One drawback to all of this growth, however, has been an occasional lack of scholarly rigor. Precisely because crime fiction is a popular genre, people may feel enabled to jump into the conversation without having the requisite background in the field or, in the case of translated texts, in the original language and/or culture. This tendency, in combination with the imperative to engage crime fiction from other national traditions (particularly Nordic noir) can lead to distortions, awkward errors, or a lack of usefulness to crime fiction scholars and students. Teaching crime fiction criticism in the current climate, then, it is crucial to frame that criticism for students in ways that inform them, and enable them to formulate the right questions for assessment of the criticism.

I regularly teach a dedicated crime fiction course, a course I revised out of an old-fashioned literary genre course that had not been offered in years; my revisions included converting the course to fully-online delivery. The course is cross-listed at both advanced undergraduate and M.A. levels, and the contents change as much or as little as I like from offering to offering. At my graduate institution, I taught a lower-division course on "genre and theme" as a course in crime fiction. An entire course in crime fiction, under a heading that points to popular genre, creates a distinct set of expectations for use of crime fiction criticism. In addition, I have used crime-fiction syllabi in rotating-topics courses at the undergraduate and M.A. level: these course titles include Major English Authors and Seminars in American Literature and World Literature. I have taught Contemporary

Literature under the subtitle "Detecting Spirits," bringing together literary fiction, crime fiction, and poetry that played with multi-faceted notions of "spirit" and "detection." Finally, I have incorporated individual crime novels in courses dedicated to more traditional subjects or non-popular culture objectives. For example, I have used one of Sharan Newman's well-researched historical crime novels in a British Literature 1 survey course to help students engage the medieval period; I usually incorporate one crime novel whenever I teach a course in women's literature; and I have included crime fiction in rotating-topics courses focusing on literature of the First World War, the 1930s, and a postgraduate seminar on technology in mid-twentieth-century literature.

I have found that teaching crime fiction in different course contexts impacts my own understanding of an individual work. Even though text selection is informed by the specific goals of the class, the process of teaching the text and interacting with students around it, can change one's valuation of a text. As the emphasis and perspective shift, books that are less satisfactory specifically *as* crime fiction are revealed to have other merits. For example, as reader I found Agatha Christie's *Death in the Clouds* (1935) to be an implausible, over-plotted outing. When I included it in the seminar on technology in mid-twentieth-century literature because it was one of the objects of study in David Trotter's *Literature in the First Media Age: Britain between the Wars* (2013), another book was revealed. So much period detail about airline travel! So many connections between the conventional clue-puzzle transit mystery and the kinds of social history to be gleaned from more literary fiction! This observation has implications for the teaching of crime-fiction scholarship in terms not only of how, but also how much and what kinds of criticism students are asked to engage. Teaching crime fiction criticism requires deliberate attention to framing techniques, specific assignments to promote productive engagement, and the underlying rationales for these.

Students, Courses, and Sources

Teaching crime fiction criticism often requires greater attention to goals and context than is the case with more traditional subjects of literary study; it can also require a more explicit rationale for the assignment(s). Our students expect to be asked to use literary criticism in literature courses, but they need to see why we are using it with a popular genre like crime fiction. They know how to locate appropriate critical sources for canonical literary texts, too, but they may need more help from us to locate quality crime fiction criticism. They may also need to expand their understanding of the range of criticism available, from readers' responses to scholarly studies, and to practice evaluating sources. A student seeking a required number of sources for an assignment on the work of Virginia Woolf, for example, knows where to look and may need guidance primarily in narrowing the results. In contrast, with crime fiction, students often need useful tools to expand their search as they locate, evaluate, and incorporate criticism.

Dedicated crime fiction classes warrant an up-close, directly focused engagement with criticism, in addition to its supporting role in research projects. For advanced students in a traditional classroom setting, I assign a monograph review-essay, which requires them to negotiate a full-length study and then share their knowledge with the class. For the online class, I ask students to perform similar work with one scholarly article or, depending on course material, with a major review, suggesting places where they should look for substantial reviews. When the subjects of study range from older works such as the Sherlock Holmes stories to contemporary titles in translation such as Henning Mankell or Anne Holt, I offer general suggestions for searching through the campus library and online, and I require pre-approval of their selection. I have used this assignment variously as the focus of one week's online discussion forum (with settings making the other postings visible only after the student has posted his/her own), as part of an exam, and as a free-standing assignment.

Models for using critical sources are also useful in this context. Students who are accustomed to a direct match between the criticism and their topic need encouragement to cast a wider net, but they also benefit from seeing *how* general sources may be put to use productively, *how* to extract illuminating material from books or article focusing on other primary texts. This is one aspect of teaching crime fiction criticism that calls for a more direct engagement with parts of the process that are taken for granted, or occur behind the scenes. Understanding the functions of peer review, and awareness of the different layers of editorial shaping represented by (for example) blogging, fan-oriented sites, and publication in the *London Review of Books*, helps students select among the results of their broader searches. It is also helpful to build on the kind of assignment described in the previous paragraph: once a student has located a source, analyzed it, and captured its main points, he/she is ready to consider what applications that source might have. Are there other writers mentioned in the discussion? Even a brief treatment as an aside offers material. Are there qualities—formal or thematic—or contexts presented that could be brought to bear on the works of other writers or on other topics? Slowing down to ask these questions, and making room for shared information and discussion of research strategies, is beneficial. (And these benefits carry forward, I have noticed, improving students' research in later classes. They learn more about how research works, and have benefited from practicing these skills directly.) I also use my own published work as a model. I share an article with the class not so much as a source itself, though it is that, but as a model of using other sources. Pointing to items in the bibliography and highlighting how they are used in the article demonstrates how to draw and adapt material from secondary sources whose application may not be apparent at first glance.

While in many classes more taxonomical works may not merit student engagement, earlier critical works on crime-fiction classification and definition are often worthwhile. These can benefit students directly as they begin to learn more about subgenres in popular forms and the genealogy of crime fiction, and also indirectly as they see for themselves important shifts in both critical practice and academic values. As works move from basic classification to more sophisticated analyses of subgenre and cross-pollination, students encounter foundational bases for the critical enterprise writ large. They also discern how apparently neutral terms can be laden with value judgments, and observe how scholars engage in conversation over those terms, corroborating, contesting, redefining, or advancing them. Noting and discussing such terms as "golden age," "clue puzzle," and "whodunit," for example, not only encourages deeper understanding of the crime fiction genre, it provides a model for how humanities scholarship goes about its business.

The so-called golden age writers provide another kind of glimpse into broader cultural patterns. These writers and the high modernists they co-existed with are revealed to have engaged in simultaneous production of texts—whether those be detective novels or modernist poetry—and of critical standards by which to understand and evaluate those texts. Crime fiction criticism and modernist theories of culture both flourished in the inter-war period, offering genre-shaping criticism in apparently "low" and "high" modes. In the previous century, Edgar Allan Poe was deeply committed to shaping critical standards concerning ratiocination, horror, and the inter-connections between true and fictional crime even as he was producing texts exemplifying those standards. Poe's statements about shaping a national literature are also illuminating not just for crime fiction—and his ideas on this matter have a new currency in the twenty-first century as crime fiction in translation is booming—but for literary and cultural study more broadly.[2]

What about classes where crime fiction is only part of a broader theme or period focus? Is it okay if a student taking the class does not engage any crime fiction criticism? My practice there has been to ensure students are exposed to it, though they may not be directly engaging it in their own research and writing. Furthermore, there are opportunities to bridge gaps between crime fiction criticism and scholarship on more canonical literary texts. Reading Sayers' *Strong Poison* (1930) as part of a class on the 1930s, for example, it is not difficult to show how some aspects of the scholarship addressing Sayers' work as crime fiction speaks in concert with criticism of (for example) Orwell's inter-war fiction and essays. There are articles offering comparative analysis of crime fiction and "highbrow" literature, such as my "Dorothy L. Sayers and Virginia Woolf: Perspectives on the Woman Intellectual in the late 1930s" (*Virginia Woolf Miscellany* 2015), and students can be shown how crime fiction features in broad-ranging cultural studies, such as Allison Light's *Forever England: Literature, Femininity and Conservatism between the Wars* (Routledge, 1991) and David Trotter's *Literature in the First Media Age: Britain between the Wars* (Harvard, 2013). Studies such as these show students how crime fiction can contribute to literary and cultural study alongside more traditionally prestigious work; they also affirm the value of crime fiction criticism as such, as these scholars are well-versed in the genre and can articulate its contributions.

It is striking that Pyrhönen's study dates the concern with crime fiction's shift from periphery to center as early as 1981. Unlike the metaphysical detective narrative, valorized by high theory but not transforming the genre as anticipated, this issue has continued to grow in importance as we have moved into the twenty-first century. Discussions of the cross-currents between crime fiction, literary fiction, and best-selling fiction recur in criticism and popular reviews; Magnus Persson's 2011 article, "High Crime in Contemporary Scandinavian Literature: the Case of Peter Høeg's *Miss Smilla's Feeling for Snow*," is a useful case study. Students can readily identify examples of the increasingly fluid boundaries between crime fiction and other modes, as these abound in contemporary culture: not just literature, but film, television, even journalism and news coverage, reflect the mainstreaming of crime stories for a variety of purposes. Some of these stories are click bait, or an old-fashioned titillation of prurient curiosity that sits queasily alongside celebrity stalking, but a considerable portion is doing interesting cultural work. Crossovers between true crime and literature have a long history, but students can readily engage a constellation of material such as Margaret Atwood's *Alias Grace* (1996), Susanna Moodie's *Life in the Clearings Versus the Bush* (1853), Atwood's *In Search of Alias Grace: On Writing Canadian Historical Fiction* (1997), and criticism specifically about Atwood's works. Adding crime fiction criticism, such as that on historical crime fiction and literary adaptations of true-crime cases, offers students terms, approaches, and a different kind of context for *Alias Grace*. As of this writing, *Alias Grace* is being filmed in Canada, adding yet another mode for consideration; delightfully, Atwood herself has a cameo as Disapproving Woman.

I have found it particularly valuable to include crime fiction in classes about women's literature, whether those have been specifically entitled "women writers" or the broader "women and literature." Feminist scholarship shows how women's success in a genre often leads to its de-valuing by the male critical establishment, and crime fiction provides both an example and a counter-argument to this tendency. Using crime fiction by both women and men in concert with crime-fiction criticism allows students to better understand this dynamic. Supplementing crime fiction by Sayers, Christie, Hammett, and Chandler with short critical pieces such as Edmund Wilson's "Why do People Read Detective Stories?" (1944) and "Who Cares who Killed Roger Ackroyd?" (1945) plus Raymond Chandler's "The Simple Art of Murder" (1950) makes visible the gendered critical/artistic nexus. Author biographies, with the publishing history they provide, can offer invaluable framing for dismissal of best-selling authors such as Christie and Mary Roberts Rinehart, sneeringly dismissed by the "Had I But Known" tag. Historical crime fiction has provided my women's literature students with the fruits of research, suggestions for how to continue that research independently, and (literally) clues to understanding women's place in social history. The junior-level class I taught at a large R1 institution was one of a handful of courses that could be selected to meet a required diversity option; crime fiction succeeded in engaging some of the more reluctant students who were resistant to Edith Wharton and Virginia Woolf. Learning about the importance of genre fiction for women in the marketplace added another layer to course objectives.

Crime Fiction Criticism in the Wild

The ever-increasing number of book-length studies of crime fiction, articles in journals oriented toward popular culture, and substantial reviews of both primary and secondary sources: these are all central to teaching crime fiction criticism. Additionally, as students engage crime-fiction criticism, part of learning how to evaluate it is learning what is behind it, what informs it. My experience has been that crime-fiction criticism is a natural location for drawing back the curtain on the publication process, and fostering awareness of how much range there is in pre-production selection and evaluation. The basics of peer review, and of alternative review processes for public scholarship and commercial publication, can be presented in as much depth as seems appropriate for any particular set of students. In teaching crime fiction criticism, we begin with our own working knowledge of the field and are well able to assist students in their research process. Recent developments in the field are reflected in increasing outlets for quality work, however, and I would like to offer some thoughts and suggestions for finding relevant secondary material.

There are scholarly journals whose missions provide platforms for crime-fiction criticism, such as the USA-based journals *Clues* and the *Journal of Popular Culture*. Fan and reader-oriented outlets run a broad range, and some blogs offer substantive material beyond friendly reviews and event promotion. By their nature, internet sources are changeable; blogs that have been useful to my students may change or disappear while new ones will materialize. While I am hesitant to name many specific internet sources, two long-standing ones that offer accurate and up to date material are http://www.eurocrime.co.uk (run by Karen Meek for more than ten years) and http://crimealwayspays.blogspot.com (run by Declan Burke since 2007). Major literary reviews such as the *Times Literary Supplement*, the *London Review of Books*, and the *New York Times Book Review* include regular attention to crime fiction (although students sometimes need guidance in evaluating their biases and/or knowledge base), and the *Los Angeles Review of Books* features reviews, review-essays, and author interviews (http://www.lareviewofbooks.org).

Full-length studies and collections of essays on crime fiction subjects find their way onto the lists of many academic presses; the current state of the field suggests that there is not one particular press to whose catalog students would turn to discover new work. The *Crime Files* series, based in the UK office of Palgrave Macmillan, has been going since the turn of the century under the general editorship of Clive Bloom. The titles of that series offer a snapshot of the kinds of topics that fit under the umbrella of crime-fiction studies, including books on major authors, connections with other genres (gothic, film), feminist readings, historically-situated analyses, and even some books that are more readers' guides than scholarly studies (suggesting the close links between critical modes). *Crime Files* titles include both monographs and essay collections, and its offerings continue to grow in concert with developments in the field.

It is also useful to encourage students to look beyond obvious venues, showing them crime fiction criticism appearing in journals such as *Modern Fiction Studies* (USA) and *Mosaic* (Canada). Crime fiction makes its way into broader period studies and in theoretical explorations such as Franco Moretti's model of distant reading.[3] The presence of crime fiction in such outlets illustrates the connections between the genre and broader concerns of humanities scholarship. Sometimes these non-crime-fiction outlets are essential for teaching crime fiction. In my seminar on contemporary Scandinavian crime fiction, for example, articles on crime fiction in *Scandinavian Studies* were essential. Sometimes negotiations with library staff are required in order to provide access to necessary material. Even with shrinking budgets, libraries are receptive to requests that will benefit students.

Archival material can be valuable as well, depending on the readings being studied and access to library and/or archival holdings. As more material becomes available online, students can be directed to good resources, and the researcher's own material can be drawn on. For example, students can be directed to the UK National Archives (http://www.nationalarchives.gov.uk) for material such as images of maps or the online available records for "crime, prisons and punishment 1770–1935." From my own research, I have shared data from the Mass-Observation Archive (University of Sussex, UK) relating to reading and to attitudes toward capital punishment; material from unpublished letters in the Sherlock Holmes Collections (University of Minnesota, USA); and information about "pulp" editions housed in the Russell B. Nye Popular Culture Collection (Michigan State University, USA). We want our students to learn in our classes—new material, new ways of thinking, new questions to ask—and we want them to leave ready to learn more. Sharing aspects of research that go beyond processing already processed products like journal articles can contribute, by providing tools and the motivation to use them.

Conclusion: M.A. Seminar in American Crime Fiction

I would like to use my M.A. seminar as a closing case study, as it pulls together the practices presented in this chapter and demonstrates some of their implications. Let me begin by quoting part of the course rationale, as it indicates my priorities in teaching crime fiction and reflects my understanding of its importance to literary and cultural study:

> Crime fiction is a popular genre known for its strong narrative arc and material specificity. The genre's detailed presentation of society, from its material circumstances to its values, makes it ideal for the study of context-rich literary history. It has also been the basis for important theoretical work in literary study, such as 1970s and 80s structuralism and Franco Moretti's twenty-first century hypotheses about "distant reading." Crime fiction has been an international literary phenomenon from its inception, and American writers have played an influential role in its development. This semester's crime novels reward study, and they represent authors who have contributed to genre developments in the US and internationally.

This seminar is one of the required courses for my university's M.A. degree in English, and its course number is for American Literature. Although all of the literature we read is American, I emphasize the international nature of the genre. Even in the earlier days, the Anglo-American cross-currents were vital to genre developments; in the twenty-first century, broader internationalization is shaping the genre. The rationale's dual emphases on material culture and theoretical models play out through discussion and research.

One means of getting students deeper into these two emphases is a monograph review-essay and presentation, an assignment I use in a variety of upper-division and postgraduate courses. Because the development of the genre and its critical history are important for a full understanding of American crime fiction, each student chooses a work from a list of scholarly studies, writes a review-essay of 4–6 pages, and prepares an informative 10–12-minute presentation for the class. The essays present key features of the book and indicate connections to course readings we've done, while the presentations pool our knowledge. I remind students that the audience for these two components is slightly different; while the audience for the review-essay is familiar with the subject text, the presentation is bringing the news to the rest of the class. Students are encouraged to provide a handout or submit material to be posted on Blackboard.

This assignment fulfills several objectives. First, it gets the students to come to terms with one full-length study of crime fiction. I place the assignment about two-thirds of the way into the semester, effectively launching the research for the final seminar essay with a thoughtful engagement of a monograph while also pooling student knowledge of these professor-selected works. Through the content-rich presentations, students receive grounding in the wealth of approaches that scholars have taken to crime fiction; in some cases, they also find specific scholars and texts that will inform their own research. Through in-class interaction among students whose reviews cluster around similar topics, everyone advances their discernment of utility and value. In the cluster of texts on the hardboiled subgenre, for example, students began to see differences in approach (varying degrees of reliance on theory, cultural history, and/or archival material) and in subject matter (books only, related ephemera, and/or film). Guided discussion of these findings enables students to practice evaluating crime fiction criticism—what kinds of judgments are rendered on what aspects of the criticism?—and to begin shaping their own approaches. They begin the research for their seminar essays from this foundation, and it provides a platform on which the professor can build through examples of scholarly articles, essay collections, and mainstream or popular reviews. While this is an assignment I use in other classes, for crime fiction I provide a list of possible monographs and I place greater emphasis on the sharing of basic knowledge via the presentation. The list of monographs provided ensures breadth of engagement; while I always include more options than there are students in the class, there are never so many that an important category goes unrepresented. Furthermore, the list includes both important "classics" in the field and more recent studies, helping students gain a sense of how crime fiction scholarship has developed since the early academic work of scholars such as John Cawelti, George Dove, and Kathleen Gregory Klein. My selection is broken into subcategories of "literary history," "theory and criticism," and "subgenres and topics." When I distribute the list, I briefly describe the books, placing them in an overall context of crime fiction criticism and identifying the primary objects of study (course authors, well-known films, etc.). As much as possible, I avoid signaling my own take on these works or directing students toward or away from individual titles; they all meet standards of significance for inclusion on the list, and the presentations and discussion will illuminate their contributions and limitations.

The essay at semester's end offers students the opportunity to pursue independent research and contribute to ongoing critical conversations around crime fiction. Topic selection is open, as long as the primary focus is on crime fiction, and students make choices in line with their commitments. Some students have pursued additional historical and cultural research; others work comparatively and include other crime fiction (sometimes works they have encountered in classes taken with me previously); still others pursue a theoretically-grounded reading such as feminist readings of texts with the grain, or against it; some interrogate (sub)genre definitions and boundaries. A common student response at the end of crime-fiction courses is that crime fiction did not seem like something to be studied before they took the course, but they discovered that it rewarded their study by providing cultural insight, offered valuable opportunities to sharpen their critical tools, and was enjoyable. These rewards are shared by the professor, too.

Crime fiction criticism, like crime fiction itself, continues to evolve. The Pyrhönen study, excellent as it is, cannot predict new directions, and we do not ask it to do so. On top of the clear, rich presentation of the critical heritage it provides, it also shows how criticism is time-bound. Just as the periods traced in the study, the "moment" of 1994 is characteristic of its time. We also see how quickly subfields can develop. For example, within twenty years of the ground-breaking book-length feminist study of crime fiction by Kathleen Gregory Klein, *The Woman Detective: Gender and Genre* (1988), publishers' lists include specialized books that marry feminism with subgenre (Johnsen, *Contemporary Feminist Historical Crime Fiction*, Palgrave Macmillan, 2006) or theme and period (Godfrey, *Femininity, Crime and Self-Defence in Victorian Literature and Society: From Dagger-Fans to Suffragettes*, Palgrave Macmillan, 2012). The big movements right now are the international awareness and increasingly multi-directional traffic among authors and scholars, crime fiction's clear relevance for what is being called "the new realism," and the rapid progression of crime fiction's mainstreaming. The broadening of the term "noir" is one symptom of this shift, as those discovering crime fiction adopt a term that used to have a sharply-defined meaning; while "noir" can begin to seem like all things to all people, it also reflects the high value being placed on the genre and, after all, it is only the latest iteration of the perpetual quest to name the genre: detective fiction, mystery, whodunit, crime fiction, noir. So let us teach crime fiction criticism as being rooted firmly in its time, and trust that some of our students will make the next generation of criticism significant and relevant.

Notes

1. Heta Pyrhönen, *Mayhem and Murder: Narrative and Moral Problems in the Detective Story* (Toronto: University of Toronto Press, 1999), 8.
2. See, for example, "American Literary Independence" and "National Literature and Imagination" in *The Portable Edgar Allan Poe*, edited by J. G. Kennedy (NY: Penguin, 2006), 582–84 and 594–95.
3. Moretti argues that "both synchronically and diachronically ... the novel is the system of its genres" (*Graphs, Maps, Trees* [London: Verso, 2005], 30) and he uses the Sherlock Holmes stories as one of his central experimental examples.

Works Cited

Atwood, Margaret. *Alias Grace*. 1996. New York: Anchor, 1997.

———. *In Search of Alias Grace: On Writing Canadian Historical Fiction*. Ottawa: University of Ottawa Press, 1997.

Bertens, Hans, and Theo D'haen. *Contemporary American Crime Fiction*. New York: Palgrave Macmillan, 2001.

Burke, Declan, ed. *Down These Green Streets: Irish Crime Writing in the 21st Century*. Dublin: Liberties, 2011.

Cawelti, John G. *Adventure, Mystery, and Romance: Formula Stories as Art and Popular Culture*. Chicago: University of Chicago Press, 1976.

Chandler, Raymond. "The Simple Art of Murder" (Preface). *The Simple Art of Murder*. 1950. New York: Vintage, 1988

Christie, Agatha. *Death in the Clouds*. 1935. New York: Harper Collins, 2001.

Clarke, Clare. *Late Victorian Crime Fiction in the Shadows of Sherlock*. Basingstoke: Palgrave Macmillan, 2014.

Dove, George N. *The Police Procedural*. Bowling Green, OH: Bowling Green State University Popular Press, 1982.

Dussere, Erik. *America Is Elsewhere: The Noir Tradition in the Age of Consumer Culture*. Oxford: Oxford University Press, 2014.

Godfrey, Emelyne. *Femininity, Crime and Self-Defence in Victorian Literature and Society: From Dagger-Fans to Suffragettes*. Basingstoke: Palgrave Macmillan, 2012.

Horsley, Lee. *Twentieth-Century Crime Fiction*. Oxford: Oxford University Press, 2005.

Johnsen, Rosemary Erickson. *Contemporary Feminist Historical Crime Fiction*. New York: Palgrave Macmillan, 2006.

———. "Dorothy L. Sayers and Virginia Woolf: Perspectives on the Woman Intellectual in the Late 1930s." *Virginia Woolf Miscellany*, no. 87 (2015): 23–26.

Klein, Kathleen Gregory. *The Woman Detective: Gender and Genre*. Champaign: University of Illinois Press, 1988.

Knight, Stephen. *Crime Fiction 1800–2000: Detection, Death, Diversity*. New York: Palgrave Macmillan, 2004.

———. *Form and Ideology in Crime Fiction*. Bloomington: Indiana University Press, 1980.

Light, Alison. *Forever England: Literature, Femininity and Conservatism Between the Wars*. London: Routledge, 1991.

McCann, Sean. *Gumshoe America: Hard Boiled Crime Fiction and the Rise and Fall of New Deal Liberalism*. Durham, NC: Duke University Press, 2000.

Merivale, Patricia, and Susan Elizabeth Sweeney, eds. *Detecting Texts: The Metaphysical Detective Story from Poe to Postmodernism*. Philadelphia: University of Pennsylvania Press, 1998.

Moodie, Susanna. *Life in the Clearings Versus the Bush*. London: R. Bentley, 1853.

Moretti, Franco. *Distant Reading*. London: Verso, 2013.

———. *Graphs, Maps, Trees: Abstract Models for Literary History*. London: Verso, 2005.

Mullen, Anne, and Emer O'Beirne, eds. *Crime Scenes: Detective Narratives in European Culture Since 1945*. Amsterdam: Rodopi, 2000.

Nestingen, Andrew. *Crime and Fantasy in Scandinavia: Fiction, Film, and Social Change*. Seattle: University of Washington Press, 2008.

Nickerson, Catherine Ross. *The Web of Iniquity: Early Detective Fiction by American Women*. Durham, NC: Duke University Press, 1998.

Persson, Magnus. "High Crime in Contemporary Scandinavian Literature – The Case of Peter Høeg's *Miss Smilla's Feeling for Snow*." In *Scandinavian Crime Fiction*, edited by Andrew Nestingen and Paula Arvas, 148–58. Cardiff: University of Wales Press, 2011.

Poe, Edgar Allan. *The Portable Edgar Allan Poe*, edited by J. Gerald Kennedy. New York, NY: Penguin, 2006.

Pyrhönen, Heta. *Mayhem and Murder: Narrative and Moral Problems in the Detective Story*. Toronto: University of Toronto Press, 1999.

———. *Murder from an Academic Angle: An Introduction to the Study of the Detective Narrative*. Columbia, SC: Camden House, 1994.

Reddy, Maureen. *Sisters in Crime: Feminism and the Crime Novel*. New York: Continuum, 1988.

———. *Traces, Codes, and Clues: Reading Race in Crime Fiction*. New Brunswick, NJ: Rutgers University Press, 2003.

Sayers, Dorothy L. *Strong Poison*. 1930. New York: Bourbon Street Books, 2012.

Thompson, Jon. *Fiction, Crime, and Empire: Clues to Modernity and Postmodernity*. Champaign: University of Illinois Press, 1993.

Trotter, David. *Literature in the First Media Age: Britain Between the Wars.* Cambridge, MA: Harvard University Press, 2013.
Walton, Priscilla L., and Manina Jones. *Detective Agency: Women Rewriting the Hard-Boiled Tradition.* Berkeley: University of California Press, 1999.
Wilson, Edmund. "On Crime Fiction." Accessed October 1, 2016.

CHAPTER 13

Teaching Contemporary US Crime Fiction Through the 'War on Drugs': A Postgraduate Case Study

Andrew Pepper

There is a familiar look to the syllabi of most introductory 'crime fiction' courses at undergraduate level: a few weeks at the start on the 'classics' (e.g. Poe, Collins, Doyle, and at a push Anna Katharine Green), followed by a section on the American 'hardboiled' novelists (e.g. Hammett and Chandler) and/or the English 'Golden Age' writers (e.g. Christie and Sayers) and a few weeks at the end examining more recent female/feminist and non-white appropriations (e.g. Paretsky, Vine, Mosley). There is necessarily nothing wrong with such an approach and it gives students a good introduction to some of the genre's canonical novelists but it closes off opportunities to explore other manifestations of crime fiction. For example, the move from the English Golden Age to the US hardboiled tends to produce its own account of the genre's developments that overlooks emerging crime fiction cultures elsewhere or crime writers that are perhaps harder to classify (e.g. Josephine Tey or Patricia Highsmith). Furthermore, such an approach produces a set of narrow assumptions

A. Pepper (✉)
Queen's University Belfast, Belfast, UK
e-mail: a.pepper@qub.ac.uk

C. Beyer (ed.), *Teaching Crime Fiction*, Teaching the New English,
https://doi.org/10.1007/978-3-319-90608-9_13

about the genre's emergence and development: that this can be understood as a straightforward passage from 'classical' crime fiction which is figured as 'conservative' to hardboiled crime fiction which is characterised as 'radical', and that the genre becomes synonymous with a set of Anglo-American writers, thereby excluding whole swathes and traditions of fiction set and/or written outside this critical lens. This essay concerns my efforts to teach contemporary US fiction at postgraduate level in ways that push against some of the more ossified assumptions about what the genre is and how it functions politically—and to challenge postgraduate students to think critically about their own understandings of the genre and its complex discursive formations and to read crime fiction through a set of conceptual frameworks.

Specifically, my essay focuses on the challenges and potential benefits of teaching contemporary US crime fiction through the 'war on drugs' and vice versa: how we can use the 'real' context of the contemporary drug wars afflicting the Americas and beyond to, firstly, ask far-reaching questions about the complex relationship between the true crime and crime fiction; secondly, consider what crime fiction can say about this 'real' context, or how crime fiction can make interventions, that other modes of discourse and other disciplinary perspectives cannot; and thirdly, examine the complex formal and political implications at stake in these interventions. There are other advantages of beginning a course entitled 'Contemporary US Crime Fiction' with a section focusing on the 'war on drugs' or the 'drug wars': it immediately places us on the margins of, or outside, the geographical confines of the US insofar as the related issues of policing and trafficking require us to consider the US's relationship with Mexico especially and the rest of the Americas. To teach US crime fiction in ways that decentre rather than reinscribe the exceptional status of the United States of America is to make an important political statement. But to teach US crime fiction through the lens of the 'war on drugs' also demands that we pay attention to current affairs and the contemporary news agenda and to reflect upon their own practices and views of the world in terms of their reading. This is of course something that we ask of undergraduate students too, but the onus on postgraduate students to critically reflect upon their understandings of the relationship between fiction, theory and the(ir) world is especially pronounced.

Reading fiction of any kind can sometimes seem, to students, like an activity wholly divorced from their own lives and experiences, and the tendency of much crime fiction towards resolution (whether clear-cut or otherwise) often reinforces a gap between their reading habits and the typically messy open-endedness of their lives. As such, they often comment on the 'realism' of 'war on drugs' fictions which cannot offer such assurances and do not usually bring their narratives to straightforward resolutions, not least because the 'war on drugs' itself is unwinnable and hence limps on ad infinitum. Moreover, while few of my students have any direct experience of life in Mexico or the US-Mexico borderlands, many have read about the violence afflicting Mexico (e.g. the kidnapping and presumed murder of forty-three students in Guerrero in 2015, or perhaps Sean Penn's unwitting role in the capture of Mexican drug-lord, Joaquín Archivaldo Guzmán Loera, aka 'El Chapo', in 2016). This, in turn, gives them some sense that crime fiction focusing on the contemporary drug wars is urgently speaking to and about our world, not least because the question of 'our' complicity as potential purchasers of illegal drugs is directly raised in the works themselves. For the purposes of this essay, the set texts I'll refer to are *Sicario* and *Cartel Land*, a mainstream Hollywood movie and a high-profile documentary both released in 2015, and Don Winslow's epic crime novel, *The Cartel*—sequel to *The Power of the Dog* (2005)—also first published in 2015. This mixture of film and fiction allows us to consider how the 'drug wars' currently playing out in Mexico, the US and elsewhere are depicted in different forms and media and the implications of these differences for our consideration of the genre's politicisations. My examination of strategies for teaching crime fiction here are based on my experiences at Queen's University Belfast teaching these materials on a final-year undergraduate module called Contemporary US Crime Fiction and an MA module called The Thriller in an Age of Global Insecurity—and as such I would like to thank my students for their unwitting assistance in helping me formulate my thoughts on this subject.

True Crime and Crime Fiction

There are advantages and disadvantages of focusing on 'real' events or circumstances and using these to somehow assess the crime fiction that emerges out of them. For a start, the notion that the fiction may be 'based on real events', or in the case of the documentary *Cartel Land* (this film juxtaposes the story of the Autodefensas movement in Michoacán, Mexico, a citizen-group established to oppose drug cartel violence, and a vigilante group in Arizona, USA, patrolling the US-Mexico border), may try to capture this reality, gives the material additional charge or relevance for students. One of the dangers of course is that students will assume the facts to be inviolate and will use these to assess the purported accuracy of the (crime) fiction. This in turn runs the risk of calcifying rather than unsettling the rather more slippery distinction between the reality and artifice. Yet the contemporary drug wars—for the designation 'war' is by no mean an overstatement—is useful here because its appalling, bloody excesses allow or require us to think carefully about 'the fact/fiction thing' as outlined by Mark Seltzer:

> No doubt true crime puts in doubt from the start the line between fact and fiction. The very notion of true crime, I have suggested, proceeds as if 'crime' itself were assumed to be a fictional thing, such that the word 'true' must be added to bend it toward fact; the line between crime fact and crime fiction is in play from the start.[1]

In other words, and insofar as it may not be possible to properly distinguish between crime fact and fiction, the drug wars that flared with particular brutality from 2006 to 2012 (un-coincidentally the years of the Calderon presidency in Mexico) presents us with a compelling case of this semantic degradation.[2] Students perhaps already know about the scale and extent of the bloodshed, but when they are told that 100,000 or more people have been killed by cartel and government violence between September 2006 and September 2012, it puts this violence into sobering context.[3] To really make the point, and having given the students due warning, I also show a small selection of images of the violence—bodies hanging from bridges, headless corpses—to underscore the idea of excess as well as the issues raised by a new development in Mexican journalism colloquially known as the 'noja roja' whereby graphic images of cartel violence are posted in the internet for vicarious consumption.[4] This, in turn, requires us to think about, from the point of view of novelist or film-maker, how to make sense of a 'reality' that seems so grotesque, so excessive, so overdetermined, that it does not in some perverse sense seem 'real' and about the ethical implications of looking at images of violated corpses—what a character in *The Cartel* calls 'violence porn'.[5] In classes I am aware of the need to handle these issues and demands sensitively and give students prior 'warnings' about any potentially offensive images that I might show but I have found that students are keen to interrogate their own responses to these images and to reflect upon the differences and proximities between images and 'the real'.

In practice, students responded more favourably to *Cartel Land*—a documentary that explores populist vigilante efforts to oppose the growing influence of the cartels in Arizona, US, and Michoacán, Mexico—than to *Sicario*, which they seemed more able or willing to dismiss as 'artifice', even if the Hollywood movie offers useful insights into the militarisation of policing and 'the merger of the war on drugs and the war on terror'.[6] 'The pleasure and appeal of documentary film', according to Bill Nichols, 'lies in its ability to make us see timely issues in need of attention .... The linkage between documentary and the historical world is the most distinctive feature of this tradition'.[7]

In this sense, the students were responding not merely to the timeliness of the issues raised (such as the legitimacy of state policing vs. populist interventions) but also to the documentary's affective dimension. This latter aspect was starkly presented in an interview with the widow of a man brutally killed by cartel violence, described by director Matthew Heineman as the film's most disturbing scene:

> She witnessed her spouse being chopped into piece and burned to death. To sit in the room and talk to this woman whose body was there, but whose entire soul had been sucked out of her; to look into her eyes and to see the hollowness there; to hear her describe the horrors of what she had witnessed; and to think we are the same species of human beings that would do that to other people. That stuck with me.[8]

But the documentary's truth-claims also allowed us to consider its status as representation and the problems of identifying with what we see on the screen as 'real'—hence Michael Renov's question posed against nonfiction film in general: 'Is the referent a piece of the world, drawn from the world of lived experience, or, instead, do the people and objects placed before the camera yield to the demands of a creative vision?'[9] This, in turn, enabled us to think about the implications of 'creative intervention' and utilising 'fictive' elements (e.g. narrative arcs, characterisations, camera angles, sound) to organise 'a presumably objective representation of the world',[10] and as a result, how crime fiction and true crime are more entwined than we might first think.

Crime Fiction as Narcoculture

At stake is the larger question of the effects of particular creative decisions and how we might read the resulting representations politically. Rather than trying to determine how well or accurately crime fiction and nonfiction responds to the complexities of the drug wars, we should focus on what they tell us, as representations, about the discourses that act or impinge upon their constructed-ness. In other words, we accept that these texts do not show us the 'real', however seductive this idea might be, and instead we think about how the formal and thematic decisions taken (what to film, how to film, what kind of story to tell etc.) have particular effects, intended or otherwise. In the context of the contemporary drug wars, this is in effect what Miguel Cabañas calls 'narcoculture' or 'the complex network of cultural practices and representations, ambiguous and sometimes contradictory, that has become our "truth" about that world'.[11] A documentary like *Cartel Land* might in one sense show us the 'real'; for example, what it is like to be caught up in a shoot-out. However, we also need to think about its political meaning and implications, and as such we talked in class a lot about whether its determination *not* to offer a commentary or position on the violence or to give us a larger framework or context to understand this violence means that its politics are, in the end, confused and confusing. As such we wondered whether the 'reality effect'—this need to document rather than to comment—meant that *Cartel Land* was not able to offer a successful, fully realised critique of the violence and its multiple causes. I'm aware here that this last point may have been my reading of the documentary rather than my students', but they were willing to entertain the idea, especially retrospectively after we'd read *The Cartel*, which offers us a more sophisticated contextualisation of the violence.

If part of what we tried to do in class was to explore the slippery nature of the distinction between fiction and nonfiction (crime fiction and true crime) we also thought about whether the fictional could give us insights into the 'real' that are somehow beyond straightforward modes of objective reporting. To put this another way, why might it be the case that 'it is through the "fictionalized" narratives that one learns most about the world of drugs'?[12] Mexican novelist Yuri Herrera has an answer: 'What art can do is offer an alternative discourse that accounts for the complexity of the phenomenon, of its long history, its many complicities, and the need to reflect again on each individual's responsibilities. Good literature ... surpasses all Manichaeisms'.'[13] Herrera's remarks of course implicitly resurrect well-worn arguments about what constitutes 'good' literature, as opposed to 'bad' genre fiction but part of my argument here is that crime fiction is able to surpass or indeed unravel these Manichaeisms just as effectively as Herrera's 'good literature'. This was the jumping-off point for our in-depth consideration of Winslow's *The Cartel*—an epic account of the failures of the US-led war against drug trafficking and the drug cartels, and one that places an emphasis on complexity, history and indeed complicity in the manner that Herrera indicates. At stake is not simply the question of what fiction can do that other forms of reportage cannot, but rather what kinds of fictional forms are best able to critically interrogate these kinds of complexities?

One particularly gruesome incident of cartel violence occurred in Morelia, Michoacán, on 6 September 2006 and is described by Saviano: 'twenty men dressed in black, their faces covered in ski masks, burst into the discotheque ... opened black plastic trash bags, and rolled five decapitated heads across the dance floor' (97). On its own the act is symptomatic of a generalised savagery, or as Saviano puts it the perception of Mexico as 'a place of unending and incomprehensible violence' (59) but we decided that what Winslow does so well is introduce us to one of the perpetrators—Jesús 'Chuy' Barajos—thirty pages prior to the act itself. As such we thought about the act as part of a more complicated story that cannot be reduced to the actions of a single bad or defective person. Rather we see how Chuy is sequestered into the brutal and brutalising environment of the cartels, how he is trained and indoctrinated and how this context drives him to do what he does. As such we talked about how what we do, especially in contexts as fraught, complex and violent as Chuy's, is never simply the result of individual pathologies; rather the way we act in the world is shaped by the systems we are a part of. This shift from individual action to systemic context is arguably best served not by a single narrative that follows one character and line of enquiry but a series of multiple, overlapping stories that develop in complex ways across time and space. Or as Zavala puts it, referring to Winslow in particular, 'only a particular narrative trend of fiction and non-fiction published in the United States has been able to articulate a necessary, critical, and subversive view of the official discourse on drug trafficking and its related organizations in both countries'.[14]

Crime Fiction: Systems Versus Individuals

In my own work on crime fiction I am very keen to explore how 'individual action is always socially and economically situated' and how the 'systemic is always privileged over the subjective' so that 'what keeps us reading, typically opens out to interrogate the nature of society itself, and of the systems – of state power and capitalism – which simultaneously envelop and govern us, and those in the stories, as subjects'.[15] I do not ask students to read my work because such an approach tends to produce stilted exchanges in which students are typically embarrassed about quoting my words back at me but rather try to engage them with the attendant ideas—in this case, that crime is best understood in a systemic rather than individual context. In the case of *The Cartel*, and indeed of cartel violence in general, this shift of emphasis from individuals to systems allows us to think through two related propositions: first, that the violence afflicting parts of Mexico and also the US should be seen as a consequence of capitalism (rather than as something capitalism can cure or make better); and second, that drug cartels are not readily distinguishable from state structures and activities to the point where it is hard to tell where the licit realm of politics, business and law ends and the illicit realm of organised criminality begins. Summarising both positions, Saviano puts it as follows: 'it is not the mafia that has transformed itself into a modern capitalist enterprise, it is capitalism that has transformed itself into a mafia. The rules of drug trafficking … are also the rules of capitalism'.[16] This, then, is the starting point for our consideration in classes of the wider implications of the cartel-related violence: what it tells us is not just about contemporary Mexico (and the US) but also about the world we live in more generally. Here in our class we returned to some of the images of mutilated bodies and hanging corpses we had considered at an earlier moment and asked how the embodied violence might perhaps speak to or about Saviano's formulation of organised crime and capitalism. The best answer we could come up with related to the use of violence as a form of advertising and brand differentiation and to the logic of deregulation and expansion—and the acquisition of new markets—which in *The Cartel* becomes the driving force behind every violent act. If Ed Vulliamy gives us the most succinct account of this developing logic whereby 'the greed for violence reflects the greed for brands, and becomes a brand in itself' so that 'Mexico's war' is 'the inevitable war of capitalism gone mad',[17] the best conceptual framework is offered by Slavoj Žižek's distinction between 'subjective violence'

('violence performed by a clearly identifiable agent') and systemic violence understood as 'the catastrophic consequences of the smooth functioning of our economic and political system'.[18]

Some students struggled with this notion of violence not as aberrant but rather as the product of 'the smooth functioning of our economic and political system'. However, we considered the role of the state and state institutions in *The Cartel*, either as well-meaning players in the battle to quell cartel violence or as bodies or entities that are centrally implicated in the escalation and intensification of the violence. Here almost everyone in the class agreed that it was the latter rather than the former and hence, as Zavala puts it, 'that drug trafficking exists within the community and is not a criminal force attacking the community from the outside'. Rather, 'it is a social construct always inside the state, with organized structures that also fulfil the roles of the state when needed. Narcos are not invading criminals; they occupy the top strata of power and civil society'.[19] In the novel, Winslow gives us numerous examples of corrupt policemen and politicians, but this dense supersaturation of graft has become *de rigeur* for the crime narratives that deal with the contemporary drug wars. As such we considered what makes *The Cartel*'s treatment or thematisation of the relationship between the state and criminality different. Here we focused on the structural aspects of these connections or as Dawn Pavey puts it, in her book *Drug War Capitalism* (2014), how the violence of the cartels 'interacts with capitalism, state power and resource extraction'.[20] Winslow suggests, for example, that particular cartels, such as the Zetas, cross a line not when they massacre entire villages or torture innocent people but rather when they threaten the interests and activities of multinational oil companies—at which point these interests, in consort with elements in the Mexican and US state, are prepared to act with rival cartels using extra-legal violence and methods to do so. Hence we paid a lot of attention to what Art Keller, a DEA agent in the novel, describes as the 'psychological leak from the war on terror into the war on drugs'. He states that:

> The battle against Al Qaeda has redefined what's thinkable, permissible, and doable. Just as the war on terror has turned the functions of intelligence agencies into military action, the war on drugs has similarly militarized the police. CIA is running a drone and assassination program in South Asia; DEA is assisting the Mexican military in targeting top narcos for 'arrests' that are often executions. (392)

Holloway argues that thriller fiction tends to function conservatively or even neo-imperially to legitimise 'human rights abuses by the West, particularly state sanctioned torture, by depicting the West, rhetorically, as the virtuous bringer of rights'.[21] But in class we agreed that a novel like *The Cartel* offers a more critical perspective on US and western complicity and does so by suggesting that Keller and others belong 'to a wider network of systemic violence, of which the international drug trade is a part'.[22] *The Cartel* also suggests that the 'war on drugs' is not ultimately a war against the product itself or even a war against the cartels but rather a vicious, bloody asymmetrical conflict where 'the pain, fear, and suffering resulting from militarization and paramilitarization are experienced in large parts by poor and working people and migrants'.[23] But this, in turn, raised the question of what the crime novel can do in the face of these discriminations and brutalities. What kind of resistance can a novel like *The Cartel* enact in the face of such concentrations of power and violence? What hope can it offer 'ordinary' poor and working people caught up in the violence? And how does Winslow, a US citizen, write a novel that doesn't simply lay bare US complicity in and with the escalating violence but pays proper attention to the involvement of individuals and groups in Mexico in the struggles against the cartels? These are difficult, far-reaching questions and while I wouldn't expect my MA students to come up with fully-developed answers in class, my hope would be to encourage further reading and exploration in preparation for essay-writing exercises.

One of the bigger issues I try to encourage students to think about in my classes is how far we can expect crime fiction to further progressive politics or indeed whether the genre, which is typically orientated towards the logic of explanation and resolution, inevitably supports a more conservative politics. In my own work, I try to emphasise the tensions and ambiguities produced as a result of the genre's complicated relations with the state and capitalism:

> If there is a populist scepticism in crime fiction from its earliest incarnations towards traditional modes and figures of authority, any overt political radicalism is contained by the accommodations crime stories must make towards the articulation of law and the restitution of order. In the same way, this conservative impulse is itself undermined by the crime story's typical refusal to turn a blind eye to institutional failure and corruption.[24]

In classes we tried to think about how this same dynamic is identifiable in the crime narratives produced by, and in relation to, the contemporary drug wars. In the first class, where we discussed *Cartel Land*, we considered how the legitimacy of the vigilante actions established in Michoacán by Dr José Mirales and the Autodefensa group, is gradually eroded as members of the group are sequestered into the cartels and thereby become complicit with the very thing they were set up to oppose. This led to a discussion of the film's final scene where the meth cookers we saw at the start are revealed to be part of the local police force and their spokesperson (concealed by a ski-mask) suggests that the cartels can't be stopped because everyone is complicit in their activities. In doing so, texts like *Cartel Land* and *The Cartel* challenge the typical logic-resolution imperative of much crime fiction or at least show students that not all crime has to conform to this pattern. The larger political point is made eloquently by an online blogger, the Wild Child, in *The Cartel* who extends this idea of complicity even further (to include those who consume the drugs and those who profit from the laundering of cartel profits) while at the same time identifying those most in danger from the ongoing violence and in doing so reconstitutes the 'war on drugs' as a 'war on poverty':

> I speak for the ones who cannot speak, for the voiceless. I raise my voice and wave my arms and shout for the ones you do not see, perhaps cannot see, for the invisible. For the poor, the powerless, the disenfranchised; for the victims of this so-called 'war on drugs', for the eighty thousand murdered by the narcos, by the police, by the military, by the government, by the purchasers of drugs and the sellers of guns, by the investors in gleaming towers who have parlayed their 'new money' into hotels, resorts, shopping malls, and suburban developments .... This is not a war on drugs. This is a war on the poor'. (582)

The notion that the 'war on drugs' is really a war against the poor really underscores the political dimension of Winslow's novel and demonstrates, more eloquently than I am able to, that crime fiction does not have to be an escapist, politically conservative form but rather can engage in anti-capitalist thinking without being 'preachy'. The blog-post is moving rather than propagandist because Wild Child's brave opposition to the power of the cartels ends up costing him his life. If this is part of Winslow's response to the thorny and fraught question of resistance and the capacity of the genre to stand in opposition to conglomerations of power and violence understood as systemic rather than subjective, to use Žižek's terms, we also discussed the time and space that Winslow devotes to thematising this resistance and to exploring the potential for collective action. Here then we returned full circle to the issue or question that I raised at the outset: what can fiction, and specifically crime fiction, do that other forms of fact-based reportage cannot? Certainly *The Cartel* brilliantly illuminates and interrogates the complex alliances between states, drug cartels and businesses and in doing so allows us to see what would otherwise be invisible. But in the end what we thought the novel does best is to give us insight into the everyday lives and experiences of those caught up in the violence and either succumb to the coercions and temptations offered to them or try, often in vain, to stand up to the aggressors. As such, in the final part of our class, we considered characters living in Mexico, especially in the Juárez valley, such as Marisol, Jimena, Erika and the other 'women of Juárez', who demonstrate considerable bravery and pay a heavy price for it. Winslow doesn't suggest that their interventions will necessarily produce 'good' results—and there is no naïve faith in the capacity of individual protagonists, even vigilantes, to deliver justice—but implies that the world would be a bleaker, less hospitable place without their efforts. Perhaps this is the only realistic hope that crime fiction about the contemporary drug wars can offer us.

Conclusion

This was the first year that I have taught these texts and that I have organised the first half of the module specifically around the 'war on drugs' in crime fiction, and hence it remains to be seen just how students respond to the issues raised both in their assessments and in end-of-semester questionnaires. On the evidence of their enthusiastic response to the texts, even to a 600-page novel like *The Cartel*, and the attendant and related issues of state power, capitalism and violence, I am encouraged that they are keen to make connections between the crime fiction we examine in classes and the world that we are all a part of. To this end, as well as requiring students to write an academic essay on a subject or topic of their own choosing, I am asking them to produce a digital map (e.g. either a mind or geographical map) that thematises or indeed visualises a particular aspect of a crime narrative or a series of crime narratives in order to find new ways of further demonstrating the genre's capacity for engaging with and intervening in the world that produces it. Certainly there is much for the students to ponder in terms of what the violence means, how it is represented and to what end—and in turn to think about how or how far the scale and scope of the violence, the further opening up of social divisions and inequalities, and the thematisation of the changing relationship between state and capital puts pressure on our preconceptions about the formal and political properties of crime fiction as a genre. For example, what are the implications for the genre of the sheer scale and extent of the violence—especially if there is no chance of bringing the attendant crises to some kind of order? And if the complicity between drug cartels and state actors and between the licit and illicit realms runs so deep, what happens to the possibility or hope for justice, even a flawed justice, that is so central to the genre?

But this is only part of what I want my postgraduate students to do or only part of what I want them to reflect on. The richness of the 'war on drugs' as a case study is evidenced by the proliferation of new crime fiction that addresses it as a subject but also by the scholarly materials produced about it, much of it coming from disciplines outside literary studies, for example Sociology, Criminology, Security Studies, International Relations. Indeed this move beyond or outside the 'safe' domain of literary criticism—whereby students are asked to make connections between literary and visual narratives and critical work and theoretical perspectives from other disciplines—is one of the key attributes of successful postgraduate work, not least because it requires students to think about how the resulting exchange of ideas asks far-reaching questions both of crime fiction and of these other disciplinary perspectives. For example, crime fiction can explore the human consequences of the violence and exploitation discussed in sociology or the difficulties that individuals face when trying to manoeuvre within larger institutions. Looking ahead to the ways in which the study of crime fiction at postgraduate level might develop in future years, I would point to two related aspects: firstly, as the 'drug war fictions' demonstrate and even enact, we will be thinking about the global proliferation of crime and policing and of the increasing difficulties of distinguishing legal and illegal domains and even of being able to 'see' how power is wielded, by whom and for what ends. And secondly, as crime fiction becomes one of the key vehicles for staging and critiquing these manoeuvres, we will be in a better place to think about the complex relationships between theory and practice (and fiction and the 'real') and the ways in which interdisciplinary studies can help interrogate these relationships.

Notes

1. Mark Seltzer, *True Crime: Observations on Modernity and Violence* (London and New York: 2016), 38.
2. See Persephone Braham, 'True-Crime, Crime Fiction, and Journalism in Mexico', in Andrew Pepper and David Schmid, eds., *Globalization and the State in Contemporary Crime Fiction: A World of Crime* (Basingstoke: Palgrave, 2016), 119–140.
3. Roberto Saviano, *ZeroZeroZero*, trans. Virginia Jewiss (London: Penguin, 2013), 105.
4. See Braham, 'True-Crime', 120–121.
5. Don Winslow, *The Cartel* (New York: Alfred A. Knopf), 312. All further citations refer to this edition.
6. Emma Björnehed, 'Narco-Terrorism: The Merger of the War on Drugs and the War on Terror', *Global Crime* 6:3–4 (2004), 305–324.
7. Bill Nichols, *Representing Reality: Issues and Concepts in Documentary* (Bloomington and Indianapolis: Indiana University Press, 1991), ix.
8. See Corrine Gaston, 'Inside the Drug Wars: A Conversation with "Cartel Land" Maker Matthew Heineman', International Documentary Association (3 February 2016). http://www.documentary.org/feature/inside-drug-wars-conversation-cartel-land-maker-matthew-heineman (accessed 22 November 2016).
9. Michael Renov, 'Introduction' in Renov, ed., *Theorizing Documentary* (London and New York: Routledge, 1993), 2.
10. Renov, 'Introduction', 2.
11. Miguel Cabañas, 'Narcoculture and the Politics of Representation'. *Latin American Perspectives*, 41: 2 (2014), 7.
12. Luis Astorga qtd. in Cabañas, 'Narcoculture', 8.
13. Yuri Herrara qtd. in Oswaldo Zavala, 'Imagining the U.S.-Mexico Drug War: The Critical Limits of Narconarratives', *Comparative Literature,* 66:3 (2014), 345.
14. Zavala, 'Imagining', 342.
15. Andrew Pepper, *Unwilling Executioner: Crime Fiction and the State* (Oxford: Oxford University Press, 2016), 3, 12.
16. Roberto Saviano, 'Foreword', Anabel Hernández, *Narcoland: The Mexican Drug Lords and their Godfathers*, trans. Iain Bruce and Lorna Scott Fox (London: Verso, 2014), x.
17. Ed Vulliamy qtd. in Rebecca Birron, 'It's a Living: Hit Men in the Mexican Narco War', *PMLA*, 127:4 (2012), 822.
18. Slavoj Žižek, *Violence: Six Sideways Reflections* (London: Profile, 2008), 1.
19. Zavala, 'Imagining', 349–350.

20. Dawn Pavey, *Drug War Capitalism* (Edinburgh and Oakland: AK Press, 2014), 26.
21. David Holloway, 'The War on Terror Espionage Thriller, and the Imperialism of Human Rights', *Comparative Literature Studies*, 46:1 (2008), 20.
22. Zavala, 'Imagining', 354.
23. Pavey, *Drug War Capitalism*, 35.
24. Pepper, *Unwilling*, 2.

Works Cited

Birron, Rebecca E. "It's a Living: Hit Men in the Mexican Narco War." *PMLA*, 2012, 127:4, 820–834.

Björnehed, Emma. "Narco-Terrorism: The Merger of the War on Drugs and the War on Terror." *Global Crime*, 2004, 6:3–4, 305–324.

Braham, Persephone. "True-Crime, Crime Fiction, and Journalism in Mexico." In *Globalization and the State in Contemporary Crime Fiction*, edited by Andrew Pepper and David Schmid, 119–140. London: Palgrave Macmillan, 2016. Print.

Cabañas, Miguel. "Narcoculture and the Politics of Representation." *Latin American Perspectives*, 2014, 41:2, 3–17.

Gaston, Corrine. "Inside the Drug Wars: A Conversation with 'Cartel Land' Maker Matthew Heineman." International Documentary Association, 2016, (3 February). http://www.documentary.org/feature/inside-drug-wars-conversation-cartel-land-maker-matthew-heineman (accessed 22 November 2016).

Hernández, Anabel. *Narcoland: The Mexican Drug Lords and Their Godfathers*. Trans. Iain Bruce and Lorna Scott Fox. London: Verso, 2014.

Kraska, Peter B. "Militarization and Policing – Its Relevance to 21st Century Policing." *Policing*, 2007, 1:4, 501–513.

Nichols, Bill. *Representing Reality: Issues and Concepts in Documentary*. Bloomington and Indianapolis: Indiana University Press, 1991.

Pavey, Dawn. *Drug War Capitalism*. Edinburgh and Oakland: AK Press, 2014.

Pepper, Andrew. *Unwilling Executioner: Crime Fiction and the State*. Oxford: Oxford University Press, 2016.

Renov, Michael, ed. *Theorizing Documentary*. London and New York: Routledge, 1993.

Saviano, Roberto. *ZeroZeroZero*. Trans. Virginia Jewiss. London: Penguin, 2013.

Seltzer, Mark. *True Crime: Observations on Modernity and Violence*. London and New York: Routledge, 2016.

Winslow, Don. *The Cartel*. New York: Alfred A. Knopf, 2015.

Zavala, Oswaldo. "Imagining the U.S.-Mexico Drug War: The Critical Limits of Narconarratives." *Comparative Literature*, 2014, 66:3, 340–360.
Žižek, Slavoj. *Violence: Six Sideways Reflections*. London: Profile, 2008.

Filmography

Cartel Land. 2015. Director: Matthew Heineman.
Sicario. 2015. Director: Denis Villeneuve.

Index[1]

[1] Notes: Page numbers followed by 'n' refer to notes.

C. Beyer (ed.), *Teaching Crime Fiction*, Teaching the New English,
https://doi.org/10.1007/978-3-319-90608-9

CPI Antony Rowe
Eastbourne, UK
May 08, 2020